THE LOST KINGS

THE ROYALS OF RAKE FORGE
BOOK ONE

ASHLEY MUÑOZ

Cover Design: Neptune Designs

Content Editor: Memos in the Margins
Editor: Rebecca Fairest Reviews
Proofread: All Encompassing Books

 Formatted with Vellum

To the darlings who have always felt the tug of the moon in their chests and the heart of the meadow in their blood. You were never meant to choose only one to love when they both make you feel alive.

Spotify Playlist
Pinterest Inspo Board

CONTENT WARNING

This book is intended for mature audiences of 18 and over.

Mild violence and one scene with depictions of gore.

Children trained in utilizing artillery and weapons.

References to thoughts of suicide (extremely brief and the person is over 18 years of age)

Romantic situations between teens that do have on-page physical interactions, and while it's not sex, some scenes are graphic.

Mild cliffhanger- this is duet and written as though the story isn't complete until the end of book two.

The use of sedatives on a minor (17 years old)

The use of sedatives on animals.

Sexually Explicit Scenes that include MFM (while the males do not touch in any way, it's essential to understand they're both present.)

An Additional Note:

This duet is based on the characters created in The Rake Forge University series. (Wild Card, King of Hearts, and The

Joker) While this series is second generation and can be read without reading the first gen series, there will be references to their parents, who have their own stories. You can go find them in Kindle Unlimited and Audio on Amazon or in print on my website.

FAMILY TREE

MALLORY & DECKER
JAMES
⌄
CARTER MARIE

TAYLOR & JUAN
HERNANDEZ
⌄
ALEXANDRIA (ALEX)
GIOVANNI (GIO)
KINGSTON (KING)

RYLIE & KYLE JAMES
⌄
PRESLEY

SCOTTY JAMES: UNCLE TO
⌄
DECKER & KYLE

MALLORY & TAYLOR ARE STEPSISTERS

THE LOST KINGS

ASHLEY MUÑOZ

KYLE
13 YEARS AGO

Presley's lashes fluttered against her freckled face while she clung to her stuffed animal. She slept in complete peace as if she hadn't snuck out of her bed yet again. I'd smile at her determination if it weren't for this new feeling cracking my chest open. Seeing her between the twins, in what she had called "her favorite place in the whole world." Perhaps it was because she'd just turned five, or maybe it was the argument I got into with Juan, the twin's father, but I finally had a name for that new feeling.

Fear.

"It's normal, Kyle." My wife's soft voice brushed against my ear as she stood on her toes to reach me. The twins' dinosaur lamp was on in the corner, providing plenty of light to see the boys' faces while they slept in the large king-sized bed that they shared. Juan had said they weren't ready to sleep apart yet, but I had a suspicion it had more to do with the girl who lived across the mansion who always found a way to sneak into their room.

I leaned over them and gently tugged down the blanket that covered Presley's face. Her hair was dark like her mother's, her lashes were long and she had the same freckle on her cheek that Rylie had.

The boys took after Juan with the same inky hair and long lashes, with the same warm brown skin. They all looked so tranquil, and yet that fear came back in full force.

My voice was nearly as soft as Rylie's as I muttered in response, "She's getting too old."

Kingston and Gio certainly were. They would be seven in less than six months.

Rylie sighed while squeezing my arm. "They're best friends. She feels safe with them."

That word "safe" felt like a sucker punch because my daughter often felt afraid. From what my wife and I gathered, it had to do with how frequently we moved around and that she didn't have roots. Seemed she made her own between the twins.

Presley's nose twitched, but she was tucked under Kingston's chin, so it made his lashes flutter. Gio was behind her, wrapped in his own tattered blanket, while a piece of Presley's braid was looped around his finger.

"They're too old to be sleeping in the same bed." Not to mention spending every waking hour together. The three were completely inseparable, and while it was cute when they were little, it was starting to make my stomach bind into an invisible knot. I was about to pull my daughter into my arms when a familiar voice stopped me from the doorway.

"Never thought I'd see The Joker panicked over something so innocent."

My wife released a small chuckle while shaking her head. "You two have fun, I'm going to bed."

"Night, little one," Juan said warmly toward Rylie while she exited the room.

The nickname he'd given my wife years ago steadied me, reminding me how much history I had with this man. He may be the twins' father, and responsible for these two little boys who couldn't seem to stay away from my little girl, but he was also my friend.

Juan pushed off the doorframe and walked over to where I stood, staring at our kids.

"You're overreacting."

I glanced up, seeing Juan's messy hair crowding his forehead. He wore black sweats and a white T-shirt with no socks. He had likely been sleeping or at least trying to. Lately, things had been so stressful for all of us that it was difficult to find any rest.

"My gut tells me I'm not."

"They're children. Practically siblings, let them support one another. They need it now more than ever."

I was reminded of our argument from earlier. We would need to run again, but Juan wanted to remain in North Carolina. He had his wife, Taylor, and their three kids to think of. Their daughter Alex, and then the twins Gio and Kingston...even Juan's mother and step-father had started tagging along wherever we would go. I understood their need for stability, but we both still had enemies which required us to remain hidden.

I had them from my connection to the mafia...and he had them because of his role in leading El Peligro, a gang that originated from the cartel.

We'd both attempted to leave our lives spent killing and defending our names when we became family men, but we were fools. Our enemies were determined to never let us forget and refused to let us move beyond it without paying for every single thing we did.

"I can't fix this, Juan. I tried. Fuck, you know how often I have tried to untangle this fucking mess. No matter what I do, how many enemies I defeat, it's like a new family pops up with its sights set on murdering everyone I've ever known."

Our friendship had started by accident when a deal had gone bad and instead of killing each other, we killed the other men in the room and became allies. That was almost ten years ago, and while we'd been running ever since, we hadn't gained any space from our problems. They only grew, and in turn, we did too...we became closer as a family, traveling together and watching one another's backs.

Juan continued to stare down at our kids before giving me his thoughts.

"Perhaps we need to unify our families then. If it's getting this bad, use El Peligro, just as an extra layer of protection."

A sour feeling overrode that fear working through me.

He'd managed to take the gang his father had led, and with his wife, Taylor, they'd turned the entire thing into a charity. El Peligro didn't strike fear into people's hearts anymore; it gave them hope. I hated the idea of taking what he'd changed for the betterment of the community and turning it into something lethal again. El Peligro was dismantled from the top down and reconstructed to be a tool for the powerless. They were getting insulin to people who didn't have insurance. Homes for those who couldn't afford rent. Clothes and school supplies for low-income families, and funding for the local schools.

El Peligro had started buying up property so they could offer housing to those who needed it most instead of corrupt billionaires buying out of greed. El Peligro was a thorn in the side of any politician or real estate mogul who wanted a foothold in North Carolina. Juan and Taylor wanted to stretch their hands further and cover a broader scope, but it would take time.

Time they didn't have if we had to continue running.

While they were playing Robin Hood, I stabbed everyone who dared to breathe wrong in their direction. Juan didn't realize this, but even he had accrued several enemies by standing on the right side of the law. Those real estate moguls wanted blood, and I was the person who took the hits. I did it because I'd created so many other messes that Juan had to save me from. It was an honor to have his back.

"I don't want to use El Peligro unless we have no other choice."

Juan dipped his head and shifted closer to me to quiet his voice.

"Once upon a time, we talked about who would take over for us. Do you remember that?"

A fist gripped my heart as I watched Presley sleep. Back then she wasn't even a thought. I had assumed one of Juan's kids would lead or take over, but now my daughter was here, and there'd been a separation in how we led and what we did. Juan was the good guy and had a community to protect. He'd become a symbol of hope for so many, there was no way I could ask him to sacrifice his sons to fix all the shit I'd started with these families.

I had envisioned having my own outfit...stealing from the other families in the mafia and creating a large enough one of my own so that I would be invincible. I wasn't the head of any family; I had no ties anywhere...I was The Joker. Someone who crept into the underbelly of society and tricked them out of their holdings. While I was prepared to walk away from all of it entirely, I fucked up.

I fell in love, and when her life nearly became forfeit because of my role in the mafia world, I stepped away. I was prepared to never step back into that life again, but it yanked me by both legs, not giving me any choice.

The threats were endless, and I wasn't sure we'd ever be able to outrun them.

Not unless something drastic changed...

"We've been running for five years straight."

Juan turned toward the door, ready to head back to bed no doubt. His raised brow encouraged me to continue.

"We need a new plan..." I trailed off.

He glared at me then flicked a gaze over at the kids who were still sleeping.

"What sort of plan?"

This could be insane. It could be the worst idea I ever had or the only option we had for survival.

My fists clenched and unclenched at my sides. "First, we consolidate, give our kids roots. The manor...it's large enough to give each of our families privacy. We move here, permanently."

Juan's eyes were dark in the muted room, but I noticed as they narrowed on me angrily. I knew what he was worried about: that I'd drag his boys to the front of the line to go to war for us. It was a thought we had years ago when the idea of who would take over was brought up. But this was my plan, and it had to be me who was willing to take the risk.

"Okay...and then what?" Juan asked cautiously.

I paused, letting my mind work. Rylie was going to kill me, but Scotty would have my back. My uncle would understand, and deep down I knew I was right about what I had in mind.

We could do this.

"They're going to grow up understanding the dangers we face."

Juan shook his head, stopping me. "That's too vague...what exactly do you mean?"

I turned so he caught my expression. "Every family now knows my playbook...we aren't establishing a foothold anywhere as an official family would. Unlike the Costa Nostra or the Bratva...we have no place at any table."

Juan's eyes narrowed on something behind my shoulder. "You burned the table and killed most of the players. Now you're dealing with their relations and offspring. Hiding in your hole like a snake who swallowed his meal."

A smile curved along my lips. "Exactly."

"Are you going to tell me what the new plan is beyond all of us moving into the manor and raising our kids together?"

My mind began to churn out scenarios and ideas of how we could get out of this, and all of it revolved around that image of me being in a hole, devouring my meal. I wondered what would happen if I were given enough time...

"Just keep my kids out of it, whatever it is you're planning," Juan grumbled one last time.

"They won't be involved..." I assured him, still staring down at Presley tucked between his two boys. "But they're already extremely protective of her..."

Juan's head snapped up as if he'd just realized what I was hinting toward.

"What are you going to do, train her the way Scotty trained you?"

Juan never knew the depths of what my uncle had put me through. He had an idea that it was rough, but I'd never really opened up to anyone other than Rylie about how gruesome his methods could be. While I didn't want to consider my own child going through something that painful, I also knew firsthand how protective my uncle already was of her. Besides, there wasn't anyone on this planet I trusted more than Scotty. The second he defied a direct order to hand me over to his boss, he'd earned my loyalty.

My body shifted; my eyes meeting his. "He's the only person who could ever prepare her for what's to come."

Juan searched my face, understanding dawning on him. "You'll allow him to essentially raise her, Kyle. Think that through."

A strange throbbing sensation began in my chest at the idea of Scotty raising Presley. "Rylie and I aren't going anywhere. We'll be there to ensure she's safe, that he doesn't go too far. Besides, the boys will always keep her safe."

"See what you did there by bringing my boys into it?"

Juan's glare was severe as we stared at one another. He knew as well as I did that there would be no escaping the fact that his boys would naturally be drawn to protecting her. They already were and they hadn't even turned seven yet.

The silence expanded only to finally burst as Juan shook his head. "Then perhaps I need to take them away from her."

That throbbing in my chest became tighter just at the idea of him and Taylor leaving. We'd been through so much together, and while most of it was shit that got me shot, or nearly gutted like a goddamn pig, at least Juan was with me through all of it.

"You can't separate them. You know that as well as I do."

It was the only card I could really play. He and his family were free to leave, and they'd be fine, but Presley was an only child, and the kids here made up her family. Not just the twins, but their older sister, Alex, and Presley's cousin, Carter.

"Will you help me or not?" I interjected again, this time too loudly. Kingston stirred, which made Presley's eyes flutter.

Juan stepped closer and softened his voice. "My boys are not to be a part of this. Any of it."

"Understood." My voice was gentle, but the way Giovanni's eyes snapped open, you'd think he'd heard me.

I lowered my arms and pulled my daughter out from between them, which forced Kingston's eyes to open as well, and now both twins were glaring at me as if I'd just stolen something from them.

Deep down I knew this bond between them would keep my daughter alive. Just as long as nothing happened to make them ever feel anything more than sibling affection toward one another, then we'd be safe, and this entire plan would work.

CHAPTER 1
PRESLEY
AGE 16

Green stained the tips of my canvas shoes, effectively ruining them.

But I remained seated on the tiny knoll that faced the twins' section of the manor. From this vantage point, I could see their back patio and I had a clear shot of Kingston's garden. If they were to walk outside, they'd see me right away. Hell, even if they looked out their living room window, they'd see me.

I could walk up there, knock on the glass and have them open the door but that would require far too much pride. I couldn't muster it after all the things I learned, and everything they said.

Please come out.

Please come out.

My fingers raked through the longer blades of grass as I waited, staring at the patio furniture outside their kitchen doors. Lights were strung up, stretching to cover the garden area too. I had a million memories of playing under those lights, of waiting for them to turn on so we could have s'mores together and plant things under the moon.

Now, I glared as if they were a problem about to disrupt my life. If they came on, it meant my best friends had already left, and they'd done so without coming out here and telling me goodbye.

The blue in the sky turned into a dark pink, then to an orange. The cicadas sang around me, along with a few bullfrogs welcoming the night. My heart ached as if I'd physically pulled it from my chest and they'd taken it with them, packed away in one of their messy duffle bags, stuffed under a hoodie and discarded.

Forgotten.

My phone remained dark beside me, fully charged, with the volume up. No one had called. No one had texted.

They'd just left.

The lights around their patio flickered on, and a light inside their living room turned off.

A sob broke free from my chest because this wasn't real. They would never just leave...not me. Not ever.

The argument we'd had flashed in my mind, but we always argued, and while I was hurt and they owed me an apology, I still wanted a goodbye.

We were supposed to wake up this morning and go renovate the farmhouse. I was going to give them the silent treatment for a week, and they were going to try and get back into my good graces by visiting the baby Highland cows with me. We had plans next week to go swimming up in the mountains, and we were going to take a tent and camp.

It wasn't until the patio door opened that I registered I'd been outside for too long. The sky was nothing but inky black and a tiny crescent moon interrupted the darkness above me. Something felt oddly ironic at the lack of stars being out, as if Gio had taken all of them with him.

The man walking toward me was lit up by the string of lights and looked so similar to the twins that my breath hitched. He was gentle with his daughter, wife, and mother but held a razor-sharp edge with everyone else. I always respected that about him.

Juan dropped into a squat in front of me and searched my face.

"Hey, kiddo. You okay?"

No. I wasn't okay.

"They're gone?" I asked as another sob crept into my throat.

He nodded, but his eyes were red, and his Adam's apple bobbed as if he were holding back emotions just like I was. A few stray tears slid down my cheeks as I processed how different things were going to be for all of us.

"You need to get up and go home, Pres." Juan held his hand out to me, and I numbly accepted it. He pulled me to my feet and then cradled me to his side just like he had done a thousand times since I was a kid.

"They'll be back before you know it." His tone was full of encouragement but deep down I knew better.

Deep down I knew things were never going to be the same. My best friends were lost to me and it was all my fault.

CHAPTER 2
PRESLEY
AGE 7

The center dipped, making Gio roll toward me. I nudged him with my elbow, so he'd give me some space as Kingston crawled next to me.

"At least this place has a cool trampoline," Kingston said while stealing some of my blanket.

I tugged back, hitting him in the side until he finally let go.

"Gio, find us the twins." I finally settled and pulled my stuffed cow closer to my neck.

Kingston made some sound then shifted next to me. "Probley can't cause it's a different sky."

We had left the manor, even though I wasn't sure why. Mom and Dad just said we had to all leave on a trip, and then we packed all of our bags. I tilted my head to the side. "I think it's the same sky."

"A different patch of sky." Kingston sighed like I should have known what he was saying. "Found it."

Gio raised his finger and then I put mine up, but I must not have pointed in the right place. "You don't see it, Elvis."

I cut my gaze over to the boy next to me. "That's not my name. It's Presley."

Gio rolled his eyes while Kingston scoffed. "We knowwww."

I knew his mouth couldn't form the R in my name the right way, so he didn't call me Presley. He called me Elvis, but Kingston called me *mi reina.* He only did that because I made him play dress-up where I got to be the queen, but it didn't bother me as much as the nickname Gio gave me.

I sat up, my hair sticking up everywhere behind me. "Then stop calling me Elvis."

"Look! It's right there, the Big Dipper." Gio grabbed my hand and made me point in the right place, which made me fall back to the trampoline.

I sighed, "I thought we were looking for the twins. Castor and Pollux." I didn't really know what it was, but Gio had once said there were twins in the sky and ever since, I had wanted to find them.

"I'll keep looking," Gio replied.

"Do you think we'll always be under a different sky?" Kingston asked, pulling my hand into his.

Gio quickly grabbed my other one until both my hands were clasped by two warm palms.

My fingers wrapped around theirs as we all watched the familiar stars light up the sky. It made me think of all the times I'd drawn my farm and the cows I'd have on it. How they'd be so happy under a sky like this, and how there'd be open space for them and for me. I'd invite Gio and King to come visit but they'd have to promise not to ever be mean to my cows.

I let out another little sigh, feeling content. "Yeah, cause there's so much of it. It's like all the roads that lead to everywhere we go."

Kingston explained, "We'll always have to find the Big Dipper, then we'll be under the same sky."

Gio sat up and stared over at his twin. "What if it's daytime?"

"Duh, only during nighttime," Kingston argued.

"Maybe there's a Big Dipper in the clouds somewhere," I suggested, "Or maybe the twins are up there."

Gio rolled his eyes. "It's hard to find that one and you're acting stupid. Of course the Big Dipper isn't in the clouds during the daytime."

My nose scrunched in irritation. "You're stupid. If we ever get split up, I'm not looking for your stars, so we won't ever be under the same sky."

Gio crossed his arms and said, "Then I'm not looking for you."

My eyes burned and before I knew it, I just needed him to understand how big of a deal that would be to me.

I took my brown cow stuffy and shoved it under his neck while crawling onto his chest. "You take that back, Giovanni. Right now. You have to always look for me because what if I get lost? You have King, I have no one to find me."

Kingston pulled me off and gently said, "I'll look for you, *mi reina*."

Gio glared until he realized I was crying and then he pulled my hand into his and whispered, "I'm sorry, I'm just joking. I'll look for you too."

I sniffed. "Promise?"

"I promise."

THE NEXT NIGHT we were back home, and I was being tucked into bed while my parents tried to make me feel better. When we traveled, no one seemed to care if me and the twins slept on the floor together but whenever we got home, we weren't allowed to. The twins always made me feel better, but Mom and Dad said I had to start growing up.

"Goodnight, sweetheart. We love you." My dad said, before hitting the light.

I didn't say it back.

Why couldn't I just sleep with my best friend, just like always?

Once the light clicked off, I clung to my stuffy. I tried to prepare for the fear that always came when the darkness hit but this time, there was a strange green glow that appeared above my loft.

I crawled out of bed and then climbed the stairs up to my second-story loft. Mom had set up a painting area for me, where I created pictures of the farm I wanted to live on one day. The ceiling had never glowed, but now it was covered in green stars.

Someone tapping against glass had me turning around.

I walked over and pushed the window open, only to have Gio duck his head and step on the seat, and then the floor.

"What are you doing here?" I whisper-shouted at him.

Dad was going to be so mad if he heard him.

Gio's eyes rose to the glowing stars and then he smiled. "I felt bad about what I said when we were on the trampoline. I made you a sky that we will always share now, no matter what."

Squeezing my stuffy closer to my chest I tilted my head back and smiled.

"This way you'll never leave me."

Gio reached out and held my hand. "Never, ever."

CHAPTER 3
PRESLEY
AGE 17

Growing up I learned how to take a hit, probably harder than was necessary, but my uncle's methods were unconventional. Frayed knuckles I could tape up, glue together in some cases. Ice baths were helpful for the bruises and aching ribs I'd earned over the years. There were tools for every injury. Scotty taught me how to endure, how to eliminate weakness, and live without it myself.

Unfortunately, no one ever once considered that I might need to learn how to break.

Perhaps if they had, then I wouldn't be tucked in my best friends' empty bed, staring at artwork that we'd done together when we were kids. I wouldn't be trying to take a hit off their pillows as if they were a drug just to feel as though they were still here.

I wouldn't be doing this every night instead of sleeping.

If my parents or Scotty knew I was merely placing things inside of tidy compartments in my head and pulling them out to grieve over later, maybe they'd realize I needed help. I could complete the lessons given to me in a timely fashion and with precision, but then I was left alone. Left to wander the halls of a mansion that was split into four family wings, two of which were empty.

A salty tear slipped into a crack along my lip that hadn't healed yet from my last training session. The sting was a reminder that I was human.

Alive.

Kingston used to say, "Plants can breathe, Presley, and if you're ever unsure, just hide it from the sun and tear out its roots."

I had argued something stupid just for the sake of arguing. Probably because I just wanted him to keep talking to me and I couldn't stand the idea of him ever stopping.

The picture of the farm I drew as a kid taped above his bed shifted as the AC kicked on and it made my gaze wander over to the opposite side of the room.

Navy blue bedding was draped over a queen-sized bed; Gio's posters were mostly related to star systems and how to navigate them. Moon rocks, glow worms, and a few NASA posters from when he wanted to be an astronaut.

Gio used to tell me I was the brightest star in his universe, then he'd pretend to blast me with some homemade star-blasting machine. He'd joke that I was so bright I needed to be broken into tiny pieces and shared.

The memory had my fingers curling tightly into the covers. Wetness tracked down my face as I glared at the ceiling. A flame burned deep in my belly to stand up and rip the image away from any place that anyone could ever see it again. Especially one of the brothers that had a hand in ruining me.

Because really there wasn't one person who had a hand in breaking me...there were two.

MY COUSIN CARTER was the same age as the twins, which meant she was a year and a half older than me. When we were younger, she liked to rub that in my face and remind me that she was in charge. However, Alex, the twin's older sister, would then remind Carter who was actually in charge, so while my cousin and I should have bonded, I drew closest to Alex and the twins.

Throughout the years, Carter and her parents would come and go, not really living in the manor like we did. It became easier to feel detached from her, and she didn't understand why I was always training, nor did she care to know. She would typically arrive like a hurricane, toss her things, dump all her drama, and then make the weekend all about her before leaving again.

It used to bug me when I was younger, because I felt like I had no room to fit inside her larger-than-life world. She traveled more than me; she went to school. It wasn't exactly public school, but private school was still better than doing your homework at the kitchen table while your uncle fed table scraps to the dogs.

Now, seeing her come in wearing a pair of two-hundred-dollar sunglasses, with extensions in that went past her ass, I was beyond grateful for her antics.

"Oh my god, did someone die? Why are you hugging me?" Carter was stiff, with her arms dropped to her sides as I squeezed her.

Finally releasing her, I let out a sigh. "Just so glad you're here."

She threw her purse, which was practically a duffel bag to the couch, and plopped down. "Well at least someone appreciates me." She crossed her arms, and I took in how her reddish-brown hair had gotten lighter while her self-tanning applications had gotten darker. She'd inherited the James' family mossy eyes that my dad, her, and Uncle Scotty all had. I was insanely jealous of that fact.

I sat next to her, tucking my feet up under me. "Why do you say that?"

"Because my parents left me here. They literally dropped me off and said they had to go to Belize without me. Like, what the fuck could they be doing that's so important? Whatever, at least this place is big, and I'll have my section of the manor to myself. Where are the twins?"

That's when she really inspected me, as if I were missing two sets of arms and legs.

"Wait." She swung her head around the room, then stood up. "It's your birthday, they aren't here?"

Just then, Alex walked into the room from the terrace and plopped onto the couch across from me.

"My brothers are idiots."

Guilt sprung up like a resilient weed, and in my silence, I was grateful that Alex never looked at me or acted as though I was the reason her brothers had left.

Carter placed her hands on her hips, her black leggings were paired with flip-flops and a crop tank, revealing her toned stomach. "I figured they'd be back by now...especially on your birthday..."

My gaze met hers and while I tried so hard to tamp down the emotions surfacing, my eyes began to water.

"Oh shit." My cousin dropped into a crouch in front of me, and while we'd never been close, not really, she threw her arms around me.

"I'm so sorry, Pres. You three were inseparable. Annoyingly so, but I can't believe those idiots still haven't pulled their heads out of their asses."

"Carter, stop reminding her that my two moron brothers left. I've been trying to cheer her up, but it isn't working." Alex sighed, and it made me laugh because what the hell else could I do?

She pulled away from me and eyed the blonde on the couch across from me. "Well, I'm here now. We're going to have a girls' night. My side of the manor is empty; we're going to party over there."

I was only seventeen. Carter was almost nineteen, and Alex was twenty-one...but we'd never really followed any of the rules. There was enough alcohol in this house to have a fun night alone in the empty part of the manor, so I perked up and swiped at a few stray tears.

"I'll grab some nacho cheese from my pantry. And chips!"

Alex sat up and held her finger up. "I want margaritas, and only margaritas."

Carter rolled her eyes but agreed. "Fine."

An hour later, I was stirring nacho cheese in a saucepan while Carter turned on *13 Going on 30* at the same time she attempted to use some new, trendy workout machine. It looked like an ironing board and a thigh master had a baby, and while Carter used her knees to pull herself up, she kept crying out each time the thing wobbled.

Alex was blending the margaritas, and something in my chest loosened. I had needed this.

Six months without them, and every day I felt like I wouldn't make it without breaking down. With Carter and Alex, I at least felt like I could breathe again.

After finishing off two drinks and a pile of nachos, things were beginning to wind down. Alex had turned off the blender, double fisting two of her own drinks while reclining on the couch.

"Okay, I have a question for you, Presley!" Carter laughed while sipping the last of her drink. She was on her third margarita and had apparently hit her limit based off how frequently she was laughing.

"Yeah?" I called over my shoulder. I was now trying out Carter's work out machine. The thing really was unstable, but it was also sort of fun.

Carter crawled next to me on the floor and whisper-shouted, "I think I finally figured out what Uncle Kyle does for work."

"Oh yeah?" I pulled my knees up, gripping the handles. Shit the whole thing nearly toppled over again. Carter was never invited into the confidential details of what our family did. Mostly because her family left too often and didn't want to live in the safety of the manor. Because of that, Dad always said it was imperative that Carter never learn what anyone did.

"He's in the mafia!"

I fell off the machine and rolled onto my back. Alex's eyes grew from her spot on the couch, but she didn't say anything.

"Why would you think that?" I slowly got to my hands and knees and tried to get up.

Carter smiled and tapped my nose. "How does anyone think that? I don't think it, I know it."

I hated drunk Carter. "Okay, but how do you know it, then?"

She dropped to her butt then sprawled out on her back. "Because I saw something I wasn't supposed to...isn't that how all these things start? I saw your dad shoot someone...do you think that means he'll shoot me too?"

Her words were like shards of ice being tossed at my chest. Memories of when I had found out clouded my mind, making me nervous about what would happen to her. This was a major breach if she truly did see something she wasn't supposed to.

"Carter, what did you see?"

She was already relaxing with her head on a cushion and her eyes closed, but before she fell asleep, she muttered something that had Alex shooting up from her seat and running to find Scotty. As for me, it sent a cold chill down my spine as a memory surfaced.

"The Joker."

CHAPTER 4
PRESLEY
AGE 8

I loved Halloween.

It was the only time we could go into town without using fake names or keeping our faces low. When I had asked once about why we did that, my mom had hugged me really tight and said we were just being cautious.

I wasn't sure what that meant exactly, but my family was cautious anytime we were in public. They were careful when it came to me going to school, or even attending sporting events that my cousin Carter played. She had so much more freedom than I did, or even the twins and Alex.

But on Halloween, everyone dressed up. Even the parents.

We went into town and into all the neighborhoods, just like all the other kids, and we got to trick-or-treat. My mom and dad went as Harley Quinn and The Joker. I wasn't sure why but the twins' dad, Juan, got really mad at them for it. Kept telling them they were being reckless, but I wasn't sure why.

I was dressed like Kora, one of my favorite Avatar characters, and the twins dressed like Minecraft characters. One was a zombie and the other was a villager. Carter was dressed like a baseball player, just like her parents. Dad said his older brother, Decker played baseball in college, so when he and aunt Mallory decided to dress up, it was supposed to be funny.

I hadn't had so much fun in such a long time, and I didn't want it to end. Red leaves crunched under my feet as I ran down sidewalks, knowing other kids were living the same life I was. For one night, we weren't any different, and I wasn't this bird caged in a manor, without friends except for the ones that lived under the same roof.

For one night, I was completely free. I didn't even mind that the twins and Alex had left early. Carter and I kept inspecting each other's candy buckets, while our parents walked behind us. Every now and then aunt Mallory would play with Carter's hair and I would get mesmerized by how similar they looked with reddish brown hair and the same smile.

I looked back seeing Dad had his arm over Mom's shoulder and she kept laughing into his neck. Scotty walked behind them, dressed like Alfred from Batman. It had been my idea and I knew he'd only done it to see me smile. "Can we go get ice cream?" I called from over my shoulder.

My dad's laugh was the one he used with only me and Mom. I once heard Scotty say that my dad diced up versions of himself and handed them out to different people, depending on what they needed from him. I once asked him what my dad gave to me, and Scotty had pulled me into his arms and promised me that my dad only ever gave us the truest version of himself, or whatever was left of it. I didn't know what that meant, but it made me grateful for the times I saw him smile and laugh with us, knowing he didn't do that with anyone else.

"All this candy isn't enough for you?"

"No!" Carter yelled back and uncle Decker snagged her bucket from her in response.

"Carter Marie, your bucket is completely full." His laugh

reminded me of my dad's. They looked similar but Uncle Decker had darker hair and he was taller. Aunt Mallory hedged closer to see inside the bucket and then let out a sigh.

"We should actually get back. I have an early call in the morning and then we have to get back to New York."

I glanced over at my cousin, seeing her eyes drop to the ground. Sometimes I wished she could live in the manor with me, like the twins did. Even in their own wing, at least I'd see her more often than I did with her parents always going back to New York. Anytime I got sad about it, my mom would remind me that they were doing important things that helped people. I waved to my cousin as she walked off with her parents and tried not to feel sad over the loneliness.

Red leaves swirled around my ankles as the wind picked up and I smiled, almost feeling like it was a hug. Nature always seemed to find a way to remind me I wasn't entirely alone, even if I felt like it.

"You still want some ice cream, Kiddo?" My dad called to me.

A black car sped past us, but I didn't pay attention to it as I turned around with a smile, about to explain that I thought Ice Cream would be a great idea, but my dad had stopped walking.

"Dad?"

It was as if time stood still and completely froze in place.

"DOWN!" Scotty shouted and lunged for me right as my dad fell and red began ruining his white shirt. My uncle's arm came up and covered my eyes, but I felt his other arm extend out, and then more shots rang out.

Tears streamed down my face as I screamed for my dad. I wanted to see him, but Scotty completely blocked my vision. I heard my mom screaming too, and then there were people running toward us, their voices washing out the echoes in my head.

"Call an ambulance!"

"Ma'am, are you hurt?"

"Wasn't there a child here, is she okay?"

Then there was screaming, which is when Scotty finally moved off of me and I was able to see what had happened. There was a body lying a few feet from us; he had a hole in his head, his eyes were wide and staring right at me.

I got to my feet and moved over to where my dad was and found my mother with her hands holding something to his side. Her makeup had begun to run from how hard she was crying.

I held my father's gaze, his green eyes that I loved so much locked on me. His hand covered my own and he smiled.

"You know how we live separate from the rest of the world and we use fake names in public?"

I nodded, pressing my hands into my daddy's chest, doing what my mom told me. She had taken the extra fabric from my costume and slid it over his wound then told me to hold down as hard as I could.

Dad smiled again, this time blood smeared his lips. "This is our secret, honey. People want to hurt us."

"Why?" My voice felt strange, like I hadn't spoken a word in hours, and yet it felt like I'd been screaming for just as long.

"We ruin empires."

Red and white lights lit up the darkened neighborhood as the ambulance pulled up and two people in uniforms ran toward my dad. Scotty pulled my hand, so I was leaving my dad's side. I watched as they hovered over him and then loaded him into the back of the ambulance. Mom ran over to me, kissing my forehead.

"Stay with Scotty, Presley."

I nodded but noticed Scotty tug her hand. "Don't."

Mom shook her head as her lip wobbled. "I can't leave him."

"You think I can?" Scotty argued, pulling me closer to his side. "Do not make your daughter an orphan tonight. They're going to follow him to the hospital."

"Then do what you've always done, Scotty, and protect us."

She turned back toward the ambulance with a sob, which had her hands up and covering her mouth.

I glanced up at my uncle and saw the way his jaw moved, realizing this was the closest to crying I'd ever seen him. He held my hand and finally glanced down at me with a smile.

"I need you to be brave, Presley. Can you be brave with me?"

I nodded.

Scotty guided me toward our car and told me to get in next to him in the passenger seat, which wasn't where I'd been allowed to sit yet.

"I used to take your father on trips like this with me, and he learned how to be brave by being with me. You're going to as well, okay?"

Pulling the belt over my chest, I nodded and sank down into the seat as he drove off.

"I'm going to tell you a story, Presley, and I need you to remember this story and promise me that you won't share it with anyone, even the twins."

"I promise."

"Okay then, I'm going to tell you a story about how your father once protected the twins' mother, and in order to do that, he had to kill a bad man. This bad man was the boss of a very bad group, and after he killed him, all of that man's men and employees wanted to hurt your dad."

I thought that over, and asked, "Is that who those men were, in the black car?"

Scotty glanced at me and nodded. "Yes, that's exactly who they were...they've been after your dad for a very long time, and now they're after you and your mom. It's my job to help keep the family safe. It's why we live in the manor, and why we work so hard to keep everyone together."

As we drove, Scotty pulled out a gun that had a long barrel on the end and laid it in his lap.

"Presley, you're going to see something you don't want to see. I tried to protect you from it, but it's going to happen, and I could use your help."

"Me? What am I supposed to do?"

He kept his eyes on the road in front of us. I realized we were following the ambulance, but there were a few cars in front of us.

"You're going to do something that will scare you, and I know you're afraid, but I promise you that nothing will happen to you. You're going to help me keep your mom and dad safe, okay?"

I nodded, trying not to be scared.

"This car is protected with armor. They can't shoot us in here, but I need to stop them before they get to the hospital."

"Okay." My voice was shaky, and so were my hands, but there wasn't anything I could do but be brave like he'd said because I didn't want anything to happen to my parents.

"You need to do exactly as I say." He opened the moon roof until the cold air began blowing inside.

"Unbuckle, Presley."

I quickly did as he said and unlatched the metal.

"Do you remember when we rode down that road that had the trees you loved so much and your dad and mom asked if you wanted to fly?"

I had placed my feet on the leather compartment in the middle and poked my head through the moon roof, flinging my arms wide.

"Yes." My stomach tilted as understanding dawned.

"You're going to do that but instead of flying, you're going to protect your mom and dad."

His eyes remained on the road as he trailed them close. "You're going to pull the trigger on this gun I'm about to hand you, and you're going to make their car stop. Do you understand me?"

Panic surged. I shook my head as a few tears fell from my eyes. "I can't do that. I can't shoot a gun, Scotty. I can't—"

He kept his eyes on the black car in front of us but quickly glanced at me. "You can, Presley. You can do this, because if you don't, then that car is going to arrive at the hospital at the same time as your parents, and they're going to kill everyone inside. Your mom, dad, and all the people who helped them. We have to stop them."

A tiny fire lit up my chest as I swallowed my fear and agreed.

Scotty placed a black gun in my lap. It was metal and too big for my hands. It felt weird and heavy.

"You'll pull this as tight as you can." His hand directed my finger over the trigger, lightly showing me how to pull it. "Never point it anywhere but at what you intend to shoot. Keep your arms straight, don't drop it."

"Okay." My voice shuddered.

Scotty showed me exactly how to grip it and then ordered me to get up. The car suddenly sped faster and we veered to the side of the black car, right by their back tire.

"Now, Presley! You have to do it now. Stand up, and then shoot, don't stop shooting until the gun stops."

I placed my feet on the leather console and with the gun in my hand, the weight of it was distracting. The wind rushed through my hair, tugging it behind me as if the sky wanted to lift me from the car and carry me off. I watched the ambulance's lights flash and counted to three.

I thought of my mom.

I thought of my dad.

Then I brought my hands up and did exactly what Scotty told me to do. I squeezed as hard as I could and felt the gun lightly kick, but it was more of a jolt up my arm. From here I could see through the window, there was a driver and someone next to him. Then the back window rolled down.

"Hold it steady, Presley. Shoot that window!"

I closed my eyes but did as he said and just kept squeezing, and with every jerk of my hand and every window that shattered, I screamed. I screamed so loud that I pushed out the noise of tires squealing, of glass breaking, and of metal crunching.

I was yanked down hard enough to fall into my seat seconds later, and Scotty maneuvered the car around the black SUV that had just run off the road and slammed into a cement barrier. It burst into flames seconds later and I watched the fire lick at the sky from my side mirror. It felt like I was dreaming.

I'd done that.

I had—

"Let go, honey. It's okay." Scotty tried to pull the gun from my hand, but my fingers were gripping it so tight, I wasn't sure how to open them.

A tear slipped off my lash, and it hit my cold face. "I can't."

"You can, it's okay," Scotty encouraged, while watching the road.

I didn't let go until we veered off the exit and the scenery changed. The ambulance was still in front of us, red and white swirled in front of me. I stared down at the metal in my hands and thought about what I'd done.

"You're letting us go to the hospital?" I assumed he'd take me home.

Scotty adjusted his hand on the wheel before glancing over at me with a smile. "Figured you'd want to see your parents. It's our job to keep the family safe when there isn't anyone else to do it. No one will ever keep them as safe as we will, Presley."

Something about that struck at that fire that had been lit in my chest. I didn't understand why bad people wanted to hurt us, but I understood what my uncle was saying.

"Dad said we ruin empires." I spoke softly, inspecting the dried blood on my costume.

"What do you know about empires?" Scotty flicked his blinker to follow the ambulance. They drove toward a side entrance, but we continued toward the parking lot.

"You taught me about the Romans and a few others, but I don't really know."

"Your father has a dream, Presley. He wants to remove the bad people from this state, maybe even this country. To do that, he must take out their leaders and the way they make their money. We call that an empire."

"So my dad is sort of like Batman?"

Scotty laughed while shaking his head. "Ironic because his name in their world is 'The Joker.'"

"The Joker?" Now dad's costume and why the twins' dad was so bothered made a bit more sense.

"He went by a fake name so people never knew who he was. He stole from bad people and stopped the bad things they were doing. But to keep your mother safe, and now you...he never gave them his real name. He was always just 'The Joker.'"

My mind began to piece small things together, one by one. "Is that why we never use our real names in town?"

Scotty nodded. "We're trying to keep you safe."

"Will my dad die?"

Scotty glanced over at me, then ruffled my hair. "No."

"Why?"

He smirked. "I trained him. I'm going to train you to be exactly like him, only better. You up for that?"

I wanted to be like him, to be able to get hurt and not die. I wanted to be strong like him.

"Will you show me how to shoot without feeling so cold and scared?"

The rush of the wind in my face, the way the car crashed was still echoing somewhere in my soul, and I worried at what point that would try to sneak out.

"I'll teach you, *lánya*. You'll be better than even me, be able to see those coming from far enough away that the people you love never get hurt."

He had the same eyes as my dad, and they seemed to cloud as he watched the road. I wondered if maybe he was worried about my dad and didn't like that we were so close to getting hurt today.

"I'll learn then."

Scotty found an open spot and parked, then turned off the engine. "It'll be hard work, you sure you're up for it?"

"I'm sure."

He gave me one last smile before unclicking his seat belt. "You'll hate me for what I turn you into."

I could tell he meant it in a very serious way, and since Dad got shot, maybe it would be safe if I just did what Scotty said. "Won't it be worth it if I can help save the family?"

My uncle never responded before opening the door.

CHAPTER 5
PRESLEY
AGE 17

The afternoon heated my hands as I pulled on the rotting wood.

Dust erupted from the last board being dropped and the sunlight cast an eerie glow through the gaps in the walls. The pile on the floor of discarded wood had grown so much, it would take well over an hour for me to pack it all up and move it to the burn pile.

Taking a step back, I glared at my lack of progress and scanned the rest of the wall and all I had left to do. The old farmhouse was strong even after all the weather and neglect it had endured. But I was determined to rip out every single board until there was nothing left, and I could start fresh.

The heat practically suffocated me as I moved through what was once the living room. Swiping at my brow with my forearm, I paused at the sight of someone standing in the open doorway.

Ashy chestnut hair cropped high and receding from a too angular face. Green eyes I wasn't lucky enough to inherit, and a muscular frame hidden under a set of black clothes far too thick for this heat. I rolled my eyes and continued past him as if I hadn't seen him.

"You're being stubborn."

I ignored my uncle and dipped down to retrieve my water bottle.

"You're acting like this wasn't something that could happen at some point."

My eyes remained on the wreckage. I was going to put up shiplap I had decided, but only in certain parts of the house. Not throughout.

"Lánya."

I had never asked why Scotty called me that, but I'd once overheard Taylor asking him about it. *Why do you call her daughter?*

I had no idea what language he used, but I knew for certain he wasn't my father. I had a feeling it was deeper than that for him, that he cared for me in a way that meant he loved me like how my dad loved me. Speaking of my dad...

"What has *The Joker* said about all this?" I spun away, rearranging more rotten pieces that would need to be tossed.

Scotty remained quiet, unphased. "You mean your father?"

"No. I mean The Joker. That's who's pulling all the strings, right? The one who has the enemies and the one I'm stepping in to replace?"

My father hadn't handed me a crown; he'd given me no other choice but to accept it. Ever since that night when I was just eight, I had felt the burden of being *The Joker's* daughter.

"Your father is against it. He doesn't want you anywhere near the Adesso family."

My chest squeezed the smallest bit with relief.

Scotty followed me from one room to another, taking his time as if he had no agenda at all. I knew him better than that.

"But I happen to think this would be the most peaceful outcome after the mess Carter created for us."

My beautiful but very stupid cousin had indeed started a shitstorm for us. According to Scotty, who I had called after her reveal of my dad's criminal alter ego, she had somehow fallen in with a rival family. Roscoe Ferro, who had been trying to get information on us, had wiggled his way into her life with the help of his mildly attractive and now dead nephew. My dad caught on before the rest of us did because he managed to catch her while he was out on a supply route.

My dad stepped in and killed Ferro's nephew, who had been pretending to be Carter's boyfriend for the previous month. The man had called my dad, "The Joker," right before a bullet landed between his eyes. Carter crashed out, and her parents, unsure of what to do, dropped her here after my dad suggested it.

Finding her had put our family on the map, so now our enemies were circling like sharks in the water.

"Why can't *you* set up the alliance, why does it have to be me?" I asked.

My uncle surveyed the room before toying with a loose board. "Adrian Adesso has specifically requested you be the point person between our families."

I turned and raised my brow. "And you trust that?"

It was dangerous that the young head of the Adesso family was able to reach out in the first place, although I wouldn't pretend to understand how vast or deep my uncle's connections went. He'd worked in a few different crime families throughout his life and had made more allies and enemies than I cared to keep count of.

"I trust you. If you were to go into enemy territory, you'd be fine. You've been taught how to withstand whatever he throws at you. We need an ally, Presley, and he's the most powerful one we could ever hope to get."

I shook my head, unsure why my uncle was suddenly acting so stupid. "We can't trust him, which means there'd be no alliance that we could create that would ever last."

Scotty stared at me.

The silence grew and suddenly it clicked.

"You think I can win him over, make him like me." My tone was unsure because of how embarrassed it made me feel to even say that out loud.

My uncle didn't reply right away, but I knew that was his plan.

I ignored him, digging back into the rotted wood. Anger stirred like a dust storm in my chest, clogging my airways and tear ducts. Why did I have to be the one to clean this up? I knew I'd been training for it my whole life, but I signed up to shoot and kill whomever threatened our family. I never agreed to go play dress-up and smile at the enemy.

It only proved as a reminder of why the twins had been so upset that night when—

"I'm not asking you to do anything that you don't want to do. Maybe you go and you meet him and he's not horrible. You inspire loyalty in people, *lánya*. Even if you merely become friends, that could ensure we have him as an ally."

Friends.

Didn't he realize that I was incapable of keeping those? My only friends left me. They abandoned me, and without so much as a goodbye.

I began focusing on the house once more, but the thought of doing this, of helping my father kept creeping back into focus. The longer we drew all this out, the less of my life I'd get to live. I had made a promise that I would help set things right and end the threats. Then I could have my farm and start my life.

I could get my dad an alliance and make sure he would be okay. I could help end this war that had been waging for all these years, and then I could settle down.

"Where is this guy?"

Scotty's eyes flicked up while his dark brows rose. "Italy."

Of course he was in Italy. I'd always expected to be sent away to fight for the family; I just assumed it would be with my gun, and maybe a knife at my rival's throat. I didn't think it would be to meet with the head of a family and play nice. "I will travel to Italy for one week, and only a week. One of those days I will meet with your guy. That's all I'm offering."

"Fine. Would you like to take any backup with you?"

I assumed he meant his dog Reaper but was shocked when I saw him pull up his phone and show me the string of texts. A vine on envy and malice twisted around my heart and squeezed.

They were texts from the twins...and they were meant for me.

My voice was so small as it squeezed past my lips. "How come those are going to your phone?"

They'd been texting me.

All these months, they'd been reaching out, and I hadn't known.

Scotty acted blasé, as if this wasn't earth-shattering information. "I had our tech guy set it up...whenever they text you, it forwards to me. Same with calls. The only thing I can't control is if they find you on social media."

I wasn't on social media.

My uncle had been doing things like this my entire life, so it shouldn't have been a surprise. I shouldn't have felt the bone-deep pain of betrayal scraping along my veins, reminding me that this man who had a hand in raising me would never hesitate to ignore how badly my heart would take the hit. "Scotty, what the fuck?"

He shrugged and pocketed his phone. "They were a weakness, and you needed the time to get past your infatuation with them."

My chest felt like it had caught fire with how easily he'd dismissed what I had felt for them, and how he acted like he had any real clue how deep it went. "I wasn't infatu—"

He scoffed and spun around, about to leave. "You forget that I have eyes everywhere, *lánya*."

My face heated, realizing what that meant. I was on his heels, practically chasing him as I asked, "So what...they're offering to suddenly come back and be my security?"

"They haven't offered anything other than apologies but as I said...you inspire loyalty. They'd go with you in a heartbeat."

No, I didn't inspire loyalty; I was the spoiled brat who required constant observation. The twins did what they had to...it was better that I couldn't see their texts because anything they'd have to say would be an excuse or justification as to why they felt like they had to hurt me the way they had.

"No backup. I'll be fine."

Scotty's eyes found the gravel at our feet and then he stopped.

"Would you like me to show you what they said?"

I continued walking toward the large field that separated the farmhouse and our manor. Gravel crunched under my shoes and the sun warmed my skin, but it was the frustrating tears in my eyes I needed to hide.

Without looking back, I replied, "No. You can delete them."

I figured that would be the end of it, but Scotty's next words froze me in place.

"You ever wonder why they have such a hatred for me, your dad, and this life?"

No, I didn't want to dig into any of their whys. Not when any of them had been reason enough for them to keep me. Whatever they did see was enough for them to lump me in with everyone else and dismiss this entire family.

My throat was tight as I shook my head.

Scotty's feet scuffed the rocks as he drew closer. "You might want to ask him some day."

My head popped up as I watched my uncle pass me.

"Who?"

He replied, tilting his chin over his shoulder, his mossy eyes landing hard on me. "Kingston."

CHAPTER 6

KINGSTON

AGE 10

I knew I wasn't supposed to be downstairs.

It was one of the only rules we had in the manor, and I was always the one to ensure none of us ever broke it. But two days ago, Presley got into trouble and her dad got so upset that he took her favorite stuffed animal away. He said it was gone for the month, and since she was nine years old now, she needed to start growing up.

It wasn't really her fault for sneaking into our room again. Her dad had made it really clear that she wasn't allowed to anymore, but there was a really bad thunderstorm last night with so much lightning, the electricity went out. Presley cracked our door around midnight and both me and Gio had taken all of our blankets and piled them in the middle of the floor so we could both protect her.

The next morning, her dad was standing over us with his arms crossed and he looked really upset. Our dad didn't seem mad, but he did shake his head like he was disappointed in us. I didn't really care that much, not when it came to keeping Presley safe, and making sure she didn't need us. Now she needed us for a different reason.

That stuffy meant the world to her; nine or not, she couldn't go a whole month without it. Presley had already checked their entire family wing, and all the cars, which meant there was only one place it could be.

Gio had gone into town with everyone else, same with Presley and my big sister, Alex. Our families were shopping or going to dinner, but I had faked being sick. My abuela was here and offered to watch me, but she was already asleep on one of the outside loungers, listening to one of her audiobooks.

I'd snuck past the big windows in our wing that revealed the loungers and darted down the hall until I was out of sight.

The door to downstairs was tall and heavy, but I pulled it open and took the stairs two at a time. I had to be quick if I was going to find her stuffed cow and get it to her room before anyone came home. The stairs were made of concrete, and the basement was too, but large, thick rugs covered most of the open space, so it didn't feel like a dungy basement. It felt like a library with leather couches and two large desks. The main space wasn't where her dad's office was though, so I kept walking until I turned the corner to a small hallway.

The door was black with a gold knob, which reminded me of something from a pirate ship. I gently twisted the handle and pushed the door open. The room was lit by a dim lamp somewhere off in the corner, but directly in front of me was a half wall that I quickly ducked behind as someone in the room started talking.

Who the heck was here...everyone was supposed to be in town.

My fingers tunneled into the rug as I crawled forward, peeking around the wall. I saw a man sitting in a chair, his wrists were secured with zip ties and so were his feet. He was crowded by Presley's dad, his uncle Scotty and...my dad.

My eyes narrowed as I took in my dad's dark hair, which wasn't styled and had pieces falling over his dark brows and nearly cutting into his amber eyes that matched mine.

He had a sneer on his face as he stared down at the man in the chair, and his fists...they were dripping with blood.

It made me focus on the man in the chair, seeing that he was also bleeding. His lip was busted, his eye was black, and his cheek was cut. With his head drooping, he looked like he could barely sit up.

"For someone who keeps begging to keep his life, you sure are making this extremely difficult." Kyle joked with a smile slipping up on his face like this was funny. His smile was different though from when he was around us...cruel and almost evil.

Scotty stood at the back of the wall, one of his dogs next to him, alert and watching the man in the chair. He looked like Presley and Carter in a way, with dark hair and fair skin. I didn't particularly care for the way he went so hard with training Presley; I knew he would never hurt her, but he was always so intense it made me a little afraid of him.

My stomach dropped as my dad pulled his arm back and slammed his fist into the man's face again. He groaned and spit out a blob of blood. "Please, I'm begging you. I have children. Don't you have kids...can't you understand?"

Tears started in the corners of my eyes as I watched my dad laugh, and then Kyle pulled out a knife. "We don't have kids, Frank. Not a single one, but something tells me yours would be better off without you."

"I didn't know she was that young—" The man choked on his blood, while tears streamed down his face.

"You stepped foot into my community, Frank. El Peligro had no choice," my dad said, grabbing the guy's jaw.

Kyle inspected his nails. "Honestly, even if you hadn't, your connection to the Yullivi family is a complication."

"I can—I can tell you who I'm working for. I know I messed up. I won't ever go near—"

"No, we'll send your body as a message to your boss. That's really all the use we have left for you," Kyle said lazily.

There was a thickness in my throat, making it difficult to swallow. What was I seeing? Why was my dad and Presley's like this... why were they the bad guys?

"I'm begging you." The man screamed, which made me flinch.

"Scotty, I think we'll let Reaper have fun with him."

Reaper's sleek black fur gleamed near the lamp light as his head tilted toward the man in the chair.

Scotty quickly muttered something in a different language and Reaper lunged. Within seconds, blood sprayed everywhere as the dog dug into the man's throat.

My stomach tilted and I vomited.

I had no idea if anyone saw me, but I had to get out. I scrambled back and fell to my butt before turning on all fours and running toward the door. The second I was out of his office, I threw up again.

Then I ran and kept running. I just kept going until I got to my bedroom and slammed the door behind me.

"KINGSTON?" I heard Presley's soft voice from the door and turned over on my side.

She knocked again.

"King-ston?"

I hated when she drew my name out like that, as if it were a song or something.

I didn't want to see her, or anyone. "What?!" I yelled over my shoulder.

The door pushed open, and I could hear her bare feet gently slap against the floor, and then something warm was being pushed against my face.

"I got you dirt."

I lifted my hand to feel along the glass jar and pulled it away from my cheek. She'd filled a glass jar with dirt.

"I saw the sun hitting it and I know you like to touch the garden dirt when the sun heats it. I brought it to you, so you'd feel better."

Angry tears wanted to fall, but I held them back. It wasn't her fault that my dad had lied to me, and her. It wasn't her fault that I had to see that dog rip someone's throat out.

My stomach tilted and I felt sick all over again, but I managed to whisper, "Thanks, *mi reina*."

I thought she'd leave, but she crawled onto my bed and over my legs until she was tucked against the wall facing me. She had her stuffed cow in her arms, and a sad smile on her face.

Blue eyes. Dark hair and a freckled nose.

"Hi." She blinked, lowering her long lashes.

"You're going to get in trouble again for being in here."

She just placed her hand over the jar of dirt and continued to stare at me.

I didn't want to talk anymore, so I shut my eyes.

I felt her palm move to my cheek and for some reason that felt nice. She had no idea that her father led a different life, or that Scotty did. She loved Scotty almost more than her real uncle, Decker. They were liars.

My dad was one too.

I let the tears fall and finally let sleep pull me under.

Sometime later I woke up and found she was still across from me; her hand curled around mine. Gio had crawled onto the bed too and was asleep slightly angled between both me and Presley with his face up toward the ceiling.

Taking in a deep breath, I realized I'd be okay as long as I had them. I could face our family being liars, and I'd protect them from it, no matter the cost.

CHAPTER 7
PRESLEY
AGE 17

Adrian had apparently offered to send his private jet to pick me up, but I wanted to use this rare window of freedom to refuse and fly there myself. Scotty would never approve of me flying commercial, or without someone following me. However, since I was doing him a favor that I'd never wanted to begin with, I explained I'd be going alone and in my own way.

Once the plane landed, I secured my carry-on and found a taxi to the cute hotel I had booked myself. Then showered before dropping into bed.

I stared at my dark phone, willing my best friends to figure out what Scotty had done and bypass it. More than six months had passed since they left, and things weren't getting easier; they were getting more complicated and dangerous. I knew they had their reasons for crashing out the way they did but honestly, would it have killed them to just fight me in the training ring so we could get past it? I missed them.

I needed them.

Alex had trained in the gym with me the day before yesterday and asked again if I had heard from them. My throat had practically closed over the question, and when I saw her disappointment, I felt like I had failed her and everyone else in the house. They hadn't just left me; they'd left all of us. I had asked her if they were anywhere on social media because I'd gotten desperate for any crumb about their lives. She'd informed me what I had already assumed; they weren't anywhere, not anymore.

All of their socials were deleted, nothing new had been created.

If only I had told Scotty to show me the texts...

Turning on my back, I stared at the ceiling and willed sleep to claim me. When it finally did, it was to the image of someone standing over me with a smile.

I woke to the sound of someone singing.

Groggy and jet-lagged, I wasn't sure what exactly was going on as I gathered my surroundings and tried to piece together where I was.

I wasn't in my hotel room anymore...

Which suddenly had me shooting up in bed...except I wasn't on one.

The couch I was on was royal blue and velvet soft. The blanket over me was down feathered and plush. The light in the room was all natural, and someone was cooking bacon.

"Good morning, *Bellissima*."

A man came into view wearing a simple black T-shirt that was tight enough to reveal sculpted abs, defined biceps, and an Adam's apple that had to be three times bigger than the average male's.

I tried not to linger on any other details, like the fact that he had thick, chestnut hair that was long enough to fall over a pair of stunning blue eyes or that his face was so handsome my jaw actually lightly dropped.

"Where am I?" My voice was too quiet for how I felt, but my gut told me I was in the home of Adrian Adesso, which meant I had been moved against my will and ultimately kidnapped by the don of the Adesso family.

The man drew closer, holding a spatula in one hand and letting his other dangle at his side. "I'm Adrian. I apologize for the way in which I brought you here but the invitation I had extended strongly encouraged you to take me up on being hosted while visiting."

His *methods* in which he got his way, regardless of what I had chosen, reminded me of Scotty, which made me viscerally angry for utterly no reason other than being bested.

"You kidnapped me. I'm a minor you know, you could go to jail for that."

Adrian smirked, and I hated how the sight of it made my stomach do a tiny twist.

"Yes, you're seventeen. For now. No one will be touching you, or hurting you...do you know how old I am?"

Young. Far too young to be the head of one of the most powerful families in Italy.

His smile widened as he dropped into a crouch before me. "I'm nineteen, not too much older than you."

"Oh goodie, should I be thanking you for drugging me?" I lifted my middle finger.

How did I get out of here?

Adrian's smirk faltered the smallest bit. "An extremely small dose of ketamine, only so you didn't wake up and hurt anyone before we were able to get you to safety. You're probably wondering why I took you, and the answer is simple: There are other families that know about your arrival and a few who had even tracked you to your hotel."

Scotty had done worse than drug me with a low dose of ketamine in some of our training sessions, so while that part should piss me off, it didn't. The other families being there however, that got my attention.

Adrian stood and pulled out his phone then turned it toward me, showing camera footage playing. There outside my hotel were two black cars, and out of them five men exited, two of which attached their silencer barrels as they pulled open the glass doors.

The angle of the camera switched to the staircase outside of my room, and the men came into focus. I recognized them.

"They're from the Yullivi family."

Someone who had been at war with my dad for several years...I had done some research on them because their methods in reaching my father became aggressive nearly nine years ago. They said there was a debt Dad owed, but my father owed several debts to too many families.

Adrian kept his phone in place as the camera revealed a secondary set of men who entered the hall from a room across from mine. They quickly disposed of the Yullivi men and pulled the bodies into the room they'd left.

The footage went black and Adrian's gaze on me was severe as I tipped my head back and locked my eyes on his.

"You're not safe in Italy. Unless you're with me."

Bullshit. I refused to believe him. "Just because they don't want to play with their food before they eat it, doesn't mean I'm any safer with you."

He let out a small laugh before sauntering back into the kitchen. "Come eat, *Bellissima*."

"Stop calling me beautiful and maybe I will." I kicked my legs over the covers and relaxed at seeing my clothes in place. They'd kept me clothed, and safe...although I had no idea if he'd placed trackers in me, or on me...

Shit, what a nightmare. I was going to have to let Scotty deal with all of that because this was all his fault.

My stomach grumbled so loudly that I slapped my hand over it. I was going to have to eat, and I was going to have to remain here with him for the week, hearing him out or whatever it was that he wanted. I had no idea why he'd even be interested. It wasn't as if my father had anything of worth that he'd benefit from. We didn't have our own made family, which meant no access to men or weapons or even money.

Slowly sliding off the couch, I walked into the bright, oversized kitchen. The island was nearly ten feet long, topped with thick quartz, and the floors were a beautiful wood that gleamed under the sunlight cutting through the windows. "Why do you even want me here?"

Adrian's eyes remained on the food as he replied, "I guess pity, and another reason that I'll share with you at a later time."

"Pity?" My fingers curled over the back of the leather stool tucked under the island.

"Yes." Adrian's eyes met mine. "Your father was very young when he created his Joker persona. I understand why he stole from everyone...he was backed into a corner and really had no choice. Scotty explained that the family he worked for demanded your dad be handed over to be held accountable for killing their boss; he essentially was told to accept his death. I would have done what he did, and I respect him for that. Now, I see that he wants to keep his family safe, and for that, my respect for him only grows."

I watched him carefully as he moved around the kitchen, plating the bacon and eggs and applying butter to the toast. Questions lingered on my tongue, but something told me to wait to ask them because as sincere as Adrian seemed to be, and as touched as I was that he had a decent disposition toward my family, something in my gut told me he was lying.

I just had to wait him out until I was able to prove it.

Unfortunately for him, I'd been training my entire life to do exactly that.

CHAPTER 8
PRESLEY
AGE 11

My hand hurt, but I just shook it and jumped in place.

"Do you want to wrap them?" Scotty asked, lifting a dark brow.

I *should* cover my knuckles; I knew that, but since I had started learning these combos, it was easier to land them and memorize them if I felt the bag against my skin. I wasn't hitting it hard enough to do much damage, just learning the positions, but after an hour, there was a sting and the tiniest amount of blood left behind.

I shook my head. My uncle Scotty just moved to the side and placed his hands in front of him while gesturing for me to continue.

My fingers curled into a fist and the punch landed against the bag in a soft thud.

"Again," Scotty ordered, and my mind began to go where it usually did when I started these combinations. Somewhere warm, that smelled like freshly cut grass. Somewhere hidden from the world, where animals lazily dozed and flowers bloomed. To the farm that I would one day live on.

One with animals and golden flowers.

"Begin with the kicks," Scotty directed me. He checked the dogs lying next to him and whispered something in German.

He'd taught me which words would get them to do what. I knew if I wanted Rex to sit, I had to say, *sitzen.*

And if Scotty wanted one of the dogs to attack, he merely said, *töten.*

He practiced on the dummies at the farm sometimes, and I got to watch how terrifying the dogs were when ordered to kill. The most terrifying of all of Scotty's dogs was Reaper when he tore into one of the dummies. Stuffing would fly everywhere, and his lips would peel back, revealing rows of dangerously sharp teeth.

"Now mix it up, punch while—"

"There you are." My mother interrupted Scotty, pushing through the gym doors.

She eyed my knuckles then the dogs near Scotty's feet. Her jaw did that thing that I noticed when she was mad at Dad or Scotty, and usually it only happened when she found them training me. It would set into a firm line, and her lips would push together as if she were holding back a million thoughts.

"Scotty, can I please talk to you out in the hall?"

My father's uncle wasn't much older than Dad or Mom, but sometimes the lines near his eyes and mouth made him seem ancient. He argued with anyone when they tried to interrupt my training, except for my mom. She, he would never argue with...at least not in front of me.

"Sure." Scotty gave me a look that I'd seen a million times. It was to clean up the small amount of blood my knuckles left behind on the bag, and then to go soak my hands in disinfectant.

I did as he wanted and began cleaning the bag while the dogs remained with me, but after a few seconds, I heard my mom yelling, which piqued my curiosity. I dropped the spray bottle of cleaner and tiptoed over to the gym door. Soft mats lined the walls to dull the noise, intermixed with mirrors. The floor was also a mix of mats and thin black rubber, which muted my steps as I trailed closer to the doors.

Through the crack, I saw my mom's eyes wide and round. Dad said I inherited the blue from her gaze. Her hair was the same color as mine, and nearly just as long. She wore hers down and straight, while mine was usually tucked into a braid.

Mom had on leggings and a tank top while her feet were bare. Which meant, she likely walked over from our wing of the house.

"This was never run past me," she yelled. Her chin wobbled, which had my focus back on their argument.

Scotty's back was straight with thick lines of definition.

"I assumed Kyle told you."

My mom laughed, but it didn't sound funny.

"He said she was training, but no one ever said my daughter would be punching a bag without gloves until her knuckles bled." She pointed at the door, knowing I was behind it. Her face was starting to get red.

Panic flipped around in my chest. I didn't want her to take away my training; it was the only thing that seemed to be an outlet for me, and it was the only thing that felt like it made sense. I knew my mom wished I was more like her. She probably wanted me to be like my cousin Carter and the twins' sister, Alex, but that didn't feel right. I liked running around the property line wearing a weighted vest. I enjoyed shooting and throwing knives. I liked learning to fight.

"This needs to stop, Scotty."

He stepped closer to her, putting his hands out. "You agreed to this, Rylie."

"I never agreed to *this*. Look at her, Scotty. She has bruises on half her body; her knuckles are shredded."

My mom's eyes watered, her arms came in and tucked in close over her chest.

He stepped closer. "You placed your life in my hands once upon a time. Trust me with her, Rylie. I would never do anything to hurt her."

I'd never witnessed Scotty sound so...soft. He seemed like a human with her; whereas with everyone else, he was cold and gruff. To be fair, he was that way with Mom most of the time too, but something about her fear seemed to force out this side of him.

"I'm sorry, you're right. I just—we almost lost Kyle and hearing what she saw and had to do that night...it keeps me up at night. I hate what we're subjecting her to. She doesn't get to just be a normal little girl, Scotty."

"What does anyone know of what normal constitutes, Rylie? There is no way for any person, especially a little girl, to be normal. No code, no law that suggests how they should be or who they'll become. Presley *is* normal because she arrives every day with a smile on her face, and the day that changes, I will pull her out. I swear that to you."

Uncle Scotty stepped closer and pulled my mom into a hug, which made my eyes go wide. I'd never seen him hug anyone before. Her arms came around him as she hugged him back, and suddenly Dad walked into the hallway, watching them with a smile.

It was muffled, but I heard Scotty say, "This is a risk and it's taking a toll on all of us."

My mom had tears streaming down her cheeks as she nodded, then she sobbed.

"What if we're making a mistake by allowing her to train like Kyle trained?"

My dad's uncle didn't get to respond because my dad finally stepped forward, away from the stairs.

"Scotty, you're such a softy. Don't let anyone see you or else your cold-hearted cover will be blown."

Scotty finally let my mom go and then ruffled her hair. "She's still the only person who's ever stood up to me. She's earned my respect, and a few hugs."

"I stand up to you all the time," my dad argued and it made me smile.

Scotty shook his head and turned back toward the doors, where I was spying. I started running back, but the dogs were right behind me, which made it awkward when they started running after me.

I heard laughing and then my dad ran after me, catching me mid-run.

"Caught ya."

And just like that, I remembered exactly why I was enduring the training Scotty put me through. Why I hit the bag until my knuckles bled, and why I endured bruises and broken fingers. I did it because one night my dad was nearly ripped out of my world, and I'd do anything to prevent that from ever happening again.

I ARCHED the line into something that resembled a barn and then bit my lip while I erased it, only to reshape it again. I was with the twins, trying not to think about how badly my hands hurt, or how frequently they kept glancing at them. I just wanted to forget for a while and be their friend who liked fluffy cows, the farmhouse next door, and stargazing.

"What animal is going to sleep up there?" Gio slid into the chair next to me, moving my paper toward him.

I pulled it back and shrugged. "Charlotte."

Gio's brow lifted, while his eye narrowed. Just the left one. It was weird that only his left eye moved when he did that with his eyebrows, but it's how it always had been.

"A pig?"

"The spider." Kingston's smooth voice cut into our conversation as he peeled an apple by the sink.

I saw luggage being pulled out of storage and left near the family wings, which meant we would be leaving again. My parents told me we were headed out on yet another vacation, but I caught Uncle Scotty packing weapons, some similar to the one he'd placed in my hand and others that were larger but just as deadly.

And just like that my bubble had burst. In the manor it was easy to forget that there were people out there who wanted to hurt us. That all the training I did had a purpose behind it.

It was possible that I didn't know everything about Dad and Scotty's business, but I understood enough to know that our world was a sandcastle built on a beach with choppy waters and unpredictable tides. Any second and it could wash away.

Gio slid my paper closer and then took my pencil. He started marking the white sky with little dots and a large moon. "Now, it's for stargazing. Your spider can live up there, but so can a pig if it wants..."

King laughed while shaking his head. "You and your stars."

Sometimes the fact that they were twins made me look at them longer just to piece out the differences. They both had black hair that made me think of raven feathers. Their skin was the warmest brown that was most similar to their dad's and grandmother's. I once overheard Gio's mother saying that when he was born, he had stars in his eyes. His were more silver and grayer than blue. It looked like trapped starlight.

King's eyes were amber, like a muted fire, trapped behind glass.

I turned around and watched Kingston who was now eating his apple. The boys were almost thirteen, and I found new pieces of them that had started changing. Like the way their jaws looked different, making a ridge along their faces, pulling their smiles wider. I heard their mom talking about braces and how they'd both be getting them soon. It made me want to go back in time to when we were younger, when the boys would play pretend with me.

My memories had me asking, "What would you use the window for, King?"

His amber gaze landed on me in a way that made me feel like he wasn't going to answer. He was starting to do that more. Instead of being all laughter and smiles, like he used to be... he'd suddenly become so serious. Something dark had found a way to crawl into his heart and it seemed to rot there.

"It looks like a good place to..." he hesitated, then with a flutter of his lashes, continued, "shove someone...I'd call it the murder window, and no one would ever question me because it would be easy to fall from that big of a gap."

Our eyes locked in a game of who would break first. This was his new game with me, and I didn't like it. He wanted to bring clouds over what slices of sunshine I could find. I hated it. So did his brother.

"Someone's gonna push you out of a window if you don't stop being so serious. Have you considered maybe going for a walk, seeing if you can find a girl to flirt with?"

My eyes were back on my drawing, ignoring the brothers talk, but when Gio mentioned Kingston finding a girl to flirt with, something strange pricked at my chest. Like a weird awareness that had never been there before, a pain that had always been inside me but chose this moment to alert me of its dreadful existence.

"Dad is coming back soon, asked that we all stay here." Kingston tossed the core of his apple and then turned to leave.

Gio picked up an extra pencil from my little canvas bag and then started filling in more of my picture while leaving me room to draw on the other half.

"Come on, Pres, finish our farm. What else is on it?"

He always knew how to draw me back, like a light in the storm. I also loved that he always called it our farm, not mine but ours. We'd wanted the farm next to the manor to one day belong to all of us, and while I liked to draw it and even pretend I lived on it, deep down, I believed that maybe one day we'd really live there. "Chickens."

Gio's laugh was infectious. "I can't draw chickens to save my life, what else?"

"Marigolds."

His laugh made me laugh. "Aren't those just flowers? Why do they have to be specific?"

Kingston suddenly returned, grabbing a glass for water as he watched us.

"Anyone ever tell you that your laugh sounds like a tinkling bell? Like something from a book or some land with fairies?"

Gio and I stared at him from across the kitchen, confused. I moved on, ignoring him.

"Marigolds aren't like every other flower."

Gio shook his head but started drawing the shape of a marigold and I smiled, realizing he already knew what they looked like. I continued to draw with my best friend, feeling sunshine invade my heart like I always did with Gio, but there, lingering around that odd prick of pain in my chest, was worry about the shadows that lingered over his twin.

My eyes lifted again, only to find Kingston's already on me. He stared long enough that Gio finally kicked me under the table, forcing my attention back on the drawing. When I finally looked up again, Kingston was gone.

———

Mom and Dad were cuddled up on the couch watching a movie when I tiptoed past the hall. I knew Uncle Scotty's routine, and since it was well past ten, he was already in bed, likely reading, but he wouldn't come back out until five in the morning to prepare us for our trip. I should have been clear of anyone noticing my departure, but Reaper padded over to me, his steps quiet on the carpet. His snout was in my face, his tongue lapping at my cheek as he whined, probably to play.

I pet him, while trying to push him away, but he wouldn't budge.

"Go lay down, Reap," I whispered.

His tongue came back out in a few swipes over my face.

I was never going to sneak out at this rate. I just wanted the chance to go see the moon over the farmhouse. Tonight, we had what Gio called a Hunter's Moon, and I knew it just had to be beautiful seeing it from the hayloft over that empty field.

Remembering that I hid treats near the foyer table, I gently slid it open and pulled out a small bag of elk jerky and tossed a piece as far away from the door as possible. As soon as I found my window, I ran for the door and slipped outside of it. Cold wood floors ran beneath my feet as I exited the wing of our family home and ventured toward the main artery of the house that connected us all.

While the twins lived on one side of the house, and even my cousin Carter lived in another, we resided along the western half of the estate. The central area was all thick rugs, polished side tables, standing, bronze lamps, and expensive drinks that I was always told not to touch. Green vines hung over the glass doors that led to the outside terrace. While that would lead me directly outside and near the path to the farm, it would also alert my Uncle Scotty that someone had opened one of the doors, and there was probably a camera aimed at the exits, so he'd know it was me.

No, I would have to go through a different exit that didn't have an alarm rigged to it...at least that was assuming they hadn't fixed it. My steps were quiet as I walked toward the training gym, a level below us, only to be stopped by a firm hand on my wrist.

"What are you doing?"

I spun around, a breath caught in my chest as I came face-to-face with Kingston. His amber eyes were narrowed, his clothing dark, like mine, and his expression thunderous as if I'd interrupted him.

Pulling at his hold, I whispered, "I want to go see the moon Gio talked about."

There was never any use lying to the twins; they knew almost everything about me, and typically I would have invited them to come with me, but I knew Gio was already in bed and I was still mad at Kingston for how rude he'd been earlier about my picture.

"Gio is asleep."

I rolled my eyes, pushing past him, descending down the steps. "I know."

He quickly followed after me. "How come you didn't ask me?"

The training doors loomed ahead of me, but I sidestepped them and went down a different hall, so not to enter the actual facility.

"*¿Mi reina?*" Kingston tugged the ends of my hair.

I didn't like hearing him call me that, not when I was so hurt over how he'd behaved.

"Because you're rude, and you hurt my feelings," I snapped.

The singular metal door sat darkened at the end of the hall, no cameras in sight...unless they were on the other side.

"Stop, Scotty hung cameras outside of that door. You have to use the window from the locker room." He gently tugged my wrist and pulled me off to the side.

I followed him but pulled my wrist free.

"I wasn't rude. I was myself...since when does that bug you?"

I glared at him. "It's always bugged me, King. But today it just hurt a little more than usual."

We slipped through the wood door separating the locker room from the training mats and kept the light off. There were lights outside, illuminating enough of the room for us to see. We walked past the few lockers until we faced a window large enough for us to slip through.

Kingston flipped the lock at the top of the window, and the secondary one at the base, then shoved the pane glass up, creating a crack for us to slip through. The warm night air rushed in, coasting over our fingers and faces. I realized too late that I probably smelled like Reaper, which had me swiping at my face. The last thing I wanted was for Kingston to think I smelled like dog.

"Follow exactly where I walk," Kingston ordered from over his shoulder.

I mimicked everything he did. Lifting my leg, crawling through the window and then landing on the patch of gravel underneath it. King ducked and remained low as he ran straight forward. I did the same as him, until we hit a tree line, at which point he finally relaxed and stood straight up.

"You sure that worked?" I asked, glancing back over my shoulder.

He kept his focus forward. "I come out here quite a bit. I've never gotten caught."

We walked in silence, the shadows in the trees gathering and making me grateful that I wasn't alone. It wasn't until we broke past the tree line and came to the field between our properties that the large moon overhead lit up the land enough for us to see by. Gio was right, the moon was magnificent.

"Why do you come out here a lot?"

Kingston glanced over at me but kept walking. "Just to think."

We crossed the field and slipped through the broken fence, rounding the large barn. It was in shambles, but the stairs inside were sturdy enough to lead up to the hayloft. Kingston took them first, and I followed behind him, until we reached the top, and I quickly found the blanket I'd kept laid out for whenever I wanted to come up here.

Dipping down, I sat cross-legged on the dusty blanket while Kingston copied me.

I didn't want to talk, so I just stared at the full moon, wishing Gio were here with me instead.

Kingston reached for my hand and gently pulled it into his while inching closer to me.

"I'm sorry I hurt your feelings."

My pride was like a wall of granite, unwilling to crumble even for him, but I relaxed my shoulders and allowed him to trace lines over my skin.

"You can't make fun of me when I dream, King. You're one of my best friends, and they don't laugh at each other's dreams."

He let out a sigh before dipping his head. "I have dreams too, you know."

I glanced over, seeing the way the moon highlighted his profile and his strong jaw and dark brows. Something stirred in my stomach, like a batch of butterflies being released with nowhere to go. My face warmed, and my palms suddenly felt sweaty.

"What's your dream?"

He faced me, a smile sweeping his features and transforming his face from handsome and broody to so remarkable that my breath hitched. "I dream of marigolds too...ones that sit on a kitchen table, plucked from the garden I grew. Wallpaper that has little prints of Highland cows and a pantry full of organic Cheetos. Sunlight soaking into plants in a home that smells like coconut and oranges."

Just as fast as he'd faced me, he left me. Releasing my hand, he stood and walked closer to the edge. Meanwhile, I sat there, staring up at him, desperately trying to untangle his words.

Because his dream sounded an awful lot like...it was me.

CHAPTER 9
PRESLEY
AGE 17

"You're welcome for not coming with the jet to get you." Adrian's words dripped with sarcasm as he took my suitcase from me and walked us to his car. Two men waited outside of it, just like they always did.

"Hello, Benni. Renzo." I smiled and ducked my head to slide into the back of the armored vehicle. Benni entered after me, sandwiching me with Adrian. Renzo slipped into the front seat.

"Hello, Ms. Presley. How was your holiday?"

"Thanksgiving was wonderful. Thank you." The lie slipped from my tongue as easily as any others had. While I did just celebrate Thanksgiving, it was far from wonderful. The twins hadn't come home, and I still hadn't mustered the courage to ask Scotty about their texts. The entire manor was sad and empty, so I left early and decided Italy wouldn't be so bad to spend some time in.

Anything to get me out of that house.

This marked the fifth trip I had made to see Adrian. Each month he'd send his jet and request that I visit for a week. Most of the visits I'd argue that I didn't want to, and then Scotty would have to force me for the sake of creating an alliance. This time, however, I had asked Scotty to set it up.

"I never understood the appeal of that holiday," Adrian mused, sliding his knuckle under his jaw while looking out the window. He was baiting me into conversation and while I typically fell for it, I wasn't really in the mood. I hadn't ventured onto this trip because I enjoyed Adrian's company. I hadn't fallen victim to his outrageously good looks. I just needed out of the manor, and working on creating an alliance for my dad seemed to be a better use of my time than digging into the rotting wood of the farmhouse. Especially now that November had arrived and it with it, a deluge of rain that made tearing out old wood almost unbearable.

"You cut your hair." I lifted my chin toward the man next to me and hated the flip in my stomach when he smiled back at me.

"You noticed."

My eye roll wasn't severe enough. I needed to punch him or kick him, but I wouldn't. "Your hair was nearly longer than mine last time I saw you, so yes, I noticed."

His chuckle was smooth and dark, and I had to remind myself not to trust it. He was playing me as much as I was playing him.

His villa was set against a sheer cliff with white-capped waves that roared beneath it. Two stories tall, with only a three-car garage, which meant this home wasn't his primary one. It simply couldn't be. He was worth well over twenty-five million, if not more, and between the staff he kept and the various businesses he ran, I knew he had various homes, including a few in the U.S. Yet he always made me come here to see him in Italy.

The car slowly veered in through the tall gates guarding his estate and pulled in front of the outlier garage. Once we parked, I slid out after Adrian and followed him up the cobblestone steps into his home. The foyer boasted with warm lighting, gleaming marble floors and extravagant artwork. I loved how peaceful his house felt, and while I knew I should go grab my things, I immediately started for my favorite view.

"I set your things in your room." I heard Adrian's soft voice from behind me while I stood on his balcony watching the ocean. Had enough time truly passed that I now had my own room in his house? A shiver worked up my arms as I tried to think back to our other visits. Late night evenings were spent by the fire playing chess. He took me to several vineyards and orchards...he'd taken me to a nearby stable and let me ride his favorite horse. I had accidentally left behind a set of my favorite leggings one time, and a pair of slippers another.

Shit. I had created a tiny space here in his home, and he'd let me.

Turning on my heel I gave him a friendly smile. "Thank you."

His dark brows rose in surprise. "No eye roll or punch to the arm...shit, should I be worried about a knife in my chest tonight?"

That was one thing that I hated about Adrian. He knew I was skilled in combat and shooting. I had no upper hand whatsoever with him, and I blamed Scotty entirely for it.

"I'm not nearly as immature as you make me out to be." Yes, I was, but I owned it.

Adrian followed me as I walked toward the kitchen. I loved his chef, Leon, and enjoyed hugging him whenever I came to visit.

"You're not immature in the least, *Bellissima*."

Leon was chopping vegetables as I walked up to him and gave him a hug. He wrapped me up nearly as tightly as my own dad did. He was old enough to be my grandfather, and suddenly I ached with the grief that I had never known mine.

"Tell him to stop calling me beautiful," I muttered into Leon's neck.

His body shook with a laugh as he pulled back and held me at arm's length. "Can you blame him? You have a heart that's built for a man like him, that paired with your pretty eyes, he's a goner."

I glanced over at Adrian who was blushing.

I'd never seen him blush before and it did something strange to my chest. I was still seventeen for another several months, but it didn't change the fact that he was only two years older, and that sometimes I caught him staring at me in a way that made me think of someone else who used to get caught doing that.

The ache in my chest grew as I fought to push out memories of the twins and focus on the here and now. This was a distraction, that was all.

———

"You're really good at tracking the stars," Adrian praised me from the cushioned patio lounger next to me.

We were outside, listening to the waves crash below the cliffs and staring at the glimmering stars set against the navy sky above. I had a blanket wrapped around me while I ate freeze-dried Skittles. Adrian acted appalled at my snack choice then continued to steal them from me every few minutes.

"My best friend taught me how. He is really into astronomy."

Adrian paused for a second before replying, "I didn't realize you had a male best friend."

I let out a tiny laugh while locating the Gemini cluster. "I have two actually."

"Two best friends?" The bag of Skittles was gently tugged from under my arm as Adrian began munching.

I glanced over at him. I liked that he didn't turn on any lights and none of his staff was out here with us. It made this feel more intimate and relaxed. It was stupid of me, dangerous even. No one here to stop him from tossing me off the cliff, other than my sheer ability to stop him myself...but I felt relaxed enough not to worry about it.

"Two *male* best friends. They're twins."

I couldn't make out his expression, but Adrian hummed something as if he were surprised.

"You made it seem as though you grew up in somewhat of a secluded environment. How did you meet these incredible men?"

Hearing them referred to as men reminded me of their birthday, and how they'd turned eighteen on the last night that I saw them.

Maybe I was just being worn down by Adrian's kindness and the way he knew I loved a certain kind of pasta and always had Leon make it, or that I enjoyed my coffee strong, with cream, and made sure it was ready every morning for me...but it had my inhibitions low enough that I opened up.

"The twins grew up with me in the manor. They were like my family...but not actually related to me, if that makes sense. Their dad and mine became allies in a strange sort of way; at least that's how I heard it, but they've been with us since before I was born."

Adrian hummed again while popping another Skittle into his mouth. "So how do they feel about you coming to visit me?"

A sour taste seemed to fill my mouth, something that wasn't from the sweet treat I was eating. The twins would always remain my best friends no matter what, but how did I explain that they hadn't spoken to me in over ten months?

"I wouldn't know. We sort of had a falling out several months back."

The waves crashing against the rocks below shut out the sound of anything else until Adrian tossed the bag of Skittles back over to me.

"I'm sorry, *Bella*."

I smiled, finding his use of beauty vs beautiful, cute. I pushed a few pieces of freeze-dried candy into my mouth, choosing not to say anything this time.

"Would they like me though?" Adrian moved from his seat and was suddenly crowding mine, shoving his hand back into the bag of candy. I tried to pull it away to prevent him from eating any more.

"Heyyyy."

"Share," he laughed, and I tried to wrestle the bag away from him, but we just ended up laughing while he slid closer. Before I knew it, his arm was around me, pulling me closer into his side.

Sighing, I answered him, "I think they'd hate you but only because the only people they like are each other and me."

"I wouldn't blame them for hating me. I sort of hate them too but mostly because they have a piece of you that I could never have."

He didn't elaborate and neither of us clarified what he meant. I hadn't ever told him the specifics of what broke up the twins and me, but maybe he didn't need to know.

"They haven't ever given me Italy. That's all you, Adesso, and I fear it always will be."

He was quiet again until I felt something like a kiss against my head.

"I fear Italy would never be enough. They have a past with you, and something tells me somewhere along the line that they might have developed more than friendly feelings for you."

I toyed with the fringe on the blanket. "What makes you say that?"

The stars winked above, and the wind rustled through my hair as Adrian stroked my arm. "Because I did."

CHAPTER 10
GIO
AGE 13

Dad told me that Kyle was in private security and because of who he protected it warranted extra people to be stationed around the manor. Armed people, men and women who wore tactical gear and had helped train Presley how to shoot those weapons.

When we realized how much Presley was being taught, both King and I asked if we could train as well. It took a while, but our parents finally gave in, and while we didn't get to train with half the artillery that Presley did, I was never jealous. Especially not when I saw how many miles Scotty forced her to run around the property, or how long she had to box without gloves or any kind of wraps. Mostly I felt bad for her, and it angered me, but I'd never been envious.

Not until now.

"Dude, there's no way her dad is training her to drive that." I gasped, wide-eyed as the gleaming Dodge Hellcat rumbled down the road.

Kingston didn't say anything, but he'd watched the taillights disappear as it exited through the main gate.

I jumped down from the cement half wall and ran toward the

opposite end of the fence line, where we could see the street that circled our manor but wasn't inside the boundary line. It was often used when my mom and dad had big renovation projects done on the manor. There were four feet of solid brick that encompassed our property. Above that was two feet of iron fastened to the top, but we could see through the slats.

"There they are!" I pointed, seeing the car come back into focus.

Presley's dad was in the passenger seat while the window was rolled down; his smile was probably something that would stick with me for a long time. I hadn't ever seen him smile like that. The car wasn't speeding, but then through the window I saw Kyle say something and Presley downshifted, and the car shot off quicker than a bullet.

"That's way too fast for her," Kingston shouted while we both moved down the fence line to try and keep up with them.

A tight curve was up ahead, and my heart began to thrash in my chest like a fish out of water. "She isn't slowing down!"

My brother's fingers wrapped around the iron in a tight grip as he watched the car, and I moved farther down the fence until I found a spot that we could probably climb over, that is if we had a way to soften the fall, but even if we didn't, would a broken arm be that bad as long as it meant we could stop whatever it was Kyle was doing with her?

We both seemed to hold our breath as we watched the car slide to the side and glide over the gravel. Dust kicked up, and rocks flew behind the car, but within seconds, the car straightened and increased in speed.

"Did she just drift?" I asked, feeling confused and mildly alarmed.

"Pressy finally did it!" A familiar voice sounded behind us, and both my brother and I turned to see Carter walking up. She had her hair in a tight ponytail with shimmery strands of blue and gold intertwining with her reddish-brown hair.

Kingston turned back toward the empty road. "What do you mean she finally did it?"

"She hates that nickname, by the way," I reminded our step-cousin because if Presley heard her call her Pressy again, she'd probably punch her. Carter's existence in the manor was always a little confusing. While Presley felt like family, Carter actually was. Her mom, Mallory, was our mom's stepsister, but Carter's dad, Decker, was Kyle's brother by blood. So, Presley and Carter were cousins by blood, and Carter was ours only by marriage and yet throughout our lives we did way more with her than Presley did with her.

Carter stepped closer, getting a better view of the road. "Presley has been working on drifting for over a year, took her forever to get that. Uncle Kyle took me a few times when they came to visit us in LA last year, but I got really bored with it all."

My confusion only deepened. I'd lived around Kyle and Presley my entire life, and I had no clue either of them was into cars like that.

"Why would Kyle teach either of you?"

Carter's expression crumpled into total confusion. "Uncle Kyle used to be into street racing. He was really good, actually. My mom and dad said he won like every race he ever participated in. It's partly what got him in trouble. They never told me what that meant, or what sort of trouble, but I just assume everyone we know has had some brush with the law at some point."

Dad hadn't...as far as we knew at least. Mom once told us that he'd been really close to having a professional hockey career, but they never explained why that didn't work out, other than the community needing help with El Peligro. I know the gang our grandpa once led was somehow involved, but I wasn't sure how.

Carter let out a sigh before pulling out her phone. "I'm shocked Pressy never told you two. Makes me wonder what else she hasn't shared."

We must have remained quiet for too long because Carter got bored and wandered off.

Kingston was glaring at the road again, but I knew he was as frustrated with Carter's comment as I was. Presley, King, and I, we shared everything. We never kept secrets from each other, so her being able to drift around a corner in a Dodge Hellcat had me wondering what else she wasn't telling us and why.

***

It was after dinner when King and I decided to sneak out our loft window and walk the small pathway along the top of our roof, down to the west wing of the manor. The tall glass windows were covered in gauzy white curtains, and beyond them, you couldn't make anything out. King pulled out a small knife and slipped it through the small gap, sliding up the golden hook that kept the panes together.

I gently pressed against the glass and crawled inside.

My foot landed on her cushioned window seat, then her carpeted loft. Ours had a couch and extra gaming stuff, along with a place for me to map out stars, but her loft had craft supplies scattered along a long table. She didn't have a lot of time to spend on her crafting, but I liked that she had a whole loft dedicated to when she could. There were pieces of barnwood scattered over the table and scraps of rope.

I knew she'd be creating a picture frame or two based on the printed images of the farm and the Highland cows she loved so much. There were a few pictures of her family, and then several of me and Kingston too.

"Elvis?" I walked over to the stairs that led down to her room and took them two at a time. Kingston was right behind me as he skipped the last step and landed in front of Presley's queen-sized bed. She had on a pair of headphones while she flipped through one of her school books.

Kingston took the book from her, which had her tearing at her headphones while spinning around. "Hey!"

"We need to talk." I slipped out of my slides and sat on her bed.

My brother did the same, sitting opposite of me.

Presley rolled her eyes but moved her books out of the way for us to sit. The comforter was a teal color that matched the barn wood theme she had going throughout the room. Presley was a cowgirl born without the ranch or cows and that reality never stopped devastating me.

"You could have sent a text." She set her headphones on the shelf behind her bed and then pulled her knees up under her chin before facing us.

Kingston ignored that and launched into things faster than I anticipated. "Since when do you race cars?"

Her eyes always reminded me of tiny flames. Not the red or orange part of the flame, but the hottest part, the blue that revealed total combustion. Her eyes were like that, wide and always completely undoing me in ways that I didn't think were possible but now they were framed with thick, black lashes that I never remembered being so long.

"What are you talki—"

I cut her off, because irritation scratched at some place in my chest. "We saw you today, and Carter did too. She told us that you've been trying to drift for over a year."

"Carter said that?"

Kingston flicked his eyes across the room toward her closet and suddenly got up.

She quickly untangled her feet and followed him. "What are you doing?"

"We don't keep secrets, Presley." King pushed her closet door open and flicked on the light.

"What are you looking for?" Her eyes searched the space, but I didn't miss how she kept focusing on the shelves.

King noticed too and moved toward them. "What else, *Elvis*?"

She stepped in front of him with her eyes narrowed. He never called her Elvis unless he was trying to irritate her, which she only proved with her tone. "What do you mean?"

"I mean, what are you hiding?"

"Nothing!" Presley cried, but King jerked open the drawer and began pulling out the clothes and throwing them on the ground.

"Kingston!"

I started looking through the other side of her closet, already knowing pretty much everything that was in here. Being around someone your entire life meant you knew what their blankets, sleeping bags, slippers, and clothes all looked like.

Presley grabbed my brother's arm and held on to it as he pulled on a drawer and something loud thumped inside it. He paused and quickly glared down at her before reaching inside.

"Wait...just—"

"What is this?" He pulled out a gun...

Presley ran a hand over her face. We knew she'd been training with weapons, that was no secret, but we were informed that all artillery would be kept in designated weapons' rooms, where they'd be locked up and managed by someone with a key. Why would she need one in her closet?

"It's mine," she argued, reaching for it.

King pulled it back, anger twisting his words into something harsh. "You're twelve years old, why the hell do you have it?"

The fire in her eyes burned as she stared at him. She looked like she wanted to fight him.

For a second I wondered if the two would spar like they did in the training room. There was some edge that Kingston was riding, and something deep down told me it had to do with whatever happened when he was a kid. The thing he never shared with us, and while I maybe should bring that up to leverage her telling us, I wouldn't betray my brother like that. Whatever it was had imbedded inside him like a thorn, and I worried if we tugged, it'd cut an artery and he'd bleed out, or in this case, become someone we didn't recognize.

"Pres." I softened my tone and tugged on her hand. "We're trying to figure out what you're keeping from us. We just care about you. You know that."

Her head swung in my direction before she dipped her chin, tucking it to her chest.

"Fine. I'll tell you guys but...you can't say that you know. I was told not to tell you, that was years ago, so maybe it's not as big of a deal now but just in case, you have to keep it a secret."

I nodded, while Kingston angrily shook his head but set the gun on a shelf. The three of us sat down on the carpeted floor and we waited for Presley to explain herself. She tucked a few chocolate strands behind her ear before setting her hands in her lap and wetting her lips.

"I have that gun because it's a memory...a reminder."

"Of what?" Kingston snapped.

I glared at him right as Presley did. "I can't talk to you if you're going to be a jerk."

My brother took a long look at Presley, never wavering from holding her stare until he finally lowered his chin. "This stuff is hard for me to hear...there's things I haven't spoken of and I'm not sure I ever will, but I'm afraid of what you're going to tell me."

Presley reached her hand out and grabbed my brother's, pulling it into her lap. She stroked soothingly over his knuckles and the back of his hand while she glanced over at me.

"My dad isn't in private security."

Kingston squeezed her hand but didn't interrupt.

"When I was eight, there was an incident where my dad was shot...do you remember that?"

I thought back and remembered a time that my dad was panicked and rushed out the door, heading to the hospital. Kyle came home a few days later, wearing a sling and looking sickly pale. They'd told us that he'd taken a bullet for one of his clients.

"I remember that."

Presley checked Kingston's expression before continuing. "He was shot by a rival family...someone in the mafia. It all happened right in front of me...I am pretty sure Scotty saved my life, and Mom's too. But when the ambulance got there, Mom rode with Dad and Scotty knew they'd follow them."

My brother pulled his hand free and ran it through his hair. I noticed he was shaking.

"Rival family?" I asked, still trying to follow what she was saying.

She nodded. "My dad started working for a family back when he was a teenager...I think it had to do with shadowing Uncle Scotty while he worked for a really dangerous family, but he did...something that had a lot of people angry and wanting his life for what he'd done."

"What did he do?" I was curious what a teenager could have done that would have warranted such a reaction.

Blue fire met me; in the dim lighting of her closet, her eyes seemed extra bright. Her scabbed knuckles rose as she tucked more hair behind her ear in what seemed like a nervous tick. "He killed your grandfather...he was a bad man, someone who was going to hurt your mom and your sister. My uncle Scotty and Decker showed up to help your dad when he went to get her...my dad killed him. He was a very powerful man, and because of what he did, my dad sort of became this other person. He brought on this disguise after training for a long time...he was called The Joker."

I scoffed, reeling at how crazy this all sounded. "The Joker? Really?"

Presley flushed pink. "I guess he used it as a calling card for people...he tricked families into working with him and stole from them. He made a lot of enemies by playing them against each other. When he wanted to finally step away, I don't think he could...he's been trying ever since."

"Get back to the gun, and why the hell you have it," Kingston grumbled with a glare at Presley.

"That night that Dad got shot, Scotty knew they'd be followed. So, he drove behind the ambulance and we came upon this SUV that was behind them."

"You were in the car?" My voice was too loud; I felt it, but I couldn't quite piece together what she was saying.

"My parents were in an ambulance, you guys had all gone home. Where else was I supposed to go?"

I locked eyes with my brother, feeling like my heart had dropped into my stomach. We'd let her down, and we hadn't even been aware of it.

Presley pushed on, dropping even more bombs that I felt hit my chest.

"Scotty needed help..."

Kingston stood to his feet and began rambling curses in Spanish while he ran his hands through his hair. "Tell me he didn't place that gun in your hand and tell you to shoot someone."

I watched Presley's face carefully as a small red blotch started near her jaw.

"They were going to kill my parents...I didn't have to see them or anything. I shot through their windows, made sure their car stopped."

"Do you hear yourself?" Kingston yelled before storming out of her closet.

We both quickly stood and ran after him.

"Bro, what the hell?"

My twin spun around and I noticed there were tears burning in his gaze.

"So does this mean you're in the mafia now too? Is that what you're training for? You're going to join them as they murder and kill people?"

Presley's thick lashes fluttered against her cheek, and I couldn't seem to stop staring at her eyes. "I'm not in anything, but I am learning how to protect my family."

He walked closer to her, his chest heaving, then his voice rose. "Are you or aren't you joining them? Is that why you have bruises all over your body?" He gently took her hand and lifted it between them.

"Why you're constantly tearing open and pushing yourself to every limit imaginable?"

Presley winced and tugged her hand free. I stepped closer and put my arm around her.

"Dude, chill."

My brother's eyes blew wide as he stared at me. "No! She can't be like them. I won't let her be like them."

"I'm still me!" Presley screamed back.

My brother stepped even closer. "You're not you. You're the sunshine that warms the earth. You're the breeze that lifts the scent of flowers. You're the stars in Gio's sky. You're everything good in this world, Presley. That's you. You're not the weapon they're forcing you to become."

Presley's face had more pink infused in her cheeks and neck, but her lips pursed in anger. Her fists were clenched at her sides, and her jaw was set as she watched my brother walk away. He ran up the stairs to her loft and crawled back through the window.

I pulled my best friend into my arms and held her.

She shook under me, inhaling a shuddery breath, and then her arms came around me. "I may be your stars, Gio, but you're my sky. I look up and know if you're there, then I'll be okay."

"And I always will be." I held her tighter until I finally let go and eventually followed my brother out the window and back to our room.

CHAPTER 11
PRESLEY
AGE 18

I sat cross-legged in the hayloft, watching dawn claim the sky.

The cool air caressed my skin, making me tug my sweater tighter. The farm was beautiful at various parts of the day, but nothing aside from starlight beat the dawn cresting over the hills.

My eighteenth birthday had finally arrived and with it a wave of grief unlike anything I had experienced since the twins first left. I had two twin holes in my heart, both of which obstructed any happiness from taking up that space.

Tears gathered in my lashes like little clusters and then dripped down my cheeks in a cascade of sadness.

I was supposed to be with them when I became old enough to allow this tiny flame in my heart to flourish. The crush I'd grown on my best friends was unforgivable, and the reminder that their absence was entirely my fault was growing to be too much.

Lately, my only way of dealing with this pain swirling in my chest, breaking me open and pulling the cords of my heart out was to go see Adrian.

I'd be there now if it weren't for some business he had here in the States.

The memory of him first explaining that he'd begun to develop feelings for me was the tinder to a friendship I desperately needed. Trust was the thin membrane of our relationship. I knew I shouldn't, but I had fallen for him anyway, in the sense that he was dependable, kind and considerate. I didn't feel romantically any way toward him, but he'd claimed part of my heart regardless, merely by being there.

Unlike my best friends.

Tugging my phone free, I stared at the text thread between the twins and me from the last time we texted one another. It was a joke we'd made about Scotty eventually getting some sort of hairpiece because his head was balding so rapidly.

I knew they would have texted me today. I knew Scotty's phone was lit up with a string of messages from them, and all this time they just assumed I was ghosting them. Isn't that what I had said I'd do?

Shouldn't it be what I wanted after all they did?

A tear slipped off the tip of my nose and I swiped at it aggressively, while dialing a number I shouldn't.

The whole time it rang, I inwardly shouted at myself to stop, but I just let it keep going until...

"Presley?"

I paused before letting out a shuddery breath. "Adrian?"

"What's the matter, is everything okay?"

The sun crept through the clouds, illuminating the sky, which reminded me how early it was. "Sorry, were you asleep?"

"No, *Bellissima*, I was on my run. What's wrong?"

A tiny hiccup escaped me as I tried to reel in my emotions. "Are you still in New York?"

"Yes, for another few days." His voice was stern, like he wanted to know why I was upset. "Tell me what's wrong."

The sun moved past a few lingering clouds and was so bright I closed my eyes. "It's my birthday today. I wanted to know if you could take any time—"

"Yes." He cut me off and began barking out orders in Italian to someone in the background. "Can I come to you?"

I hesitated. Scotty would kill me if I allowed Adrian to come here, but wasn't this what he wanted to begin with? Wasn't I the one tossed on the stone altar of sacrifice to keep this family safe, even when my cousin so carelessly tossed us to the wolves? Why was I the one who kept being held accountable and no one else cared? The twins bailed, Carter did whatever the fuck she wanted, and Alex just hid away in the manor, helping her mother with their charity.

I cleared my throat and replied, "You can come here."

I MET Adrian at the gate, so the guards posted there didn't shoot him. I didn't tell anyone that he was coming, but it felt safer this way. When he pulled up, he was alone, which made something in my chest crack.

What the hell were we doing?

The second the gate opened, and he drove in, he pulled closer for me to get into his car. We drove toward the larger garage that housed our armored vehicles and faced the opulent rolling hills behind the manor. The tree line was dark as a few wisps of fog clung to them.

"A spring baby. Who knew." Adrian laughed and I found myself smiling too.

"Technically it's still winter for another few weeks."

He turned the car off and faced one another. I tried to relax into the plush leather but the way he was watching me had my stomach flipping.

"I got you something." Adrian lifted the middle console hatch.

I smirked, moving the smallest bit so he had more room. "Swing by a gas station on the way over?"

His eyes lit up with humor as he smiled. "No, I got this for you when I last visited Spain. I saw it and instantly knew it was yours." Pulling out a velvet box, he opened it, revealing a necklace connected with just a singular diamond circle.

"You're complete, Presley. You act like you're not, but it'll be my goal to prove to you that you are." He pulled it free from the plush setting and leaned closer.

I watched as he placed it around my neck and then gently traced my shoulder, encouraging me to turn so he could clasp it. "Thank you, Adrian. I love it."

His lips were near my ear as he whispered, "Happy Birthday, *la mia Bellezza*."

I closed my eyes, willing the tears to stay in place. Adrian had been hinting at feelings for me, but I'd been too young. Now, I wasn't sure he'd continue to play games; he was the sort of man who just claimed what he wanted, and it was clear he wanted me.

I just wasn't in the place to be claimed.

I needed a friend, and I hoped that's all he'd be for me right now. To ensure he didn't kiss me or do anything else, I spun around and threw my arms around his neck, then just as quickly, jumped out of the car.

Once he was outside with me, I headed toward the front door of the manor.

"Come on. I have a movie marathon on the horizon for us."

He smiled at me, then tucked his hands into his pockets before walking toward me. "Okay, but no vampires."

My hair lifted as I spun around, and I caught his broad smile as I did. "Definitely vampires and a few zombies too but only the kind that can fall in love."

"Of course." Adrian laughed, and when I went to open the front door, I felt like my smile had finally returned too. Even if it was short-lived.

ADRIAN LEFT around eleven at night after spending the entire day in my room, watching movie after movie with me while we ate pizza, salad—for him—and drank our weight in strawberry milk.

Reaper's gentle trot warned me that my uncle would arrive soon. I sucked in a deep breath and counted to three.

One.

Two.

Three.

"What the fuck did you do?!" His voice was a thunder crack in the room.

Turning toward him, I made sure my mask was in place as I feigned confusion. "What do you mean?"

"You brought our enemy into our *home*. He now knows where we live. How could you be so reckless?"

"Me?" I gestured at my chest, feeling it heat with anger. I walked around the coffee table and pointed at him. "You're the one who pushed me and pushed me over there and told me to create an ally. Well, I did! How can you be upset with me?"

Scotty's eyes were burning as he glared at me. "You revealed where we live, Presley."

"What exactly did you think an ally would do, Scotty? We're supposed to trust him."

His jaw clenched tight as Reaper watched us argue, before lying down and placing his face on his paws.

"I wanted you to gain his confidence, be casual and reel him in. I didn't want you to fall for him."

"I didn't fall for him!" The shock that he assumed that felt like a crack in my ribs, but perhaps it was the shame of how close his statement landed to the truth. Was I falling for Adrian?

Scotty stepped closer, his nose flared in obvious frustration. "Then why the fuck did you invite him here on your birthday and spend all day with him in your bedroom? The entire manor was on high alert all fucking day, Presley."

"Because I have no one else, Scotty!" I sneered, while a few tears slipped down my face. "I have no one else. The twins aren't coming back. Carter and Alex are hardly ever here. I'm alone. I have you and my parents, and that's it."

My uncle was quiet as he watched me cry, and then after enough silence had passed between us, he pulled out his phone and pressed a few buttons.

"Fine, Presley. You're lonely? I'll fix that...don't blame anyone but yourself for this."

"What do you mean by that?" I searched his face, panic filling me.

He kept pushing buttons, and my anxiety continued to rise.

"What do you mean, Scotty?"

He finally dropped his phone and glared at me once more. "I mean your little friendship with the head of the Adesso family is over."

The echo of his steps reached me before he did, and when he held his phone out to me, I wasn't sure what I was even looking at but as he walked past me, I realized exactly what he'd done.

He'd been texting the twins from his own number, the most recent message was a picture of me lying against Adrian's chest while he played with my hair in my bed. The television played against the far wall, and our snacks were strewn next to us.

The text below it read:

Get home now.

New emotion clogged my throat as my head whipped up and I watched Scotty walk away. A sob worked into my voice as I dropped his phone.

"I hate you."

He didn't turn around, but I heard him as clearly as if he had. "That's fine, Presley. Hate me all you want, just take that fucking necklace off while you do it. It's probably a tracking device."

"They are only going to be coming back because you ordered them, just like one of your dogs."

His feet faltered for one second before his head dipped. "At least they're obedient when it comes to protecting the family. Something you still need lessons on."

"Fuck. You."

Suddenly Scotty spun on his heel and glared back at me. "You forget that I never had to order them to protect you, Presley. You forget that I nearly died at their hands because of that instinct. Never pretend like I am not aware of what's at risk, but more so, stop pretending like they aren't in love with you."

"They aren't!"

"You are not stupid, Presley. Stop acting like this before you get someone killed, or did you forget you've already done that too?"

He disappeared around a corner before I could reply that it wasn't my fault...all the times they'd tried to protect me. It was his.

CHAPTER 12

KINGSTON

AGE 15

This plant was going to die. My mother had tried so hard to keep it alive and tend to it, but I knew it wasn't going to make it, which would devastate her. She was weird like that, had seemed to let go of the concern of actual people dying, or the bodies that our father helped pile up, but plants dying fucking destroyed her.

"Kingston, do you know what I did wrong, honey?" My mother's soft voice sounded exasperated as she tilted the leaves of the plant. My hands were behind my back as I stared down at the peace lily almost scoffing at the irony of her choosing this one to try and keep alive.

"Perhaps it died of hypocrisy."

My mother's eyes lifted slowly, meeting mine. Her blonde hair was long, kept back in a low bun, but pieces touched the sides of her face. She had blue eyes, not like Gio; some people said they were, but if you actually took two seconds to compare the two, they were nothing alike. My older sister, Alex, had my mother's eyes, but Gio had some strange blend of fuckery that didn't exist in anyone I'd met in either family tree yet.

Mom's lips pursed. She knew exactly what I was talking about, and if we were the kind of family that embraced therapists hearing our problems, then perhaps, she'd know why I was constantly so pissed off.

"Are we doing this again, son?"

I smiled, leaning closer to the plant, feeling a small pinch of regret pull at my heart. I loved my mother, and my childhood was full of joy and memories of her being present, happy and truly the sort of mother that anyone would hope to grow up with. It wasn't her per se I took issue with; it was this life we led. The one we'd finally sat down and talked about as a family.

The night I'd come back from Presley's room, I'd burst into my parents' bedroom and demanded my father explain it to me, this story Presley had shared. I knew she didn't want me to, but I had to understand my father's role in it without telling him what I saw. I had to know what he'd be willing to share with me. All I'd gleaned was that our lives were fucked, and this existence was our way of creating a family of our own. One that remained safe and had each other's backs.

"Too much sun, Mom. This plant needs more shade; you'll have to set a timer to move it around a bit."

My mother held my wrist in gratitude and walked off.

I watched her go, already knowing I'd take the plant and go bury it in the garden. It was a stupid thing I'd started doing as a kid, feeling like it was my way to atone in some way for the lives our family took. The blood we shed. I often mentally walked back into that room where I witnessed a man's life end so horrifically and I allowed the moment to linger.

Something that shaped me as effectively as a carving knife peeling back layers of my skin until I bled the secret out.

Memories surfaced of Presley's face when she'd brought me that jar of dirt to cheer me up, and how she still had no idea that her offering was the only thing that saved me from drowning. She was the rope in my ocean, pulling me to shore. She wasn't the little girl who brought me a jar of sun dirt; she was already changing into whatever they were molding her into. Since that day in her closet, when we'd discovered the gun in her closet, things between us were strained.

She hugged me the very next day and I hugged her back, but how was I supposed to explain to her that I needed that girl back who had thought of me when I needed her the most. Back when she knew I needed warm dirt and brought it to me, placed it against my cheek and told me everything would be alright. I wanted her back, and the more time that passed, the more I knew I might not ever see her again.

Sometimes I wondered if she had given up on her dream of a farm, with fluffy cows and marigolds. I was curious if she wanted to ever return back to who she once was, but like some doors, they were sealed shut.

Maybe she needed both me and Gio to pry the seal off and bust it open for her.

Alex suddenly burst into the room, and the look of panic on her face made me freeze in place. My sister was three years older than me and Gio and was almost an identical replica of our mother. She had blonde hair, fair skin, blue eyes and long delicate limbs, but it was the expression on her face that seemed the most familiar.

I already knew what she was about to say, which was why the plant slipped from my fingers and smashed to the tiles beneath me.

"How bad?"

Alex's mouth parted as she tried to inhale a gasp. "Scotty has five of them fighting her."

Son of a bitch.

"Where's Gio?"

Alex was on my heels, jogging with me. "I can't find him. I texted her parents, but I'm not getting a response yet."

"Fucker is going to stop doing this."

"Kingston, part of this is on her. She needs to know when to stop." Alex's tone shifted, as if she was trying to tell me something I didn't want to hear.

I knew that she was right, but how did a fourteen-year-old girl stand up to a grown man and tell him no?

I shoved the doors open to our in-house gym, hearing the echo around the room of men yelling and jeering on the spectacle in the center of the room. I could hear Scotty's voice over the others', barking out commands. His harsh, demanding tone was all directed at Presley.

There across the room was something that would be ingrained in my mind forever.

Long, chestnut hair braided down her back, while her fists were up, protecting her face. She had a busted lip and a cut near her eyebrow. She didn't look afraid; she looked determined, and a tiny flicker of pride flared into life as I took her in.

Five of Scotty's best fighters circled my best friend, taking turns as they lunged toward her with different hits. They were barefoot, but one of them landed a hit to her side, which made her go down, but Scotty merely yelled for her to get back up. She jumped to her feet and went on the attack, landing a powerful kick combo on the man who'd kicked her. But someone else came up behind her and kicked at her legs, swiping them from under her.

Scotty was barking more commands: some for his fighters, and others for Presley.

I ran across the room, hearing my sister yell from behind me.

Scotty's eyes lifted. His expression was murderous as I neared.

"Get her out of there, she's going to break!" I pushed against one of the fighters, watching the match and seeing Presley duck, barely missing a massive fist that would have landed in her face. Her braid whipped around as she jumped back up and did a back kick. Another man's fist landed in her kidney a second later, making her cry out.

My vision went black, and the same panic I felt when I was ten years old, watching Scotty order his dog to murder someone came back. Rage barreled through me with a roar and aggressive shoves at the people in front of me.

"SCOTTY! GET HER THE FUCK OUT!"

Panic was hammering at my chest so hard that my entire body shook. Presley puked up blood onto the mat.

Blood.

Fucking blood.

"Kingston," Scotty snapped, then he glanced at Alex. "You could have said something to me, Alexandria."

I heard my sister scoff. "No one can say anything to you, Scotty."

Presley wiped her mouth and got back into her combat stance. She was going to keep fighting. She was going to kill herself and Scotty wasn't going to stop her. Using my shoulders and my elbows to shove, I hit flesh as hard as I could until there was an opening and I lunged forward.

Presley's eyes grew wide in horror. "King, get out of here."

"No." I raised my fists in a defensive stance, but within seconds, someone landed a blow to my side, like they did to Presley. I went down instantly, but I rolled out of the way and jumped up.

"Kingston!" Presley's worry had her turning toward me, allowing someone to land a hit to her stomach, which had her doubling over.

My body was shaking so badly that I felt like I was going to throw up. I think I was screaming, but I wasn't sure. Scotty was yelling something too, but the men kept coming for us, so it wasn't to stop. Suddenly someone's fist landed in my face, near my eye. I winced in pain, trying to roll, but their fist came back down.

I heard Presley screaming, but my vision was coated in blood. Their fist came down again, and I knew something was wrong; there was too much blood. My eyebrow had completely busted open.

I knew people were still yelling, but suddenly it all stopped, and it was just Presley's hiccups that I could hear, and then there was Scotty...he was angry.

The pounding against my body stopped and I felt Presley crawl over to me. "Oh, King, this is going to scar."

Her fingers were gentle on my face, but I was still confused how she'd made everyone stop. That's when I felt soft fabric wipe my eyes, and I was able to make out what happened.

There were two men lying in puddles of blood on the mats and my brother stood over me, holding twin knives, dripping red.

My brother's glare was pinned to Scotty, with a murderous expression. He'd stabbed them to get to us.

"You want to try and kill my brother and Presley, then fine, but you'll have to kill me too."

Scotty gestured toward me on the ground. "Kingston thought he could interfere as well but lasted all of two seconds. Meanwhile, Presley has lasted an hour."

She'd been at it for a whole hour? Fucking shit.

"Yeah, well, my brother plays by the rules. I don't."

Scotty let that hang in the air between them, knowing two of his men had already been stabbed.

Scotty's men groaned from the ground, trying to hold their sides together. There was so much blood that I wasn't sure who or how we'd clean all this up. "She can be done for the day. But let me be clear about one thing. Presley will not break unless it's you two doing the breaking."

The men around the ring had already dispersed, and the threats were gone so I rolled over to check on Presley. She'd shed her shirt to help me wipe my eyes and was in just her sports bra, but she had her arms crossed over her stomach and was turned away from us.

"You hurt anywhere else, *mi reina*?" I gently touched her face and prodded at her arm.

Gio was next to her too, and we looked her over. She winced as she tried to move, which had Gio gently pulling her closer. Her entire left side was black and blue.

I didn't process it fast enough, but Gio's eyes narrowed on the bruise, his nose flared and then he spun and let his hand fly. A knife sailed from his hand and was buried in Scotty's shoulder within the blink of an eye. Reaper, the fucking dog I'd witnessed rip out a man's throat, turned its head and darted for my brother.

"Gio. Kill him!"

"NO!" Presley screamed, trying to sit up. She was worried about the dog.

The fucking demon that ripped someone's throat out. He was still running toward us when Scotty yelled a word in German and the dog immediately stopped and laid down.

"What the fuck is going on in here?" My dad appeared with Alex on his heels, tears streaming down her face. I felt bad for how panicked she must have been.

"A training session that your sons infiltrated and now stopped," Scotty said with a bit of a gasp. "If you'll excuse me, I need to go see our doctor."

He walked past us with the dagger still protruding from his shoulder like it was nothing at all. Gio's fingers were shaking as he watched him walk away, and that's when I felt Presley's hand close around mine.

I looked down and saw tears gathering in her eyes all while Dad carefully took the other knife from Gio's hand. "Son, why does this have blood on it?"

My brother's eyes were still on the door where Scotty walked through. He wanted to murder him, that much I knew.

He wasn't going to speak up, so I did. "Scotty wouldn't let us get to Presley."

Dad's eyes went round as he looked back over his shoulder. "So, what, you stabbed someone?"

Gio finally looked up at Dad and smiled, using all his teeth. "Look at Kingston. Those fuckers busted his eyebrow to shit; he's going to scar. I should have stabbed more of them."

Dad's muttered "fuck" was all we needed to hear for him to realize that something had shifted in our family and that we might have started out on a path he never wanted us to walk. But how could you assume a monster wouldn't also breed monsters?

Presley got up and held her side.

"Thanks, guys. I love you."

I watched her walk away, feeling her words hit my chest like a piece of dynamite. She loved me.

I'd always known she did...but for some reason it felt different now that I was fifteen. Different now that I realized I wanted her love.

THAT NIGHT I LAY AWAKE, staring at my ceiling.

There, taped above me was the wrinkled picture I'd drawn to imitate Presley's farm last year. She'd found it under my bed and because I was too embarrassed to just admit that I'd had my own dream about our lives and how that barn window would be the perfect place for us to see the trees and plants during the day, and the stars at night, I had lied instead.

After she saw me toss it in the garbage, I walked back into my room and pulled it out, smoothed it and then hung it where only I'd see it. Presley hadn't been to our room since that day, as far as I knew at least.

My brother and I were traveling less but somehow Presley was gone more. I didn't like the way change felt inside my chest, as if there was a crevice forming between the three of us, increasing every day. Gio had mentioned it too that this felt like a long-drawn-out goodbye. We hadn't really talked about it, but we felt like it started last year when we'd fought over the reality of our parents' jobs.

Gio was in his bed, watching something on his phone, when someone filled the doorway of our room.

"We need to talk," Dad said, pushing his shoulder into the wood frame.

Gio dropped his phone with a sigh and I sat up.

Dad locked focus with us both before moving to my desk and

pulling out the chair. Once he was leaning forward with his elbows on his thighs, he sighed.

"What happened today was too far over the line for either of you to ever go."

I flicked a quick look at my twin and saw his eyebrow twitch. He was thinking about how he hadn't gone far enough.

Speaking up, I chose my words carefully, so it didn't seem like we were trying to get out of trouble simply by blaming Presley.

"He has her training to fend off five grown men at once."

Dad let his head bob, his eyes on the carpet. Mom once said we were walking replicas of how he looked at our age, but I'd seen photos, there was a similarity, but we looked like her too. We had the shape of her eyes, nose and mouth. I thought of what I had said about her plant earlier this morning and suddenly felt guilt push up like a weed in whatever soil surrounded my heart.

"Scotty's training methods are unconventional, which is why he isn't in charge of yours."

Gio swung his legs over his bed and scoffed. "You expect us to just excuse his behavior because it's unconventional?"

"No, I don't expect you to excuse it, but you do need to accept it. Presley is being trained to become someone significant for their family. Mostly, Kyle doesn't want her to ever be at the mercy of her enemies without a chance at survival."

I shook my head, not liking that explanation. "She's being killed slowly now so no one else can kill her abruptly later?"

Dad didn't respond to that, but he knew I was right.

"Bottom line, boys. You need to understand that Presley isn't ever going to live a life that others would call normal. She's not ever going to be the girl that's carefree like Carter is. She will always be held to a higher standard, and if that's going to be a struggle for you both to be around, then we need to discuss the possibility of sepa- rating ou—"

"No!" Gio shouted right as I shook my head.

Dad stared us both in the eyes before gnawing on his lip like he wanted to say more but was holding back. "I can't have you stabbing people in this house because you don't agree with how Presley is being trained."

Gio threw himself back on his bed with a huff. "Fine. I won't ever stab him again."

"Not just him." Dad swung his gaze over to me. "I know you don't particularly care for her father either. We live in peace, or we don't live here at all. Respect how she's being trained or I'll remove you from her life."

"Dad, you can't do that!" I yelled right as Gio sat up in a panic.

My brother's voice broke as he stood to his feet in front of Dad. "We're just worried about her; she's our best friend."

"She's like your sister, I get that," he corrected Gio, but it felt strange, almost like he was trying to remind us. But I didn't think of Pres as a sister; it felt infinitely different with her than it did with Alex.

"She's ours," I muttered, but Dad's glacier expression told me that was the wrong thing to say.

He shook his head and snapped a little too aggressively. "She isn't yours."

Yes, she was. but I wasn't going to argue that with him.

Our dad stood and heaved another sigh. "I just need to make sure you both understand. Presley isn't going to change her training, nor will the methods used to help her get there. You need to accept it, or I promise you, we will leave."

My stomach tilted in the wrong direction, but I gave him my agreement just the same.

CHAPTER 13

PRESLEY
PRESENT

I stole Scotty's phone.

He must have disabled the password, or he never set one up, which was possible because he frequently used burners. Didn't matter. I had it, and I had finally succumbed to reading through the messages that had been forwarded to his phone ever since the twins left.

Anger was a twisted root around my heart as I thought back to what Scotty said. As if he didn't play a role in how things ended with my two best friends. As if he hadn't been the reason it all got messed up.

My thumb slid along the screen as I went back to the texts that had come in all those months ago.

They'd created a group chat and aside from calling, all the communication seemed to be there.

I clicked on the thread and began reading.

Kingston: Pres, can you please answer one of our calls.

Gio: We said some things that we need to explain...please answer the phone.

Kingston: Presley, please.

Gio: We need to explain why we left early...it wasn't our choice.

Kingston: We're both pretty fucked up not getting to say goodbye.

Kingston: we're sorry, mi reina.

I scrolled down seeing more from the months that passed.

Gio: The stars out here where my uncle and aunt live are on another level, Pres. Wish you could see them. How are the stars back home?

Kingston: How's my garden? I was hoping you wouldn't mind keeping it alive for me. My mom would do it but she couldn't keep a plant alive if my life literally depended on it. She's a plant killer.

Gio: Please pick up, Pres.

Surely they would have texted me privately as there would be things they didn't want the other to see. The more I swiped, the more I realized the only thing left was the group chat, and a few voicemails... which made me wonder if Scotty had deleted certain messages.

I swiped over to the voicemails and placed it on speaker phone so I could listen while I did my nightly skincare routine.

"Hey this is Kingston...I just was hoping to hear your voice. I know I have a lot to explain, Pres, but if you just give me the chance to do it then I will. I'll tell you what I meant to say that night instead of how it all went down. I wish you'd just answer. Please pick up."

The next voicemail started playing automatically.

"Pres, did you know that Kingston dream talks? It's funny as hell. He's

remembering a time that you lost your favorite stuffed cow and tried to help you find it. I texted you the video so if you wanted to text me back about how funny it is, that would be cool. But if not, then I get that too. Please just answer one of us."

I paused mid-drip as the face serum trickled down my face. There was no text with a video, which meant my assumption that Scotty had deleted messages was true. What had they said?

There were only two voicemails, one from each of them...surely there would have been more.

Just out of curiosity, I made my way down to the blocked callers and sure enough, there was an endless list of messages from each brother dating all the way back to the first week they left. I fought a smile and lost.

Once I finished up my skin routine, I snuggled under my covers and hit play.

I didn't realize how much I missed their voices and how their laughs were so distinctly different.

Hours likely passed as each message played and the next started, until finally I drifted off to sleep to the sound of Kingston explaining exactly how all of this was indeed Scotty's fault.

I fucking knew it.

CHAPTER 14

GIO

AGE 16

Our big sister, Alex, was turning nineteen and we were celebrating it away from home.

We didn't have to travel a ton anymore, not nearly as much as when we were little, but every now and then we'd still pack up and get on a plane. While our family typically ventured down to see my dad's extended family, this time Presley and Carter's families joined us.

"Mexico is my favorite place on the planet." Presley sighed from the pool lounger she was sitting on. She was difficult to look at today, or if I were being more honest, it would be that she was difficult *not* to look at today.

She wore a two-piece bathing suit, similar to about a billion other times we'd gone swimming together, but there was something about how she looked now that was so different from how she used to that made things annoyingly confusing for me.

She had a bigger chest, and her stomach looked different. I'd seen her abs a million times, never caring about them or the way her belly button dipped inward the slightest bit, which made water pool there when she'd get wet. Her hair was another thing; it was long and usually braided; but here, in Mexico, for some reason she'd let it down as often as she wanted.

It was soaking wet, resting against her back while the sun baked her already tan skin. Her lips looked more pink than normal as well... and bigger. Her lashes were thicker and seemed to frame her eyes in a way that made her look like she was wearing that dark eyeliner stuff, but she wasn't.

"Gio, stop standing in the middle of the walkway." My dad gently smacked my back on his way past me. He was carrying a tray of drinks over to my mom, Aunt Mallory and Presley's mom, Rylie. Aunt Mallory and Uncle Decker were here visiting with us for once. They'd been hit or miss quite a bit over the years; there was a stretch of time they were back for good, then they started leaving again.

Glancing over at Carter, I saw her in a similar position as Presley and realized I didn't notice anything about her that made me feel uncomfortable, which made me worried all over again. Carter wasn't my biological cousin; we weren't blood-related at all, so if I wanted to look at her in that way, I could...I just never had the desire to.

"I've been here so often, it doesn't really feel that special anymore," Carter remarked while scrolling on her phone. She traveled more than any of us did, but I doubted she'd been to Mexico as frequently as I had.

I sat down next to Presley and shook my hair out, getting droplets on Pres and Carter's phones. Carter shrieked and jumped up and ran for her towel.

"That was mean." Presley laughed into her hand while shoving me with her foot. My eyes trailed up her leg and landed briefly on the way the green fabric on her bottoms hugged her hips. Since when did I care how her swimsuit fit her?

"She was being rude," I muttered in defense. My gaze was on my best friend's face, but it kept dipping lower to her bottom lip.

Suddenly it spread into a smile. "Where's Kingston?"

Something in my chest deflated, but I ignored it and pointed over my shoulder with my thumb. "Getting food."

Presley slid off the lounger and stretched. "I'm gonna go find him, see if he wants to race in the pool."

My voice felt funny, so I didn't respond. I watched as she walked past me and tried to stuff the feelings exploding in my chest back into whatever box they'd crawled out of. Jealousy wasn't completely uncommon for my brother and me to feel, especially when it came to Presley. It's just that we typically felt it around who got to be her partner on video games, or who sat next to her in the car.

This...whatever this was, it was new and it was terrifying.

———

LATER THAT NIGHT, the lights around the pool were soft as I watched Presley and Carter swim with Kingston. I had joined a few times throughout the day, and each time I felt that strange feeling return, I would push it away. Only to see Presley get closer to King. When they'd laugh or joke together, my chest would feel tight all over again.

I'd been trying to work through it all day, but it hadn't gotten any better.

"Let's play something," Carter suggested, getting out of the pool and wrapping up in a towel. Alex, and all the parents were inside somewhere, leaving just us kids out here. Kingston was on his phone on the lounger next to me, but he set it down right as Presley exited the pool.

"What do you want to play?"

Carter's reddish-brown hair almost looked black from being wet and the dim lighting. She shrugged and then glanced at both me and King, then back at Presley.

"Actually, I have an idea."

"What?" Presley asked, wringing out her hair. She'd also wrapped up in a white towel. The air was still warm enough that we weren't cold, but I was grateful she covered up so I didn't have to sort through all of my feelings over seeing her soft skin or counting her freckles.

Carter's eyes nearly gleamed as she said, "Let's play Truth or Dare."

"That's so lame," Presley sighed.

She sat down next to me and continued to wring out the water from her hair.

"That's only because you always chicken out." Kingston mocked Presley.

He wasn't wrong. Presley could do almost anything, but if we dared her to try something gross or to jump off of something really tall, she'd chicken out and get mad that she lost.

"It's still lame, let's think of something else."

Carter sat down next to Kingston and pulled out her phone.

"Well, we can't play anything that's physical because you'll beat all of us," Carter complained, clearly talking about Pres. She was scrolling through her phone again, which made me curious if she really wanted to play something or if she had other plans. Kingston and I weren't allowed to have social media yet, and I was fairly sure Presley wasn't either. We challenged each other on Duolingo on our phones and watched copious amounts of YouTube; otherwise, we didn't have accounts anywhere because our dad was worried we'd accidentally leak where we lived or post where we were in real time and somehow get kidnapped.

Presley glanced over at me and gave me an expression that meant she was about to reply to Carter and it wouldn't be good. "King and Gio are stronger than me; you're the only person who wouldn't win, Carter."

Her cousin paused mid-type and slowly raised her eyes.

"I'm not nearly as weak as you guys think I am."

Kingston sneered, "No one said you were weak, Carter."

"Let's just play Truth or pass then, Presley. If you pass, you lose."

The two girls stared at one another, glaring until Presley's jaw slid to the side and she gave in. "Fine."

Carter beamed, clapping her hands. "Perfect, okay, we go by age."

King and I looked at each other right as the girls did.

"Who came first?" Carter waved between us.

It was Presley who smiled and pointed at me. "Gio did."

We actually had no idea who had come first since our mom had never told us. We had a theory that she honestly didn't know because of how stressful her labor was. She always told us she was just grateful we were okay, and that everything was sorted out later.

"Gio, you'll go first then King and then me, and last will be Presley."

I wasn't particularly in the mood to play this game, but I also didn't want to leave if Presley was still out here. Which was another realization that something had shifted between us, and she wasn't even aware that it had. Kingston's gaze kept lifting to Presley every few seconds, and even if he hadn't told me, I had a feeling he had the same struggle.

"Okay, Gio, your question is: If you had to choose between saving Alex and Kingston, who would you save?"

My nose wrinkled at the stupid question. Presley looked nervous as she inspected me and glanced over at Kingston, then back at me. She hated anything that made me uncomfortable, as if I couldn't handle it, but this one was easy.

"I'd give my life trying to save them both."

Everyone made a booing sound before Carter moved to Kingston.

"Okay, if you had to choose between never being able to see or hear again, which would you choose?"

He made a sound that indicated he was thinking, which came out almost like a sigh. "I'd choose not to see."

"Why?" Presley asked, screwing her nose up. "Wouldn't you want to be able to see your loved ones and colors?"

He stared at her long enough that something in my gut shifted around. It was tied to that block of cement that had recently surfaced when it came to him and Presley.

"There are certain sounds I've grown accustomed to. Someone

can change their appearance, but I'm positive that I'd always know someone's voice. And then there's laughter…someone's laugh could pull me out of the darkest head space. I wouldn't have to see them— just hear that tinkling sound they made when they were happy. It would be easier to be grateful for your life if you only had your hearing and not your sight."

He was talking about Presley.

A memory surfaced of him talking about her laugh like it was a tinkling bell.

I couldn't control how soon everyone's eyes were on me, but my face felt too hot and my chest was too tight.

"Carter, it's your turn." I cleared the knot from my throat, realizing they wanted me to ask her a question.

"Would you rather eat a moldy piece of bread covered in peanut butter or jelly?"

Her gasp was obnoxious. "Ewww that's disgusting. Why would you ask me that?"

Her question was easy in comparison to what we'd been asked.

"Answer the question, Carter," Presley teased.

With a sigh and an eye roll, she replied, "Peanut butter."

Presley laughed and Kingston's eyes found hers instantly, locking onto her as she tipped her head back.

I didn't want him looking at her.

I didn't want him falling for her.

He couldn't.

Not when I was fairly certain I already had.

Something seemed to come over me as Pres continued to laugh, and Kingston continued to watch. I lunged forward and pushed my brother as hard as I could off the pool lounger, which forced him to fall back and into the pool.

"Gio!" Presley shrieked right as Carter stood and covered her mouth.

My fists were clenched as I watched my brother break the surface and gasp for air. "The fuck, Gio?"

I didn't respond. Our eyes locked, and he only held my stare for a moment before flicking his eyes over to Presley then back over to me. He knew, and while I hoped he'd shake his head or act outraged by the idea, he smiled instead.

It was a devious smile that told me he'd be getting me back, but it wouldn't be by pushing me into a pool.

Something told me it would be worse.

"Psst." A hiss echoed through the room and then something shoved my shoulder.

"Gio!"

I sat up and looked around the dark room, finding someone kneeling next to my bed.

"Presley?"

Her hand moved to my mouth, covering it. "Come on, let's go."

I moved the sheet off and slid out of bed. I was in a pair of basketball shorts, but my shirt was still off. The air was hot and humid. I glanced at Kingston's bed, seeing he was still asleep.

"Where are we going?" I whispered back, but Presley merely grabbed my hand and pulled me with her as she moved over to Kingston's side of the room. I ignored the fact that she was including my brother in whatever we were doing and focused on how warm her hand was in mine.

"Kingston," she whispered, rousing my brother from sleep.

Once he was awake enough to sit up, she tugged his hand.

"Gemini is out!" she said excitedly, leading us out of our room and down the hall. The place we were staying had polished, wood floors that creaked ever so slightly whenever we stepped on them, but right at the end of the hall was a door that led out to a huge balcony.

Kingston was holding Presley's other hand, and right as he saw me, he delivered that exact expression he'd given me when exiting the pool. Presley's head tipped back as she stared at the sky. Her pajamas were cotton shorts and a thin tank top, which made that concrete block return to my gut.

Why did it feel so strange seeing her like this?

She was freshly fifteen and still had her braces. She'd always just been Presley...even though if I were to really remember and think back, she'd always been more than that to me.

"Right there, Gio!" She pointed up, and I stepped next to her until I saw where she was pointing.

Sure enough the complex system was there, the two twin heads at the narrow opening.

"You found it, Elvis." I draped my arm over her shoulders and tugged her into my side.

Her smile was infectious as Kingston stepped closer to her.

"Show me, *mi reina*. I can't find it."

Yes, he could. He may be into plants, but we'd both been in the same astronomy class last year, and we'd both learned how to read maps.

Presley left my embrace and gently took his wrist until her hand hovered over his. "Look, right there." Their heads were bent closer, as she leaned into him, trying to get him to see the right group of stars.

"Oh, I see it now."

Idiot.

Presley let him go and then brought her hands together. "It's so beautiful. I can't believe we finally found it."

"You found it, Elvis," I said, tugging on the end of her braid.

She turned and smiled at me then reached for both of our hands and intertwined her fingers through ours.

"One day I want to come back here, when we're grown-ups. I might even want to live here."

Kingston and I followed her to the ground when she decided to lie on the balcony and stare up at the constellation. We never let her hands go while we lay next to her.

"What about your farm, Pres?"

She let out a heavy sigh. "I can have a farm here in Mexico, can't I?"

Kingston broke the silence. "I think we'd miss you."

"Can't you guys follow me here?"

I smiled, turning my head. "Both of us?"

She tilted hers to match my gaze. "Yeah, can't just have one of you."

Kingston tugged her so she turned her face toward him. "We'll always have the sky, Pres. Even if you choose Mexico and it doesn't choose us. We'll have the sky."

"I can't imagine a world without you two," she whispered after the breeze skimmed over us in cool waves.

Glancing over at my brother, I suddenly wished I hadn't looked. Pain that mirrored something in my chest stared back and suddenly us fighting over her felt stupid. I didn't know what her future held, but I knew who controlled it.

Scotty would get to determine where she ended up, and deep down I already knew it wouldn't be with either one of us.

CHAPTER 15
PRESLEY
PRESENT

The mood in the manor was strained and awkward, at least in our family wing.

My mom sipped her coffee while sneaking glances at my dad, who was already watching her. He did that sometimes, and the secret smile between them was always something I hid away in my own mind as something I wanted when I found my forever.

Scotty was in the kitchen, making eggs, while Reaper and Rex panted near his feet.

Still in my pajamas and wearing slippers that looked like miniature Highland cows with fluffed little horns, I padded toward the family room and paused in front of my parents.

"I'd like to speak with you both about something important to me."

Mom set her mug down while Dad did the same with his phone. "What's wrong, honey?"

I'd been thinking about this all night, well, as soon as I woke up and realized what I'd heard through all the deleted voicemails. Aside from the distance between the twins and me, they were likely under the assumption that I had merely been ignoring them all this time.

Unfortunately, part of that was true, as I could have approached Scotty much sooner regarding the messages; I just didn't, and for that reason I was not prepared to see them.

"I plan on traveling to Italy for a while...perhaps a few months this time."

I heard something crash in the kitchen as the skillet was tossed onto the counter. Scotty slowly made his way into the living room, dogs on his heels. I refused to look at him.

"Why the sudden desire to stay there for so long; you've only done a week at a time previously." My mom's brows caved like little caterpillars. I looked like her, almost identical if you asked some people. All of dad's DNA was inside me, where I withstood all of Scotty's torture.

Glaring at my uncle, I explained, "I just think it would be best if I took some time away from the manor for a bit. Scotty wanted me to create an ally with Adrian, and I have."

"Like hell are you leaving. You're staying right the fuck here," Scotty seethed, pointing at the carpet.

My dad glanced between us, his forehead mirrored my mom's, crumpling in confusion.

"What the hell is going on?"

All at once Scotty and I started yelling at the same time.

"He's been keeping all the twins' messages from me!"

"She brought Adrian here, to our home, where we live!"

My mom winced then moved to grab her mug while Dad rubbed his forehead.

"Okay, stop. Jesus. Just stop."

He stood between me and Scotty as if we'd attack one another or something. I was tempted, but the old man would still put me on my ass faster than I cared to admit possible.

"Scotty, you wanted her to get close to Adrian, why are you upset about this?"

His green eyes burned as they focused on me, his jaw popped. "She was supposed to get close to him as a cat would with a mouse it wanted to eat at some point. He was supposed to be toyed with, kept at arm's length. She was not supposed to fall for him."

"For the love of God, I didn't fall for him!" My hand cut out in front of me, my anger barely leashed.

"You invited him into our home, Presley. This is where your family sleeps. While you may be creating an alliance with him, we do not trust him. We don't trust any of them."

I knew he was right, and deep down, shame threatened to break me open and reveal exactly why I was curling inside the shelter of Adrian's existence. Was I using him as a means to escape?

Yes.

Was that just as bad as what Scotty had suggested when he mentioned toying with him?

Also yes.

"Look. I'm not ready to see the twins, and you summoned them home because I pissed you off. It's going to be a mess, Scotty. A fucking mess. I need to leave." My voice wobbled the smallest bit and I sucked in a sharp breath to keep it from cracking.

Dad scoffed, and it had me glancing over quickly. "So what, this is just how it's going to be? They stay away because they're upset or whatever reason they're using to remain gone. You leave because you're upset? At what point do we just go back to being a family?"

Scotty and I didn't speak, but my mom made a humming sound before standing from the couch. "Kyle, you're the last person to preach about this. You went three years without talking to me. If your daughter needs the space, then she can have it. Of all the things you've forced her body to endure, you have no right whatsoever to force anything on her heart."

Dad's expression crumpled a bit while Scotty's didn't change at all.

I didn't need his approval. I ducked my head and backed out of the room before anyone else could argue with me.

My room was a mess with clothes strewn about everywhere, but

I just continued stuffing my suitcases. I paused for a second to text Adrian.

Me: Can I fly back with you?

I needed my...what did I even need? Adrian had my preferred shampoo and skin care products. I even had clothes there. Honestly, I could just get on the flight and be fine.

Adrian: Don't tease me, Presley. Are you really wanting to come to Italy with me?

My thumbs swiped quickly before I could think any more about it.

Me: Yes. I'm ready whenever you are.

Adrian: Dare I ask for how long?

I glanced over at the burner phone that Scotty had used and closed my eyes.

Me: A few months, I think. Maybe longer.

Adrian: I'll be there to pick you up in thirty minutes.

A STRANGE ACHE unfurled in my chest, one that had been there the night the twins left. The same one I had when I realized how they felt about me and how things really were between us.

It didn't matter.

They had left and now I would too.

I zipped up my carry-on right as my door opened and Scotty entered.

"I know you're mad at me, but I want you to know that everything I've done has been to protect you. I don't want you to trust Adrian implicitly...he's grabbed hold of some piece of your heart, *Lánya*, just don't give him the whole thing."

It enraged me that he could be so cold with me one second and then call me daughter in the next.

"I'd rather risk my heart with someone who wants it than live a life without one, like you."

His gaze was soft as he stared down at me as if he realized he'd pissed me off enough that there was no coming back. I had forgiven him for holding their texts from me for several months. But calling the twins back here just to keep me in place was too much.

Turning my back on him, I continued to pack. Ignoring him, I didn't watch to see what he'd placed on my bed, but as soon as he left, I turned around.

There on my luggage was a flower crown. It was one that I had made when I was little, made mostly of twigs, and woven in between the sticks were dried flowers that were crumpling and breaking.

That ache in my chest turned into a void.

CHAPTER 16

KINGSTON

AGE 17

Presley used to make crowns out of flowers and twigs, then she'd wear the thing on her head and pretend she was a princess. It would always be this big production where she'd ask me and Gio to be knights. I never really cared because I'd talk her into letting me be the dragon, and I'd find some tall place to jump from that I wasn't supposed to.

Now she was wearing a diamond tiara with a dress that made her look like real royalty, and it was making me feel weird.

She was only sixteen, but there was something about how her smile stretched over her braces that had my own smile coming out. These days it didn't feel like anyone could get me to do that, but Presley always could.

I watched as Presley sipped something clear and bubbly from her glass. I knew it was Sprite, but she was probably trying to act like it was champagne. I knew her well enough to know she was trying to give the impression that she was mature for sixteen. I could tell by the way she kept glancing at the boy near the corner that kept looking at her. He seemed similar to my age or older, with shaggy blond hair and a tux that was too big for his frame. It was only a matter of time before he saw her watching him, and then he'd walk over and speak to her as if he had the right.

The discomfort I felt over observing her flirting with her eyes had nothing to do with the fact that she'd snuck into our room last night and slept on our floor just so she could spend the first moments of her birthday with us. We'd stayed up all night, sneaking out onto the terrace, watching the stars.

Presley's sixteenth birthday had arrived and with it, an insane idea from Scotty. While we'd been hiding from rival families all our lives, he suddenly wanted to play with this idea that we could emerge into their society and dance right under their noses without them ever even knowing it. We went by different names and floated about the party as though not a single person would notice, but the entire idea had me on edge.

The boy across the room finally made his move toward Presley, holding out a plate for her that contained a piece of chocolate cake. She accepted it with a delicate smile and a small blush that crept under her thick lashes. Something stirred in my chest seeing it. Knowing she was so focused on this boy who wasn't me or Gio.

What did she think was going to happen here, at a party we were hiding in plain sight just to attend? Aside from that, what could he be saying that had her laughing so much?

My brother found me sulking against the wall and shoved my shoulder.

"Stop staring at her."

I glared ahead, locking my jaw over how the idiot talking to Presley just tucked a piece of her hair behind her ear. The ear that I knew had an infection when she was seven, then again when she was eleven. She'd had them pierced when she was twelve, and the first pair of earrings she got were two little cows.

I directed my question at my brother as I asked, "No one should feel comfortable enough that they can just walk up and touch her. Doesn't anyone realize how fucking dangerous this entire thing is?"

There were rival families here for fuck's sake.

Gio let out a sigh before tucking his hands into his suit pockets. "He's not touching her."

"He just touched her ear."

Why did it feel like someone had placed a river rock baking in the sun all day right there on my sternum? I'd always watched over Presley, always been aware of her movements and remained near enough that if she were in danger, I'd be there to help, but this was different. She wasn't the one I worried was in danger; it was me that I feared for.

Me that felt out of control watching her.

Me who was messed up in the head for looking at her the way I was and thinking she was pretty. Beautiful even.

I'd counted her freckles the last time we were on the couch watching a movie. She assumed I was playing a staring game with her, but she wouldn't engage. It was better that way because it allowed me to scrutinize her every dark spot, every thick lash, and the way her cheek dimpled on only the left side of her face.

"Can you see Scotty from here?" Gio asked, bringing me back to the girl across the room now taking a photo with the stupid boy.

That was enough.

I snapped harshly enough that my brother pushed off the wall, "He can't have photos of her."

Scotty was already watching us from across the room with a hard set to his jaw as we approached him. He wore a fitted suit, all black, of course, because God forbid the man wear anything aside from that color. I knew he'd snuck in weapons, even if we'd been checked at the door. This whole night was one of Scotty's sick and twisted games. We'd parade around in front of the very people who were trying to kill us, while pretending to be someone else, just to see if we could get away with it.

Since discovering our family's proximity to organized crime, my brother and I became students of their world. While we were here pretending to be a part of a family that no one ever heard of, all so Presley could have this mirage of a birthday party, we knew better.

Scotty planned this, and he was likely testing us like he tested everyone.

"This is reckless," I hissed, close to Scotty's ear.

He glared down the length of his nose at me like I was shit on his shoe. "Kingston. Giovanni."

Gio glanced at me like he wanted permission to hit Presley's uncle. Instead, he stepped closer and matched my pitch as he repeated, "This is dangerous and stupid. The guy drooling all over Presley is part of the Milano family."

Scotty sipped his liquor then with more ease than I cared for, and said, "If you two are so worried about Presley, then perhaps you should take it upon yourselves to protect her. She'll go places I can't follow. If you're so inclined, you can trail her. Watch her. She'll never be able to date, not anyone regular that is. She'll get them killed, so maybe you're doing her a kindness by stepping in."

"So you're asking us to go and take care of this?" Gio asked, seemingly confused.

I was too. Why not just stop all this and get her out of here?

Scotty took another sip of his drink. "I'm telling you that if you're worried, then simply take care of the threat yourselves."

With that, he slipped through the crowd. We turned back toward our best friend and found her smiling at the Milano kid. He was closer to her now and touching her hip.

Red hot rage lit me up and that's all I could see as I turned toward her. Gio followed, only to bump my arm seconds later. "I'll distract her."

My eyes didn't leave the couple as they continued to laugh. One of the Milano soldiers stood close enough to them, telling me he was likely the son of someone high up in the family. Possibly even the don of the family. Good, maybe this would warn enough of them to stay the fuck away from—well, we had no family name here.

We were pretending, acting out exactly what Presley's dad used to do. We'd dug into his background once the news landed that he was a part of the mafia but had stolen from them. The Joker surfaced and we realized exactly how fucked up of a legacy Kyle had left for Presley.

"Elvis," Gio sang, walking up behind her and grabbing her attention. Her expression was reluctant, but she turned away from her admirer and gave her attention to my brother, which gave me enough time to move in.

"Gotta talk to you for a second, Josh." I pushed on the kid's neck, and right as Presley turned to see what was happening, my brother pulled her in for a hug.

It allowed me the chance to push the kid behind a corner, without the soldier near him seeing.

"My name isn't Josh!" His face was red as he tried to push at my hands.

I let him go but quickly swiped his leg, so he fell on his ass.

"Hey!"

Bending down, I plucked his cell phone out of his pocket, turned his face to unlock it and then found the pictures he'd snapped of Presley. Her smile was infectious, her eyes sparkling and even her skin was glowing. Whatever that presence was on my chest became heavier.

"Sorry, Josh, it isn't personal, but you can't have these."

"What the fuck is your problem?!" he yelled, pushing his palms into the marble floor, elevating his chest. His face was tomato red. There were words on my tongue that I wanted to spout off at him about touching Presley, about thinking he had the right, but I realized it wouldn't matter.

"Stay away from that one."

His eyes narrowed; his lip lifted with a sneer. "Fuck you. Which family do you belong to, we're going to fucking destroy you."

He was exhausting.

With a heavy sigh, I pulled out one of my knives.

"Can you understand what I'm telling you?"

He tried to push me again, but it only had me moving the blade to his throat.

"Try it and you'll be dead in seconds. I have men stationed every-where, they—"

My mind merely replayed the way his hand splayed open on Presley's hip, and the way she had given him one of those smiles she'd never given me, and my hand moved on its own, plunging the knife into the palm that had spread over Presley's body.

His mouth opened and closed like a goldfish as he gaped at his hand.

"You scream and alert anyone and I have another blade for your tongue."

His whimper was quiet, but he pulled his hand to his chest in agony.

"A kindness from me. You touched her, you're lucky all I settled for was stabbing you. I could have taken it clean off."

I smirked before standing above him, and right as I did, Presley and Gio rounded the corner. Her eyes widened at the sight of him, then flicked angrily over to me as if I had been the one to fuck up tonight.

My jaw clenched, and before she could say anything, I pulled her farther into the hall and disappeared behind a door.

Gio would fix my fuck-up by alerting Scotty to my little blunder.

"Why did you do that?" Presley spat at me as she spun around in her dress, letting it flare around her legs. I watched her, as entranced as I'd ever been by anything that I'd ever witnessed grow from the earth or bloom under the sun.

"Kingston." She said my name again, and I finally sighed, giving her my answer.

"You can't get that close to people here, Pres. He was dangerous. You told me there were enemies after your father. Be smarter than that next time you want to cozy up to someone who could hurt you."

She crossed her arms, which pushed her chest up, and my eyes betrayed me by lingering on the plump flesh that her dress dipped to reveal.

"I was only talking to him...why do you care who I talk to?" Her blue eyes flashed the smallest bit with curiosity, and it felt like a ripe, red apple in the hands of a delicate sinner. I would be the corruptive snake that shed some artificial light on her.

Stepping closer, I smirked. "Maybe I was jealous, *Elvis.*" I slowly dragged my finger across her collarbone, and along the column of her throat.

I watched as she swallowed and her chin wobbled. "Jealous in what way?"

Tilting my head, I toyed with her. "What way do you think?"

She tried to take a step away from me, but I held her in place with a palm to her hip.

"Do you..." Her pink tongue came out and wet her bottom lip. "Like me?"

Like her? I thought over how I'd woken up early just so I could walk along the ridgeline and hide amongst the brick chimney to watch her walk with her cute little slippers out on her balcony and smile at the sunrise. Her hair always blew around her face like she'd made an invisible friend and it had waited all night to greet her.

At night I'd occasionally make my way there and crouch near that window just to ensure she was tucked inside, safe and protected. With a strange jolt in my chest, I decided this was enough.

A laugh escaped me as I stepped back. "You should see the look on your face, Pres."

Her shapely brows curved in, crowding her cute forehead and the three freckles that rested near her hairline. That strange shudder in my chest returned tenfold, making my airway feel too tight.

"You were joking," she said matter-of-fact and then she lowered her face as if to hide the blush that crept into her fair skin.

"Of course I was. You're like a sister to me." I stepped forward and gripped her chin between my fingers and then shook her head as if to dismiss this entire thing. "Doesn't change the fact that you have to be careful in places like this. Nobody gets to touch you."

Her eyes burned with ire, and I welcomed it because I liked warm things. I enjoyed the heat Presley gave to me when she burned hot enough to give it. It made me think of the jar of dirt she once gave me; all warm sunshine baked into the dust of the world that so consistently failed me. She had no idea how impossible she made existing.

Her presence was a thorn, puncturing and piercing my chest, but I learned to live with the pain. Even as kids, I had learned to tolerate how painful it was to look at her and not become completely undone by her, but then she grew, and she became more beautiful than I had ever imagined she'd be. She grew fierce and bold and completely perfect.

Now she stood there, glaring at me with hate and anger radiating from her in waves. I was crazy because I was half tempted to hand her the knife and ask her to cut me, just so I'd always remember this moment. This one time in space where it was just us, not our family, not Gio, no one. Just a glass jar, like a flower, trapped and protected.

"How about you not fight my battles, King." Presley finally pushed past me, digging her shoulder into mine.

I laughed, gripping her wrist and tugging her back. "Oh no, and why not?"

Within seconds, she had a knife at my throat, pushing me back, her teeth bared. "Because I'm more skilled at battle than you are."

Our lips were mere inches apart and I had to push down the way my fingers ached to grab her face and pull her closer. I knew it wouldn't be welcomed. Presley wanted a stranger, someone to come in and sweep her off her feet. She didn't want her best friend who spent more time in the dirt than most flowers. My fingers had a permanent layer of dirt under them; my clothes smelled like soil, and I was as positive as the diamonds that gleamed from her tiara that Presley James would never belong to someone like me.

She was a star, the sun...the skies we spent our childhood searching.

But one thing she'd never become was mine, so I ducked my head and let her release me. Then I watched as she opened the door without looking back.

CHAPTER 17

PRESLEY

AGE 16

Rain fell at an angle, coating my window in fat droplets.

I was perched on my window seat, staring at the soaked world as my mood continued to sour, and I ignored my life. I'd forgone training for five days, and I'd ignored my best friends nearly just as long. I needed to forgive Kingston for what he'd done, but I wasn't just mad at him. I was devastated that he'd toyed with me the way he did.

It was bad enough that the twins were able to get Snapchat recently and they both had started making online friends, most of which were girls based off the giggles and laughs I heard coming from their screens.

Kingston confused me, more frequently than was kind. My feeble crush on him had weathered indifference from him for so long, but to have him pretend, or even act as though he'd acted out of a place of jealousy, it was too cruel. He said it was because he wanted to protect the family, but since when had he ever cared about that?

"Presley?" My mother's voice had me turning, seeing her with a plate of apple slices and peanut butter.

I ignored her too. She'd done nothing wrong, but I was angry with her for keeping me here, just like I was at my father and Scotty. I understood the gravity of what was going on and how we couldn't simply exist outside of these walls without retribution, but the interaction from my birthday only proved that I'd never make any friendships or lasting relationships for as long as I was trapped in the manor.

My mother made her way up the stairs to my loft and gently sat next to me, placing the plate between us.

"Missed you at breakfast this morning, and lunch."

She was worried about me, and part of me revolted at the idea of causing that, but I was too disappointed to empathize.

"Talk to me, honey. What's going on?" She gently toyed with the ends of my long hair. I wore shorts, long socks, and a hoodie, but my hair was washed and styled, so it hung in a long sheet behind me. Something inside me cracked, feeling her fingers pull at a snag, as she continued to comb through it.

"I'm stuck here." My throat suddenly burned as a sob worked through me. "I'm done with my school courses, but I'm only sixteen. I've had no experiences, nothing outside of the manor and the people here. I want to make friends, go to school, kiss a boy. I want freedom."

I felt like a bird, begging for someone to open my cage.

Freedom felt so fleeting, and like such a strange concept. Of course I wasn't trapped; I was kept safe and well-loved, and yet the look on that boy's face wouldn't leave my mind. The way he looked so shocked at Kingston's behavior, and the way the realization hit me that I'd never know what it felt like to kiss a boy at a ball because the twins would step in and ruin it. It all was a ball of tension just sitting in my chest like a time bomb.

"You know why we—" my mother started, but I cut her off.

"I know, but is it really so important to prevent me from having these experiences? What if I go by a different name and I keep my head down...I'm not trying to make waves or cause issues. I just want the chance to be a normal sixteen-year-old."

My mom's eyes narrowed at that word choice, and I remembered what she'd said about me. She didn't know I had overheard her say that I wasn't normal, but now I was using it against her. Relying on the fact that somewhere, down deep in her heart, she longed for her daughter to have typical teenage experiences.

She bit her lip and glanced outside, and a fresh hope rose within me.

"I'd be safe, Mom. You know I could handle myself, and you know that I'd do whatever you said I had to. I could do a half day, since I don't really need any more credits. Scotty can forge the paperwork and all the documents for me, showing I only need a few classes. Please, I'm begging you. Ask him for me."

Her eyes searched my face, and I knew I'd gotten through to her. She was the number one fan of me having normal kid experiences. There was no way she'd deny me this.

"I'll talk to your father, and to Scotty about it, okay?"

I flung forward and threw my arms around her. It was as close to a yes as I would likely get, but it still meant the world to me.

DINNER ARRIVED and the smell of my mother's lasagna filled the room. Our table only had four chairs because we never invited anyone over to eat with us. Scotty was a private person, and my parents liked to protect him in the little ways they could since he was always protecting us.

Scotty wore a simple T-shirt, sweats, and his feet were bare. I liked when he didn't have to wear his armor here, as if this was the only place on earth that he didn't have to wear a bulletproof vest. His thinning hair was a bit mussed, which meant he'd napped before dinner.

"So," Dad started, while glancing up from his plate, "your mother talked to us about your request to socialize."

That was an interesting term for what I was trying to do. I didn't say anything for fear of what would happen if I misspoke or screwed everything up by blurting out how unfair it was that I'd been stuck here while my cousin Carter had been allowed to attend private school with other people her age.

She'd had boyfriends before.

Instead, I gracefully nodded while taking a small bite of food.

Dad continued, "I'm upset about what took place at the ball and I'm still unsure exactly where Kingston got the idea that it was his job to step in."

I had no idea either; it was like he'd just picked up this need to be my protector out of nowhere.

"He's hotheaded and doesn't think through things before he ruins them," Scotty murmured, keeping his eyes on his plate. While I agreed with him, I still felt the urge to defend my best friend, but I bit my lip instead.

"But I agree with your mother." Dad placed his gaze on me, and I tried to tamp down my hope. "I think it's time you get a little bit of socialization outside of this house. It could be good for you to be around kids your own age and learn how to be around them."

Oh my god. It was happening; they were going to let me go. Elation filled my chest like warm, fuzzy cotton. It had a squeal of happiness erupting from my throat as I jumped out of my seat and rounded the table, hugging my dad. "Thank you, I won't let you down. I promise!"

Dad hugged me to him then sighed. "Just hang on a second. Scotty has a condition."

Of course he did. Releasing my dad, I glanced over at my uncle, awaiting whatever his ridiculous condition would be.

Scotty set his fork down and gave me his full focus. "You'll go under a different first and last name. You will not drive yourself. You will carry a weapon at all times."

I moved my head, agreeing with him on all fronts because it didn't matter what name I used as long as it meant I'd get to leave and be around other people.

"Lastly," Scotty added, giving me a sly smile, "the twins must go with you."

The air nearly left my lungs. "What? No...Kingston is the entire reason we—"

Scotty put his hand up, stopping me. "Those boys would set themselves on fire to protect you. You convince them to go and they get the blessing from Juan and Taylor to go, then you'll be enrolled by Monday."

"But they've already graduated!" There was no way they'd willingly go back to high school, especially just to be my protectors.

"I can create documents that say they haven't. They're only seventeen; it won't be a difficult thing to fake."

"Don't get your hopes up, honey," Dad said, grabbing for a piece of garlic bread. "You'll have to convince two seventeen-year-old boys to babysit you, and they'll have to win their parents over to do it. I'm not sure there's much of a chance for you."

My heart squeezed tight as my hope began to plunder. "Can't you talk to Juan?"

He smirked and shook his head. "I'm afraid the twins are where my opinion stops counting. They've been protective of the boys getting mixed up in our mess since before they were born. They might relent because it's just school but still..." He took a big bite of bread. "Don't get your hopes up."

I sank into my chair again and pushed the food around my plate feeling strangely depressed. This meant I was going to have to forgive Kingston for what he did, and then beg him to help me out.

Great.

<hr>

My phone showed it was close to midnight when I finally built the courage to talk to the twins.

With a heavy sigh, I flipped my duvet back and got out of bed. During the warmer time of year, I slept up in my loft, which was smaller and had less space, but I liked being near the large window that opened out to my small veranda ledge. Dad had opted for an expensive but old piece of glass that had two pieces that opened, kept closed by a single gold hook. Just like in Peter Pan.

I hadn't walked over to their side of the house in months, but it didn't matter, I still knew the path like the back of my hand. Even in the dark, under only a blanket of stars to keep me company.

Pulling on a hoodie and a pair of slippers, I kept my sleep shorts on and pushed the glass panes open, revealing a small patch of black shingles and a dark sky. The two arches on either side of my veranda kept the wind at bay, but once I was out, I pulled my window closed and then braced my hands before stepping around to the pathway.

White light lit up a few clouds hovering overhead, and distant thunder rumbled as the wind coiled through my hair. It made the longer strands whip against my face. I pushed it back and kept my eyes down on the small pathway in front of me. My window was on the complete opposite end of the mansion, so I had to be careful as I walked. While my footing was sure, the wind was much stronger with it being close to the end of February. My hoodie was no match for the air that bit at my legs and the moisture in the air that crowded my lungs.

I moved faster, until finally I saw the ledge that led to Gio and King's room. It had the same flat veranda area in front of the window but theirs was a bit more modern. Tonight, the window was shut but they never kept it locked.

I pulled up on it right as rain started falling in heavy drops against my face. I straddled the ledge with one leg and ducked under, pushing inside and falling flat on their loft floor. I got to my knees and sat up, a plume of smoke drifted up from the corner.

"What in the fuck are you doing, *Elvis?*" Kingston rasped while tipping his head back from the two-seater couch he was reclined on.

Something fluttered in my chest at the cadence of his voice, but it dove into my stomach painfully fast when I registered he'd called me the wrong nickname. I hated when he called me Elvis, it always felt like he was making fun of me. Even being annoyed with him, I couldn't help but notice the thing swooping in my chest was the same wicked thing that had beat against my breast in that closet, when he was standing so close to me. I'd been so angry, and yet I'd burned as if he'd set me aflame.

I pushed my hair back from my face and stood, peering over the loft railing and seeing Gio playing a video game down below, their large flat-screen lit up with a myriad of colors and a car driving fast over terrain.

"I need to talk to you guys."

Gio called up from below, "Is that Elvis?"

"Yeah!" King shouted back as if I weren't here to say it myself. I rolled my eyes at their dumb nickname for me and walked over to where Kingston was sitting. He didn't lift his feet, just raised his brow in challenge as if he dared me to forgive him for what he'd done and go back to how things were between us.

That fluttering only worsened as I swallowed my pride and sat down on top of his legs, which made him smile.

"You have to stop calling me that, it's stupid."

Gio made some sort of pained sound from below followed by a loud crash on the screen.

"Fuck, that thing always gets me!"

Kingston blew out another plume of smoke and then handed me his blunt. "Haven't stopped in sixteen years. Don't think it'll stop now that we're almost eighteen."

I wrinkled my nose at his offered hand. He knew I hated weed unless it was in brownie or gummy form. I didn't smoke or vape. I ignored his comment about being almost eighteen because I still hadn't come to terms with it. I was one year and six months younger than my best friends, and I'd dealt with that disappointment my whole life, which always felt manageable. Until now. Becoming an adult felt different, as if they'd pluck out their roots from the soil of the manor and walk away from me forever.

"Still too good for our weed?" Gio asked, climbing the last step to their loft.

I shook my head while Gio made room on the armrest, his arm touching mine.

"I'm not too good for it; I just don't like inhaling substances that could be bad for my lungs."

King laughed quietly while Gio reached over and took the smoke from his brother and inhaled.

"I think one day you might like the way certain things feel on your throat, *mi reina.*"

I shook my head. "Not smoke."

"No." Gio smirked, while shaking his head. "Not smoke...probably something a bit warmer, and smoother."

Yuck. "If this is about that warm eggnog your mom tried to serve last Christmas, I stand by what I said. It should never ever be warm, it's not normal."

I heard Kingston choke, and then he kept coughing, which served him right. He shouldn't be smoking. After one last clearing of his lungs, he moved his feet, which were under me, to kick his brother but all it did was make me fall sideways. My face was suddenly in Kingston's lap, smashing against his phone or whatever he had in his pocket.

"Ow!" I sat up quickly, slapping at King's stomach. "You better not have a gun in your pocket. That's too freaking big to be your phone. Scotty will kill you if you took anything from the armory."

His eyes grew wider as a flush crept under his eyes, and that's when Gio burst out laughing. King's mouth snapped shut and he shoved me back into place so he could get up.

"Jesus. It's not a fucking gun, Pres."

Fine, his phone then. Whatever.

He was mad now, which sucked, but it wasn't my mistake. "It was his fault." I pointed at his brother. "And I'm only mad because your phone hurt my face when I fell."

Gio had doubled over laughing but I made out something he said. "Wasn't his phone."

Then wha—

"What are you doing here, Presley?" Kingston interjected snidely.

I crossed my arms and made myself more comfortable on the couch. "I came here to ask you guys for probably the biggest favor I've ever asked you."

They didn't say anything, so I swallowed the lump in my throat and continued.

"I want to enroll in the local high school next week. I'm only hoping to attend for a few months, until June."

They were both quiet before sharing a look with one another. It was almost as if they'd known I was going to enroll or something. I couldn't prove it but it was just a feeling I had. Finally, it was Kingston who spoke up.

"Why?"

My mouth parted with a response when Gio cut in. "Aren't you done with your required courses? Scotty's had you working on a crazy tutoring schedule, I think you're ahead of us."

I tugged at my pajama shorts nervously, unsure how to even explain this to them. They were my best friends, and they'd seen me in every stage of life from having the flu to wearing designer gowns to charity functions. They had never shown any interest in me one way or another, but for whatever reason my dad and Scotty seemed to think they'd follow me all the way to public school.

It was ridiculous and yet, there, buried under my heart, in soil that would never see the light of day, was a fragile and very pathetic crush that liked to linger in my lungs when I'd breathe in their scents and burn in the backs of my eyes when I'd hear them talk about a girl that had messaged them. Occasionally when they weren't looking, I'd focus on how much they'd changed, how their bodies had been honed into weapons with stacked muscle and veins running up their arms in ways that I couldn't help but stare at.

I knew it was wrong.

The shame I felt on an almost daily basis was exhausting, and the mortification was even worse. They saw me as a friend, if not a little sister, and nothing more.

With a heavy sigh, I crossed my arms. "I'm sixteen now, and if I don't get out of this house and start making friends, then my chance at dating or getting my first kiss will be nonexistent."

There was a horrible, uncomfortable silence that stretched between us. One so awkward and noticeable that I finally looked up, seeing them both silently communicating with each other. I hated when they did that.

"Stop doing the twin thing." I shoved at Gio's arm.

Kingston's jaw flexed as if he were annoyed. Gio blew out a harsh breath before looking down.

"So what do you want from us?" Gio asked.

Here it went. I inhaled a sharp breath before slowly letting it out. "Scotty said I have to convince you guys to go with me. I have no idea why, because I'm perfectly capable of handling things on my own, but he's making that a requirement."

King's amber eyes narrowed while a small smirk lifted along his lips. "So we have to go in order for you to go?"

"Yes."

Gio crossed his arms, his brows caving. "But we're already finished with all of our courses."

"Scotty said he'd forge documents for us."

Kingston scoffed and shook his head. "Wow, how kind of Uncle Scotty. He's doing all this just so you can see if your Prince Charming is waiting for you in the Rake Forge public school system."

Asshole. Obviously, I wasn't expecting my soulmate to find me in high school; I merely wanted to date or get some friends. I elbowed Gio out of sheer irritation with them both. However, because he was sitting on the arm of the couch, he started to tip sideways. Instead of embracing the fall gracefully, he pulled my arm, which had me jerking to the side automatically, forcing him to fall on top of me.

"Gio!" I mumbled into his shoulder, but I felt him laughing above me. His palm moved to the side of my face while he sat up, staring down at me.

"If you're wanting to get your first kiss out of the way, I can help."

My face flushed, the crush I harbored flared to life with excitement, which was exactly why I had to tamp it down and push him off me.

"I'm good, thanks."

Kingston glared at us from where he stood.

"You do realize most the guys in public school have already kissed girls…"

Gio scoffed, hiding a laugh, and for some reason it made me feel lame enough that my face turned red.

I shrugged. "So what?"

"So, the first time you kiss someone it's awkward. You have to sort of learn how to do it right. If you kiss some guy you're into and he's expecting you to know what you're doing, it might embarrass you."

I was already embarrassed.

My eyes were hard as I assessed my best friend from across the room. Gio tugged my hand into his lap, stroking over my knuckles. "We're just watching out for you. We don't want you to encounter something that will make you feel unprepared, or that could make people talk about you or draw attention to you. Even with a fake name, Pres, you can't draw attention to yourself."

My gut sank because I knew he was right. If I were going just to learn and keep my head down, that would be one thing, but I was specifically going to make friends, or hopefully a boyfriend.

"Besides, how fair would that be to the guy you kiss or end up dating? What if you develop feelings for him, and then he meets Scotty?"

A knot formed in my throat picturing that. Scotty would find a way to make him disappear. Anyone that would become a complication to me taking over the family would have to be removed from the equation.

"So what am I supposed to do?" I felt defeated and frustrated as I tossed my hand out toward King but glared over at Gio. "Haven't you guys kissed girls before? I've seen you Snapchat girls...can't you coach me without actually touching me?"

Their faces turned the smallest amount of pink before Kingston cleared his throat.

"Don't confuse affection with distraction."

I didn't know what that meant, nor did I care.

"It's still the same result either way. You guys get to live a life, while I don't—"

Gio cut in with a glare. "We aren't the ones being groomed to take over a crime syndicate...don't you think that might mean an arranged marriage down the line somewhere?"

I laughed, getting to my feet. "You know my dad would never agree to anything even remotely close to that."

The twins stared at each other, not saying anything out loud.

I cut my hand through the air. "Stop it."

Gio exhaled. "Look, we're only trying to look out for you, same as always. This isn't a good idea. If you need to be kissed that badly, then one of us will do that for you. No need to go to school for it."

Something throbbed in my chest. A blazing fire, cooled with the calmest rain. If I were to dig up that crush that I buried so often, then I'd confess that I wanted them to be my first kiss, but I already knew how this was going to go.

Only one of them would do it.

Just one, and whoever didn't kiss me, would break me.

I couldn't do that to us...

Forcing my eyes shut, I practically begged them. "Will you please consider going? For me. Please?"

They glanced at one another before giving me a soft nod. Gio replied, "We'll consider it, Pres. Promise."

I watched him turn to go, feeling frustrated and strangely confused.

Without waiting for Kingston to say anything, I walked over to the window and slid out onto the veranda where the rain began to pelt my face and soak my hair.

CHAPTER 18
PRESLEY
PRESENT

The small bistro café was only a few blocks from Adrian's villa, so I walked.

I wore a pair of sandals, a flowy skirt and small baby-doll tank, which allowed the warm summer breeze to kiss my skin and tangle my hair. I closed my eyes and tilted my head back, remembering why I loved this place so much.

I'd arrived almost a week ago and since then, the only person I had heard from was my mother. We'd been texting and talking almost daily with no mention of the twins, Scotty or my dad. It was nice, like a tiny reprieve.

Adrian was helpful, funny and charming as always. He was also a tiny reprieve that I hadn't known I needed. He didn't ask why I suddenly wanted to come, nor did he push for anything more than what I'd already offered him.

After taking a seat at a small table and placing my order, I pulled my phone free to check to see if my mother had sent any other messages or if there were any updates from Carter. She felt guilty about her role in all of this, but not bad enough to stay at the manor. According to Scotty, she'd already left on some girls' trip with her friends. My screen lit up, but the text on my display wasn't from my mother.

Gio: You ran.

Kingston: Never knew you to be a coward, Pres.

The twins had thrown me in a group chat, and suddenly the feelings I'd been trying to escape by running to Italy had caught up with me. Which meant Scotty had officially removed the forwarding feature to his burner. In an odd, very ironic way I was thankful he hadn't done it back when I first discovered they were being sent to him. I wasn't ready to confront them then, and I especially wasn't ready now.

Gio: Guess it's easy to be spineless when you start sucking the cock of a coward.

What the hell? Why were they talking to me like this? They'd never...

Kingston: If I find out that Presley sucked that fucker's cock, I will remove it from his body.

Gio: Based off that picture, looked like she was friendly enough. His hands were in her hair.

Kingston: For that, I will be taking his fingers, but honestly, I'll settle for Presley just coming home. We have a few things to talk about.

Gio: Do you think she blocked us?

My fingers moved over the keys, typing out an angry reply. How dare they text this bullshit to me after all this time of not—

They had been trying to connect with me; I was the one who hadn't responded. With or without Scotty's interference, I had been hiding from my best friends for over a year. My chest was warm, my lungs heating with the need to yell or scream. Leaving cash on the table for a coffee I didn't even drink, I gathered my things and darted through the door.

My gaze was still on the phone as I walked back to Adrian's house. My eyes watery and my heart thundering out a warning.

Gio: Holy shit, she didn't block us. Her dots are moving.

Kingston:...Pres?

"I had a feeling I'd find you out here, walking back from town," Adrian called to me, shaking me out of my thoughts.

I smiled up at his advancing form. He wore white linen pants, a black T-shirt and sandals. Designer shades were covering his eyes. I *had* been a coward, but only because I hadn't told him about why I'd come here.

"I just grabbed some coffee from down the way," I laughed, pointing behind me.

Right before he reached me, I did the only thing I could do regarding the twins. The only choice that really mattered because they were baiting me, and I'd fallen for that before. I wouldn't again.

Presley left the group chat

CHAPTER 19
KINGSTON
AGE 17

Having a twin had always felt like I'd been given a second set of eyes, ears, and in some cases, even a heart.

Gio was literally my other half in every way. With one look, I knew exactly what he was thinking, and I always knew he could feel what I was feeling. We were in sync, more so than what I'd read of other identical twins. The only thing that wasn't the same about us were our eyes, and if one of us decided to go with a different haircut.

Otherwise, we were the same on the outside, and while Gio pined for the stars, and I had a penchant for the soil, we were fairly close to identical on the inside as well.

Which was how I knew my brother was feeling and thinking the same thing I was as we stared at our parents.

Dad had his arms crossed while Mom merely tapped one finger on her thigh.

"To be clear, you're going for..." Dad asked, glancing between the two of us.

Gio answered, "Socialization."

134

"Right...socialization." Dad smirked, his dark hair was starting to get a silverish sheen on the sides, near his temple.

Mom gently spoke up, her blue eyes darting between us. "I guess I assumed the girls you were chatting with on your phones provided enough socialization already."

Dad dipped his chin to his chest and snorted.

Girls we made sure they saw us socialize with. Everything we did was on purpose and all of it was to always ensure it looked as though we played a part. If we had socialization skills and we made friends, perhaps we'd be given more freedom outside of the manor. Maybe dad's men would stop following us around. However, we knew their scoffs had to do with this outrageous idea to attend high school when we didn't need to.

"We aren't really asking for permission," I explained.

Dad's eyes lit up as his chin raised. "To be clear, you're still seventeen for a few more months, so you *are* asking for permission."

Fuck.

"Dad," Gio started before rubbing at his eyes.

Mom stood and let out a sigh. "Can you both just admit why you're really doing this?"

No, because Scotty gave us a command that we both saw right through. He'd challenged Presley to get our participation, but what he was really doing was giving us an order.

Go with her. Protect her. Just like I had at that dance.

Instead, I replied, "I'd honestly expected you to demand we go."

Dad laughed. "Why would we care one way or another?"

Mom glanced over, clicking her tongue. "Juan, stop it. Of course we care, especially if this is because Presley is going."

Gio was quiet, so was I.

Dad finally stood and walked until he was directly in front of us. "You're both like brothers to her, I appreciate that you're willing to watch out for her, but you've got other things to focus on. She's fine. I bet Scotty will even send Reaper with her."

Hearing that dog's name made my spine snap straight. I fucking hated that dog, and I heard Presley mention sleeping with that demon more than once.

"Just the same, we'd like to go for a while to be sure she acclimates okay."

Dad's amber eyes searched our faces before he let out a heavy sigh. "I hope you know I'm going to owe Kyle fifty dollars for this."

Fucking Kyle.

I rolled my eyes while Gio let out a snort. "Don't care."

We turned away and left our parents in the living room. Did we want to attend public high school after we'd already technically graduated? Fuck no.

But there wasn't a universe in which we'd ever allow Presley to go without us. She didn't realize this was just temporary, her wanting friends, attention. She had no idea what was in store for her the second she turned eighteen. We did, which was why we had to go.

We knew she could handle herself. She honestly could take us down with one move, but Presley had a heart made of cotton. If she were to hand it over to the wrong person, they'd pull it all out, uncaring that they'd leave her empty and hurt. She was different, and it was entirely likely that she didn't realize it. While her heart was soft, her knuckles were torn to shreds and puffy, and the bruises on her face and body made her look like she'd just left a war zone.

But she was also beautiful in a way that defied logic.

I used to think it was just a phase I was in and there weren't any other girls around for me to look at. Then I was exposed to them on Snapchat and whatever the fuck else, and nothing had made me feel the way she did when she entered a room. No person's outward appearance took my breath away the way Presley's did.

To the point where I'd get lost staring at her lips or watching how her nose crinkled when she came across something she didn't like. I found myself aligning our homework schedules just so I could watch how she examined each page. How her lip would get pulled between her teeth while she tried to concentrate. Then she'd do something like ask me to walk with her in the gardens, and she'd mention plant names because she'd memorized them.

For me.

Just like she memorized planets and stars for Gio.

Love wasn't really something I was familiar with, and I wasn't sure it's what I felt for Presley, but it didn't matter.

Nothing really did as long as she was safe.

Which was exactly what we'd make sure of.

CHAPTER 20

PRESLEY

AGE 16

Socializing wasn't as easy as I assumed it would be, and people were as cutthroat and horrible in real life as I had always watched in movies and on dramatic TikToks and reels. Rake Forge High School was teeming with kids who wore swirls of red, black and white. The cheer squad brushed past me without giving me a second glance, their hair in bouncy ringlets. The football players wore their letterman jackets, and backward ball caps, laughing and joking. Ignoring anyone who hadn't been in their group since childhood.

At least that's how it seemed.

I had been going to school for roughly a month, and I hadn't made any friends yet. Me being a senior who was just sixteen wasn't exactly going over smoothly with my peers, and I wish I had considered that before agreeing to this. That and the number of times I would raise my hand to answer a question that no one else in the room seemed to know. After a few side-glances and glares, I realized my brain wouldn't be the thing that got me asked to parties or kissed by a boy. So, I started drawing in class instead so at least I wouldn't be garnering any more glares or whispers about being a know-it-all.

I didn't actually need to graduate, so I didn't need to turn in the assignments, and I didn't need to be so smart. I also changed how I dressed, or I tried to, but that part wasn't easy either. I typically wore leggings and activewear. No one else beyond the physical education teacher wore that, so I asked my mom if we could go into town and buy me some jeans. She'd teared up, and I rolled my eyes, regretting not just asking Scotty to take me.

I could deal with the lack of friends, and the lonely lunch bench that no one ever filled, but what really dug at me was how Gio and Kingston interacted with the girls in the school. Every time I went to the bathroom, I'd have to hear about the girls' obsession with them. They had no problem becoming instantly popular with as many friends as anyone could ever hope for. They were invited to everything.

And why wouldn't they be? They were athletic and handsome in a way that reminded me of someone from Hollywood. They'd each slip on a pair of sunglasses, and you'd think the girls had lost their minds. It wasn't as if I hadn't also been impacted by their toned arms, or the way their clothes fit them just perfectly enough that they looked like models. The beautiful brown skin, the thick, black hair that still managed to look like raven feathers, styled perfectly. They both had wide jaws; their dark brows and thick lashes made them look dreamy.

It wasn't that I couldn't see what everybody else did; I simply didn't understand why everyone else got to experience them and I didn't. They'd agreed to attend school, but for the safety of our family, Scotty had suggested it would be best if we acted as though we didn't know one another. They'd merely be eyes and ears, keeping me safe from a distance.

Insecurity started to spill into my chest, infecting my lack of interaction with people and my confidence. I wanted to just hide behind the assignments and go find a spot in the library until the end of school, but that's not what I was supposed to be doing here. I was supposed to be making friends.

There had to be someone here that liked me.

Glancing around, I found a guy from my biology class staring back at me. I waved, and he waved back. Within seconds, he walked over and sat across from me.

With blond hair, swept away from his face, a strong jaw and light blue eyes, he was cute, and I liked his smile. I couldn't believe it, but I felt myself blush as he started talking to me.

Finally, it felt like perhaps I had a chance at making a friend, or better yet, a boyfriend.

I ignored the sensation that someone was watching us and tried to enjoy my conversation with Landon. Finally, things were going in my favor.

CHAPTER 21
KINGSTON
AGE 17

I'd cut off my arm and hand it to Presley if she needed it, but this public-school gig was getting old as fuck. Gio sighed, and I knew he was feeling it too. We'd already finished our courses, so the classes didn't keep our interest. The only thing that did was sneaking out to take turns to watch Presley in each of her classes.

We were only here for her, and the fact that she wouldn't even be able to complete the entire reason for attending school, was starting to frustrate me. We had to play a part, and that was fucking exhausting. Like now, as we watched some kid in her class smile at her and offer her his notes. If I wasn't pretending to be a senior in high school, I could walk over to him and explain in vivid detail what I'd do to him if he ever tried to smile at Presley James again.

Gio watched them as intently as I did, and I glanced over at my brother, seeing the same rage that burned inside me reflecting in him. It reminded me of that time in Mexico when he'd pushed me into the pool. I wasn't sure that feeling ever left him, but he'd seemed to get better at hiding or managing it.

Presley took the offered notes with a smile and the guy relaxed while the two started to chat. Maybe he'd be brave enough to ask her to prom, and we'd have to ruin that for her just like we did with anyone who ever dared to get too close to her. She'd never get that first kiss, and while I didn't mind preventing any other idiot from touching those perfect lips of hers, I did feel guilty that she had no idea she was being sabotaged. But then I'd play out the scenario of what would happen if she fell for one of these pricks and Scotty found out. He'd kill them, and Presley would blame herself.

Gio tipped his head back next to me, staring at the moon that was still visible in the sky.

"You want to do it, or me?" I muttered quietly.

"I'll do it, you took care of the last one."

Yeah, the jock who I'd heard saying Presley's ass was the most perfect thing he'd ever seen wouldn't be coming back to school anytime soon, not after I'd "*accidently*" spilled my drink on him at a party and then tossed my lit Zippo at him. When he was screaming "what the fuck my problem was," I had simply explained he needed to stay away from Presley. He didn't fight back, and he was fine. Barely a single mark on his stupid pristine face, but the thing that pissed me off was that none of these idiots ever fought us on seeing her.

I wondered what would happen when we finally found the guy who would. Not that it mattered, we knew the score.

I watched as the kid leaned over Presley's shoulder and pointed at something on the paper. My gut twisted with something unfamiliar. If I took long enough to examine what that feeling was, perhaps there'd be a way to make it stop. As it was, anytime anyone got close to her, or made her smile, it felt like I was the one burning on the inside.

Pushing off the wall, I turned away from watching her and reminded my brother to be quick as I walked toward the car.

GIO AND I SHARED A CAR, and while it wasn't brand-new, it was something we were proud of. We'd been restoring the 1969 Camaro for the past year and were finally able to drive it. We were in the student parking lot, waiting for school to be out, so we could watch Presley get picked up by Scotty, and then we could finally head home but someone slapping the hood of our car had us both dropping our phones and gaping out the windshield.

"Can you guys give me a ride home?" Presley ducked her head, staring into the passenger side window while holding the straps of her backpack. She wore black leggings, a cropped sweatshirt and Doc Martens. Her hair was braided in two symmetrical rows, and her lashes were thicker and darker than normal. In fact, her cheeks looked brighter, and her brows were fuller too. Was she wearing makeup?

Panic ran through me at the realization, but I couldn't even focus on it because her demeanor was sad and deflated. It made my gut sink as Gio opened his door and slid his seat forward for her to crawl inside the back.

A few onlookers glanced our way, likely wondering why she was with us when during school we made it a point not to be seen together. We took off and Gio spun around in his seat, facing her. His window was down, which made pieces of her hair blow around.

"What's wrong?"

We both knew what was likely bothering her. The guy who had flirted with her yesterday was now giving her the cold shoulder and ignoring her. Just like every other guy who'd acted even remotely interested in her.

Her lip trembled from where I saw in the rearview mirror. Even that looked more glossy than usual. It didn't matter that she was wearing makeup; it just bugged me because she had never needed to wear it. Ever since attending school, she was suddenly worried about how she looked, and it made me fucking crazy.

She sounded so hopeless as she tugged at her backpack strap. "I think maybe you guys were right about this being a bad idea..."

Gio glanced over at me while I kept my eyes on the road.

"They're all idiots, Pres."

She sniffed, and my heart felt like it was going to combust. I could count on one hand the number of times Presley James cried throughout her life. Never had she cried during the times Scotty had pushed her in training. She hadn't shed a tear when she was sent into the woods in shorts, bare feet, and nothing but a T-shirt on in the dead of winter. She was given two hours to secure clothing and food. I'd never forget her showing up half a day later, blue lips, bloody feet and a fucking smile on her face.

She'd only ever cried after Scotty had to put one of his dogs down due to cancer, when she watched *My Girl,* and that time Gio broke her seashells.

That was it.

I flicked my eyes to the rearview mirror and saw two salty tears trail down her cheeks and I pulled the car off to the side of the road.

"Heyyyy," she whined, while Gio cursed.

I got out of the car and slammed my seat forward, while crawling into the back seat and then pulling my door closed. Gio slid over the seat until he was sitting next to her, and I was on the opposite side, sandwiching her between us.

The tinted windows hid us as we all crowded the back seat, the low music blocked out the strange silence that hung in the air. This was new for us, and delicate...it felt as dangerous as stepping in a minefield. Something had been brewing among the three of us, and while Gio and I hadn't fought about it yet, it was only a matter of time. Because he looked at her the way I did, and I knew his chest caved in at the thought of her one day leaving us behind, just like mine did.

This was more than friendship, and it could ruin us.

"No one likes me." Presley hiccupped, swiping at her face. "I thought I could make friends, but it's been weeks, and no one likes me. No girls and no guys. I'm never going to go on a date. I'm not going to prom, and I'm not ever going to get kissed."

She was crying so hard she had begun to shake, and her voice cracked.

I glanced over at my brother, who was already watching me. It took me back two years when we were on that balcony in Mexico, and Presley had talked about leaving us behind. I'd known he'd pushed me in the water because I was flirting with her, but that moment when we'd looked at each other and silently acknowledged each other's pain still haunted me.

This moment felt the same.

"Presley, you're not crying over those assholes who can't shoot the hat off a stuffed squirrel from five hundred yards away."

She sniffed. "That's only when I have the long-range rifle."

"They still couldn't do it," Gio said, using his thumb to swipe her tear from one cheek, so I did the other. She didn't react to how we both had touched her, and maybe throughout our lives we'd given her that exact feeling a thousand times, and it didn't feel any different to her. It felt monumental to me, and I was positive it did to Gio as well.

Things were changing.

We may have agreed to protect her when Scotty had asked us, but we were already in too deep not to watch out for her. We would have done this whether he asked us or not.

Presley placed both her hands over her face and groaned. "I'm so embarrassed. I begged my parents for this opportunity, only to be a total loser and repel absolutely everyone I meet."

"Come on, Elvis, you're not being fair to yourself." Gio shook her thigh, but she only sniffed again.

"If I can't even do this, what makes anyone think I can lead a family?"

I sighed, relaxing into the seat. "Well for starters, you know how we feel about you leading a family. We think it's bullshit and you should settle down on a farm instead. However, for the sake of your feelings, you're not leading until you're old enough, and when you do lead, you won't be dealing with teenagers befriending you."

She let out a small bubble of laughter that hit me like a brick to the chest. It was that tinkling sound she'd always made, the one I could hear from several rooms over. The one that made me think of warm dirt and a gentle hand against my face. Dark hair, freckled nose, blue eyes and...*home.*

"I wanted to have my first kiss, my first boyfriend because I thought maybe it would help desensitize me to things once I am leading. What if I meet some evil mafia boss, but because I've never been kissed, I fall for him?"

Gio grunted, which I was grateful for because I inhaled a sharp breath.

We'd just recently joked about her first kiss as if it were nothing. We offered to take it as if she was offering a stick of gum when, in reality, it was nothing short of monumental.

Her head lifted and her mascara had begun to run the smallest bit, smudging just under her eyes. "You guys make it look so easy."

"What?" I asked, trying to clarify if she meant kissing or breathing...my mind was all over the place. My heart felt like it was trying to pound out of my chest; my skin felt too hot. What if she asked us to do it...to take her first kiss?

By all rights we had no other choice, but which one of us would do it?

She glanced over at me. "Being popular and making friends."

Oh, right. I cleared my throat, tugging at my jeans. "We're literally only there because of you, Pres."

"Well, then how come you're not helping me become cool? You don't talk to me or even act like you know me—" Her voice trailed off as her face scrunched up. If I had to guess, she was sorting out how impossible that would be for us.

"We're playing a game there, Pres. We can't draw attention to you in any way and we really can't be seen with you. You know this."

She nodded. "I know...I just hate this."

Gio ran his hand down the length of her braid then tucked a few stray pieces of hair behind her ear. "I think you need to go get a fix."

She perked up, swiping at her face. "I haven't been in a really long time."

"Then, let's go." I patted her knee, but she grabbed my hand and held on to it while doing the same with Gio's.

"Thank you." She pressed her lips to our knuckles, and it made my breath hitch. By the expression on my brother's face, it had the same effect on him. Her lips were touching my skin, her warm breath...fuck, how could something so innocent feel so insanely hot? I had to squeeze my eyes shut and remember that my best friend was only sixteen. I wasn't eighteen yet, but it didn't matter. She was Presley. If we did take her first kiss, there couldn't be any emotion behind it.

Once she released us, I jolted out of the back and took my position in the front seat.

I had to stop this, all of it. Right the fuck now.

CHAPTER 22

PRESLEY

PRESENT

I spent the day swimming and sunbathing with Adrian and ignoring my phone.

Not blocking the twins was the worst decision ever, further confirming my coward status. They'd added me back to the group chat three separate times until I finally just turned my phone off. I didn't need to read what they had to say. They weren't just angry over me ghosting them all this time; they were hurt and vengeful.

It was more than that though...something was brewing under their comments. It connected to Scotty and his training methods, to me and this role I was cast into. It was convoluted, and I feared that their time away from the family only worsened their disposition instead of helping it.

"You're gone again." Adrian's smooth voice cut into my thoughts as he swam up next to my floating lounger. I was relaxed, not really paying attention, but I must have missed something he said.

"I'm right here."

He drew closer, until his head rested next to my thigh. "I need you closer."

Butterflies erupted in my stomach as I stared down at his dark head of hair, my mind playing a cruel game of memory and how many times I had looked down at two other heads like this. An entire childhood spent being in love with two people I was never allowed to have, much less allowed to love.

Yet I fell face-first into the disaster that awaited me.

"I'm going to kiss you if you keep zoning out like that," Adrian murmured close to my leg, then his soft lips gently skimmed over my thigh, his tongue tracing the droplets of water off me.

"How come you haven't yet?" My smile wobbled as uncertainty prodded at my chest.

Why was I encouraging this?

Perhaps I just needed to get past the twins, and if Adrian was a boat that would take me out of the murky waters where my feelings for them remained, then I'd gladly embark on that voyage.

Adrian's blue gaze was pure fire as he stared up at me, and before I could process what he was doing, my lounger was tipped, and I was falling into the water. My hands flew wide but strong hands caught me right as the plastic slipped out from under me. I was pulled into Adrian's firm chest, and he didn't hesitate; his mouth slanted over mine in a heated kiss.

My hands went on his shoulders, drifting into his hair as I kissed him back. As his head moved to the side, I opened for his tongue to sweep inside my mouth.

A groan erupted from him as he pulled me closer, and without knowing what else to do, I wrapped my legs around his waist. Our kiss continued to deepen even with his men watching, even as I knew we weren't alone, and the erection thick in his shorts pulsed against my center. It provided enough friction to make me squirm against him.

"Fuck, you have no idea how long I've waited for that." Adrian breathed against my mouth, breaking our kiss. We'd moved closer to the wall of the pool, and I hadn't even noticed.

Heaving in oxygen, I didn't want to say anything to ruin the moment, so I just moved in for another kiss but suddenly his men began talking into their radios in tandem, all speaking Italian.

It gave Adrian pause as he watched them move back into the house.

"Come, we need to go." He let me go and I swam toward the stairs. I could hear a few of the coms going off as my feet touched the smooth concrete steps.

"Threat near the gate."

"Unidentified vehicle."

Fear threaded my stomach with fraying nerves as I thought back to the twins' threats. They wouldn't come here, would they?

No, they had no idea where I was.

Scotty knew but he'd never—

Would Scotty reveal where I was out of spite? No, he knew how delicate this alliance with Adrian was; there would be no way he'd do that.

"There's a threat near the gate. I'm going to have you come with me and we're going to remain in the safe room until we know everything is secure."

It was on the tip of my tongue to ask why he wasn't helping his men. My dad, Scotty, and even Juan would never leave their men to fight a threat alone. They'd always face it head-on, that's what I was trained for, what I was taught.

"Adrian, I don't need to be placed in the safe room but if you'd feel more comfortable..."

His hand tightened around mine as he pulled me with him, down the hall. "As embarrassing as this is to admit, I'm not nearly as skilled as you are, Presley. I don't particularly want to place my abilities to the test right now."

I wish he hadn't admitted that to me. I hated how he kept revealing his weaknesses and places that I could hurt him.

It only confirmed that I never would.

"Okay." I followed him, only to have one of his men stop us.

I couldn't hear everything they were saying because their heads were bent close together, but Adrian suddenly froze, and then looked over his shoulder at me.

"There are two people here to see you. They aren't fighting us, but they requested the chance to talk to you."

Oh shit.

"Presley?"

"I can go outside of your fence line, that way they're not brought in here." Because what the hell were they planning to do?

Adrian pulled me back to his side, and I hadn't even realized I'd begun to walk away. "No. Any guest of yours is welcome here."

He waited for me to elaborate, and when I didn't, he gave the order.

"See them in."

My face burned as I followed Adrian up the stairs, and he released me near my bedroom door. "Get changed, I'll meet you in the main room to receive your guests."

The door clicked shut and I immediately pulled out my cell phone and dialed the only person who could help me. With the screen to my ear, I began pacing and pulling on clothes.

"Hello?"

"Scotty, why are the twins here?" I whisper-yelled, glancing out my window as if I could see anything other than the back terrace from it.

My uncle waited a second before replying, "Presley, I fear I cannot help you with this."

"Oh bullshit. Did you give them this location?"

He paused while muttering something in the background. "I didn't. However, you should be aware of a few things that have developed within the last week."

I paused my pacing, staring at the side wall where the sun was reflecting off the diamond jewelry that Adrian had gifted me. "What things?"

"Things that require your removal from the Adesso residence, and while I was not the one to send Gio and Kingston to you, I would have."

My breathing slowed as I thought through the reasons that could have led to Scotty needing me away from Adrian.

"What happened, Scotty?"

He muttered another order over the phone to someone else before briskly replying, "Nothing I can share over the phone. You need to leave with the twins."

"And how exactly am I supposed to explain that to Adrian?"

"I don't know, but I know you'll figure it out. Please be safe."

With that, he hung up and I was left staring at my phone with absolutely no fucking clue what was going on.

"Just fucking great," I muttered to myself. The gray hoodie lying on the foot of the bed was pulled over my shoulders. I was about to head downstairs when I eyed my suitcases and wondered if I should just pack. Scotty was on my shit list for getting me into this situation to begin with, but he'd never lie about something as important as my safety.

I really hated Scotty for this. Really fucking hated him.

I TOOK THE STAIRS SLOWLY, holding tightly to the banister as I tried to focus on the fact that I might be in danger and not the fact that I hadn't seen my two best friends in over a year and a half.

I found two of Adrian's men stationed at the bottom of the stair-case, holding assault rifles. They ignored me as I walked past them and continued down the hall. Adrian had left the back patio doors open, allowing the Mediterranean breeze to warm the villa with a heady, salty sweetness.

Two more guards waited near the hall that led to the kitchen. My bare feet pressed into the warmed wood as I neared the main room. I inhaled a silent breath and held it in my lungs like a captive beam of sunlight, hoping it would warm me from within as the reminder of their abandonment resurfaced.

The natural light touched the tip of the hall, boasting of wide windows and a large panoramic view of the sea. I'd cuddled against Adrian's chest just last night while the stars danced outside.

A shuddery breath left me as I turned the corner, and my focus found the only two men to have ever held it captive. Seated side by side, the twins wore dark T-shirts, which looked unfairly attractive against their brown skin; they were also toned and more defined than when they'd left me. Their raven hair was nearly identical, but Gio's was cut shorter on the sides than Kingston's, his was longer in the front, brushing that scar that now cut right through his brow from that time he'd lunged into the ring to protect me.

They stood at the same time, facing me, and my heart had nearly faltered as a pair of amber eyes and starry gray ones landed on me. It took me back to being six, curled against them in a warm bed. Back to blanket forts, games of hide and seek, playing pretend and a lifetime of other memories.

"Presley." Gio's gaze took in all of me as Kingston took a half step forward before thinking better of it.

I ushered out a rusty greeting that was as painful as scraping the darkest places of my heart and tossing them out on the floor. "Hi, guys."

Adrian's cool tone held restrained anger, which was the only reminder I had that he was standing silently by the fireplace with his arms crossed. "Presley, darling...please come take a seat as we chat with your friends."

Kingston's eyes cut over to Adrian as if he was going to kill him for calling me darling. Gio kept his eyes on me, raising a brow as if he wanted to make fun of me for it. A smile nearly stole my features as I remembered how this felt, to be with them.

Just the same, I did as Adrian suggested and walked over so that I could see them better. I was about to sit next to Adrian when he pulled me so I landed in his lap as he took a seat on the chaise.

"These are your childhood friends?" Adrian asked. His unspoken question tangled in my chest like a pair of loose wires. He'd already confessed feeling insecure over these two friends of mine, and now they were in his home, without warning and taking me away.

Guilt pricked sharp and painful in my gut.

"Yes, this is Kingston and Giovanni Hernandez," I explained, giving his hand a gentle squeeze.

Their gazes were both locked on where my hand held Adrian's, and where his hand cupped my knee.

"Hernandez. That's familiar..." Adrian tilted his head, then squeezed me back, intertwining our fingers.

I was about to explain their connection to my family through the charity their parents ran when Adrian froze under me. It was as if he'd just realized something.

Kingston gave him a deadly smile. "Yes, I should hope so. We've recently had business together."

My head swung inspecting Adrian, and then Kingston. I was out of the loop in a major way. A way that might get me killed if I wasn't careful. Adrian's odd behavior only worsened as he removed his hand from my knee. "Yes, well what can I do for you two?"

I was deposited on the seat cushion next to Adrian. I ignored what it implied that he was suddenly creating visible distance between us.

The boys looked so intimidating sitting next to each other. Like two strokes of dark shadow, here to steal the light.

"We're here to accompany Presley back home. We have a bit of a family emergency."

Adrian's gaze cut over to the side of my face. "Is that so?"

My chin dipped, playing along. "Yes, unfortunately. I just got off the phone with Scotty who confirmed it."

"Well, I would have flown you back. No need to have sent these two." His jilted tone was harsh, and I could understand. This was an odd way to handle something like this; we had to assume that Adrian wasn't stupid and would see through these antics. Which he would. However, there was something else going on here that I was missing. The twins had been up to something, and my gut told me it wasn't good.

"I'm sure he didn't want to impose, knowing you have a busy schedule." I smiled, while stroking Adrian's hand, tangling our fingers together. Usually he'd hold on, and even flirt with me, but this time he pulled away and stood.

"Well, your guests just arrived, surely they can spend the evening here before flying back."

Kingston stood, then Gio did as well. I watched their muscles move under their shirts, and the denim across their legs go taut. They both had on dark boots that were unlaced and loose. They looked like they did in high school. Too dangerous and too gorgeous to be real.

"No need. We have a jet ready to go. As soon as Presley is packed, we'll be on the way."

I joined everyone by standing and let out a sigh. "Well, I already packed because Scotty called."

Adrian's gaze cut to me quicky before swinging back to the twins. His jaw popped as a muscle twitched.

"Of course, well, I certainly hope all is well back home."

Gio walked toward me first, placing his arm around me. "Thanks. We'll be on our way."

As much as I knew they were both worried about something I had no knowledge of, I couldn't just pretend like Adrian didn't exist, or that he wasn't someone important to me. He'd been there for me this past year while they had not. So, I spun under Gio's arm and walked back to Adrian until his arms came around me.

"I'm sorry." My muttered response went into his chest where just an hour ago I had watched water trickle down from the pool.

His lips pressed into my hairline as he muttered a reply, "I just want you safe, *la mia Bellezza*. Get home and call me. If you need me at all, I'll come for you."

Leaning back, I was about to thank him when he dipped his face and kissed me.

His lips were warm and firm as his hands went to my hips, but I was tugged away just as swiftly.

Fire trapped behind glass met me as my eyes flew open. Kingston's eyes burned, and it seemed as though that fire had escaped, and I was sure he'd burn Adrian to the ground where he stood. Kingston's jaw clenched, and the anger radiating from him made chills run down my arms. I was poised for whatever fight would break out between the two or if one of Adrian's men would try and shoot, but my best friend merely dipped his head then tightly held me to him.

Kingston's hand was around mine as he led me back toward the hall. "Sorry to cut all this shit short, but we have a jet to catch."

Guilt bloomed in the very place I had once nurtured my obsession for him, for his brother. I used to feel shame over feeling things I shouldn't for two people I lived with and grew up with, but now... after everything, that guilt was only pinned to the fact that the twins and I kept hurting each other.

I didn't glance back to see Adrian's reaction. Nor did I try to untangle his actions. He went from being rigid and cold, almost not wanting to touch me once second, to branding me the next. Kingston's hand remained over mine while Gio crowded the space behind us. That's when I realized there were familiar looking men heading up toward my room.

"Are those your father's men?" I asked quietly.

Gio gave me a soft reply as we exited Adrian's house. "Something like that, Elvis."

I wasn't sure what to make of that, but there were three cars waiting for us. Right as I slid into one, and moved over for the twins to follow, they glanced at each other and seemingly had a silent argument before gently shutting the door in my face.

Once again, leaving me alone.

CHAPTER 23

GIO

AGE 17

My brother stood next to me as we watched Presley pet the baby cows roaming the pasture. The sun was bright, the field was green and lush, and we weren't supposed to be here. We'd broken into the pasture from the east gate, and wandered in, so our best friend could see all the baby Highland cows.

"There's so many babies!" Presley practically squealed as she stuck her hand out and pet the calf that had shaggy brown fur and a massive nose. She wore a pair of jeans, ripped in the knees, and a cropped T-shirt that rose every time she clapped her hands. A smile had tugged on each of our mouths as we looked down and realized she wore her cowboy boots out here.

Like always, a warmth unfurled in my chest like spun gold. Looping and tying around my heart in a tight vise.

Clearing my throat, I quietly addressed my brother, "Dad wants us to stop attending classes. Says he wants us to start helping with the soup kitchen, and whatever the fuck else El Peligro is doing."

King glanced over at me in confusion. "We already explained why we're going to school...and he already gave us his blessing."

His gaze returned to Presley as she continued to talk to the baby cows, petting their heads and...naming them. She'd taken out her braid, which left her dark, long hair wavy and annoyingly gorgeous. Two days ago, we'd driven her out here and watched her do the same thing, and the entire time we hadn't spoken about how it felt to be in that back seat, or how she'd kissed our hands.

Or how right it felt.

My gaze darted to the girl a few yards away and then back to my brother, keeping my voice low. "Dad's cousin was drunk the other night, out near the staff quarters. They were having some kind of party. I overheard some stuff about Dad's charity...and the fact that several of the members are starting to defect and want to go back to the power the gang used to wield. Sounds like a lot of them are tired of the Robin Hood routine."

Dad and Mom had never been completely honest with us about the gang they were both seemingly attached to. It was Hector who shared things with us. He and our abuela would occasionally share a story or two. We'd heard enough to deduce that when our grandfather, Manny, had run it, things were dangerous, and the gang was feared. It had roots in the cartel, which gave them an edge that rival gangs didn't have, and frankly didn't mess with.

Kingston shifted against the fence. "Do you think Dad wants to pull us in and help maintain the image he's been upholding all these years?

Wouldn't that be exactly what Kyle and Scotty were doing with Presley?

I scratched the back of my neck. "Fuck if I know, but I'm not going to stop attending school to find out."

Kingston continued to stare at Presley, and all it did was take me back to a thousand other times I'd watch him stare at her throughout our lives, worried he'd be as in love with her as I was. Things had been tense between us for years as we'd circled this one issue.

This one person.

This feeling I'd had for so long never left, and it continued to feel heavy and terrifying. The fear of Kingston kissing her, and not me.

It would break me, but I knew he cared for her the way I did. I knew, deep down, we both selfishly wanted the same thing from the same exact person, and I had no idea what that would do to us. My brother was the other half of my soul, and I had no intentions of doing something that would separate me from him...

Yet if he had her. And I didn't.

I couldn't let that happen.

We'd been fighting over Presley since we were old enough to talk. Since that first moment she came crashing into our block tower on wobbly legs, with a smile that seemed to brand itself on our hearts.

"What if Dad forces it?" I asked, kicking at a clump of dirt.

My brother didn't stop staring at Presley while he let my question hang in the air. I knew how I would respond, which meant that was likely his answer as well. We simply wouldn't listen to our dad, and we'd never leave Presley, so things would get fucking messy.

Presley finally turned away from the animal pen and let out a deep sigh.

"That was exactly what I needed. How can I ever repay you guys for taking me twice in a week?"

I smiled at her and tugged on the bottom of her shirt; it showed her purple bra strap, and more of her shoulder, but she didn't seem to notice as the three of us turned and started back toward the car. Her hand suddenly wrapped around mine, and I returned the gesture. Glancing to the side, I saw she was holding Kingston's as well.

She would never understand that she was the sun to both of us.

For me, she was the brightest star in my universe, and for Kingston, she was the light that drew life from the ground. She meant more to us than she was supposed to.

"I know you guys just did me a solid and helped me through this horrible week, but I wanted to see if—" She stalled and slowed down. It forced us to slow with her and then turn as she stopped completely.

Her blue eyes were downcast as a flush of red lit up her narrow cheekbones.

"What is it, *¿mi reina?*" Kingston asked, using his free hand to tuck a stray hair behind her ear.

Her flush deepened again, and I wanted to remember this moment when the sun lit up her face and made her hair look like there were little strands of gold woven through it. Or the flush in her cheeks from the happiness she felt around the fluffy cows. This was Presley being happy, in her most natural state, and I was starved to see her like this more often.

"It's just...um, I was wondering if you guys could help me maybe meet someone in school. I'm embarrassed to even ask, and I know we can't act like we know each other in person, but maybe if you know someone who you could introduce me to and maybe say I'm your cousin or something?"

Fuck. Why did she keep coming back to this?

Kingston let her hand go and took a step away. "You want to be kissed that badly, you're willing to have us set you up with someone?"

Presley tried to release my hand, but I wouldn't let go. "Just answer the question."

She looked a little shocked as she tugged to be released again. "It's something that's important to me."

I shifted so she was forced to step closer to me. "But why are you so set on it, Elvis? What will kissing do for you?"

She finally tugged her hand hard enough that I let her go and she started walking back to the car. "Just forget it."

Kingston and I both took long strides to keep up with her. "Explain it to us."

She crossed her arms over her chest but continued toward the car. "No, just forget I said anything."

We were right behind her, and the second she reached for the door handle, I grabbed her belt loop and pulled her back.

"Just wait a second."

Tears gathered in her eyes, and it tore at me in a way that nothing ever had. It was like Presley was evolving into a completely new person, and I had no idea what to do with her.

Kingston moved behind her, opened the door, and pushed the driver's seat forward. "Get in the car, Presley."

"No, honestly at this point I want to walk." She raised her chin and shifted away from the door.

I had yet to release her, so I led her back to the car by the back of her jeans. "You don't have a choice, Elvis. Get. In. The. Car."

"Fine!"

I let her go right as she darted for the opening. Once she was inside, I shut the door and then stared at my brother from where he moved to the opposite side of the car.

"You getting in or am I?" Kingston asked.

My fists clenched tightly as worry gnawed at me. I knew exactly what would come next. It was a humming in my blood, an echo in my chest of something I'd wanted for years but had never caught or examined. Like a loose butterfly in my chest that finally landed somewhere that I could inspect it.

Swallowing the thickness in my throat I replied, "I think we both know neither of us can get in there."

Kingston paused then shook his head. "Don't really think either of us has a choice."

My eyes snapped up, meeting his. We silently glared at one another in challenge.

"Are you suggesting we both get in there?" Because if we did, then...there'd be no turning back.

My twin didn't reply, but his jaw ticked a few times. "It's neither of us or it's both of us."

My stomach might as well have turned into a hollow pit for how empty it felt. My heart hammered out a warning in my chest, but my twin just kept his gaze on me. He offered me a silent assurance that we'd be okay, and I chose to cling to that look. That glint in his eye said that he had some plan, or some idea of how we'd make it out of this intact and still best friends.

It wasn't until he opened the door and slid inside that I moved and did the same exact thing on the opposite side.

The interior of the car was dark because we'd parked in the shade, but it smelled like Presley's shampoo. She used something that had coconut and oranges in it, and ever since I was young, I'd been addicted to it.

"Why are you guys back here?" Presley asked, angrily. Her arms were still crossed over her chest and her face was red. The piece of hair Kingston had tucked behind her ear had come loose and was now resting against her cheek.

Kingston caught my eye from over her head, and I realized then and there this was going to require us both to put our pride aside and just focus on her and what she needed.

"Presley, we weren't making fun of you about your request to be introduced to someone."

She sniffed and I nearly pulled her into my arms.

"Fuck, Pres. Don't cry."

She turned to look at me, her lips pursed, and her brows knitted. "I'm not crying. I'm angry. You guys have so many friends, and all I wanted was for you to introduce me to one of them."

"Did it ever occur to you that perhaps we don't want you to be introduced to anyone else?" Kingston started tracing a path over Presley's hand.

I added, "We aren't going to entrust you to some idiot high schooler. You want your first kiss, you'll give it to one of us."

She threw her head back against the headrest and let out a heavy sigh. "I'm not kissing one of you."

"Of course you're not. You're kissing both of us."

Her head snapped over to Kingston, but he didn't wait for her to come to terms with it. He pulled her over his hips until she was straddling him. Her brown tresses fell, and the ends kissed the top of my brother's thighs. I focused on her nails, and how her hands went to his shoulders to balance herself.

"No one will ever know, *mi reina*. It's our secret, just relax and close your eyes, okay?"

Her chest was rising and falling so fast, it was impossible not to stare at or feel my own pulse begin to race. This was what I had wanted for so long, but it felt horrifying that I was watching it all unfold with someone else. I had dreamt of those hips cradling mine. I had dreamt of that hair tickling the tops of my thighs and those pert breasts heaving in front of my face.

"Okay," Pres finally whispered, keeping her gaze on Kingston, but then her brows knitted. "What if I don't know what to do and what if—"

Kingston pulled her chin down until their lips met. Everything seemed silent and loud at once, maybe there was something erupting in my eardrums or my heart. Everything felt too reckless as I watched my brother move his jaw to the side and take Presley's face to help her match his rhythm.

I had to push down the anger and the jealousy and remember that this was for her. All of this, every second of it was for her. We were the only two people in her life who would push down our own needs and our own desires and put her first.

So I tried to encourage her by scooting into the spot she'd vacated. "Does that feel good, Pres? You look perfect from here."

Presley pulled back, breathing hard. "Yeah, it feels good but, King, your phone is digging into my thigh."

I gave a little snort while Kingston pulled her chin back in and resumed kissing her.

"Why don't you try to rub against his phone, Pres. See if it makes you feel good."

Presley froze for a second and I worried I'd freaked her out, but then she slowly shifted her hips the smallest bit and my brother let out a groan.

"Can you rub faster, Pres?" I asked, before deciding to place my hand against her ass and guide her. If this was as close as I was going to get, then I'd fucking touch her.

Every time she moved back and her ass pushed into my palm, I'd push her forward again. I had no doubt that my brother was about to cum in his jeans any second at the rate Elvis was going and how hard they were making out. Had she even noticed how comfortable she'd gotten with kissing and how naturally she was flowing with Kingston's movements?

Smacking and sucking sounds filled the car as the two began to get lost in the chaos of their lips, the touch, her pussy moving over his cock.

Kingston finally pulled away, looking slightly dazed and a lot like he was in love. Presley's eyes were still shut as she panted and traced her tongue over her bottom lip.

My brother didn't glance at me as he ground out. "Now let Gio taste you, Presley. Remember, we don't have to tell anyone this happened. We can feel what we feel and just let go. You're still uptight. I want you to try and let go with Gio, okay?"

I was already hard from watching her kiss my brother; she'd feel it instantly.

Finally her eyes opened and her lashes fluttered. "That was okay?"

Kingston placed his hands under Presley's ass and pulled her back over himself with another groan. "It was fucking perfect, Pres. Wanna know a secret?"

She nodded while crawling off his lap and slowly getting into mine, mirroring the exact position she'd had with him. The second she'd settled over me, her eyes went wide, feeling the exact thickness she felt under him.

"That wasn't my phone," Kingston whispered, "it was my cock."

Her mouth parted while her blue eyes grew wide; those thick black lashes fluttered against her freckled skin, and I grew even thicker underneath her.

Kingston added, "You made me hard, and I bet you made Gio hard too."

She looked down at my mouth and I didn't wait for her to connect all the dots. I just pressed my mouth to hers.

Smooth and perfect, her lips molded to mine as her hands went around my neck. She seemed instantly more comfortable having already done this with Kingston. She tasted like berry lip balm and smelled like fresh cut grass: a day spent in the sun and something that itched under my skin that felt like home, like forever.

She began rocking over my hardness like she had with Kingston.

"Just let go, Pres. No one ever has to know what we do in here. Do whatever you want to do," Kingston encouraged her with a low murmur.

I had a feeling he was going to pull himself out any second and begin stroking his erection. If he was as hard and as aching as I was, then I didn't blame him.

His words seemed to land because Presley spread her legs wider, which allowed for more contact between her thighs and my aching cock.

Presley's hot tongue swept into my mouth as she dry-humped me.

"Just like that, Pres. You're so perfect," Kingston praised.

Presley began moaning into my mouth and it was so fucking hot that I wrapped my arm around her waist, holding her to me so tight that it pushed her tits closer and encouraged her to move her hips over mine faster.

Suddenly she tipped her head back and let out a loud gasp before a slew of curses left those perfect lips. Her hips snapped forward and slid back so fast, she had to be coming.

"Shit," Kingston muttered before letting out a groan. "I'm going to pull myself out, Pres, I have to. We're never gonna fucking talk about this, but I'm about to come and I'm not doing it in my jeans."

"What do I do?" Presley rasped, slowly coming down from her orgasm.

Kingston had already started stroking himself.

"Move back, let Gio pull himself out. You can watch us…"

She was mesmerized watching him, her eyes wide and mouth gaping.

"Should I move?"

She sat back enough that I could unzip my jeans and ever so slowly, I pulled my throbbing cock out of my boxers. The tip was soaked and weeping with precum.

"Stay exactly where you are, and just watch, Elvis."

Presley's eyes grew as she slid her gaze from my engorged erection to Kingston's. Being nude around my brother had never bugged me, and I'd caught him jacking off more times than I cared to admit, but this…this felt different. I didn't dare look at him. Didn't want to pop whatever strange, perfect bubble this was where the girl of our dreams welcomed us both to that lustful, yet curious gaze of hers.

I desperately wanted her eyes on me. I needed her to watch me as I came from what she'd done to me. My hand moved faster, the strokes growing shorter but firmer as I watched her pouty bottom lip get sucked between her teeth, and then the tingling started in my spine, and I grew desperate.

"Unbutton your jeans, Pres, and lift up your shirt. We need a place to release," I whispered, still stroking my dick. I imagined what it would be like if she touched me, or she licked me. I could hear my brother's moans and the sound of his hand moving over his slickness while I watched Presley do exactly as I said.

"Get back in the middle, on your back," Kingston rasped. "Keep your shirt lifted."

She did exactly as Kingston said, as we adjusted for her to fit back in between us. She watched us both with an awestruck expression on her face.

"I'm gonna come." Kingston swore and then shifted so he pressed his knee into the seat and held his cock over Presley's stomach. I was right behind him, mirroring his movements.

With one hand, I held my cock, and the other, I pulled the top part of Presley's jeans down so when I came, it was all over the lacey black part of her underwear.

"Fuckkkkkkkk."

Right as I came, my brother did as well with a heaving curse and ropes of white seed that coated across Presley's belly button.

It was quiet in the car, only our breathing could be heard as we all remained still.

Finally, Presley delicately touched her stomach and over her mound, which was covered by lace.

"Is this normal, what we did?" she whispered, smearing her fingers into the mess.

It made me hard again, but I had to put myself away before we did something even worse.

Presley inspected her fingers while her chest still heaved. My brother had put his cock away too and was now adjusting himself.

"Yes, it's normal," I explained even as lust still coated my voice.

She continued to stare at her fingers. "I mean this part...the...on my stomach and over my underwear."

"Yes, Pres. Although, I'd preferred to have come on your face or even across your tits. I can assure you, it's very normal."

She stared at me, then Kingston, and then slowly brought her fingers up to her mouth and muttered quietly.

"We're never talking about it outside of the car, right?"

I swallowed thickly, while Kingston nodded. "Never."

Then she slowly began cleaning the mess off her fingers by lapping at it with her tongue.

"Shit," I rasped while King muttered something else.

"Do you—" I started, still completely mystified and unsure if what happened had really just happened. "Do you have any questions about any of this?"

She slowly began buttoning her jeans while pushing her shirt down over the mess, which made me feel guilty. We should have brought something for her to clean up with, but it wasn't like we were planning for this to happen.

"No...but if I have questions, and we're not supposed to ever talk about it again, how does that work?"

"Google?" I joked, which had her smirking and lightly hitting my chest.

I smiled, and as we drove home, things felt different but not wrong.

Then, as we walked up the steps to the manor, Presley lightly touched our fingers with hers before quietly saying, "Thank you for giving me that. I'll cherish it forever."

I stopped walking because the weight of her words felt too thick and heavy. It was a weight that I wasn't sure what to do with, but at the same time, I felt like I could fly, if only I were brave enough to try.

She made me feel all of those things, and when I looked at the pained expression on my brother's face, I had a feeling he felt the exact same thing.

Which meant we were completely and utterly fucked.

CHAPTER 24
KINGSTON
PRESENT

I crawled into the SUV in front of Presley's, while Gio occupied the one behind her.

My fingers tightened around the gun in my lap as I stared at Adrian Adesso standing on his balcony, behind his ten-foot-tall gate. He was surrounded by armed men, the sea at his back, and the entire village on his payroll.

Presley had no fucking clue how dangerous this place was, or how much danger she'd willingly stepped into. I had no clue why she was even with him at his home in Italy, or why he'd been in North Carolina, with her.

Seeing that text from Scotty was like someone stabbing me in the chest with a rusty blade.

Even if I didn't bleed out, I'd be infected, and the wound would linger.

As much as it hurt to see her laying on his chest in her room—I was also angry.

So fucking angry.

The call I'd been expecting came through and I answered it on the second silent ring.

"You fucked up."

Scotty only waited a second before he replied, "I'm aware. A year ago, we had different intel."

"Isn't she your little super soldier? We should have just let her stay here."

Even saying that felt like I was pulling that rusted blade further into my chest.

Scotty let out a sigh, which meant he was exasperated with me. "I never asked you to get her. Nor did I ask Gio."

"You sent us the picture of him in our home, with *her*."

"And you took that how you wanted. Perhaps it was merely a test to see if you'd gotten over her." Scotty's snide reply had my fist clenching. What the fuck did he know about what we'd had with Presley?

"We came home because our intel is more up-to-date than yours. We protected her, just like you always demanded of us. Hope you're fucking happy."

"Happy?" His scoff was incredulous. "You both *ruined* her...She's cleaning up this family's mess. He was a viable option for her, and until we can find another alliance for her to—"

"What the fuck do you mean, find another?" He would not be doing this shit again.

Scotty barked out a command to someone in the background, but he came back with a simple, "She's a weapon, Kingston. She'll be used as such."

I squeezed the handle of the gun in my lap so tight, I felt the indents from the grip form to my skin. "You raised us to believe she was the whole goddamn war, so why are you suddenly downplaying her to merely being a weapon?"

"Her heart. She gave it to you two, and it broke. Now, she's frail."

My next words were cut off as he barked out another command and then cut the line completely, leaving me staring at an empty screen.

"Fuck." I tossed the device and watched the side mirror, seeing Presley's car.

Henry, the man next to me, glanced in the rearview mirror as well.

"She might have a tracker."

My fist fell under my jaw as I continued to watch the car follow us. "We're not going anywhere that she hasn't already invited him. Although, knowing Scotty, he'll be scrambling to get us all out of the manor and hiding somewhere new."

I felt Henry's gaze on the side of my face. "That wouldn't be necessary if you succeed in taking your father's place."

Henry spoke of a simmering rebellion that had been birthed in our absence from home.

A tease.

Merely an idea.

But one that had been growing wings powerful enough to lift from the ground with each passing day.

CHAPTER 25
KINGSTON
AGE 17

I hadn't stopped watching Presley any differently than I had before.

I was always aware of her presence in the manor. Even with it being massive enough to allow each of our families to disappear, I always managed to find her.

When she decided to skip her training and sneak over to the farm, I was aware of it. When she was in school, I haunted her every step. When she trained with Scotty, I observed just as I always had before. Gio was with me, and if he wasn't, I knew he was equally as aware of her movement, like a second pair of eyes and ears.

But within the past three days since the incident in the car, there were new things I had started hyperfixating on. Like the way her mouth twisted into a sneer when Scotty pissed her off, or how her tits fit in that one black tank top she had that pushed them up in a way that showed anyone who was watching way too fucking much.

I noticed how sweat dripped down that little slit into her cleavage, and I was frustratingly aware of how enticing it was because after the incident in the car, I now knew what was possible.

I knew what could be if I simply let it happen.

"Kingston, did you hear me?" My dad gently gripped my shoulder to turn me away from the sparring ring. I was still in my shorts, sans a shirt, dripping with sweat.

"What?" How long had he been talking to me, and where the hell was my brother?

Dad's jaw ticked, and I marginally felt guilty. "I asked if you were free this afternoon. I'd like you to come down to the soup kitchen in downtown Rake Forge. Your mother has been there this week with your grandmother, and they could use some extra hands."

"I thought you had men for that." It was a dick thing to say, but Hector's stories had been increasing in flare. I had no idea how true they were, but this entity, El Peligro, was once something so influential it had the crime syndicate's running in fear. How had he taken something so powerful and reduced it down to a soup kitchen?

"Men are free to leave El Peligro; no one is forcing them to stay," was Dad's quipped remark. Which told me he had more and more men leaving, which meant they weren't loyal to him, but to the name and the original idea that my grandfather had. The memory of when I was a kid came back in glaring clarity. Dad had caught someone harming his community and killed the man for it. I'd resented him almost my entire life for that...until now.

My eyes flicked over to where Presley was training. She'd been kicking and punching for well over an hour. Her knuckles were torn the fuck up as per usual, because she didn't bother wrapping them, and she never used gloves. She was being trained for a war that no one else was preparing to fight in. Scotty, Kyle and Dad were all seemingly fine with tossing her up on the chopping block, even when my father had access to something as powerful as El Peligro.

I shrugged his touch off, unsure why it suddenly bothered me so much. "Perhaps you should get back to your roots and see if you invoke some loyalty again."

His jaw went slack, but I saw his fists clench tight. "You don't know anything about the roots, Son. Not how twisted or poisonous they are."

I'd heard enough though, and regardless of how deadly or toxic, Dad once wielded El Peligro. So well he'd doubled the pledges and maintained their loyalty for nearly eighteen years. That spoke of something larger than him, than my grandfather. That was a legacy, and it was one he was willingly trying to drown.

I knew it was a waste of my time to try and convince him. "Sorry. If you need help, I can head down there. But I wanted to shower first."

Dad glanced over at Presley briefly before nodding. "Okay, can you take your brother when you go? I have to head there now, but I'll see you both soon."

I agreed but was still curious where my brother was. "Is Gio at home?"

Such a weird term to use while standing in the manor, but it was so fucking large, the only place that actually felt like home was our family wing.

Dad shook his head and then walked out of the gym.

Scotty was telling Presley to cool down and start medicating her knuckles. She'd rinse them, put on ointment and then wrap them. I decided to hang around while she went through the process. Mats were cleaned and equipment was shelved before Scotty glared at me, then exited the space just like my dad had, which left me alone with Presley.

I wound up my jump rope and wandered closer to her.

"You went pretty hard today."

She glanced up at me and gave me exactly what I was hoping for. Something that told me she was still affected by what we did in the car. Something that showed that regardless of what we'd said, there was no way we'd just pretend it never happened.

Her cheeks flushed pink and then when her chin dipped, a smile crested and curved along her lips.

"You did too."

I had gone harder than usual, mostly because I knew she was watching me.

"I need to shower." I wasn't sure why I stated it like that; I'd showered a million times without broadcasting it. She'd never cared.

I hadn't either and yet now...standing here with her, without anyone else around.

Fuck.

Her lashes fluttered while she tugged her bottom lip in between her teeth and then her lustful gaze landed on me like a feather. *Tentative. Nervous.*

"I actually need to shower too."

There were cameras in the gym, but not in the locker rooms. There was a door that typically remained locked, which connected the two spaces. All Presley would have to do is unlock her side and slip inside the locker room with me, and no one would ever see us.

"Well, enjoy your shower." I smiled and she smiled back.

"You too."

I stepped away first, heading to the locker room, and once I was inside, I locked the door.

I started the shower in one of the stalls and let the water warm, and then I waited.

My chest warmed with the anticipation of her finding me, but there was a nagging dread that kept circling the back of my mind.

Gio.

Would he care if we did this?

Would it hurt him if—

There was no sound, no warning at all when I felt her behind me. I shut out the worries and concerns about my twin and I turned around.

Presley's dark hair was in a braid but pieces had fallen out and were now stuck to the sides of her face and neck. Her eyes looked electric in the low lighting of the overhead lights. I clung to that hungry look as I pulled her closer.

Her head tilted back, and I moved in, starved for her touch. My mouth met hers in a clash of tongues and teeth, and a breathy moan escaped her as I palmed her neck. Her hands were on my chest as I moved her to the wall and continued to kiss her, sweeping my tongue inside her mouth.

Years of wanting her.

Years of longing and denying and feeling like utter shit for thinking about her in ways I never should have allowed myself. For touching myself to thoughts of her.

For being so fucking desperate for her that I was pulling her bra up and over her head.

It fell to the ground, and I stared at her in awe, her tan skin, her pink, rosy nipples. The sweat that had dripped between her breasts and down her neck. I gently gripped the column of her throat and leaned in with my tongue, tracing a path down her salty skin.

She was smooth and perfect, and as I continued to lick her, a jealousy consumed me so intensely that I covered her body with mine. I wanted her to feel every thick inch of me and how badly I needed her. Capturing her lips again, I began pushing down her shorts until they too fell to the ground like her bra had.

Both our chests rose and fell in heavy rhythm while we stared at one another. She stood in front of me in just simple white underwear. There was nothing specifically sexy about them; they covered her hips and even her ass, but they still made my mouth part and my cock swell.

The space under her lashes flushed pink and it made me smile because it took me back to when we were kids and each time I saw her, I had the same thoughts run through my head.

Blue eyes. Dark hair and a freckled nose.

I walked us backward into the hot water, and our mouths met once again, while our hands began to roam. She pushed my shorts down, leaving me in my boxers and I began to undo her braid, until her hair was completely freed and completely soaked.

Her fingers wound through my hair, tugging lightly while our bodies slid against each other. I gripped her hips and slowly slid my hands under the fabric of her underwear, which made her lips part, and her eyes grow wide.

I stared at her, unsure how far I was willing to take things. I was seventeen and a half, she was sixteen...it was wrong but so was everything we were doing. We were raised together; we'd spent almost every waking moment of our lives together. I should view her as a sibling, family, and yet my cock swelled, and I nudged her legs apart as I kissed her again.

Our movements were heated but also clunky with inexperience, neither of us had ever done this before so every few seconds I'd laugh into her mouth, and she'd smile into mine; it was fun and exhilarating, but most of all, it was distracting.

Which is why I didn't realize someone had come into the room. It had to have been someone who crawled through the locker window and knew of that entry point if there wasn't a way in through the main locker doors, and there was only one person beside me or Presley that would know that.

"What the hell are you two doing?" His harsh reprimand had us separating and Presley briskly backing up.

"Gio."

His eyes were narrowed, his arms crossed, and there was a slight flush to his face, giving away that he wasn't just angry, he was hurt.

"It's not what you think." Presley bent down to grab her shorts and brought them up to her chest to cover herself.

My twin kept his glare pinned on me as if I were the person who had betrayed him. Technically I did, but only because the way we'd started things with her, it didn't feel like she belonged to just me or to just him. She felt like she was ours, and whoever found her first would have her.

"What is it you think I assume is going on?" my brother finally asked.

Presley drew closer to him. "That we're leaving you out or sneaking around without you."

Gio laughed, but I knew it was the kind of laugh that led to him pushing people into pools and him sinking knives into people's sides. "Was I here between you two and I not know it?"

Presley was standing right in front of him now, trembling because she was no longer under the hot water. "No, I just mean that King was here, and if you were here, then I would have gone in with you. I started with both of you, and—"

"How nice of you to think of us as so interchangeable, Elvis. Really fucking nice."

He turned away and swiftly exited the locker room, letting the door swing open and risking us being discovered.

Presley had angry tears gathering along her lashes as she bent to grab her bra before dashing off toward the other locker room.

I was left standing there, feeling like the shittiest brother ever.

OUR ABUELA WORE a vibrant pink apron over her clothes. Her dark hair was pinned back and the veggies in front of her were being diced faster than anything I'd ever seen on television.

"Corta, Gio. Si sabes usar una espada, úsala," she yelled at my brother in Spanish.

Chop, Gio. You know how to use a blade, use it.

Gio reached for another tomato and began dicing as he was told, but his chin remained pinned to his chest, his eyes narrowed. I stood next to him, dicing onions and piling them into a bowl. Our mom was across the kitchen next to Alex where they were making tortillas, and Dad was somewhere in the building giving orders and helping move canned goods.

I needed to talk to Gio, but it had to be where no one could hear us.

"Kingston." My grandma clicked her tongue and I moved faster, knowing she was about to get after me.

Alex did something that drew her attention, which pulled her away from our station.

"I wasn't trying to steal her," I muttered quietly.

My brother kept chopping and ignored me.

"You know you would have taken the opportunity if you were me."

That made his hand pause mid-swipe. I knew he would have, which was why I didn't feel guilty about what I had done. Presley belonged to us both, but that didn't mean we both had to be present every time we wanted her.

Gio finally replied with a snide tone, "I thought we weren't going to talk about what happened in the car."

I tried not to smile but failed. "We didn't do any talking."

He paused and swung his head around, eyes narrowed again. "Fuck you, King."

"Stop it, look at me, Bro." I set my blade down, but he didn't.

"I would have waited to talk to you; I wouldn't have just taken her into the locker room and fucked her," Gio said angrily.

I moved with him down the station as he tried to get away from me. Lowering my voice, I said, "I didn't fuck her. There was no fucking whatsoever."

Gio stared at me for so long I thought perhaps he'd relent, but instead, he pushed me, forcing me back into the metal table. The bowls we'd filled with chopped veggies spilled all over the floor. Our grandmother cursed in Spanish and our mom wiped her hands on her apron before quickly moving around the counter.

I took advantage of the delay and punched him in the jaw.

He drove into my chest, pushing me into another table, which made a mess of even more of the food. Mom was screaming at us, so was our grandma, but it wasn't until our dad came in that we finally broke apart.

"The fuck is going on here?" he roared.

He yanked me by the shirt and shoved at Gio's chest until we were separated.

I was breathing hard, and Gio still looked murderous.

Dad asked again, his voice echoing around the room. "What's going on?"

"Nothing!" I screamed while wiping at all of the onions and tomatoes that had fallen on my shirt.

"Gio?" Dad asked, but he pushed out of our dad's hold and stormed out of the kitchen.

"He gets five minutes, then he's back here cleaning this mess up. You both will be here until midnight replacing all the food your mother and grandma have been preparing. Do you understand me?" Dad's grip on my shirt tightened until I agreed.

Once he finally let go, I stared after the door my brother had exited through.

I HAD FINALLY FINISHED CLEANING everything and replacing all the food by one in the morning. My arms were tired, my fingers sore, and as I got into my dark room, I dropped into bed.

"You actually cleaned everything on your own?" Gio's voice echoed from across the room. If I had any energy at all I'd throw a pillow at him.

"Clean? I had to clean *and* replace all the shit we spilled. You were supposed to come back and help me."

His chuckle grated against my nerves.

"Presley snuck through our window tonight. She was crying and begged me to listen to her."

That had me alert, but I didn't show it. I remained face down on my bed, pillows practically suffocating me.

Gio continued, "I heard her out. She said all this stuff was confusing to her, but she figured we were all three just messing around. She didn't think it meant anything to which I had to agree with her and stop being such a little bitch about things."

"But it does mean something," I replied, muffled and strangely annoyed.

Why would she chalk it up to us messing around? Probably

because I had alluded to that by not talking about what we were doing outside of the car.

My twin let out a heavy sigh, which made me open one eye and take him in. He was in a white tank top and black boxers. His face revealed too much, and that had always been his downfall.

"I think we need to maintain that this is meaningless, Bro...so we don't scare her off."

That made me move my head to the side so I could see him better. "So now there's a we?"

My brother smirked. "Since you did all the work tonight, I've decided to forgive you."

I did throw a pillow at him then. Then another.

His laugh was a ray of sunshine that always seemed to move away my clouds.

"So, where does that leave us?" I finally asked once my brother turned his light off.

Gio waited a few seconds before replying, "I think we just go with the flow. If you do what you did today, I promise not to lose my shit. Just know that I'll be stealing moments with her too."

"We're usually always together, the three of us. What then?" I risked asking, afraid of what it would mean if my brother shut this down. I didn't mind having him with me in that car. He'd been my teammate in absolutely everything I'd ever done. Sharing wasn't an uncommon feeling, and while I didn't really pay attention to what he did with her, it didn't bother me that he was doing something with her at the same time.

Gio let out a small sigh before lobbing another pillow back at my face.

"Then we do what we did in the car...figure it out, I guess. I'm not ever fucking touching you though and if you touch me, I'll stab you."

He threw another pillow and I caught it. "I'm not holding back with her either, Gio. If the feeling is right, then I'm—"

"Not touching me. Do what you want with Presley, and we'll figure it out. But that part needs to be clear."

It was my turn to laugh because this seemed to really be messing with him. We'd never been shy with one another. I openly masturbated under my covers from the time I was eleven, and he'd asked me to check something on one of his ball sacks before. He was my brother. My twin. We kept nothing from one another, but I agreed with him on this. I had no desire to ever intersect while enjoying Presley.

"As long as she never chooses anyone but us, I don't really care what happens, but yeah. No worries, Bro. We won't touch."

"Good," Gio mused then laughed again, before throwing yet another pillow at my face.

CHAPTER 26

PRESLEY
PRESENT

I gripped the leather armrest as if it could somehow take the brunt of all my frustration and all my anger that had built up over the past year. The twins sat toward the front of the private jet while I took residence up near the back.

They talked and laughed together as if I didn't exist. Their men filled in the empty spaces in between, and while each person either slept or played on their phone, I understood exactly what was happening.

They were isolating me. As if I hadn't been isolated enough in the past year and a half.

As if they hadn't punished me enough and for what? They were the ones who left, and who hurt me. The anger in my stomach tightened into a painful knot, making me feel queasy and a lot like I was about to burst into tears.

Instead, I bit my bottom lip and stared out the window. I would not give them the satisfaction of seeing me break. I had endured enough in my life to withstand this too.

I thought of Adrian and his easy smiles, the way the skin next to his eyes crinkled when he laughed and the way his touch set me on fire. I thought of how we'd yet to cross any boundary that would have left a lasting impression on me. He hadn't taken anything from me that I didn't offer, and I'd never once offered him my body or my heart. Not fully.

The plane suddenly rocked to the side as it hit a patch of rough air, but it was enough of a jostle that it made my cup of coffee spill from my tray and ruin my jeans.

"Shit." I quickly stood and began dabbing at my soiled clothes. It drew the attention of the twins, who had stopped talking at the sight of me standing. Their burning gazes were on me in seconds, and while Gio's jaw ticked and Kingston's eyes seemed to beg something from me, I pushed out the image and walked to the bathroom with my backpack.

I always hated fighting with the twins growing up. It didn't happen often, but when it did, it was always excruciating because the two always had one another, and I was always the one left out all alone. Even now, as adults, it burned through my chest like a dry, painful heat, scorching up pieces of hope that I'd always carried regarding my relationship with them.

Foolish stupid hope.

The only extra pair of clothes I'd packed in my bag were pajamas. The rest were all in my large suitcases, which were tucked away in the cargo. With a sigh, I peeled my jeans off and pulled on my sleep shorts. They were on the shorter side, but at this point I just simply didn't care.

I decided to complete my pajama set and pull on the button-down matching shirt and then tugged up a pair of tall socks. Once I was dressed, I took two seconds to inspect myself in the mirror. My face had somehow kept a warm glow from the irregularly warm winter, leaving my freckles splattered across my nose and cheeks. Thanks to Carter, I had started using a plethora of beauty products that actually worked for me. My lashes were thicker, thanks to some serum that I applied every night, and my lips were stained after applying a lip mask. Even my face was smoother after applying creams and using some jaw smoothing device that I didn't take enough time to actually read about. I typically just listened to my cousin and used whatever she put in my hands.

I liked myself.

I had to remember that as the twins' glares would hit like a boulder and their silence would cut like a knife. I liked me, even if they didn't.

Pulling the bathroom door open, I stepped out and ran right into a solid chest.

"Sorry." I automatically apologized before realizing the chest belonged to a twin.

Once I stepped back, I found starry gray eyes and a dimple that had popped out because of Gio's reluctant smile. He didn't seem to be able to help himself.

"Saw you go back here, you okay?" His tone was soft and kind, and confusing.

I nodded, tucking a piece of hair back. "Fine, just got coffee all over myself."

Gio inspected me from head to toe, taking a step back. I felt mildly self-conscious but brushed it off. His jaw ticked once, twice, and then he laughed.

"That's what you changed into?"

Glancing down at myself, confusion set in. "What?"

This was a modest sleep set. Cotton, light, with buttons that trailed from just above my breasts all the way down past my navel, and a pair of shorts that stopped mid-thigh.

Gio used his thumb and forefinger to pinch a tiny piece of the fabric between his hands.

"There's Highland cows printed everywhere."

He knew they were my favorite animal, why did that shock him? "So?"

His smile faded as something more serious took its place. "Just wasn't prepared to see you back in something like this."

"Well, I had nothing else to change into." I tried to step past him, but he moved with me, tilting his head.

"Just, try not to walk past Kingston if you can help it," Gio warned, lightheartedly.

I ignored him, pushing past him again. I didn't care what concerns he had, the two of them were completely avoiding me, and I wasn't about to play this game.

With my head down, I returned to my seat and set my bag in the one across from me. Two seconds later, the bag was being tossed to the ground and a tall lean form had taken its place. I glanced up and locked eyes with Kingston, whose amber gaze was heated while slowly traveling down my pajama set.

"It's the middle of the day."

I quipped back, "Not by the time we land."

His jaw moved as if he wanted to say something else but thought better of it.

"You seem comfortable with the time change and flying to and from Italy. How frequently has that been happening over the past year and a half?"

His tone was sharp, and it had me gripping the armrest again; otherwise, it'd be his neck.

"I've gone several times over the past year, Kingston."

I didn't owe him why I was going or the fact that Scotty had to persuade me to in the beginning. He could think what he wanted.

Focusing on my phone, I typed in my password about to navigate over to my emails when Kingston leaned over and pulled it out of my hand.

"What the—"

"Just making sure our texts and calls came through okay because while you seemingly replaced us with that fucker, Adrian, we've been reaching out to you, only to be completely ignored." Kingston's thumbs moved over my screen as he navigated to my text thread.

Heat barreled into me, not because Scotty had blocked them or because I had chosen not to know what they had to say, but because this was all sitting too close in my chest. Like a stick of dynamite just waiting for a spark to dance along the floor of my heart, only to land on that damn ignition wire.

"How come the only texts on here are from the most recent ones we sent you?" Kingston flicked his eyes up, watching me.

I stared out the window, inspecting the clouds.

His boot slid forward until he touched my foot, but I pulled it back.

"Presley."

I ignored him.

Then Gio came and sat down next to me and I muttered a curse.

"What are we talking about?"

Kingston glared at him, but explained, "She only has texts on here from what we sent her this week. None of our voicemails... nothing else."

Gio's face swung over and that heat digging into my sternum became unbearable.

They stared as the silence grew.

"She didn't get them," Gio finally said, as if he'd finally pieced it together.

My eyes closed as I tried to push out their stares.

"Think about it. She didn't text us back a single time, but Alex had mentioned once that the day we left, Pres was waiting outside for us. It wasn't until Scotty texted us that picture that she replied."

"She didn't reply," Kingston droned, obviously irritated.

Gio shifted next to me, but I moved closer to the window, wishing it would somehow open and pull me out.

"She left the group chat."

I felt Kingston's eyes prance over my face and drop lower to my legs, and that's when his boot gently touched my foot again.

"Elvis, that true?"

Pulling my legs up under my chin, I held them while ignoring how it hurt to hear Kingston call me Elvis. An old wound seemed to tear open, not just with them in front of me, but with that little dig.

They'd made their decision, and while they had tried to reach out, now they were being just as cruel.

Kingston suddenly reached forward and tugged my knees down, placing his large palms on either thigh while his nose was practically pressed against mine.

"Presley, did Scotty do something?"

Fuck. "Yes, okay?" I shoved his hands away and he let me.

His jaw went slack and Gio's head whipped over.

"What the fuck did he do?" There was so much gravel and anger in his tone that it made my eyes water.

"He did something so when you texted or called my number, it forwarded to one of his burner phones."

"I fucking knew it!" Gio whisper-yelled, leaning closer to his brother. His gaze intent.

"I knew Scotty did something because in what universe would she just cut us completely out of her life?"

Kingston didn't reply; he just continued to stare at me as if he could pry back every layer of hurt that the two had delivered to me over the past year.

He finally returned to his seat and just continued to stare at me while angry tears gathered in my eyes, and while the truth of how soon I'd discovered they'd been texting him sat like lead inside my chest.

A truth that could divide us once again, and one that they'd eventually discover.

***

THE SILENCE in the car ride back to the manor just seemed to blend in with all the other things we weren't saying. I kept catching Gio's sad gaze, and Kingston kept flicking his eyes over me then opening his mouth as if he wanted to say something but would stop.

I watched the town of Rake Forge fly by, and then the trees as we drove closer to our manor, and then through the gates. Scotty was outside with at least twenty armed men, which had me on alert. He practically had a militia with him, and when I had left, we didn't have that sort of manpower roaming the property, so what the hell had happened?

"Why are there so many men here?" I asked no one in particular.

Gio moved so his hand landed on my thigh. "We weren't told."

I glared down at his hand but we'd parked so I didn't move it. I just jumped out of the car and rounded the hood.

Scotty's men eyed me, and I recognized a few of them from when he'd put me in the ring with them. "What's going on?"

My uncle's gaze was cold and calculated as he held his assault rifle to his chest, as casual as any soldier would, except Scotty had never served in any war.

"These are the new precautions because you brought Adrian Adesso here."

My chest pinched as humiliation clouded my thoughts and my reasoning.

"So there's no threat?"

"Oh, there is," Scotty said with a bit of a sneer then glanced over my head at the twins. "But I'm taking it one problem at a time. We'll discuss more later this evening. Please go get settled into your room."

My fists clenched tightly as I bit my lip. It wouldn't do any good to fight with him out here. There was too much at risk to reveal any sort of dispute in the open. We had no idea how loyal these men were, so I pushed past the group and went straight into the manor.

My mother was walking out of our family wing right as I was walking in.

"Presley?" Her dark hair lifted as her head turned, and confusion marred her face. "Why are you back so soon? I thought you were staying until next month."

Did Scotty not tell them?

"The twins brought me back, said there was a threat."

Mom's face did something that I knew mine did when I got angry with a sneer and widened gaze. "Scotty did this, I know he did. He sent them, didn't he?"

She stormed past me. I turned with her, trying to stop her because it wouldn't make a difference.

"Mom!"

She kept moving, her bare feet barely a whisper over the wood floors she hated so much and her hair flying like a sheet of midnight behind her. She had on a simple T-shirt and a pair of jeans shorts but right as she was about to exit the house, she pulled something familiar from her purse that hung near the front door and my heart sank, but my feet moved faster.

The front door was thrown open and she was on him quicker than I could blink. Her foot connected with the back of his leg and within a single heartbeat she had a Glock pressed to the side of his head. Her lips peeled back as she seethed, "I'm so fucking sick of you interfering with her life. I won't have you do any more damage. You think you know what's best, but you don't. I won't accept it anymore."

The click of someone's rifle had my gaze snapping up. The men surrounding Scotty all had their guns pointed at my mother. I didn't have a weapon on me. How could I not have a weapon on me?

"Mom, please," I begged, my chin wobbling.

My vision blurred, all I could see were the men in front of me. Where was my dad?

One of the men narrowed his eyes as if he were aiming and I moved without hesitating. I bolted so fast toward him that I couldn't even think through how I would take him down. I just knew I couldn't risk my mother getting hurt.

Scotty had his arms up, but when he saw me running, he began screaming. It didn't matter; I was barreling toward the solider right as a shot went off as loud as a crack of thunder.

Several things happened too fast for me to process.

Someone pulling me to the ground, a hand covering my head, another wrapping around my waist. People shouting, my mother screaming. I forced my eyes up just in time to see a bullet fly through a man's head, making him jolt to the side. Then the other men in the circle began going down, one after another.

I remained on the ground, breathing hard as I stared at every man who had dared point their guns at my mother, as if they were moving in slow motion until they were all down and my mother had finally released Scotty, stumbling backward.

I watched as my father slowly made his way up from the lower parking level, his gun still aimed as if he weren't finished shooting. He had an odd look on his face, as if someone had just dug into his chest and attempted to rip his heart through his rib cage. His eyes were blown wide, and his face was pale, so fucking pale.

"Dad?" I weakly called for him, but his focus was on Scotty.

"Seven of your men, Scotty. Seven of them had a weapon pointed at my wife!"

Dad's voice was murderously loud, the tendons in his neck strained and even spit came from his mouth as he screamed.

My uncle glanced around as he finally got to his feet, but my dad kicked his chest until he was faltering down to his knees once more.

"I spared you one time and only one time when you put her life in danger. I have ignored the liberties you've taken with my daughter because I understood what it took to withstand your training, but your men just aimed their fucking weapons at my *wife!*"

Scotty's eyes flashed over to Mom who was shaking her head, tears gathering in her eyes.

"Kyle."

I glanced at my uncle, realizing too late that the arms that had pulled me to the ground were familiar. Gio and Kingston were on their knees, holding me close while this all played out, and I was too numb to process or even react to that.

Dad pressed the barrel of his gun to Scotty's temple.

"Seven of your men in exchange for seven bullets in the head. I think that's fair, don't you, Uncle?"

Mom reached forward and pulled his arm. "Kyle. Don't."

Dad was about to pull the trigger; I could sense it. The only person I had ever seen pull him out of this bloodlust was Juan.

I squeezed the twins' hands as tightly as I could. "Go get your dad!"

Gio moved, but Kingston didn't.

I glared at his profile. His hand hadn't left mine, nor had he stopped squeezing while his gaze remained on my dad.

"Kings—"

He turned his head and quickly snapped, "I'm not leaving you."

Juan wasn't going to make it. I had to stop my father.

"Dad, don't kill him, please don't kill him." I was angry with Scotty, but he was a part of me. I couldn't lose him.

"You know he would have killed those men himself if Mom hadn't had a gun to his head. He would do anything for us."

Dad finally dropped his hand and released Scotty.

Only to return with his clenched fist landing in my uncle's face.

AN HOUR later we were sitting in the main common area, where we typically gathered for joint dinners. Tonight, there was no food regardless of what Anna, the twins' grandmother, had hoped for when she started unpacking various things wrapped in tin foil.

No one moved from whatever seat they'd grabbed.

Scotty held an ice pack to his nose while my mother sipped straight from a bottle of Crown, then chased it with a sip of her Diet Coke. The twins' mother, Taylor, was seated in one of the larger, plushier chairs, with a glass of something clear.

The twins each nursed beers, and my father wouldn't stop staring out the back patio doors.

"We need to talk about Adrian Adesso," Scotty finally spoke up.

I sat on the same couch I always did whenever we had family talks, or on the rare occasion, played a game. There were two seats on either side of me, and I hadn't even meant to do it; it was just habit after years and years of tradition.

Dad finally turned around, stuffed his hand into his pocket and waited for Scotty to continue.

"We've gotten intel regarding his plans. He'd essentially come to us with an offer of friendship in hopes that we'd become his ally. For the past year, Presley has built a connection with him and fostered that alliance."

Both Kingston and Gio snapped their heads in my direction.

I refused to be ashamed of what I'd done, especially because it was exactly what I'd been trained to do.

"Is he playing both sides, or what changed?" my dad asked, taking a seat on the armrest of the chair my mom sat in.

Kingston spoke up, shocking me into silence. "The Adesso family has grown larger than what he's led anyone to believe, not through alliances but through blood. His father may be gone, but he has brothers who have been building their presence in various parts of the world. Layering his defenses in a way that prevent them being infiltrated. He's essentially building a tower."

There was a long pause in the room, full of heavy silence when Gio added, "A tower of power if you will."

An unladylike snort left me, which I quickly covered with my hand. Gio glanced back at me with glee, fully delighted by his own antics. Kingston ignored us.

"One of his brothers has ten times the force growing over in Russia. His other brother has at least five hundred men employed, operating out of Canada, and Adrian is holding firm in two locations, Italy on the smaller scale, with most of his numbers in New York."

Scotty adjusted the ice pack and squinted at Kingston. "How do you know all of this?"

"You're not the only person who has intel and connections, old man," Gio replied on behalf of his brother.

I stole a quick glance across the room and noticed Juan and

Taylor give one another a loaded look, one full of concern and mild panic if I was reading the way Juan's jaw pulsed correctly.

Scotty shook his head before standing tall and tossing the ice pack down. "Don't stick your hand in the fire, kids."

Gio snickered again, shoulders shaking. "Why? Because we'll get burned?"

"No." Scotty paused before glancing at me. "You'll get branded. That world is a curse, and once you dip so much as a pinky in, it'll never let you go."

Kingston snapped back, "Then why the fuck have you raised Presley inside of it?"

My face flushed the smallest amount, knowing their concern was right but also knowing I'd made my choices, and I was okay with them. No one forced me to do anything I didn't want to do. But did that mean the boys had started getting involved with the mob?

My mind played back the conversation they'd had in Adrian's house when he'd said their name was familiar.

"*We've recently had business together.*"

What had they done?

"So what's the plan then...you pulled Presley. Is there an immediate threat to her that we should know about?" my dad asked, his gaze softening as it landed on me.

Scotty shook his head. "Other than his initial request at needing an alliance was disingenuous. It makes me nervous that he has an ulterior motive."

Kingston scoffed, finishing off his beer. "Of course he has an ulterior motive, he wants to fuc—"

"Find another way to say that, Son," Juan quickly interjected, with a bite to his tone.

Kingston's jaw feathered but continued on. "I saw the way he acts with Presley. I believe his feelings for her are real, but I'm also positive he has an ulterior motive. I doubt you all knew the town he's in is completely under his employment. The bistro café, the bookstore, the market...even the vendors. They all work for Adrian, every single place you went, you were being watched, Elvis."

Something cold and foreign moved through me, almost like a snake had found sanctuary between my ribs. Adrian hadn't lied to me, but he hadn't once told me about any brothers, and he feigned that he pitied my father...maybe that was more true than I realized, and he didn't need an alliance.

Maybe he had been telling me the truth this entire time.

My uncle adjusted his ice pack. "Well, for the time being we're on high alert. He knows where we live, which means we need to leave."

That was on me, but I still didn't have a bad feeling about Adrian. No matter how hard I tried to muster up the things he could be capable of, or all the horrible things the head of a mafia family could do, I still had affection for him.

"He's not a threat." I found myself arguing. Everyone swung their gazes over to me, and two pairs of eyes burned as they pinned me in place. I slowly stood and tried to explain where I was coming from.

"Ducking back underground isn't the answer here. Adrian and I have a real connection, and I'd like to tug on the thread a bit before you bury us, Scotty."

Scotty gave me one last look before walking toward the main hall. "What did you have in mind?"

"I want to bring him here, invite him to meet all of you and see if anything shifts. If he's going to draw his brothers into it, then we'll be ready, but if not, then perhaps there's still an alliance on the table here."

"Over my fucking dead body!" Kingston yelled.

Gio briskly stood. "You swore she'd never be subjected to an arranged marriage. She's eighteen years old."

"I'm old enough to make this decision on my own," I argued, stepping closer, "And you two have been gone too long to have a say about this, one way or another."

"It's not like we didn't try to get in touch with you," Kingston sneered.

I ignored him, keeping my focus on Scotty. He watched me carefully before giving me a simple nod.

"I trust you, Presley. If you think it's a good idea to invite Adrian here to meet your family, including the twins, then by all means, arrange it."

Glaring over at my two previous best friends, I pulled out my cell and headed toward my wing of the house, ignoring the arguments breaking out behind me.

CHAPTER 27
GIO
AGE 17

There were several dangerous things my brother and I had done throughout our lives. Surviving our family had always been at the pinnacle of that list, but then so had surviving Presley.

It was hell, and each day tested our resilience to watch her become the person Scotty wanted to twist her into. The torn knuckles from training, the blood on the mats, the busted lips and broken nose. There were several times I was positive I was going to murder Scotty. Nights I would slip through the shadows contemplating it, even occasionally staring at his back while I decided his fate.

But Presley cared for him. Worse, she trusted him.

And after the incident in the car and finding her with Kingston in the showers after...a strange sort of peace now filled me when it came to her and this new reality we existed within.

This new terrifying world that we'd opened up and walked into that absolutely no one could ever find out about. They were training her for war, and somewhere deep inside me needed to bring her peace in whatever capacity that would come.

School had just ended, and when Presley had walked past us in the hall, I'd tugged her inside an empty classroom.

"Gio!" she whisper-yelled while I pressed closely into her body. My lips at her ear, I muttered, "You wore a skirt today."

"All the other girls have been."

I licked along the shell of her ear, letting a small groan slip past my lips. "But it only matters when you do it. I want you in the back of the car today. We'll stay parked, just get into the back when you get to the car."

With that, I left her there, and exited the building.

Kingston and I hadn't talked about what we wanted to do, but after we discussed where we stood with Presley and each other, I knew he'd want me to do this. The car was now our sanctuary, where we'd worship Presley and where we'd shed our fears and worry over what our families might think of us.

She crawled into the back seat like she did the time before, but this time Kingston drove, while I joined her. The car flew down an abandoned road with the windows down and I'd slid my hand behind Presley's head, drawing her mouth to mine. Her hands went to my face, holding me there while we made out, our tongues at war, desperate for each other.

Her body felt so perfect against mine, her curves seamlessly in my palms as I pulled her into my lap. Her legs spread over my hips like before, but this time, she only had underwear separating her bare pussy from feeling me.

"Do what you did last time, Elvis. Rub against me until you come."

She didn't hesitate or hold back. Her hips rocked back and forth, and my hands went to her bare ass, gripping her and pushing her to slide over the bulge in my jeans faster.

At some point, the car had pulled off onto a road, but I wasn't paying attention. Not until my brother traded his place in the driver's seat for the passenger, reclining it all the way. I somewhat noticed him unzipping his jeans and gripping himself. His head was angled so he could watch us, and when his hand lifted, it moved to Presley's left butt cheek.

I stopped watching what he was doing and focused on Presley's' mouth. I slid my tongue against hers and we made out while she dry-humped me. It felt so good that I was barely holding it together, and my breathing had staggered. Her moans increased, and her hips rotated quicker and quicker until her head tipped back, and right as that pouty mouth of hers dropped open, I came hard in my jeans.

Kingston's hand was moving fast in my peripheral, but he'd gently tugged Presley's hand and encouraged her to leave my lap and crawl into the front. It was fine, my jeans were soaked, and I was fucking uncomfortable now.

We'd modified most of the interior of the Camaro, making it a bit more modern, which included a cushy leather console separating the two bucket seats, big enough for Pres to sit on. Kingston had her facing him while he remained in the passenger seat, her feet pressed into the seat, legs parted wide, so he fit between them. His cock was still stiff and weeping at the tip.

He was on his knees, facing her with his cock in his hand. Flipping her skirt up, King leaned into her, pressing his mouth to hers, and a deep groan left his chest the second his dick touched the edge of her underwear. It pulsed and then he came, with white, sticky seed coating the inside of Presley's tan thigh. Her eyes were dazed and her cheeks flushed pink, and I wanted nothing more than to pull her back and have her feel the mess she'd made of me.

Instead, I watched as my brother leaned in and kissed her while drawing up his release from her leg and smearing it over the wet spot along the center of her pink panties. It made Presley roll her hips forward as if she were ready to ride him like she'd ridden me. Her pouty lips parted as his fingers moved, pressing against that spot, and she'd rocked into it, over and over until he eventually sat back in the chair and just pulled her over his lap.

"You like this, don't you?" King asked, while Presley agreed with a moan.

The asshole muttered encouragement for her to find her release yet again while she rode his hand, and he kept his cock out, letting it rub against her leg while they moved. I tried to block out her sounds, the way she told him how good the extra wetness felt against her clit, and how he kept hitting the perfect place. I guess his thumb slipped past her panties and slid along her pussy lips, because that really had her hips moving and her begging for him to give her more.

"You're soaking me, Presley. Fuck, you're gushing all over my hand," Kingston rasped while pulling her back for a kiss.

Fucker.

I ignored how her shirt dipped and showed her cleavage and how seeing her move over him had me hard again, but with my jeans soaked, I couldn't exactly enjoy it, so I just sat there and watched as my brother practically fucked her in front of me. I watched as they both gasped, kissed, and then came again. This time, he had the decency to finish inside of a Kleenex I had no idea existed. Apparently, there was a whole damn box on the floor. Once they cleaned up, he tossed the box back to me the second Presley crawled into the passenger seat he'd vacated, and the car began to move again.

DINNER WAS TENSE, and I wasn't even really sure why.

Mom and Dad smiled as usual, Alex droned on about dance and some tech analyzation she was working on with some of the tech guys from the charity. Kingston stared down at his food, and I watched the windows outside.

I couldn't stop thinking about Presley.

The way her hair felt in my hands, or the way her body felt against mine. Even the way the jealousy over seeing my brother touch her had lessened. It felt almost normal to see him kiss her and touch her the way I did. Like she truly belonged to both of us.

The problem was, I wanted more than just back seat kisses. I hated that I came in my jeans. I wanted what Kingston had with her in the shower and then the car; I wanted her in more places than just the car. But I knew how dangerous that was. I knew it was reckless, and yet...

I pulled my phone out and shot her a text.

Me: come over tonight

My mother spoke up about some family trip, but I ignored it until my phone vibrated.

Elvis: What does King say about it?

Irritation chafed enough that I set my phone down. I had agreed that we would do this for her, and that I could set my feelings aside. I agreed that I wouldn't make this about me, and we'd put her needs first but fuck, it hurt.

An hour passed, and I'd gone through the motions of helping clean up dinner, and then watched a movie with my big sister. King noticed something was up, but I ignored him. I couldn't figure out why these emotions continued to creep up every time he was brought up. The memory of finding them together in that locker room still played on a loop in my head, and it was torture each time I remembered how she looked, backed against the wall, half naked, and in his arms.

I hated that even when I did get her, he was present too. I wanted her for myself.

Finally, it was late enough that I showered and slipped into bed. King stayed up for a while longer, but eventually his phone went on the charger and his side of the room went dark. It wasn't long after that when I heard our loft window open.

Her steps were nearly silent, but I still heard her coming closer until she was directly next to my bed, pulling the covers back.

"You never texted me back," she whispered as she slid in next to me.

I automatically opened my arm and cradled her to my chest as her hand covered my stomach, and her cheek found a place over my heart.

"I didn't know what to say," I answered honestly.

She gently stroked over my pecs, and then pressed a kiss there.

"I don't want to come between you guys."

I played with her hair and stroked down her arm, thinking over what to say so she believed me.

"Just need some alone time with you like he had. I think as long as we balance that out, it'll be okay when we're all together."

She pressed another kiss to my chest, and I felt like my heart might try and break through the skin just to feel the place her lips were.

"Well, King seems out of it, which means I'm all yours tonight... what do you want to do?"

I should try something...maybe eating her out or finishing on her thighs like King had but having her this close to me felt just as imperative as having her in all those ways was.

"Sleep and let me hold you all night. That's all I want."

I could make out the little furrow to her brow as she stroked my chin. "But you wanted to be even with King and what we did in the locker room."

"This is better. I just want to hold you."

She melted into me, and I pulled her closer. My heart was in free fall and in danger of being destroyed, but I decided to be reckless with it anyway and close my eyes.

CHAPTER 28

GIO

PRESENT

Being back in our room felt weird.

It was true that after enough time there were some spaces that you just simply outgrew, and my bedroom felt like one of those places. Especially my bed, which oddly smelled like Presley's orange and coconut. The room had been cleaned of any dust and vacuumed, which I knew was thanks to my mother, but everything else was exactly the same, including the teal hair tie that had been left behind by Presley.

I glanced over at my brother's side of the room and saw the same vacant look in his eyes.

The truth of what we'd done, who we'd become over the past year was something neither of us had time to confront. We were different people now, and our ties...the choices we'd made without our father's approval would blow up in a very dramatic way if we didn't leave again soon. We had no intention of coming home, not because we didn't miss Elvis, but we understood better than anyone else what this family was capable of and what our hearts could endure.

"Smells like her," my brother murmured, bringing his pillow up to his face.

I ignored him because I didn't know what to say. And the gash in my heart still hadn't healed.

"What's our plan for when Adrian arrives?"

My brother sat down on his bed and let out a sigh that could topple a government.

"He has leverage on us...he could use it, especially if he thinks we're a threat to his relationship with Presley."

"Are we?" I asked, gripping the hair tie and squeezing it in my fist.

Kingston stared at the wall behind me, working his jaw back and forth. "I let her go."

"Did you?" I didn't believe him for a single second.

He tugged his shirt over his head and tossed it to the ground then ripped the pillowcase off his cushion and let it fall to the floor as well. It made me wonder if his bedding also had Presley's scent all over it.

"I did. Let Adrian come."

I scoffed and shook my head. "Bullshit."

He closed his eyes before blinking up at the ceiling.

But I wasn't done. "Everything we've done this past year and a half was because of her. Was for our future. You didn't let her go; you nearly lost your shit when you saw them kiss in Italy."

"She's not going to give a single fuck about what we did for her future. She's got the head of an Italian mafia family at her feet. She could be rich and have a farm in Italy. She doesn't need the farmhouse...probably doesn't even care about it anymore."

"You're being stupid." I pulled my shirt up over my head and tossed it to the ground like he had and then walked into our bathroom. The space was white subway tile and black iron fixtures. I started the hot water and stood under the spray longer than I needed to because there was a moment that kept replaying in my head that I wasn't sure I could continue seeing without throwing up.

The guns were aimed at Rylie, but for a single second I worried that one of them would shoot Presley...at that last second when we'd run back outside, she started running and I thought...

I thought that would be the end.

She'd never hear how I spent every night under a different sky thinking of her, or how my soul felt like it had cracked when she hadn't replied to a single one of our texts or calls. Or how there were a few nights that I stood on the edge of a steep cliff and stared down at the bottom, wondering what it would take to get her to talk to us. For a few dark days, I wondered if at least I could get her to talk to Kingston, then maybe that would be enough. Perhaps my death would bring them together.

Blinking away the memories, I scrubbed my hair and then rinsed off before finishing up.

I needed to see her, but I had no idea what I'd say...I didn't know where to begin.

I just knew that I needed to see her. I was this close, and yet she seemed so far away.

Fuck it.

I pulled on my sweats and skipped the shirt and shoes, then took the loft stairs two at a time, which got my brother's attention.

"Where are you going?"

"You're done. I'm not. I need to see her."

Kingston cursed and jumped to his feet. "You obviously knew I wasn't telling the truth about that, but we can't go see her. We have to let her go, Gio."

"No, the fuck we don't. I haven't seen her in over a year...I want to talk to her."

I didn't wait to hear what my brother would say to that, so I pulled up the window and slipped out. It felt strange, fitting on that terrace being older and bigger. An entire year and a half had passed, and I felt like a different person now as I felt the cold air brush against my face and the rain pelt the surface, making it slick.

Her window arrived with a warm orange glow against the dark

sky, and something fluttered in my stomach at the prospect of seeing her again. I had no idea if Kingston was behind me or not, but I didn't care. I just needed to try and get us back to where we were before this fucking mess nearly ripped us apart.

I pressed on her window to see if it was unlocked and found that it was. The glass panes parted, and I moved the gauzy curtains out of the way as I placed my foot on her window seat.

Her room was warm and inviting, the loft looked somewhat the same, except she'd cleaned up most of her crafting supplies and had her yoga mat and a few weights scattered around the space now.

I walked forward and peered over the railing of the loft, seeing her down on her bed. She was lying on her stomach, kicking her feet while talking on the phone.

"I think I should stay here, but I will come visit you," she said flirtatiously.

Then she laughed and my chest felt like it cracked open.

"Adrian, you aren't sleeping here. It's a big deal that my family is willing to let you come back and meet everyone. I messed up by letting you come here, and Scotty is freaking out."

She toyed with her stuffed cow while she kicked her feet some more and then she laughed again. "Yes, you were the threat. Everyone sort of collectively freaked out."

A pause and then a breathy sigh. "I have been thinking of that kiss too."

Someone's hand came over my chest, pulling me back toward the window. Kingston dragged me back through the window and I couldn't seem to catch my breath or my footing.

The rain fell in angry, cold sheets as I pushed my twin's hands away and stared at his glowering expression. The storm picked up, making it dangerous for us to be out on the roof, but something kept me rooted to the spot outside of her window.

"She's moved on from us, brother. We have to accept it."

I shook my head, feeling something shudder in my lungs. I wanted to cry, or scream...fuck, I wanted to punch something.

"We didn't leave her because we wanted to. We had no choice, does she know that?" My voice cracked as I raised it to be heard over the rain.

Kingston shook his head, which had droplets of water clinging to his nose. "I don't think it matters. She never saw the messages or got our voicemails. She doesn't care."

"I'm not giving up on her. I can't."

Kingston shrugged and he looked so small and frail doing it. As if he'd finally run out of ideas, and he always seemed to know what to do.

No. I wouldn't accept that. "We fight for her. One last push...we make sure she understands everything, and then if she chooses him and we know he's safe for her—that he's good and will protect her the way we would—that's when we agree to walk away. But I won't walk without a fight."

Kingston's eyes were clear as he watched me and then he lowered his chin and agreed. "Fine...but you can't get your hopes up again, Gio. You scared the shit out of me when we were in Mexico... you got dark a few times...I can't lose you. I love Presley, always will, but I'd cease to exist without you. I need you in my life, Bro."

I clapped his shoulder, and we began walking back to our room.

"Love you too, Bro."

He laughed then shook my hold as he mumbled something that sounded like "idiot."

I smiled and followed my twin back to our side of the house where I hoped we'd make a plan on how to get back the girl of our dreams before we lost her for good.

CHAPTER 29

PRESLEY

AGE 16

The branch cracked as I tried to weave it into the crown I'd been crafting. With a heavy sigh, I tugged it free and searched for another that was fresher. The sun was out already, high in the sky, warming the garden and all the plants within.

I was tucked away behind a stalk of sunflowers, putting together two crowns for my best friends to wear on their birthday. A gentle flutter near my heart had me smiling as I realized they'd both become so much more than my best friends. Memories fluttered through my mind of the nights they'd hold me close while I was tucked under a firm chin, or wrapped in a pair of strong arms.

The twins never joined the same bed at the same time when I crawled through that loft window at night. Some nights it was Gio's bed I'd take refuge in, and other nights it would be Kingston's, but regardless of which brother I slept with, sleep was truly all we did. Never once had either brother pushed things while I was under their covers. Not like when we were in the car, or if we'd manage to sneak off to the locker rooms again. But it was always just heavy kissing and rubbing.

With Gio, we'd often sneak over to the farm and lay out a blanket under the stars, and there he'd kiss places on my body that I never imagined anyone would touch, much less kiss. Other times, Kingston would hold my hand and take me through his garden, and more often than not, we'd end up in a patch of soft grass, my arms around his neck while his lips devoured mine.

I was completely in love with my best friends, and while each and every day seemed to lead us further into uncharted waters, I had no doubt we'd be okay. Even when I noticed Gio glare at where Kingston's hand would linger when he needed to touch me. Or how Kingston's jaw would work when we were in the car and he'd watch Gio pull me into his lap, where I'd begin rocking my hips and getting lost to the sensation of having him throb underneath me.

I caught their glances that they sent to one another as sharp as the knives they always practiced throwing. I felt the tension, and while a better person...a better friend, would do the right thing and step away, I only burrowed deeper. I craved them, individually and explicitly. Gio was the cool breeze on a sweltering summer day, and Kingston was the sun that brought the heat. I needed the warmth as much as I needed the cool relief, but the longer we snuck around our families' backs, the more tenuous things felt.

We'd successfully kept our secret for nearly four months and now, not only had graduation arrived, but with it, the twins' eighteenth birthday. The manor was a buzz this morning with Anna, Taylor and Alex all discussing the party the twins would throw that would include kids from school. I had no idea why it was so important for them to host something that would be so public, but I had to remember that while they lived with us, they weren't held to the same extreme privacy conditions that I was.

Although, in school, they were going under different names so maybe they felt that anonymity was allowed. I also heard the party wouldn't be held in the manor but an older home that still belonged to Juan and Taylor that they occasionally still frequented when they needed a getaway. Apparently, there was a nice sized pool there that the high school kids would all love.

I planned on going, but I was a little frustrated because when we were around school kids, that meant we couldn't be ourselves, and we certainly couldn't act like we knew each other unless they snuck away. I wouldn't be asking them to do that at their own party, and that's what I had to keep in focus. This was their celebration, and it wasn't about me.

Finished with the crowns, I gathered the dejected pieces and tossed them to the side about to stand up when I heard my name being spoken. I was in the garden outside of the twins' kitchen and as I glanced up, I realized their window was open.

"I don't want to tell Kyle because I think he'll overreact," Juan said with a bit of a frustrated sigh.

Taylor turned on the faucet only to turn it off again. "I think this might be something worth an overreaction...they're going to get hurt if they keep this up."

"They can't both be in love with her," Juan stated as a matter-of-fact. It made my heart squeeze tight, my chest aching as though he'd just struck me.

"And why not, there were signs for years that they'd both fall for her," Taylor agreed, but the way her tone shifted made me think she might be upset about the fact that there were signs and they'd either missed them or just hadn't done anything to prevent them.

There was a long silence and then another sigh. "So I tell her father that I found his daughter asleep in my sons' room again. I tell him that Hector caught her sneaking into the locker room with Kingston, or that another person sent me a photo of her kissing Gio? How would you take that information?"

Another long stretch of silence and the entire time my face flushed the hottest it ever had. I couldn't believe they'd caught us. How mortifying.

Taylor walked closer to the window and a few glasses clanked.

"The boys are eighteen now…Presley is only sixteen. We owe it to her parents to include them on what's going on…and let them decide."

A rock fell straight into my stomach as their voices faded and I finally moved from my spot. My knees were covered in dirt; my fingers soiled from the sticks and my heart was bruised.

I knew it seemed impossible to everyone else that I could love two brothers at the same time. That my heart had room for both, but it was true. My heart was split directly down the middle, and while I knew they hadn't said it, I knew they—

My feet ambled to a stop as I made my way around the eastern side of the manor, and through Carter's terrace. Her back door was wide open, and I found her lounging on a reclined patio chair. Fingers still curled around the crowns, I made my way to her and plopped directly in front of her.

Green eyes bounced up from her phone, and then a frown tugged down her beautiful features. "What's wrong, cuz?"

Did I tell her? Would it be so terrible to have someone who could give me some advice, because how did I just now realize the twins had never one time told me this was serious to them? They'd never said they loved me or called me their girlfriend. They never once explained their plans for after graduation or turning eighteen.

I had just been blissfully going along with everything like a bird coasting on a wave, unaware danger lurked beneath me.

"You made the twins birthday crowns?" Carter sat up and pointed at what was in my lap.

I nodded, angling them in the sun. "Do you think it's possible for two people to love the same person?"

Carter inspected me then the crowns, and then set her phone aside. "I think it might depend on how old the people are. I think when people are young, it's hard to know what you really want and what's real versus what's infatuation."

That felt like a cement block to the face.

She was right, and I wasn't sure how to reconcile that. They were turning eighteen…of course they wouldn't want to continue kissing and heavy petting a sixteen-year-old...we couldn't go any further than that for another year and a half anyway...why would they stay with me?

They weren't even technically with me...they were just—

"Guys like to have fun, Presley." Carter reached forward and gently held my hand. I tried not to let my eyes water, but rejection was too close to the surface. My cousin seemed to notice as her tone softened. "Just do me a favor and only have fun in return. Don't give your heart to anyone who hasn't told you they want it. Don't expect anyone to help you achieve your dreams when they haven't asked exactly how they could make them come true. Be picky. You're allowed to have fun too, just don't get stuck."

Carter was as old as the twins, but her birthday was a few months back. Now she was flitting around doing whatever she wanted, with little to no consequences. She was free.

Truly and completely free to be who she wanted, and with whomever she wanted.

"Have you ever been in love?"

My cousin laughed, tilting her head back and everything. "No, and I hope I don't ever fall in love. It sounds exhausting as hell. Do yourself a favor and stay wherever it is Uncle Scotty has you going; at least there, you'll have adventures."

Her phone rang, and before she swiped to answer it, she ruffled my hair and then walked into the house. I sat there for a few more moments, knowing my parents were about to hear that I'd been messing around with both brothers and likely thinking the absolute worst of me. Part of me wanted to run and never see anyone again out of sheer humiliation, but the other part of me wanted the secret to come out.

I wanted everyone to know, but know what?

I'd be mortified if the twins didn't think I was worth being with for good. To keep.

I had to find out what this was to them, and plan for it so I didn't get stuck like Carter said. I needed a plan for the future in case they didn't want to be a part of it.

THE TWINS LOOKED SO GROWN up in their fitted suits.

I watched them move around the room, smiling at everyone who came up and wished them a birthday greeting. Their smiles stretched wider than normal as their friends acknowledged them. Their dark hair was swept back away from their faces, revealing wide jaws, narrow noses and a beauty that made my breath stall. Gio's blue gray eyes were lively and alert, while Kingston's amber ones were reserved and resilient.

I wanted to press pause and study their every move. Draw an image of how they looked in this moment and freeze it forever. It seemed freedom from the mansion and the chains of our upbringing suited them well. We were in Juan and Taylor's secondary home, closer to Pinehurst. It was smaller than the manor, but the pool in back was massive.

Alex and Carter were here too, somewhere, and off along the edges of the property were Juan's men, patrolling and watching. This was merely an illusion of freedom; our parents' enemies would always be watching no matter what we did.

With no parents here, and no one watching closely, it allowed me to float aimlessly around the party and not think about how I was going to explain what I'd decided to confess to the twins. I had rehearsed what I'd say, and even now as I felt my skirt twirl around my ankles as I walked around the home, I mouthed each word to myself.

Carter caught my eye from across the room and lifted her Solo cup as a way of saying hello. I lifted mine in reply but kept walking. I wound around couches with couples kissing, people jumping into the pool and clouds of smoke. There was a game of beer pong I skirted just in time to avoid being hit, then I found my way to the stairs.

I was getting tired, and I felt weird wearing heels, so my plan was to find a bedroom and take them off while I waited. The second I found a room at the end of the hall, I felt two pairs of hands at my back, pushing me inside.

"Elvis, you look fucking gorgeous," Gio rasped, before placing a kiss to my neck.

Kingston shut the door and tugged my wrist, forcing me to face him. "You do look stunning, *mi reina*, but take those shoes off, you must be miserable."

I was miserable, but only because of how hard my heart rapped against my breast and how unfair it was that it had chosen the two of them to fall in love with. Still, I bent down and slipped off my shoes and allowed my bare toes to press against the soft carpet.

"Happy Birthday!" I flung my arms around Kingston's neck and relished how he picked me up and carried me to the bed.

Gio was unbuttoning his suit jacket as he jumped on the bed, forcing both me and King to dip toward him. Then I was sandwiched between them while they both took a hand and kissed it.

"How's your birthday going?" I asked, staring up at the ceiling with a lazy smile.

They both made a humming sound before Gio replied, "Better now."

"Much better now," King added before tugging a piece of my hair up and looping it around his finger.

I needed to say it before I chickened out; I had to ask them. I needed to ask them more than I needed my next breath, but fear had me biting my lip.

"What is this, what are you hiding?" Gio asked, gently tugging my lip free before bending over to kiss it.

I let out a shuddery breath. "I need to ask you guys something."

Gio's gaze was loaded and full of concern. Kingston's was pure fire as he stared down at me. The bass from their party seemed to be a heartbeat between the walls, reminding me I was keeping them from their friends, but selfishly not caring at all.

Moving up to my elbows and then sitting up, I tugged each of their hands into my lap before gaining the courage needed. "How do you feel about me?"

Gio was the first to dip his brows in question. "What do you mean?"

"You're our best friend," Kingston started, but I didn't miss how Gio snapped his gaze up to him as if he was worried he'd say something else or too much.

"Just your best friend, or is there anything more?"

Kingston scoffed in frustration. "Of course there's more, Pres. We've been kissing you, nearly fucking you for months now, how could you ask that?"

I felt like I needed to stand so I could gather my thoughts more clearly, but I worried that if I moved, they'd pull me back and I'd start doing exactly what he'd described. Pushing my eyes closed, I moved off the bed and began pacing, and thankfully neither of them stopped me.

"You're eighteen now and I know you likely have things planned. Carter left when she turned eighteen, and I don't expect you guys to wait around for me to become old enough to—"

"Fuck?" Gio asked, ticking his brow up.

My face flushed. "Yeah..."

Kingston lifted his shoulder nonchalantly. "We want to go see Mexico for a bit, but we were going to see if you could come."

I desperately wanted to go with them. I loved Mexico, but I had to wait to make sure this wouldn't just be another memory added to the shattered pieces of my heart that I'd allowed it to endure.

"But, we know Scotty will likely say no," Gio added.

That brought me back down to earth. Right...Scotty.

"I overheard your parents talking..." I started and tried to gauge their reactions, but both were blank slates. "They were talking about me...I guess they saw us together a few times and they plan to tell my parents."

Gio flung himself back onto the bed and groaned. "Shiiiiitttttt."

My heart flipped around in fear. "What's wrong?"

Kingston murmured something before dragging his hands through his hair. "You don't understand...if our parents think there's a chance we'll jeopardize this family or you in some way, then they'll send us away."

"You just said you planned on going away," I pointed out, trying to clarify what exactly was wrong.

"Have your parents talked to you yet?" Gio asked.

I shook my head. "I came straight here after getting dressed at Carter's. I didn't see them."

King still had his hands in his hair, tugging on the ends. "What exactly did they say they saw?"

They were panicked. It was stamped clear as day across their features, and now they resembled animals caught in a trap, desperate to be free of it. And I'd asked them what I meant to them, and they'd said, "Best friend."

I had my answer; I just didn't like it.

Swallowing thickly, I stared at them, feeling my heart thump recklessly behind a bone-weary cage. I was stronger than this. I could withstand more than this. Which was why I decided to expose my heart before them and see what they did.

"I love you."

Both their eyes rapidly bounced up, landing on me in a way that I hadn't ever felt before.

My words felt rushed. "Both of you. I'm in love with you and I'm not sure what will happen to us, but I needed you to know where I was—"

"Scotty won't allow you to love us, Pres," Kingston cut me off.

My mouth remained open with the words I had planned on saying, but I shut it and stepped back.

Gio spoke next, further shocking me into silence. "We understood that from the start, Pres. What we're doing...it's fun, but it's not forever. You'll get older, and you'll have to do exactly as he says, and there's nothing we can do about it."

"That's—" My lips suddenly felt so dry they could crack. "That's not true. I have a say...I can do what I want, with who—"

Kingston laughed, shaking his head. "No, you can't. The permanent scars on your knuckles tell a different story. You're chained to the future they planned. We'll always be your friends, Pres. Always, but we knew what this was from the start."

Hot, white anger seemed to burn from my fingers up to my eyes, making them water. How dare they just assume without speaking to me...without allowing me the chance to even say what I wanted in my future.

"So that's what you think of me, that I'll just do whatever he says?"

"It's what you've done your entire life. They'll find out about the fact that you've been double-dipping with the twins down the hall, and they'll freak out, probably send you away. Next thing we know, you'll be married off to some mafia don in an alliance." King flicked his hand as if I were a mere piece of dirt caught under his nail. As if this whole thing were so simple and easy.

Cut. Dry.

Already decided.

My teeth clashed together as I stepped back. "Why go through all of this then, why help me go to school and give me my first kiss? Why bother with giving in—"

Give into what? An urge. Shit...that's all they'd done, wasn't it?

Gio stood and placed his hands on my shoulders, gently, as if I'd break if he pressed too hard. "The truth is, you can't have a first kiss unless it's us. No first date, no first anything unless it's us or someone protected well enough to defend themselves against Scotty. He made sure we'd protect you...he made it a requirement for you to even attend school, didn't he?"

He had. He'd said they would have to go and get their parents' approval.

The memory of the knife in that boy's hand at the ball came rushing back...

"You stabbed that boy at the ball because Scotty told you to, didn't you?"

Kingston dipped his chin. "He never told me to stab anyone, but he did tell us if we were bothered by your lack of protection detail to fulfill the role ourselves."

"Still, he ordered you to go to school with me..."

Had he told them to kiss me? My stomach soured instantly.

"He never told us to do what we did, as far as the car goes. We only sabotaged your relationships, so no one ever got close to you."

The air felt too hot. Too suffocating. I pulled out of Gio's hold and brought my hand to my stomach, and the other to my face, trying to piece together what that meant.

"I came to you, crying. Upset...." I heaved in a breath and tried to remember all the boys I'd thought might like me or be my friend, only to have them treat me like I had some infectious disease the next time I encountered them.

My eyes found theirs. "You humored me...pitied me. You took my first kiss because—"

Kingston stood, working his jaw. "You gave us that first kiss and all the ones after, you gave us your body, your skin, your heart. Fuck, you're two seconds from tossing your soul at our feet right now."

I was going to be sick. "You never cared about me, did you?"

Gio barked out an incredulous laugh. "Care about you? That's all we've done since the moment you existed for us, Pres. We've only ever cared about you. We're obsessed with you. Probably in love with you, but we won't ever allow ourselves to have that because you were never ours to keep. You were always going to be Scotty's chess piece to move around when he saw fit."

"So you used me? Took what you could get and now you'll toss me away?"

Kingston grabbed my wrist and pulled me closer. "We won't ever do that, but the reality is, we can't have you."

"Why not?!" I yelled, using my free fist to pound it against his chest.

I glared over at Gio and blinked away angry tears. "Why won't you fight for me? Why are you just accepting that this is how it'll be? How come you can let me go so easily when you're both ingrained in me so deeply I won't ever be over you?"

My face was wet and hot as angry tears slipped over my cheek and down my nose.

"You will be, one day there will be someone—"

"Stop it!" I pushed against Kingston again, this time gaining space. "Fight for me, tell me we have a future. Tell me you'll build the farmhouse with me, and you'll plant my marigolds. Tell me we'll star gaze at night in the field, and we'll be together, always. We'll know peace and we'll allow our bruises to heal and our hearts to mend. We'll forget the blood-soaked path that led us here, and we'll start over. Tell me there's hope."

Gio cut in and his mocking tone was another invisible gash in my heart. "And what, you'll marry us both, whose baby will you carry? Will you put up a sleeping chart for us, whose bed you'll go to, on which night?"

I blinked at him, my lashes soaked and clumpy with running mascara. "We would make it work. All of it. In time, if we had each other—"

"See, that's just it." Gio stepped closer, his cool eyes burning hot in a way that made me worry. "I don't want to share my forever with you even if it is with my twin brother. I want you for myself. I want you in my bed, carrying my kid, with my ring on your finger. That's the future I want. But I have to share you, Elvis. With this future you already accepted, with my twin who has the other half of your heart. I only have part of you, and because of that, you can't ever have all of me. I need to let you go as badly as you need to release me."

I didn't realize my head was shaking, but wetness hit my numb arms, and I realized tears had fallen from how hard I was denying this truth he'd given me.

I stupidly assumed they didn't mind me sharing their hearts.

I'd had my fingers around both since before I knew I was in love with them, and now they were prying my hands away, one digit at a time. I felt like I couldn't breathe.

"So that's it. You turn eighteen and let me go?"

Gio tried to pull me closer, but I put my hand up, preventing it.

"No. We turn eighteen and we wait around for Scotty to tell us to fuck off. We keep doing what we're doing, and eventually one day, King and I, we'll find a way to move on."

With my throat burning, and my voice trembling, I managed to form one last thing. "I wish you'd find a way to choose me, to fight for me. I wish you'd find a way to make room for this because it could have been beautiful and perfect. I wish you weren't such cowards."

With that, I spun on my heel and ran out of the room and darted down the stairs. I ran with tears blurring my vision until I found Carter, and then with her arm around me, tucked close to her side, I went home.

CHAPTER 30
GIO
AGE 18

I stared at my brother as he hung his head and propped his elbows on his knees. We were both simmering after Presley left, unsure how we'd go back to a party celebrating us. It was all just a ruse, a way for us to be alone with Presley, maybe dance with her and not have anyone question why. Our hope was to find her in here and convince her to spend time with us downstairs after Carter and our big sister left.

I love you.

"We need to go after her," I muttered quietly, a knot forming in my throat.

The look on her face, the way she dug into our chests and didn't see what we were hiding from her. Of course we loved her back; we'd both been in love with her for longer than either of us understood. We were completely undone by her and she stood there accepting the trivial truths we tossed at her as a way to guard our own emotions.

Kingston's eyes were red as he looked up at me. "And say what? We did the right thing...we can head off, let things cool down for a few weeks and come back with a new plan."

"What plan could possibly undo what we just did to her?"

My twin suddenly stood and yelled in my face. "We had no other option but to release her. The shit's about to hit the fan the second we get home. You know I'm right."

Deep down I did.

We'd tasted forbidden fruit, now we'd be held accountable for it. Our time in Eden was over.

WE ARRIVED HOME AN HOUR LATER, leaving our party early and asking all of our guests to leave. Our shirts were untucked as our heads hung low and we made our way into our living room.

Sure enough, our dad was waiting for us, so were Kyle and Scotty.

I inhaled a sharp breath as I stared at the duffle bags on the floor, packed and ready to go.

"What's going on?" I asked, eyeing the men in the room.

Kingston froze once he caught sight of the bags.

Dad let out a heavy sigh before standing. "I warned you both when you were younger that you couldn't interfere with Presley's training."

"We haven't," Kingston snapped.

Kyle glared at us as if we were enemies of his. "She came home tonight and explained that she's done training. Done with everything."

Shit.

King glanced at me, and I stared back.

"We're aware of what's transpired between you...she fell for you both, and you each allowed it. She's in a dangerous position to have her heart broken," Scotty explained calmly.

"We would never—" I started, but Scotty suddenly stood.

"You already did!" He pointed at me, glaring murderously. "You acted as protector but decided you'd slip into her heart and play thief instead. She is too young to be loved by either of you, much less both.”

My brother scoffed, tossing his suit jacket to the ground. “So what, you’re sending us away?”

Our dad’s jaw tensed as his red-rimmed eyes seized us. Something dark and dangerous swept through me, seeing him inspect us the way he was. As if we were the problem and not the reason Presley had hope. The reason she could dream and still be a girl who opened her heart for love.

“I warned you.”

“Fuck this, we aren’t going!” Kingston roared.

Kyle yelled back, “You are! She needs space, and you will give it to her or I will remove her from your life and you will never find her again.”

My heart lurched at the prospect of losing her and never finding her again. I examined Scotty, seeing the truth in Kyle’s words. His uncle would do it...he’d take her and hide her away, regardless of what she wanted.

“And if she refuses to train even after we leave?”

Scotty replied, “Then we’ll respect it, but I already know she’ll be back in that sparring ring the very next day. Give her time to work through the idea that you two could actually be her future.”

Sorrow apparently had sharp talons and teeth that could cut through skin and bone because fuck it hurt to hear him say that. I wanted to give her the future she asked for, but she tethered it to us both and I didn’t want to share her. I refused to, even if it was with my twin.

I stepped forward first and dipped down to grab the strap of my duffel bag.

“Where are we going?”

My father’s arms were tight across his chest, but as he stared at me, I saw his chin tremble. “Mexico, you’ll stay with family for a month or two. Then you’ll both come back and we’ll deal with what’s in front of us. Just take some space.”

Slinging the bag over my shoulder, I turned back toward the hall. "I have a few things to collect."

My twin didn't move. His fists curled at his sides as he held Kyle's angry stare.

"What will you tell her?"

"That's no longer your concern. *She* is no longer your concern."

"*She's* our best friend. You can't pretend our past didn't happen. She's a part of me as much as Gio is, or Alex. I want to know what you'll tell her." King's voice cracked, which made my chest ache.

Scotty smirked and threw his arms open. "Feel free to text her. Call her. She'll still be available to you to contact. We'll tell her tomorrow that you've left."

I spoke up, clarifying, "She thinks we're leaving tomorrow evening."

Kyle glanced at Scotty who gave us another reassuring smile. "I'll let her know first thing in the morning that you had to leave sooner. She'll understand. Trust me, nothing will happen to your friendship."

Kingston finally stepped up and picked up his duffle bag. "You'll tell us if she's in any danger, or you need us?"

"I doubt anything will happen in a mere two months, but yes, I promise I will let you know if there's ever any danger."

That was all we could ask for.

Alex suddenly appeared in the hall, and I walked into her arms and hugged her goodbye. My mother was there next, her blue silk robe had a hole in the pocket from when we'd used it for part of our pillow fort. Seeing her wear it made my eyes burn. Presley was the one who'd used it as a pretend sail.

"I love you," Mom whispered while holding the back of my head.

Dad came up and clapped my back before saying, "Be careful...it's easy to get lost out there once you leave home, even if it's for a small amount of time. Remember where you're anchored."

I gave him a firm nod, trying to make room for love instead of the burning anger simmering in my chest. I hated that he was sending us away, forcing it. We were going to leave anyway, but on our own terms, and we wanted to take Presley with us.

"I love you, Son." Dad hugged me and I wrapped my arms around him, wishing I could go back in time to when I was younger. Back to when I had a chance to brand myself on Presley. I would have made her fall in love with just me, and I'd never have to risk losing her to Scotty or Kingston.

She'd be mine and only mine.

I already prepared in my head what I'd say to her in the call I'd make tomorrow. I'd make sure she understood we'd be back, and this was only temporary.

Frustration burned under my chest, reminding me I had no other choice and that I could only hope she saw this the way we wanted her to. If she didn't...then we'd ruined the best thing that ever happened to us.

CHAPTER 31
PRESLEY
PRESENT

The manor felt different.

Each morning, I'd grown used to the quiet of the house that extended past my front door. I'd walk the empty halls, knowing the only sound to be heard would be the clicking of Reaper's nails as he trailed behind me.

Otherwise, it was peaceful.

Tucking my favorite book under my arm, I walked through the illuminated room and curled up on one of the leather couches. My mind was full of confusing thoughts and worries about what the day would bring. I'd spoken to Adrian the night prior and had convinced him to come visit. There was a burden on my shoulders to ensure our families maintained peace, but something kept looping in my mind. The twins saying they'd had business with him...the way they'd found where Adrian lived.

The extra men they traveled with.

All of it was odd to me.

I had just cracked the binding open of my book when I heard people cheering from the home gym.

I snapped the book shut and tilted my head, curious why there'd be so much commotion this early in the morning. It was only seven thirty, and while I knew most of Scotty's men liked to run the property at this time, not many of them used the gym.

My curiosity won out as I clutched the book and wandered down the hall. The sound only grew louder as I took the stairs down to the gym and pushed through the doors.

Men and women I'd seen protect the perimeter all cheered for whomever was in the middle of the ring. Most were familiar faces, but I realized there were several new people that had arrived with the twins. I still assumed they were attached to El Peligro somehow, but I wasn't exactly sure why they were here or how the boys had convinced them to travel with them.

Finding an opening in the people cluttered around the center, I finally saw who the focus of their cheering was.

A silent gasp escaped me as I watched the twins moving around the circle. It wasn't even that they were using moves I'd only witnessed in advanced MMA fighters, but their chests were more defined than they were almost two years ago. They had definition in places I wasn't even sure was possible; their abs had mini abs and over each ridge and groove was dark ink.

They'd gotten so many tattoos; my eyes jumped around, trying to land on where to start.

Gio had small text tattooed into his forearms, and across his chest were various symbols, images of a church, a cross, and...I narrowed my eyes on the black heart that dripped with ink... It was something similar I'd seen on Juan's chest, except his heart wasn't cut in half, and there were three smaller ones inked below his primary tattoo.

My gaze jumped to Kingston and sure enough his dripping black heart was also cut in half. They both had at least one marigold inked somewhere on their bodies. Gio had a few star systems I recognized, inked all along the expanse of his back, and Kingston had skulls with plants growing out of their heads. He had flowers dying inked all over his chest, but the marigold was alive. I found "Elvis" inked in cursive on Gio's chest, under his heart.

I was so focused on their ink that I completely missed that their fighting had upgraded to include knives. Gio threw one at his brother and it landed swiftly in the mat underneath him, just barely missing his calf. The crowd roared and I jumped back as reality came rushing back in.

What the fuck were they doing?

Gio rushed forward with his own large, serrated knife, holding it sideways as if he were about to lunge at his twin, but Kingston quickly sidestepped him. Both boys had sweat dripping down their faces and along their arms. Seeing them like that, with their raven hair messy and cutting into their eyes, their gorgeous brown skin accented with the black ink and defined muscles, they were mesmerizing. It made a simmering heat begin to build and pool somewhere low in my belly. Gio caught on that I was watching first, if his smirk was any indication.

Kingston shifted and caught me as well, then bounced on the balls of his feet, swiping his arm across his face.

"Wanna join us, *Elvis*?"

The group around them glanced at me, which made that heat inside rise to my face.

"I think she's too scared now that we're on her level of training. She's too nervous to face us," Gio sneered, while tossing his knife from one hand to another.

Is that what they'd been doing with their time away? They'd been training like I had been? Their bodies certainly showed it, as well as their precision with the blade.

I wouldn't be giving them the satisfaction of—

"Come on, Presley. Or have you grown soft in the time we were gone? Too many nights in Italy?"

"I need a knife for it to be fair." I tossed my book down and pulled my baggy T-shirt over my head, leaving me in my sports bra. My pajama shorts were long enough that I could move freely without feeling uncomfortable, so all I had left to do to prepare was pull my hair into a ponytail and stretch.

Gio glanced at his brother briefly before tossing his knife out of the ring.

"No weapons."

I shrugged. "Shame."

Then I lunged forward and kneed him in the abdomen before kicking back and landing a hit to Kingston's side. The cheering resumed as we fell into a dance where the twins would take turns delivering a hit, kick or try putting me on my back. I deflected and sank my foot into their sides more times than they probably liked, but I knew they were moving slow for me. Slower than they needed to.

"What's wrong, afraid you'll piss me off by beating me?" I smiled, tossing out a punch then moving my head to duck Gio's return.

"No. Just don't like the idea of bruising you," Gio rasped, which told me he was starting to get tired.

I spun and focused on Kingston.

"I know you can go faster; I just watched you take down your—"

Within a single breath, Kingston had moved and wrapped his calf around mine and yanked me to the mat. He managed to cradle my head, but his arm was locked over my collarbone, and his hips straddled mine. Our chests rose and fell in heavy thuds as we stared at one another.

His amber eyes were the same, and as he stared into mine, I knew he was thinking the same thing. I wanted to freeze the moment and force him to tell me why they'd stayed away for so long. I knew they planned to leave after their birthday, but they'd said a few months.

They never once said they'd stay gone for a year and a half.

My eyes caught on a set of text across his ribs that read, *"I'll carry the soil of your heart inside of mine, my very own jar of sunshine."*

Those words, it was worse than the hurtful things he'd said when I was sixteen. The false hope. Anger began unfurling in me as I watched his face lower to mine, and instead of allowing him any more space, I threw my free leg up and used it to yank his torso sideways until I was free. I needed to stop this, getting close to them and feeling them touch me wasn't a good idea. I needed to focus on Adrian.

Stepping out of the ring, I ducked to get my book and my shirt as people began making disappointed sounds and dispersing. I held the focus of both brothers as I slowly exited the gym, slinking back over to my side of the manor and as far away from them as I could possibly get.

"ADRIAN HAS a yacht he'd like to take us all on," I explained to my father and my uncle.

They both glanced at each other before replying to me, so I took a second to check with my mom. She gave me a warm smile and small nod, which I took as a good sign. My plan with this was to only take my dad, uncle and mom. That way, we kept the chances of anything negative happening to a minimum.

"He invited us to go out on the boat tomorrow, but I'd like to keep it small, and I don't really think there's any reason to involve everyone in the manor or to—"

"Does that include me?" Carter suddenly appeared near our foyer, making her way into our living room.

"Sorry, your door was unlocked." She popped her gum, then tossed her thick hair over her shoulder. She looked so much like my aunt Mallory sometimes, it shocked me, but her jawline was completely Uncle Decker.

Scotty's expression was ice cold as he replied, "But not open."

Carter ignored him and curled up on the couch. "Can I come?"

She was missing the fact that I had to even entertain this idea because of her. She'd put us at risk, and now I was the one fixing the mess, but at the same time, she was family, and her big personality filled the gaps and any awkward silences there might be.

With a resigned sigh, I said, "Fine. You can come but no one else unless your parents suddenly show up. They can come but otherwise, don't talk about our plans outside of this room."

My cousin placed her hand to her forehead and gave me a salute. "You got it."

She remained in our living room, playing on her phone while we continued to talk about the details of where we'd meet Adrian and exactly how we'd eventually be welcoming him over for dinner, but we'd build up to that.

My dad wasn't exactly happy, but he agreed to entertain this idea that I could confirm that Adrian was our ally and not double-crossing us, and that he had nothing nefarious planned. Deep down, I knew he wanted more with me, which meant he'd protect my family. At this rate with the hornets' nest that Carter stirred, this was what we had to settle for.

A tiny ping rattled in my chest, reminding me of the sixteen-year-old girl who once swore this wasn't the sort of future I'd settle for. I pushed the feeling down and changed into my work clothes. I had a raggedy pair of overalls I wore with a ribbed tank and my Converse platforms that kept me comfortable while working on the farmhouse.

The sun battled the lingering fog that clung to the trees lining the path between our properties. I was still mad at my dad for not joining the two properties with a bridge or a paved path. Dad owned the farmhouse, along with the two other properties nearest to us. Most of them were empty, save for security teams who remained with us long-term. But he'd promised me the farmhouse would one day be mine if I wanted it. All I had to do was restore it, and then use my own funds to buy it from him.

I checked the Zillow rating, and unfortunately the land alone placed it at almost a million dollars, so there was no chance of that happening any time soon, unless I started making my own money outside of my parents and the various plans Scotty had for my future.

That same sour feeling from before returned as I cleared the last small hill between the manor and farmhouse. I hadn't thought about what I'd said to the twins that night on their birthday in so long, sometimes it felt like a dream. One where they broke my heart, and I tucked all the pieces away inside of a book then secured it with a golden heart locket never to be opened again.

The barn caught my attention first as I descended the small patch of weeds and cleared the first fence. The farmhouse was second, rotting boards and dilapidated windows and all. It was old and gross, but with some renovations, it would one day be gorgeous. Tugging on my thick work gloves, I carefully made my way up the rickety porch and inside the house.

The pile of wood that I had waiting for me in the middle of the primary room was gone. That would have taken hours to clear. I glanced around the rest of the space, confused at how it was already done when a silhouette from the far room caught my eye.

"Shit," I gasped as Gio came into view. "You scared me."

Gio gave me a smirk that was familiar and yet so different. He had changed, and I couldn't quite pinpoint in which ways, but I felt like he was someone else entirely, parading around wearing my best friend's face.

"Knew I'd find you here."

I returned to the lack of walls in front of me. I needed to start replacing the gaps. "Did you clear out all the rotting wood?"

He smiled and ducked back into the room, bringing a red wheelbarrow. "Had to get back to helping you with the farmhouse."

The memory of his birthday surfaced, how he made me feel like dreaming about this farmhouse and us living inside of it was silly. That it would never happen.

I began yanking out boards and tossing them behind me. "Why are you here?"

Gio let out a small laugh. "Because I'm helping you."

I stopped and faced him, tearing off my gloves. "Why are you here, Giovanni? You left me for a year and a half and only returned because Scotty demanded that you did. Why. Are. You. Here?"

His fingers loosened around the board he pulled loose, and he let it fall to the ground, sending up a flare of golden dust.

"You going to ask why we were gone for so long?" His eyes searched mine and I had to adjust to what it felt like to have them on me again. It felt like it had been an eternity, and yet, it was as if no time had passed at all.

I shook my head and started pulling boards into my arms again. "You must have had your reasons."

He hummed while he watched me move around the room. "We did."

I didn't reply to him, but my movements became jerky and rushed as I yanked up boards, which resulted in a nail puncturing my finger.

"Ouch. Shit," I hissed while dropping the boards.

Gio stepped closer, pulling my hand into his. "Let me see."

"No. It's fine. You should go." I punched out each word between clenched teeth.

My hand was tugged into his, and he saw the blood pooling at the tip. I watched with rapt attention as he slowly brought my finger to his mouth and instead of sucking on the tip, he smeared it over his bottom lip. My eyes met his hooded ones as his tongue darted out and licked up the redness left behind.

I didn't move, and barely breathed, as I watched him lean forward and claim my finger with his mouth, fully enveloping it with a heavy suck and then gentle lap at the end. I didn't realize he was holding my wrist, or that he'd pulled me so close our faces nearly touched.

It wasn't until I felt his breath touch my mouth as he whispered, "My back."

"What?" I asked, staring at his mouth.

"There's a mark for every single day I was away from you. I had someone there that made it look like one big constellation. It represents you, and our sky that we were always supposed to share."

My breath caught in my chest as a violent heat rushed through me, warning me not to get too close. He'd break me again.

I stepped away from him, and he released me.

"I need to get back." I cleared my throat, desperate to have the burning in my eyes not turn into tears.

"We didn't have a choice that night, Elvis," Gio called at my back.

I paused in the threshold for only a second, needing to hear what else he had to say.

"The night of our birthday…we came home to an ambush. We weren't given a choice, and Scotty lied to us. Told us you'd get our texts and our calls. He said he'd tell you first thing the next morning that we had left."

I spun around; a sob caught in my throat. "I waited outside of your house for hours. No one told me that you'd already left. You didn't call or text me."

He stepped closer. "Yes, we did. I did…it was you who never texted or called. If you had, then you'd know we'd been reaching out."

"I was devasted. You'd told me you were leaving…the last thing I wanted to do was annoy you by texting and calling you. You made it clear what the future would hold for us."

He was getting closer, and my hands began to tremble. "Well, maybe I made a mistake, Presley. Maybe I messed up and haven't stopped regretting it ever since."

My chin fell to my chest and a single tear slipped down my cheek. "Maybe I'd believe that if you weren't forced back by Scotty."

My feet moved on autopilot, carrying me down the steps and through the yard until I was running back to the safety of the manor.

CHAPTER 32

KINGSTON

PRESENT

The sun glittered along the water, making the massive thirty-three-foot boat stand out like a sore thumb. I grabbed my bag, and Gio slammed the truck door on the other side.

"Think we'll get shot on sight?"

I pulled my sunglasses on and smirked. "Probably."

"I think Elvis loves us too much to let us get shot." My brother sighed while walking toward the dock. We'd beaten Presley here, so there was no way we'd miss them, but she was going to be pissed the second she realized how easy it was to overhear Carter sharing her plans with my sister.

"You think there's a chance she still loves us?"

I didn't want to think about what she'd said last night or consider that she'd moved on from us. "You can't erase what we had that easily. I think she's angry that she still loves us."

Scotty's SUV pulled up across the parking lot, and I saw Presley climb out. Her hair was braided into a crown again, with little pieces framing her face. I strangled the strap of my duffel bag as I watched her walk in a bathing suit cover-up, which didn't really cover

235

anything up at all. Her tits were visible from here under that scrap of fabric. Carter followed her, wearing something similar, but it didn't feel as revealing, nor did it make my stomach tighten when I looked at her.

"Do you think this will help win her over or make things worse?" Gio asked, walking ahead of me.

I didn't reply, just followed him. Kyle, Rylie and Scotty trailed after the two girls.

Scotty wore board shorts and flip-flops, which made me laugh even though I'd seen him on beaches before. There was something so unserious about seeing him like this, like I could finally try and take the fucker out or at least sneak in a punch.

He probably knew we were on his tail. Wasn't like we were trying to hide it, but the fact that he hadn't turned around and told us to stay meant he didn't really mind having us along. Which meant he didn't trust Presley's claim that Adrian was safe and wanted peace.

Interesting.

Why would he entertain this idea of peace if he didn't believe it were possible? He was risking the entire family by agreeing to this. He also didn't have the same intel that my brother and I had, which was that Adrian's brothers were a far greater threat than he was. They also weren't the type to cater to a love match, or any alliance Adrian created. Which is why we considered him a threat. He didn't have any choice but to bow to the majority rule of his brothers, and if they wanted a bullet in Presley's head, then he'd pull the trigger.

The yacht appeared at the end of the dock, and two men flanked Adrian as he walked toward Presley. The two were still quite a bit ahead of us, but as I looked up my feet faltered.

Gio's didn't, but I saw his head dip. "Don't fucking show it, King."

I forced my feet forward as Presley and Adrian kissed, and he wrapped his arms around her, pulling her under his arm like she'd been there since the day she'd walked out of ours.

My brother was right; we couldn't show how that affected us. We had a lot to make up for, but more than that, we needed to find a way to explain to her what our world existed of now. It was a much different place than when she was last inside of it.

It wasn't until Adrian, Presley, and her parents were on board that Presley finally turned around and realized we were boarding as well.

"Gio. Kingston." Her surprised reaction had Adrian placing his hand on her hip while twisting to see us.

"Boys...how nice of you to join us."

Boys? Fucker was one year older than us, if that.

Gio grinned and walked through his security team like he owned the boat.

"How incredibly kind of you to invite Presley's family."

Presley's face remained pleasant as if this was all a happy encounter, but I saw the way her left eyebrow twitched and raised as if it were her only way to scream that we weren't supposed to be there.

Scotty made room for us on the leather seats in the center, while Kyle merely glared, but with his sunglasses on, I couldn't make out his narrowed eyes or his pissed-off expression. I knew him well enough to know he was angry though.

Yet not a single soul here would say anything because our family could never afford to look weak in front of one as prominent or as dangerous as Adrian's. Gio and I knew this, and we exploited it.

"Such a warm day for March," I mused, settling into the plush leather.

The security team worked to bring a few trays of food on, along with prepping the boat for pushing away from the dock. One of his men sat behind the steering wheel, wearing cotton pants with a silencer parked at his hip.

"This is my father, Kyle, and my mother, Rylie," Presley introduced her parents, and it rubbed me wrong that she didn't use their typical fake names, that he was safe enough to at least share that. Adrian shook their hands and smiled warmly.

"And of course, you know my uncle," Presley introduced Scotty.

Presley moved over to her cousin, Carter, making small talk with Adrian when the boat started moving and the three of them made their way over to where the rest of the family was seated. The warm spring air blew through my hair as I watched Presley place her hand inside of Adrian's. My heart twisted in my chest, but I remembered my brother's words and tamped down any reaction.

"Mr. and Mrs. James, I just wanted to thank you for accepting today's invitation and allowing me the opportunity to meet you. Carter, Scotty, same with you. I know you each hold such a significant place in Presley's life, and I wanted to finally meet the people responsible for raising her."

A muscle in Gio's jaw feathered as Presley's gaze landed on us as heavy as one of those weighted blankets we once tried using to build a fort. We were maybe six and seven, with no clue as to why that shit was so heavy. Convinced Pres that it had come from space.

The memory had me smiling, which had Presley tilting her head.

"We're happy this worked out; we've heard so much about you throughout the year and Presley is gone so often visiting you. It only made sense that we finally made this happen." Kyle smiled brightly at the mafia don.

Rylie gave him a fake smile while pushing her shades back into her hair. "Yes, although I'm curious how much Presley has told you about us. I'm worried you might have something built up in your mind."

Adrian's face flushed the smallest bit before taking a seat in one of the leather chairs. The boat was hitting some choppy waters, but we could barely feel a thing. The wind tossed Adrian's hair back as Presley passed him to sit next to Carter, but he tugged her wrist and pulled her into his lap.

"Presley has told me that you're all very close. Rylie, she talks about how protective and funny you are. She's very grateful she has you. Scotty, she mentioned similar sentiments of you, that you're tough but fair and would do anything for the people you love. Carter, she's even told me about your parents, and how fond she is of your father, Decker, and mother, Mallory."

Rylie's countenance shifted the smallest bit with something that seemed like surprise. I was shocked too...she'd told him a lot. More than I expected of her with all her training.

Adrian's finger skimmed Presley's tanned thigh, and I nearly bit my tongue clean in half.

"What has she said about us?" I asked, giving the couple a beaming smile.

Adrian gave us more of a smirk than a real smile as he cleared his throat. "Brothers, I think...best way to describe it, although she mentioned you had a falling out of sorts, right? Which was why I was so surprised to see you arriving today."

I opened my mouth, but it was Scotty who spoke up, surprising me.

"Can't really have a falling out with family, not when they're the closest people in your life. Gio and Kingston are just as much as family as I am or even her parents. Something you should know about her is they come as a package deal."

Presley laughed good-naturedly, which had everyone else joining in, but I knew what Scotty was trying to warn. Her family would always be present, and taking her away from us wouldn't end well for him.

"Should we swim?" Presley suggested, popping up out of his lap.

Carter jumped up, setting her drink down. Apparently, someone on the boat was making cocktails and she'd found one.

"Yes!"

Music played softly so it wasn't obnoxious but still loud enough that it muffled conversations. Scotty remained on the boat, with a hat on his balding head and a whiskey in his glass. Rylie and Kyle were in the water, swimming, looking as in love and annoying as my parents always did. Carter was on board, flirting with one of Adrian's security team, and Presley was laughing...a fucking lot.

But it wasn't the laugh that I knew. It was lighter, like she'd taken the tinkling sound she used to make, ground it into dust and that was what escaped her when she opened those lips. It made me ache in an odd way. I felt something strange, as if I could capture the dust and hold it tightly enough to get her old laugh back.

I was sitting next to my brother facing the rear of the boat so we had a perfect view of everyone in the water. My reason for sitting was the semi I was sporting due to Presley slipping out of her swim cover and revealing her body in a white bikini. Her body had changed over the years. Every time she'd pull herself up on the ladder to the boat, her nipples would be hard and pushing against the fabric of her bikini top; the water glistening on her skin also made her chilled, and all I wanted to do was wrap her in a blanket each and every time she came up. I also wanted to touch her and skim each place that looked different than before.

Presley had just jumped back into the water when Adrian suddenly appeared next to where we were sitting. Dripping wet, he wore a pair of black board shorts, and his chest looked like he spent just about as much time in the gym as we did.

"She's beautiful, no?" Adrian asked, keeping his eyes on Presley.

She dipped her head back into the water then laughed at something her dad said.

Gio cleared his throat. "She's family."

"But not blood, correct?"

I smirked up at him, making sure he knew the things we weren't saying. "No. Not blood."

The unspoken challenge and confirmation that he was likely struggling with had his nose flaring the smallest bit.

"You may have known her all her life, but you haven't been around the past year. She's no longer your tagalong friend."

Gio sipped his water, keeping his gaze straight. "What exactly is it you think she is to you, Adrian?"

The man who led an entire outfit in Italy smiled deviously. "She's mine."

I tipped my head back and laughed. This poor fucker had it bad for her, but he had no idea who she even was.

"She ever tell you where those scars on her knuckles and her side came from?"

Adrian shifted the smallest bit, hand on his hip while his eyes remained on the water. He didn't reply though, which felt like a victory.

"Darn, guess she really has told you everything then," I replied, dryly.

Gio shook his head, a smile plastered on his face.

"You assume she hasn't been honest with me, but I know everything important about her."

"Yeah, what's her favorite flower?" Gio asked.

Why we were entertaining this, I had no idea, especially when we already knew she hadn't told him the truth. She didn't trust him enough.

I felt pride fill my chest the slightest bit that we knew her, and he didn't.

Until his reply hit me.

"Marigolds. She likes how they remind her of sunshine and fire all at once. She wants a whole farm of them."

With that, he walked away and jumped into the water. Then the fucker pulled Presley against his chest and kissed her.

"I can't do much more of this," I muttered quietly to my brother.

He nodded silently.

We both got up and wandered below deck where a few bedrooms were located, a secondary living room and a kitchen. Once we discovered a card game being played with a few of the staff, we joined in to pass the time.

Gio had just won an entire bag of Oreos with a victorious shout when Presley appeared in the doorway of the kitchen.

"Kingston, Gio, can I talk to you guys, please?"

The chef grabbed the deck of cards and started dispersing them to the other three staff members while my brother grabbed his prize and I trailed after him.

Gio had a cookie already in his mouth when we entered the hall, but before we could even ask what she wanted, she was pushing us into a bedroom.

"Hey!" I whispered while Gio made a muffled sound against being mauled by her.

She shut and locked the door then spun on us.

"What the fuck are you two doing?"

Gio continued eating his cookie while I stared at her. She was mostly dry now, but her hair was still wet, and little strands curled against her neck. Her skin was a warm tan from the sun, freckles appeared on her shoulder blades and across her nose. Her dark brows arched over blue eyes and thick lashes made her seem older than just eighteen. She looked so different yet the same as she always had. That mouth was the same, those lips and that chin...

"I'm eating my winnings," my brother said, interrupting my thoughts.

I let out a sigh, knowing what she was actually asking and not having the patience for games. "We overheard Carter talking and wanted to join. What's the problem?"

Her angry expression only worsened as she stepped closer to us then lowered her voice to a whisper. "The problem is, I don't want you here."

Gio smirked then tossed the bag of cookies onto the guest bed. The shade was drawn, so there was only a limited amount of light in the room.

"You know, Elvis...I'm starting to feel like you don't even want to be friends anymore and that's super shitty of you."

She shook her head as her nose flared. "It was shitty of you when you left without so much as a goodbye, then stayed gone for almost two years."

"We weren't given the chance to say goodbye to you. I told you that," Gio snapped irritably.

Presley's fists curled at her sides, and her chin lifted. "If the roles were reversed, I would have done anything to get to you. I would have ruined my future if it meant I could have kept what we had." Her voice cracked, and it only reminded me how much we'd fucked up...but we weren't ready for her to make that choice. Not then, and she was barely ready to make that choice now.

"So we just aren't allowed to be around you?" I challenged, raising my brow.

She turned the smallest amount of pink, and I loved getting to see her chest rise and fall so easily. Her tits kept pushing against that fabric of her swimsuit, and all I wanted to do was trace my tongue over the swell of her breast.

"I'm not saying that, but I don't want you here when I need to focus on protecting this alliance."

I stepped forward. "What happened to the girl who swore this wouldn't be in her future, the one who said she'd never blindly follow Scotty's orders?"

Rage burned in those irises, and it gave me pause. Was there something I was missing here?

Presley's chin quivered. "You missed a lot while you were on vacation, including the moment I got over you both."

"If you're over us, then why do you care if we're here?" Gio taunted, licking his fingers of cookie crumbs.

She scoffed and rubbed at her forehead. "Because if I can feel you watching me, then so can Adrian."

"Wouldn't it only help things along if he believes he has competition?" I asked playfully.

"Stop being idiots."

Gio started toward her other side as I carefully stepped closer. "Adrian seems to think this thing with you is serious. But he also thinks we've fucked or have at least fooled around. You tell him anything?"

"Of course not..." She paused and then bit her lip. "I told him you abandoned me, but I only ever explained that we were best friends."

"He's extremely threatened by us."

Pres let out a heavy sigh like this was taking all her energy. "I highly doubt that."

"Why? You don't think we're intimidating enough to mess with a man like that?" I asked, but I partially didn't want to hear the answer.

She tossed her shoulders back. "I think if Adrian wanted to kill you, he would. And guess what? There's nothing I could do to stop him because we aren't even close to being in a position to defy him or pick a fight with him. Please don't challenge him and don't make me witness him putting a bullet through your heads."

I stepped closer, lowering my voice. "You would never choose him over us even if it was just to make peace. The second anyone placed a gun near our heads, your fucking super soldier skills would come out and you'd start killing people. You care about us, Presley. You want us to prove that we care, I'm about to dare you to prove that you still do too."

"What does that mean?" She glanced between us, noticing how close we were getting.

"You're just going to have to find out, but if it comes down to Adrian coming for us, and you do let him kill us, then just know this one thing." I lifted my finger in front of her face, and by her comical expression, she thought I was about to make a joke. So, I softened my tone and used that finger to push some of her hair behind her ear.

"I fucking love you. I've loved you my entire life and not as a brother would. I've been in love with you since I was old enough to understand the flutter in my chest when you came near me and the way my stomach flipped around whenever you asked where I was, or what I was doing. That first day in the car was the best one of my life. I miss you, and I have every intention of getting you back."

Without waiting for her response, I pulled her hip until she crashed into my chest, and I seized her mouth. Her hands came up to my shoulders, but she didn't push me away; in fact, she paused, and when I assumed she'd pull back, she slid her lips against mine. My fingers shook as I pulled her closer. Gio moved behind her, his mouth caressing her neck in small kisses, and slow licks. We'd never both touched her at the same time. I wondered if she even processed that. It had always been one of our rules, and yet I knew why Gio had done this.

He was desperate enough to remove Adrian from the picture, and in doing so would allow her to feel us both. To remember us both and not the complicated, painful parts. Only the good ones.

Gio's fingers trailed down Presley's side while his mouth moved over her shoulder but then a knock sounded on the door. Presley pushed me away and swiped at her mouth before moving to the door. "I have to go."

Without glancing back at us, she opened and shut the door without revealing who was inside, and I heard her telling Adrian that she wasn't feeling well. Once their voices moved away, I cracked the door and crept over to the kitchen. Gio was on my heels, and the second we fell into place near the back of the kitchen and relaxed against the counter as if we'd been there the entire time, Adrian appeared.

"I was looking for you both."

Gio stuck an Oreo in his mouth, so I replied, "We've been here, gambling."

Adrian eyed the full table, where no space had been made for us and I knew it looked like we were lying, so I gestured at my brother. "We cleaned them out of snacks, so we're giving some others a chance to win something."

He paused, but I noticed the muscle in his jaw flutter. "We're about to dock."

Once he walked away, my brother stared at me then smiled.

"He hates us."

I nodded, glaring at where he'd been standing. "Might as well give him a good reason to."

CHAPTER 33

PRESLEY
PRESENT

The tree line behind our manor was riddled with thick branches and dense shrubs. When I ran the perimeter, I typically avoided going deeper into the woods simply because it was more difficult to navigate. However, my mind was an addled mess, full of its own thorns, branches and overcrowding trees.

My feet carried me over a fallen log, and I breathed steadily through my nose as I pictured Kingston's face when he made his declaration. A crack echoed through the vast space as I crushed a rotting branch under my shoes, as the image of both brothers crowding me in that room came back to mind. I pushed myself harder, desperate to escape the version of myself that had shown up last night. The one who pushed the two boys she was still madly in love with inside of a room and allowed them to touch her.

I kissed him back.

After everything they'd done, I just...they kissed me, and I didn't even hesitate to kiss them back.

What was worse was the way Adrian wrapped me in his arms and held me against his chest the rest of the trip back. He'd texted me this morning and told me I was beautiful, and he couldn't wait to see me.

I didn't deserve his texts or his alliance.

Another branch cracked under my weight, and a patch of moss had me nearly slipping, but I just kept going. My chest burned, and my eyes watered as I played the scene back through my mind. Treacherous lips. Deceitful hands, and a toxic heart...those were what the twins had left me with, and instead of making them pay for any of it, I indulged them.

My toe caught on a rock, which sent me spiraling to the ground. My chest heaved as I worked to catch my breath, and I slowly turned to my back. The sky above was smeared with low hanging clouds, and a bleakness that didn't fit how warm the air was against my skin. I decided to lay there and imagine which stars might appear once the sun went to bed.

My mind wandered to Gio and whether he'd go to the barn next door and look at the stars or if this dreary cloud coverage would ruin that for him. Thinking of him only made the ache between my thighs worse and reminded me of how I'd slipped my hand there last night when I had gotten home, and how even this morning I had rode it in hopes that this feeling would be eradicated from my system.

But it was no use.

With a groan of frustration, I threw my arm over my eyes and allowed myself to remember it again. The twins, touching me. Kissing me. Wanting me.

They'd both touched me at the same time. That was not something they'd ever done before, and it made me wildly curious how much further they'd go and why they'd erased a significant line that had once been drawn by them...especially by Gio. He'd never considered sharing me with his brother before and after not seeing them for almost two years, he was suddenly okay with it?

I needed to know what they'd been up to and why he had changed his mind.

Shit.

I was going to have to bring up last night to the twins and hopefully they wouldn't notice how insanely desperate they'd made me with just a simple kiss.

Tucked in my window seat, I bit my thumbnail while watching my cell phone screen.

I had a text to send, but I wasn't sure how to word it and if I were the one to reach out, then it would send a very obvious indication that I had been thinking about them and their egos didn't need the boost.

And yet...

My phone vibrated, which nearly made me drop it.

Kingston: Are you going to the farmhouse today?

I tried to play it cool by waiting, but he'd already seen that I read it because our text thread was open.

Me: Not sure

Kingston: You still thinking about that kiss?

Heat swarmed my face and neck, burning my lungs with irritation. Why did they have to kiss me? Why did I still have to hold feelings for them?

I began typing and then erasing the words, only to have Kingston send another response.

Kingston: Don't ghost us now...what did you think of that kiss?

Me: It confused me.

I watched his dots dance on the screen and flicked my gaze up to the window, watching as the clouds slowly moved across the sky like ships in the sea.

Kingston: How did it confuse you? I told you I'm in love with you, and then I kissed you. No confusion, Pres. You're going to be mine eventually.

My thumbs swiped briskly across the screen as my heart

hammered out a drum-like warning that this was all too close to the fire and I'd likely get burned.

Me: And what does Gio think of that? He touched me last night, same time as you...he's never done that before. I'm confused with what that could mean, or what it is he wants. I know what he said when I was sixteen, but that could have changed...once upon a time, he wanted me for himself.

Why was I even entertaining this?

Kingston: For someone over us, you sure are a curious thing but I'll ask him.

Gio added to chat.

I rolled my eyes and toyed with the curtains over my windows, waiting for his response.

Gio: You want to know how I feel about it, Elvis? Here...

Gio: >>vid link<< *winky face*

Furrowing my brows, I clicked the link he sent and immediately dropped the phone, but the moans in the video began echoing through my room.

Ohmygod.

My fingers brushed across the floor for the phone and quickly began pushing the button down to decrease the volume. Once the video was at least silent, I risked glancing at it again, feeling fresh heat hit my face and a new ache bloom low in my belly.

Playing out on the screen was a bedroom, set in a skyscraper with floor-to-ceiling windows, and there on the bed was a woman lying on her back. She had on some sort of black lingerie and heels. There was a man wearing a suit, on his knees, with his face buried between the woman's legs. Her face was at the edge of the bed, upturned, while a man dripping with tattoos, and an unbuttoned pair of jeans, stood over her with his cock out, sliding in and out of her mouth.

Curious and insanely turned on, I clicked the volume button just once to hear what sort of sounds the three of them made together. Moans echoed the smallest bit as the woman in the video rocked her hips into the man's face, and the man at the edge of the bed fucked her mouth.

Heat slid down my belly and gathered between my legs as I watched the scene unfold. Somewhere in the back of my mind I was shocked and outraged that Gio had sent me this, but there was also this irritating flicker of hope in my heart that he'd done this on purpose.

Was he telling me something with this?

I'd asked how he felt about what we had done in the room...with the two of them touching me at the same time, and he'd sent this...it had to mean he was prepared to do what he'd never been willing to before.

I held my phone sideways, continuing to watch as the woman came hard, with a muffled scream and her legs closing around the man's head, which he aggressively pushed open to lap at her release. The scene transitioned to her straddling one of them, while the other was nestled up behind her, holding her hair while he fucked her in the ass.

Slamming my eyes closed, I threw the phone down and jumped off my window seat.

There was no way they'd be open to that. Why would he send this to me as a response? How could he have gone from being so against ever sharing me with his brother, to this?

Glancing over at where I'd left the phone, I could still hear a few moans coming from the device and the ache between my legs was nearly unbearable. I couldn't keep watching that and entertaining it...could I?

Fuck it. I bent down to grab the phone and then ran down to my bed, where I slipped under my covers and slid my hand down into my shorts. I began rubbing my clit as I imagined myself in that exact position, straddling Kingston's hips, feeling his enormous cock inside me, while Gio fucked me from behind. My fingers were soaked as I continued to rub over my clit and rock my hips into my hand.

I pictured how they'd hold me. I knew they would be rough, but I also knew they'd be gentle in all the right ways. I knew they'd make sure I felt good and safe. The three people on the screen moaned as they fucked, her head was tipped back while the man behind her thrust into her, and she rocked back and forth over the man under her. She moaned deeply and begged for them both to go deeper, then harder.

I observed as the three of them thrust, rocked and slid against one another, but it was the next scene that finally had me gasping. One of them spread her ass and began licking along her crack. I rocked harder into my fingers, and then the next scene had me coming. When they both came inside her and pulled out. Thick, white cum dripped out of her pussy and down her thighs. Both men dipped their fingers into her, pulling up sticky release, and then shoved their fingers into her mouth, forcing her to suck down what she'd done to them.

I tossed my head back and my phone at the same time, focusing all my energy on my fingers and my clit. Wetness seeped into my shorts and coated my fingers as my chest heaved, and an orgasm ripped through me.

I hated this. Hated that I'd tried other videos, and they'd never made me come like this, not like watching one woman get fucked by two men. The way they worshiped her and filled her and cared for her. I just simply couldn't understand the draw of being with one man when two was an option.

Granted, I was still a virgin and maybe it did make more sense to break my hymen with just one cock versus two, but there was something in my brain that told me I'd never be satisfied with anything less than what I'd just witnessed on the screen, and the elation in my chest began to wane as I registered just how big of a problem that was.

The love I once had for the twins had to be put to rest, the fantasy of them erased and forgotten because there was only one man in my future, and I had to do whatever necessary to convince him I was worth creating an alliance for.

THE NIGHT AIR was warm against my exposed back as I walked along the white stone terrace that boasted of the best food in Rake Forge. We were near a lake resort that Adrian was staying at and he'd reserved the entire outdoor space for us to have dinner. His men were stationed every few feet, and I was surprised as I began walking past them as a few familiar faces appeared.

"Hi, Renzo, how are you?" I asked the soldier who wore all black tactical gear. Benni was stationed near him, and he gave me a warm smile. "Hello, Ms. Presley, hope you're having a nice evening."

Renzo didn't reply, but he gave me a small smile, but it almost seemed forced. I kept moving and left them at their guard posts while I moved closer to Adrian.

My hair was down, curled, and I'd applied makeup and even wore a cute, strappy dress with four-inch heels. I needed to clear my head of all things twins and all the confusion around the heartache of losing them. I had yet to text them back regarding the video Gio sent, and I had done everything in my power to avoid them in the halls and around the manor. If it were simply that they wanted me physically, then I could eventually forget it, but Kingston's confession still hung around my heart like a rusty chain.

"There you are." Adrian stood to greet me, and I fell easily into his arms and even accepted his light peck on the cheek.

"Sorry, I ran into some traffic getting here."

The traffic was arguing with Scotty over driving myself and not taking any backup.

It was imperative that I started digging under Adrian's armor to see what lay inside him. Kingston's words about how I didn't know anything about the operation or the town Adrian controlled in Italy had been running through my mind. I wasn't upset with Adrian about it, but it made me feel as though I needed to know more about him.

"You look gorgeous." Adrian took his seat across from me and a waiter rushed over to help push my seat in. The table had white linen draped over it with lit candles and mini wheat stalks stuffed inside of a porcelain vase.

"How are things going back at home with your friends returning?"

I tried to relax and sip my water and not think about the images on that video or how I kept replacing the guys' faces with Kingston and Gio's. Instead, I ended up coughing.

"Sorry. Things are okay...I haven't seen them really."

The memory of Kingston's amber eyes when he'd told me he loved me kept flipping around in my mind on a loop. As if it were haunting me. I needed to turn this around on him.

"They really are more like brothers...but we haven't exactly worked through any of our issues yet."

Adrian's lips tipped up but only halfway. I wanted to ask what was wrong, but the waiter brought over wine and bread. Adrian set a piece on my plate when he asked, "What exactly were the circumstances around your fallout?"

With the bread halfway to my mouth, I paused as Adrian smiled at me from over the rim of his glass. Setting the dough down, I cleared my throat.

"They didn't agree with how hard Scotty trained me."

It felt ridiculous to sum up so much pain and hurt into a miniscule sentence. But how else could I explain a lifetime of memories and the taboo relationship we'd developed? I had no idea what really happened, so how would I explain it to a man I was trying to convince to potentially marry me.

Adrian placed his fist under his chin, watching me, but before he could ask anything else, I shot off my own question.

"What about you...do you have any siblings?"

I watched carefully as his blue eyes flicked over my shoulder then down at his plate. He sipped his wine, then cleared his throat. "I do not. I sadly was raised as an only child."

I had to take a moment to compose myself as I watched the lie slip from his lips. "Oh...well that's too bad. What about people you grew up with, anyone that's like family but might not be blood-related?"

My smile was warm and reassuring as I tried not to seem too overeager.

He repeated what he'd done the first time. Flicked his eyes over my shoulder and then glanced down at his empty plate.

"No, unfortunately I wasn't lucky enough to have a life as colorful as yours."

He changed the subject to swimming and the yacht. We laughed and he sipped more wine while talking about Italy, his grandmother, and a few stories from when he was a child. But all the while my heart began to weave itself a tiny cocoon, protecting and shielding its tender spots from Adrian Adesso because as much as I wanted to believe differently, it seemed he was hiding something.

Which meant Kingston was right.

CHAPTER 34

GIO

ONE YEAR AGO

"Are you ready?"

I didn't look at my brother or acknowledge his question. The longer we were out here, away from home, the more lost I felt, and the tighter my chest became.

The men who once served my father now served my brother and me. Their dedication was to the name of El Peligro, not the vision or the person leading it. It's why they were so quick to abandon the charity work my mother had started, and the dream developed by my father.

I didn't blame them, not when my parents chose to take a gang, that had as much if not more power than a leading organized crime family, and turn it into a soup kitchen. The soldiers who had followed from the time my grandfather started things had all been forced to tuck away their guns and knives. They were handed hairnets and aprons and told to serve a community they didn't give two shits about.

Deep down, people wanted power, money, and security. Of course, they had a sense of loyalty but not of altruism. It was to blood, those willing to take a bullet for you, and those willing to stand when others would run. No person standing in line for a handout would care enough to have our backs. We helped a community that still saw us as rich pricks who didn't really understand their struggle.

Which was true.

We didn't understand it, nor would we ever. My brother and I were born into wealth, more wealth than we'd ever know what to do with. Being forced to serve in a soup kitchen might develop character, but it didn't have shit on the people who actually relied on that food to survive. Our parents were doing the best with what they had, but Kingston and I saw a tool rusting over due to neglect. Instead of allowing it to ruin, we chose to utilize its resources and create our own source of power.

Henry, one of the men who had helped us realize the potential to take over for our father, had laid out a map for us to inspect. We were in a warehouse; the heat soaked through the tin roof and the men bustling around the room were mobilizing on our behalf. I wasn't sure how we'd gotten here, but we'd gone too far to step back. Henry wanted to explain how a neglected piece of land could be earning the gang millions, if we'd only forcefully take it back.

Kingston glanced up at me and I remembered his question.

Was I ready?

Fuck if I knew, but there was no turning back now. Gesturing at the map, I encouraged Henry to begin.

His tattooed fingers spread out over a pair of red dots and then he pointed at the city of New York.

"The first thing we need to do is go through all the old places that we made runs. El Peligro has been around for a long time, and throughout the years we've acquired routes and even chunks of certain cities. Your father, in the past eighteen years, has given almost all of them up but legally most of them still belong to us."

Kingston glanced at the map and back up at Henry. "So we start reclaiming these spots?"

"As a start. You need to rebuild your manpower, and in order to do that you'll need cash flow. Get the routes back, start moving product again, and you'll start rebuilding that power. The good news, you have a whole ass army at your beck and call, ready to take up the colors for this gang again; they're just waiting for the go-ahead."

Kingston paled the smallest bit. "We'd be running something illegal I take it?"

Henry waved his hand over the map. "Don't worry about that part. Mostly guns, and a little cocaine. Nothing crazy but we need that route, the location of the supplier drops is imperative."

"This is shit my dad doesn't want in the city..." my twin mused, obviously conflicted with this decision. I wasn't conflicted, not when I thought about how my father had the ability to protect Kyle and Presley all this time and just chose not to use it. He had all this manpower, all these guns behind a single order, and yet he kept handing out bowls of soup as if my best friend wasn't slowly crawling onto an altar to be served up as a sacrifice to keep her family safe.

My father had dismantled this gang, tore it apart at the seams to create something good for this community, and yet within the span of a few weeks, we'd flipped it over and revealed its underbelly.

While my brother still looked conflicted, I tossed my knife onto the table. "Show us where we need to start."

CHAPTER 35
GIO
PRESENT

I kicked through a weak board in the wall and began pulling all the remaining wood apart. Kingston was on the other side of the room, doing exactly the same thing. We worked in silence as the afternoon warmed up the walls and seemed to suffocate the room.

We hadn't spoken about last night. Not other than the text I'd sent to Presley...the one she never responded to. I wasn't even sure why that bothered me so much, but I'd shown her something that took me a long fucking time to come terms with. Did I ever want to entertain the idea of sharing her?

No.

But fuck, she'd added in an outlier threat and my heart couldn't stand the idea of her choosing him. Suddenly the idea of touching her at the same time as my twin brother didn't seem so bad. Not when it meant she'd still belong to me in the end.

I cut my losses and went all in on the idea that Presley might forgive us, and then choose us, but she was honestly stressing me the fuck out with her silence.

After a handful of hours, both my brother and I took a break by eating on the front steps of the house. The air was warm, but clouds filled the sky.

"What do you think she'll do about the video?" Kingston asked.

I shrugged and tore another piece of my sandwich.

"Last night...were you okay with—"

I cut him off with a quick retort, "I've never done anything I haven't wanted to do, King. I wanted to touch her last night, so I did. I couldn't give a flying fuck that you were also touching her. If she's open to it, then that's where I stand. I want her. I know you want her. If this is what we'll need to do to have her, then it is what it is."

My brother stared at me. "At least until we get her away from Adrian."

Glancing at the ground, I kicked a clump of dirt off the steps. I imagined little feet one day running up the same steps into a house that was full of peace and happiness. A home filled with love and acceptance. A little girl with Presley's hair and my eyes. Maybe a little boy with King's.

"Honestly, even after we get her away from Adrian. I'm tired of being away from her. I'm tired of doing everything within our power to protect her, only to be forced away from her. I never wanted to leave her in the first place, and now we're here and she feels out of reach. If she chooses both of us, I'll accept it. I'll give her the future she once asked for. If that means we buy a much bigger bed, or take fucking turns every night, or it means I have to get used to seeing her be with you when she isn't with me, then I'll accept it."

My brother's throat bobbed before he ducked his face, but before he could answer, his phone rang.

I already knew who it was because that phone only went to one number.

"Yeah?"

My brother listened and then his eyes snapped to me before he pressed his thumb to the screen to end the call.

"What happened?" I began gathering all my lunch trash into the paper bag I'd brought.

Kingston ran his hand through his hair and let out a heavy sigh.

"Henry said Adrian's brothers were just identified as two men who are currently with him, acting as security."

I quickly got to my feet and pulled out my own phone, dialing Scotty's number. "That means his entire fucking family is here in Rake Forge."

CHAPTER 36

PRESLEY

PRESENT

I pushed the manor door shut and then ensured our security system was up and running. The evening had ended early, mostly because I'd feigned cramps, but Adrian had also gotten two phone calls during dinner that had taken him away from the table.

It bugged me, but I knew I had to earn his trust, and him being in Rake Forge was a step in the right direction. I didn't need to keep pushing. Still, it irked, but so did the fact that he'd lied to me. Unless Kingston was lying, but he had no reason to do that.

It made more sense that Adrian just wasn't ready to reveal certain vulnerabilities to me yet. I veered toward my side of the manor but paused before I reached the hall and glanced back over my shoulder.

I wasn't ready to face Scotty. He would ask me a billion questions about the night to try and dissect every word, and I was too tired for that. Not to mention, I needed to talk to the twins. The interaction from last night was on repeat in my mind, and I was exhausted running it through all the many scenarios I had played out. I just needed to talk to them to know exactly what they were both feeling.

So instead of going to my side of the house, I walked over to Carter's part of the manor. She was more than likely asleep, but there were several empty rooms, including one that led out to the walking path I used to cross over to the twins' side of the house. Her door was unlocked, and I knew we were the only family that was weird and locked it at night, still I felt strange invading her space.

Sure enough, she was completely passed out on the couch while a reality show played in the background.

I slipped off my heels and left them by the stairs while I climbed up to the second floor and exited through one of the guest rooms. The pathway was lightly lit from the bright moon as I placed one foot in front of the other, holding tight to the guard rails. Being closer to their side of the manor, I was there significantly faster than anytime I'd walked from my room.

Once in front of their window, I didn't waste any time with knocking. I just slid the window up and crawled inside, only to land on top of someone.

"*Ohmygoshimsosorry,*" I said in a rushed breath.

"Elvis?"

I rolled onto my back and found a pair of blue-gray eyes staring back at me.

"Gio...what are you doing?"

He held his hand out and helped me up. The loft came into focus, but I was lost on what exactly I was seeing.

"What is this?" There were blankets and two large mattresses laid out. Pillows and even a string of twinkle lights hung across the ceiling. Glancing over the ledge of the loft railing I saw they'd taken their mattresses from below and laid them down in the loft.

Gio tugged my hand until I was lying down on the bed next to him. It immediately made my heart race.

"You saw the video, did you not?"

Focusing on the bulb dangling above me, I tried to gather the strength to discuss what I'd seen in that video.

"I did."

Gio held out his hand, gesturing toward the blankets. "You'll never be asked to choose who you want to sleep with again. You'll be with both of us. Always."

The words hit like a live wire igniting my entire body. Why did that make my eyes water? Why did it feel like he tenderly handed my bruised heart back and it was stitched with careful and considerate bandages?

"Gio...that's..."

His hand found mine, and we lay there staring at the ceiling while my throat burned and a knot formed around my chest. "I need to know why you left without saying goodbye, and why you've been gone this long. I want to know why you stayed gone, and how come if you were able to come back, you didn't, until Scotty sent you that text."

I tilted my head and caught Gio smiling up at the ceiling and it was so familiar that a warm flutter erupted behind my breast.

"Anything else?"

I pursed my lips and tugged my hand free. "Yes. Where is Kingston?"

Gio sat up, perching one hand behind him for support. Running his hand through his hair, it made me focus on his arm, and the ink that now covered it. "King is handling some business, but he'll be here soon."

"What business? He said that you guys had been in contact with Adrian somehow...what did that mean?"

I saw the flicker in Gio's eyes. He wanted to lie to me; I could sense it. So I sat up and twisted his nipple the smallest amount before he could. "Do not lie to me, Giovanni. You've done enough of that."

He gripped my wrist with a bit of a shriek. "Elvis, oh shit. Let go."

I twisted harder, and suddenly Gio moved us until he was hovering over me, his hand was on my hip and his leg parted mine. "Fuck, Presley, fine. You want me to talk about all this shit, we'll start with the basics." His lips lowered until they nearly brushed mine and a whispered confession left him. "You have no idea how much I've thought of you all this time. You were an ache that never eased and now you're touching me, and while I know you're joking, I fear I have nothing left inside of me that can resist you."

I made the mistake of touching a piece of his hair and gently moving it out of his eyes. I saw his hunger and need, and then I glanced at his mouth, which slammed into mine seconds later. If I pushed him off, he'd go. Gio would never do anything I didn't want him to do and yet...this thing with the twins, it extended beyond the need to be a dutiful daughter. It had roots that ran to my very marrow and there was no ripping it out without causing severe damage. No, to remove them, I'd have to give in the smallest amount then pull, and repeat the process until they were gone.

So I gave in.

My hands wound around his neck, pulling him closer and his went to my hips, immediately pushing up my dress. The fabric was in his fingers for mere seconds before he pulled away and stared down at me as if he were just now realizing what I was wearing.

"Where were you tonight?"

Catching my breath, I tried to gather my thoughts enough to answer, but Gio must have gathered them on his own. "Adrian?"

I nodded. "Dinner."

The hurt flashing in his eyes was a gash in my heart, or maybe it tore out a suture he'd worked hard to mend himself. He had to understand why I was still entertaining this idea with Adrian, and if he couldn't then that wasn't on me to fix.

Gio had his phone in his hand seconds later, rising above me. I don't know what he sent off, but he tossed the device over to the side and then he stripped out of his shirt.

"Elvis, I hope you're okay with this, but I plan on ruining that dress."

"Well actually," I started, but Gio began pulling at the bottom slit until it began to tear. "This is Carter's dress."

"Oops." His smile made mine appear and he didn't stop ripping.

He kept going until he'd torn all the way up my hips, revealing my lacy thong.

"Fuck, Elvis." He breathed before gently running his finger down the thong, from the top of my mound over my center. The lightest amount of pressure from his finger felt so good that my eyes fluttered closed. He repeated the movement and then with his mouth next to my ear, he said, "Open your eyes, I want you to see every second of what happens next."

I did as he said and watched as he moved my thong to the side, then without any warning he tossed my thigh over his shoulder and lowered his mouth to my mound. The tip of his tongue slid over my clit, slowly and purposefully, making my head tip back and a breathy moan escape.

He smiled against my mound before pressing a kiss there, then with his fingers, he pushed apart my slit and licked along my center, catering to my clit in tiny circles before licking through me once more. It felt so good that I began to rock against his face, just like the woman had in that movie. My fingers wove through his silky hair, tugging on the strands as he continued to devour me. His eyes remained on me, as if he had to watch my every reaction.

I heard something shut form below and someone moving, and then Kingston rushed up the stairs. The second he saw us, his gaze heated, and he stripped out of his shirt.

"Came as soon as Gio told me you allowed Adrian to see you in that dress."

I couldn't really fathom what he was saying because Gio hadn't relented on how intense he fucked me with that tongue. My mouth parted, and my head dropped back.

"Look at you, Elvis. So fucking beautiful lying there on our bedding and being devoured by my twin. It's been too fucking long since we've had you between our cocks."

His filthy words had me grinding against his brother's face, harder to relieve a new ache that had crested. My head came up, taking in how defined Kingston looked against the low lights of the loft. He slipped out of his jeans, and then his black boxer briefs. My mouth went dry as I watched him stroke his heavy cock.

I'd seen them before, all veiny and velvet, but never like this. Never with the anticipation that they might actually use that glorious appendage inside me. Which brought up an entirely new set of concerns. Did they know I was still a virgin?

Were they still virgins?

Could I handle it if they weren't?

Kingston moved to support me where I could feel his thickness bob against my back, and his hands came around me. Gio continued to feast, lazily licking and using his fingers to keep me spread open.

I couldn't form coherent words while he did that so I squeezed his head to get his attention. He lifted his face, and I tried not to focus on how his lips glistened with my arousal or how it turned me on to know that he seemed to be enjoying it. I decided to keep my questions to myself until it became really clear that they planned on fucking me.

Instead, I decided to enjoy whatever was about to happen.

Kingston pushed down the top of my dress, which revealed my strapless bra, and with a hiss he quickly unhooked it and tossed it aside, leaving my nipples beading under the cool air in the room.

"So fucking perfect," he moaned, while rolling his fingers over the buds. Having him do that while Gio licked through my center was nearly too much. It had my hips lifting and my head moving into Kingston's shoulder.

"Perfect." He moved so he was more to the side and had access to my breasts, and while his twin brother fucked me with his mouth, Kingston pulled my nipple over his tongue and began to lap at each one. He played with them, palming the weight of each breast and letting them drop before lightly slapping them. "Wanna slide my cock through these and cover them with my cum."

His words made me ride his brother's face harder and had a cry leaving my chest.

"Gio, does she taste good?" King glanced over at his brother, watching as he licked my pussy.

Gio lifted his head and then lightly slapped my center. "Best fucking meal of my life."

"I had a feeling."

Kingston returned his focus to me and lowered his face until our lips met. We kissed, slow and sensual, until he pulled away and stared intently at me. "Come all over my brother's tongue, *mi reina*. He wants to taste what he's done to you."

My core clenched and then the orgasm ripped through me, making me cry out so loud, Kingston had to quickly cover my mouth with his hand. My eyes watered as I fought for some semblance of control and some balance as the waves of ecstasy lit me up from the inside out. I felt completely weightless as Kingston held me up and Gio gently licked up every drop of my release.

"Fuck, that was beautiful," Gio said, while swiping his arm across his face. "My cock is hard as hell though, and I'm either going to bury it in Presley's cunt, or her mouth."

Kingston tipped my chin up. "You ready to be fucked, Pres?"

My face heated and I knew he saw it, which meant he knew my answer.

"Not yet. We'll ease her into it."

Gio had stripped out of his clothes and held his cock in his fist while he made his way toward me on his knees. "That's okay, Pres. We're still virgins too. So it'll be like old times where we figure this out together."

I despised the relief that filled me because it meant I still cared. Too damn much.

Kingston winked at me and then helped me up. I got to my knees, feeling shaky and soaked.

The dress was fully removed, and my thong was pulled down my legs, leaving me naked. I felt sexy and confident as the twins stared at me in what felt like awe. As confident as they seemed, I could sense apprehension in them too, which made me want to be as bold as they were.

On my knees, they both watched me approach. Their cocks twitched as they sat back on their heels and stroked over their erections.

"Have you ever had them...licked?" My face warmed as the words jumbled. I was supposed to say sucked. Not licked, and I was supposed to say cock but how did someone just come out and say that?

"No, Pres. We've never had our cocks licked...or sucked." Kingston smiled at me and made something ease inside my chest.

I moved closer until I was in front of them with a foot or so of space. How was I supposed to suck them both off at the same time? I had never even taken one inside my mouth, but two?

Gio reached for my hand and guided me to his shaft, where I wrapped my fingers around him, and then Kingston did the same with my other hand. I stroked them up and down. Feeling every silky vein and how firm their cocks were with my thumb, I applied the smallest amount of pressure. Kingston let out a hiss while Gio couldn't stop watching, and then I sat back on my heels and let them go.

"Why don't you guys come to me, and you can help control...it."

I wasn't sure that was right either, but it made more sense than me bobbing from one lap to the other. Also, how come I couldn't just let go and say what I wanted to say? I had no idea how to step into this part of my sexuality without being awkward.

The twins moved and it was Kingston who went first, tipping my chin down so my mouth opened wider. Then he slowly guided his cock into my mouth. I kept my eyes on him as I allowed his thickness to glide over my tongue, then he gently pushed forward, hitting my throat.

"Oh shit. That feels so good," Kingston moaned, pulling back and gently sliding forward once more. I tasted something salty coat my tongue as he slid over it, and I realized that must be what the clear liquid beading at the tip was.

"I want to feel. Move," Gio said, while getting closer.

Kingston pulled out of my mouth and his twin quickly took his place, doing exactly what his brother had done with guiding his cock forward and into my open mouth. I tried hollowing my cheeks and even lifting my hand to hold the root of him while he moved in and out. Just as quickly as he found a rhythm, Kingston slapped his chest. "My turn."

Gio moved back and King took his place. They continued this pattern, the two of them dipping in and out of my mouth every few seconds, until Gio begged, "Please, fuck. I'm there. Let me finish."

So, Kingston allowed his brother to hold the sides of my head and slowly thrust into my mouth, where I tried to take as much of him as I possibly could. He hit the back of my throat a few times, but I coughed and kept sucking. It wasn't until he froze and began pushing deeper that I realized something warm and thick was filling my mouth.

"Oh fucking shit. Damnit, Presley. I'm coming."

What was I supposed to do? Tears filled my eyes as panic set in, but then Kingston stroked my hair and said from where he was off to the side, "Swallow it all, Pres. Every drop. Show Gio how much you love him coming down your throat. You're about to show me too, beautiful, so take it all down."

I closed my eyes and did as he said, swallowing. Once I knew that's what I was supposed to do, it took the fear out of it. Gio slid out of my mouth and fell back onto the bed as though he couldn't catch his breath. Kingston took his place even before I could swipe away the tiny strands of saliva and release left behind.

"Open up, let me see that you're ready."

I did, sticking my tongue out, and without warning, Kingston thrust forward, his cock hitting the back of my throat. With one hand in my hair, pulling tight, he executed three deep strokes before he froze like Gio had. With a groan so loud my face flushed, warm liquid filled my mouth again and this time I began swallowing the warm salty mixture down.

Kingston's gaze burned as he watched me.

"Your mom's eggnog might be better." I joked before eyeing the space between the brothers. I delicately swiped at my mouth and then decided to give in to this idea of sleeping between them when Kingston burst out laughing.

"Come over here." He pulled me between them while Gio reached for my hand.

I'd always wondered what it would be like to have them both surround me at night.

Turns out, it was perfect, and everything I ever hoped it would be.

GIO BRAIDED my hair while Kingston drew something on my ankle. He was using a black pen, and it was featherlight against my skin, so I kept jerking my foot.

"Stay still."

His hand came around my calf again and it made me smile. It reminded me of how he'd kissed along the arch of my foot earlier and all the way up my leg until he decided he wanted to taste me the way his brother had. I had no idea what to expect with someone going down on me twice in one night, but having Gio direct his brother was something I would never forget.

With Kingston's face between my legs, Gio watched lazily while playing with my hair and said things like, "Go slower over her clit, spread her pussy lips and lick through the center." It made me feel desperate, and the greedy sounds I made were muffled by Gio's hand. Kingston did something his brother hadn't though, which surprised me. While his tongue dove deep inside my cunt, his finger began prodding at the tight bundle of nerves in my ass, which was soaked from all the wetness that had dripped there.

The added pressure was incredible, and each time his tongue pushed in, so did his finger. To which Gio murmured close to my ear, "Getting that ass ready for when we fuck you, Pres."

I came that exact moment and I swear I saw stars.

Now we were naked and lying between the two mattresses. Gio and Kingston had remained as far away from one another as possible and at every move, they kept a blanket over their hips. I knew they were comfortable with one another, but I also knew there were boundaries they were extremely careful not to cross.

"I had questions that haven't been answered, you know."

Kingston flashed his amber gaze up in my direction. "Yeah, what were they?"

Gio let out a small laugh near my ear, which made his hot breath rush over my skin and goosebumps erupt along it. "She wants to know why we left, why we couldn't say goodbye —even though I've already answered that, and what we've been up to."

That's right, he had mentioned something in the farmhouse, but my emotions were running so high, it felt more like a blur. Besides, there was something about getting to hear it from both of them. "I also want to know why you were magically available to return home the second Scotty told you to."

Kingston began shading in the marigold he'd drawn on my ankle. "Do you remember that day when Gio and I broke into your training session and Gio stabbed people?"

"How could I forget?" Gio kissed my neck before tying off my braid.

"Well, the night of our birthday, our dad made us promise that if we ever interfered in any way with your future, we'd leave." Kingston gently shifted the tip of the pen over my skin while my mind wandered back a year and some months.

"That night," Gio continued from behind me, "you'd told Scotty you were done training, and because of that, our dad said we had to leave."

My stomach dropped out.

"I was the reason you were forced to leave without saying goodbye?"

That couldn't be right...no one had said anything. No one had ever warned me...

Gio pressed another kiss on my shoulder. "*We* were the reason, Elvis. Not you. But Scotty was in our living room, along with your dad, and they promised to send you away somewhere we'd never find you if we didn't go. We agreed it was best if we left that night because of your declaration and what they'd learned about our relationship."

Oh. "They likely weren't thrilled that the three of us had been together."

Kingston groaned from near my feet. "You make it sound like we're a throuple or something, and I'm definitely not fucking my own brother. So, we can't be that. You're just with both of us, and now when we want to be together, we're in the same place."

"Regardless, I'm sure our parents weren't thrilled."

"Fuck 'em," Gio sighed.

"So you left that night...and Scotty was supposed to tell me?" I searched Kingston's face and his brows crumpled. Gio's fingers stalled in my hair too.

"Yes, and your dad."

Anger swirled around like a dust storm, making my fists tighten around the blanket. "What else?"

"Scotty promised we could text you and he'd never interfere with you contacting us, and he swore that if you were ever in any kind of trouble, he'd let us know immediately."

That was a lot to process. Scotty had hidden their communications from me, lied to me about them leaving early, and threatened to send me away as a way to manipulate and control my best friends. That anger turned into rage as I thought back over how

Scotty had first told me he'd hidden their communication from me.

Scotty's text to them had said, "Get home now." So of course, they rushed back...because he'd promised to always tell them if I was in any danger.

Gio explained, "We were angry when we first got back because we'd assumed you didn't want anything to do with us after we'd spent so many months texting and calling you."

I still hadn't figured out how I would explain that Scotty told me six months in, but I was too stubborn to check after that. They'd be so hurt when they realized I *had* ghosted them. But I also felt like I had my reasons.

"What have you been doing all this time while you were in Mexico?"

I waited for one of them to answer me, but they each remained quiet. Kingston finished his drawing and then sat back on his elbows, watching me. Gio tugged me back into his chest and began kissing me.

Lightly pushing at him, I sat up and stared between them. "What have you guys been doing?"

"I'll tell you what, Elvis. Let's make a deal."

I glanced over my shoulder at Gio then over at his twin. "What sort of deal?"

"We'll tell you everything, all the things we've been up to and why..."

Kingston paused, watching me carefully.

"If I what?"

Gio finished, "Let us fuck you."

Heat flared in my core at the mere idea of them both taking me like that. The video Gio had sent came to mind, and I pictured what I would look like having Kingston under me and Gio behind me. I blinked to stop the barrage of filthy images.

"Why not just tell me what you've been up to?"

Kingston's eyes flashed with something that looked like hurt, but it was the way he messed with the blankets that told me he was nervous. Did they think I'd leave the second they told me?

It made me even more curious as to what was going on.

"This feels manipulative. I haven't lost my virginity yet, but I didn't want it given in a negotiation."

"Isn't that exactly what you're doing with Adrian?" Kingston's tone dripped with annoyance.

I pulled away from his hold and out of Gio's to inspect them.

"Are you both really going to act as though you have a leg to stand on right now?"

Gio's eyes lowered, but Kingston's remained burning directly into me. I didn't give them the chance to say anything as I pushed on.

"You left me. I've been without any friends, anyone to talk to, anyone to dream with or laugh or do anything we once did. You took that from me. While I understand the beginning and can forgive you for leaving without saying goodbye…you left me for almost two years. Now you're here judging the one friendship I made?"

"Now it's a friendship?" Gio used his fingers to make air quotes, and it made me want to throw a pillow at his face.

"Yes, whether you guys like it or not, Adrian is my friend. It's why I didn't allow Scotty to pull the plug on our alliance. I care for him."

Their gazes locked with each other and something silent passed between them, and I knew that was my cue to leave. I never stood a chance when the two of them began to silently plot against me or whatever it was they did. It's how they claimed my first kiss and everything in that car the first time. It's how we got here.

Unspoken feelings and sacrifices.

Searching the bed for clothes, I found one of the twins' T-shirts and threw it over my head. It was long enough that it covered my ass. I found my thong, pulled it on and stood up.

"Where are you going?" Gio glared up at me, still kneeling on the blankets.

I stepped over a bundle of pillows until I cleared the edge of the little nest they'd created and moved to the window. "I'm going back to my room. I made plans with Adrian in the morning, and I'd like to get some rest."

I should have known it wasn't a good sign that neither of them tried to stop me. I should have known it wasn't like them to just let me leave, but I did it anyway.

CHAPTER 37

KINGSTON

SIX MONTHS AGO

The beach was one of the only places I truly felt like I could think.

I stared down at my dark cell, and then navigated to the text thread with Presley. It was still the same words she'd texted back before our birthday. With everything that had happened on the actual day, we never ended up talking to each other via text. All my texts to her were there but with no reply.

Fuck, the urge to toss the damn phone into the water was becoming too strong. We should have gone home but now we were tied up in bullshit with El Peligro and having men call us, "Sir."

Henry kept calling us leaders, and all I wanted was to hear my best friend's voice chime in on whether she thought that was stupid or not. All I wanted was to sit down and finally tell her what happened to me when I was ten, and why the idea of leading this gang scared me so much.

Because as desperate as I was not to become like the men I'd seen in that room, as badly as I wanted no one's blood on my hands, I wanted to protect her more.

Staring at the phone, I saw Gio had texted.

Gio: Henry says there's something we need to see.

With a heavy sigh, I stood from the sand and dusted myself off, giving the glimmering waves one last glance. The drive back to where my uncle lived was quick. He was technically my dad's uncle and had once helped lead El Peligro until my father retired him and nearly everyone else loyal to the original vision.

Once I walked into the room, everyone's eyes snapped up from the table and landed on me. Out of habit and instinct, I inspected my twin's body language. He was tense, which told me I wasn't going to like whatever it was they were about to tell me.

"What happened?"

Henry's dark brows covered a pair of eyes that were usually lit with humor. He was a funny guy and always had us laughing, but even now, he seemed somber.

"We recently made a deal for weapons with the Adesso family…"

I nodded, drawing closer to the table, which showed the map of routes and trade deals. Adesso was over in Italy and New York. His brother was in Canada, and he had another operating in Russia.

"What about it?" From what I remembered it was a good deal… no issues other than the price he offered was a bit low.

Gio shifted next to me and something in my gut said if he could, he'd pull me out of the room and tell me this without an audience. "We still have ops monitoring him."

The images were shuffled in front of me and that's when my gut dropped to my fucking feet. *Blue eyes. Dark hair and a freckled nose.*

"Why the fuck is Presley in his home?" I flipped over another image, feeling heat rise through my chest and infuse my cheeks. She didn't look overly familiar with him, but she was wearing pajamas…

In another she was by the pool, dipping her feet in.

Fuck. No.

I pulled a knife out and shoved it into the image before facing my twin. "What the fuck is this?"

A muscle in my brother's jaw shifted as he glared at the image, and after working to control his voice, he explained, "From what we're gathering...they're building an alliance."

Which more than likely meant marriage.

"No." I shook my head, unwilling to accept that she'd do the very thing she swore she never wanted. "She wouldn't agree to that."

"We'll keep an eye on him...we'll know if she pops back up. More than likely this was simply a test, and she won't be back," Henry said, carefully tugging the knife I'd ruined his table with free.

Gio took the blade and gripped it. "We've got a fucking problem if she does in fact go back."

I eyed my twin, already understanding what he was thinking. Adrian Adesso was a dead man if he tried taking her from us.

CHAPTER 38

KINGSTON

PRESENT

O ver the past year and a half, there were things I'd done that I wasn't proud of. There were places in my own convictions I wasn't true to, and yet it always came back to this core belief that there was one person on this planet worth risking all of it for.

My twin and I waited in the shadows for him to come out. It wasn't easy to sneak up on Scotty James, but we discovered, through time, that it wasn't impossible. Our anger at the man demanded blood, but his dedication to protecting Presley would keep him alive.

For now.

The door clicked shut behind the manor, and we knew his dogs would sniff us out first, so we waited for them to trot off toward the opened steaks we'd left by the exterior tree line. Scotty assumed the dogs were just relieving themselves and wouldn't think anything of them heading that way or being gone for a few minutes. Gio raised his tranquilizer gun and peered through the night vision scope, then pulled the trigger twice.

Once he gave me the signal, we moved from around the house and toward Presley's uncle.

We placed our blades at his neck to keep him in place. "A word, Scotty."

Scotty's expression only revealed the smallest flinch, which wasn't nearly as satisfying to me. "What the fuck do you two want?"

"Your head on a spike would be a good place to start, but because we love Presley, we'll settle for a little blood."

He tried to move out of our hold, and I pressed my blade farther into his neck, drawing enough blood that it was making a mess.

"Gio's stabbed you before, not sure why you're doubting we'll do it again."

"Where are my dogs?" Scotty rasped, masking the pain he was obviously in.

Gio clicked his tongue a few times as if he were calling the dogs. "Shame. Guess your beasts aren't as invincible as you thought. Don't worry, Scotty, they'll be ripping throats out within three to four hours. Once they wake up, ensure they remain hydrated."

I pressed my blade a little farther now just to fuck with him. His wince made me smile.

"Why did you keep our texts from Presley? You promised we'd be able to communicate with her and yet you routed all our texts to your phone. Why do that for so long knowing we'd eventually come back?"

He winced again and I decided to lower my blade for the moment and wipe it on Scotty's jacket. "I only wanted her to have a little bit of time to get over you two. She needed some space to process what happened. Sixteen was too fucking young for her to be so infatuated."

My blade was back at his throat. "So you waited until she turned eighteen?"

Scotty made a gurgling sound, which meant I'd gone too far with my blade. I let up and waited for him to continue.

"I waited until she was seventeen. I showed her your texts six months after you left. She didn't want to know what you said then, which was around the time that I had introduced Adrian's alliance. Carter fucked us over and we needed the help."

Gio glanced over at me, but I refused to let Scotty see that we weren't made aware of any of this. Six months...it was still longer than it should have been, but it would have made a world of difference to us if we were able to communicate with her that soon.

Six months.

"So when did she see them then, because at some point they stopped going unanswered."

He gave out another little groan, moving his neck. "The night I texted you to come home, she stole my phone, which held all your communications."

She'd known six months in and didn't dare look until a year after...and instead she started seeing Adrian.

I released Scotty slowly. "Are you going to attack us or do I need to cut a tendon in your leg to keep you here?"

"Fuck off. Just let me go check on my dogs."

Gio and I both let him go and he immediately took a piece of cloth from his pocket and placed it to his neck. "You're not going to end up with her. She's outgrown you both...let her go before you ruin the family."

With that he jogged off toward the tree line where his dogs were sleeping.

"What's going through your head right now?" Gio asked apprehensively.

I was doing sit-ups, and I'd already done push-ups and a few other regular workouts, but I usually made him keep track of my time. Today, I was just going until shit hurt, and with as conditioned as I was, shit wasn't hurting nearly fast enough.

Sweat landed on the mat as I stopped moving and glared over at my twin.

"She chose him over us."

Gio dipped his head, and I hated seeing him hurt. I despised that I didn't only have to experience the pain, but had to see it on his face, knowing exactly how his heart felt because mine mirrored his.

Once his attention was on me, he tried to defend her, "She was hurt...thought we'd abandoned her; there was shit we'd said that—"

Not fucking happening. "We explained all of that to her in our calls and our texts. We've done nothing for the past year and a half but sacrifice ourselves so that there's a future we might one day have. We've done everything for her, and she still fucking chose him."

Every time she'd go to Adrian's, I'd watch through a lens how happy she looked and how more of herself she'd become. She'd shed a layer until she was stripped down to the version of herself she'd only once given to us.

I couldn't stop this feeling because even after last night, she'd left us for him.

A murderer. A man who was pretending to be someone good.

I stood and moved over to the punching bag and began to hit it.

My brother's voice followed me. "What do you want to do?"

I turned toward him and asked, "Do you honestly think she'll ever be ours?"

My brother's gaze found the floor and I left the bag, placing my hands on his shoulders. "Gio, she's toying with us. She will do anything to protect her family, including entering an arranged marriage with Adrian."

"She doesn't know who he really is." He tried to argue, but I shook my head, emotion beginning to clog my throat.

"If you try to tell her, she won't listen. I dare you to try."

Gio stepped back and ran his hand through his hair. "And if she doesn't listen?"

"I know what I want...but I also know I'll take it and walk away."

My brother scoffed and picked up a jump rope. "You'd just fuck her and walk?"

The idea of not having Presley's heart made me afraid, but the idea of her giving it to Adrian made me so angry that I gave my brother the most honest answer I could.

"Yeah...I'd take her virginity so Adrian couldn't have it and then I'd just walk."

CHAPTER 39
PRESLEY
PRESENT

Guilt twisted my stomach like a leaf in the wind.

Each time I thought of something else, the hurt and worry would return, forcing me to my window seat, staring out at the sky. I'd remained there from the moment I got back from the twins' room, until dawn.

Once the sun began soaking the earth, I showered and dressed.

I needed to talk to them and explain that the last thing I wanted was to hurt them, and then I wanted to bring them up to speed on what happened with Carter and see if they had any ideas on what I could do to keep the family safe without Adrian's help.

I knew it wasn't fair to go to Adrian and act as though he could ever fill the role the twins had always claimed. I just didn't know how to contain this pressure that filled my chest and clogged my mind with concern and fear. I was so tired of carrying the burden all on my own and I knew if I asked them to, the twins would help me.

I just needed a peace offering.

Walking down the halls toward the west side of the manor, I passed through the open foyer area that led to the back terrace. From there, I wandered over to Kingston's garden, which was mostly overgrown and dead, and dropped into a squat. Twisting the lid of the jar, I took the glass and scooped up as much dirt as I could, then resealed it.

Reentering through the terrace, I stopped when I caught who had just walked through the front door of the manor.

"Adrian?" He stood next to Scotty who was welcoming him and two of his guards into the house.

"Presley." He smiled at me and then cleared the space between us. "I hope you don't mind me changing our plans but your uncle offered to have me over for breakfast and I thought that was a wonderful idea."

I smiled as he leaned in and gave me a quick kiss. Right as he did, I practically felt their presence emerge from the gym. Covered in sweat, and in their workout gear, the twins approached our group.

"Is this dirt?" Adrian lifted my hand and acted as if he were confused.

Kingston's eyes snapped to the jar and then back to me. There was something wrong. His expression didn't lift or lighten; it hardened as if the sight of the dirt only made him angry.

"It's a gift," I said, feeling embarrassed that there were so many eyes on me.

Kingston stepped closer and I took the jar, placing it in his hand with a smile.

"When we were kids, I'd—"

The jar fell to the ground, shattering around our feet. Shocked, I stared at Kingston's hand, realizing he'd dropped it on purpose.

"Why—"

"Some shit should stay in the past, Pres." His cold tone sent chills down my spine as I watched him walk away. Gio's expression shuddered, but his glare on Adrian was severe. This was not at all how I wanted to start the day, especially with them. I was hoping to apologize and find some common ground and eventually explain that I was going to let Adrian go.

My uncle wasn't making things easy for me on that front.

Giving Adrian another smile, I stepped away from the dirt mess and followed him over to my side of the manor, where my mother was apparently preparing breakfast. Mom was all smiles and glowing skin with laughter and the most welcoming demeanor.

I liked seeing how Adrian responded to it, and how his eyes kept roaming over me as if he were trying to remember every detail. It was how he used to watch me in Italy too, and I loved it then as much as I did now. That guilt from last night twisted my stomach again, making it difficult to eat.

Why was this so hard?

I loved the twins, always had, but I liked Adrian. He made me feel different than the twins did, less fire and ice. It made me rethink everything all over again, especially with how Kingston had just behaved. I knew they were frustrated with me, but I was also angry with them. They didn't get to just act however they wanted and not expect me to respond.

Once we helped my mom clean up breakfast, I invited Adrian to my room so we could talk. I wasn't even sure what I was going to say, but I felt like I needed to confess how I felt about the twins, so he didn't think I was leading him on.

My room was bright from the loft windows above the room being open and pouring light along my carpet. I sat on my bed, and Adrian copied my movements, facing me. He tugged my old, tattered stuffed Highland cow into his large hands and smiled down at it. I thought he'd joke about me still having a few childhood knickknacks on my bed, but his face lifted, giving me a serious expression that sobered me.

"Bellissima." Adrian stroked his hand down the side of my face.

I smiled, placing my hand in his. "Yes?"

"I have been thinking a lot about this, and I think it might be time for you to understand the other reason I sought you out in the beginning. Do you remember me explaining there was another reason I'd share with you later?"

I nodded, squeezing his hand as nerves sailed through my stomach like angry birds.

Adrian's chestnut hair was cropped handsomely, revealing his light blue eyes, and I tried to cling to how familiar he looked as he took a deep breath. "I saw you once at a ball...you were there under a different name...and I'm fairly certain you were young, just freshly sixteen."

That ball.

I tried to rack my brain for whether I remembered seeing him or not. I was focused on the guy that had brought me cake, and then Kingston stabbed him...so the rest of the night was fuzzy.

"You were distracting even then. I remember wondering if you knew that you were in danger being there, that there were a few people who knew your true identity, and if I should tell you. Then I watched as the twins moved in and removed the Milano boy and realized it wouldn't be safe for me to reveal that I was aware of who you were. But ever since that day, when I saw you, I wanted to know more about you."

He moved his free hand to tuck a few strands of hair behind my ear. "You were like a loose thread that I wanted to pull on and see what lay underneath. At first, me seeing you was just to satisfy an itch, a question that I'd had burning in my mind since I first saw you, but then I got to know you and I grew to care for you. I call you beautiful because that's all I can think of when I see you. I kept asking for you to visit because the more time away from you made me realize just how addicted to you I had become. Until finally, I had completely fallen for you."

My poor tattered heart seemed too tired to absorb his words. As if we just needed some time to heal from the pain of surviving the twins. But it wanted to...so badly.

"What exactly are you saying, Adrian?" I whispered, too afraid to hear his answer.

He smiled at me again and then leaned in to kiss me. "I want to make you my wife, Presley. I know we're young, but we're both living in a world that has aged us well past what's typical. Your family needs protection and I would like to provide that."

It was everything I had hoped for since discovering what Carter had done. Since the threats had been made, and our enemies knew where we were. But my chest squeezed painfully tight at the realization that this was all wrong.

"Adrian, if I didn't care for you, I'd say yes right now and take advantage of your protection." My fingers intertwined with his and he pulled me closer until our chests nearly touched.

"Don't say no, *Bellissima*." His forehead touched mine and a tear slipped down my cheek.

"It wouldn't be fair to you, not with the way I still feel for the twins. I lied to you. They aren't merely my best friends. I fell in love with them, and while we are on the outs, I can't just walk away from that and marry you. It wouldn't be fair."

"To be frank, Presley, I don't care about fair. I just want you to be mine." He pressed his mouth to mine in a short but firm kiss then kissed my forehead. "Take time to think about it, and work through whatever you need to with them. You were falling for me the longer they were gone, *Bella*, so come back to Italy with me and keep falling."

With one last kiss on my forehead, he left my room. I remained on my window seat, knees pulled up, crying and wishing everything about my life was completely different.

I WAS LYING on a blanket in the pasture next to the barn.

The stars were above me, and tears streaked down the sides of my face. How had I gone from feeling so totally unwanted at sixteen to being loved by three men? Well, Adrian didn't say he loved me, he said he fell for me, which I wasn't sure if that was the same thing, but it felt the same.

I cared deeply for him as well, but it wasn't the same bone-deep need that I felt for the twins. The thing that made me do things that didn't make sense, or the need to make sure they saw me, or knew what I was doing. Like leaving a note for them to meet me out here taped to their loft window.

I knew they'd come, and until they did, I went back in time, remembering the way we used to gaze at the stars as kids and how we'd always talk about the sky connecting us if we were apart.

The wooden gate swung and closed near the barn, and I heard someone moving through the grass. Then a body landed gently next to mine.

Gio.

"Where's Kingston?"

I turned my head to see his eyes on the sky, but a sad smile lifted his lips. "You know, you've asked me that nearly every single time I've ever approached you alone?"

"No—"

"You have. Throughout our entire lives, if I sat down and King wasn't with me, your first question was about where he was. If I wanted to spend time with just you, you'd bring him up, and even now, after all the things we've been through." His head turned so his eyes were on me. "You're still wanting him."

My face burned all the way down to my chest. "I don't just want him, Gio. I was just curious because of him breaking the jar earlier."

Gio resumed staring at the stars but let out a sigh, "He's pissed at you."

"Why?" I was the one who had a right to be angry, not him.

"Because you chose a man who isn't good over us. A man who has lied about his identity. A man who was responsible for shooting and almost killing your father when you were eight."

What the hell was he talking about? I sat up, propping my hand behind me and glaring at my best friend. "What on earth are you talking about?"

Gio mirrored my position. "In Mexico we learned how to gather intel, Pres. We got really good at it. We knew you were seeing Adrian an entire year before Scotty texted us. We know everything about him, including the fact that he was the person who ordered the hit on your father."

"He would have only been ten years old. That's ridiculous, Gio."

Gio's eyes narrowed angrily. "The Adesso's used to be strongly linked to a family that your father targeted when he was running things as The Joker. It was your father's fault Adrian's dad died as young as he did...he made Adrian an orphan. Adrian has two brothers who travel with him, acting like security, but they're some of the most dangerous men in the world. Benni and Renzo Adesso are aware of every move Adrian makes and they don't make any decisions that aren't unilateral. So the choice to place a hit on your father was made by Benni, but all three brothers agreed to it."

That couldn't be true. I had met Benni and Renzo. There was no way they were his brothers...they looked—I recalled the blue eyes, chestnut hair. Same wide jaw.

My heart nearly landed in the soil under me. It couldn't be true.

"How could they lead in different locations if they're always with Adrian in Italy?"

"You were only visiting every few months...you're a very long game to them, Presley, make no mistake. The goal will always be the eradication of your family."

No. That just...that couldn't be true. I knew it down to my bones, it wasn't. Adrian had fallen for me after seeing me at that ball and being curious about me.

He'd never explained how he knew it was me.

"You're still finding ways to defend him, aren't you?"

I blinked, tugging at the grass beside the blanket before looking back over at Gio. "I asked if he had any siblings and he said no...I just think there might be a mistake."

The scoff from Gio had my eyes narrowing. "You know that's exactly what Kingston said you'd say."

"Since when are you guys talking shit about me behind my back?"

Gio frowned before getting to his feet. "We've never once talked shit about you, Pres. But we do dream, and when we know something that's in the way of ours, we'll discuss it. Adrian is a problem and you're not willing to see it."

Without another word he turned around, head shaking, and left me in the field that we used to lay in to stare up at a sky that we once said we'd always share. In the wake of his absence, I realized he still hadn't fully explained what he and Kingston had been up to while they were gone, and now with the information Gio shared, it had me more curious than ever.

CHAPTER 40
GIO
THREE MONTHS AGO

We had slowly regained a massive amount of fortune my father's gang once had, but there were still holes that needed to be filled and loose ends that needed finding. This wasn't about force so much as it was power. If we could create something as powerful as what the Adesso family had, then we could protect Presley from him. Because whatever game she was playing, she'd been going to Italy more and more frequently, and while my gut told me she was aware of the danger, it still made me nervous to watch.

Henry had found yet another loose end that El Peligro had neglected for years and called us in to ask how we wanted to proceed.

He stood over the map in his usual position, this time a red marker in his hand as he drew a line through Manhattan. "For ten years a motorcycle club in New York has been using this stretch of land to make runs and earn money."

"And?" I asked, ignoring the looks from people around the room. They'd likely heard the stories of my grandfather and father. From the way they were sizing us up, it seemed they were curious how we'd run things.

Henry smiled. "And it legally belongs to El Peligro. Your father never cared if they used it because they weren't running anything illegal that would interfere with his community but if we take it back, we can earn double what they are."

One of Henry's men, Santos, tossed a folder in front of us. The manilla folder flipped open, revealing images of a dark-haired woman and a kid that looked just like her...in fact, the closer I pulled the image—

"Who is that?" Kingston asked, touching an image of the woman who looked eerily similar to my father and my grandmother. She had Dad's eyes, nose and mouth. In the image, she was holding hands with a blond man, wearing a motorcycle club vest that matched the insignia of the ones we just discovered were on our property.

Henry flipped over another photo, this one of a little boy roughly five or six. He was in the woman's arms, smiling while she laughed. They looked happy, like a family. Kingston glanced at me, and I stared back.

This was one of those moments where the other shoe was about to drop and smack us in the fucking face.

"This is Wren Vasquez," Henry supplied, while a few of the men at the table whispered in private conversations while glaring at the images. A sudden urge to pick it up and hide it in my jacket surfaced.

"Vasquez...as in..." Kingston voiced, while narrowing his eyes on the picture of the woman he called Wren.

Henry nervously looked at me then the photo. "As in the daughter of Manny Vasquez."

Our grandfather...which meant...

"Shit," Kingston whispered, "this is Dad's sister..."

I locked eyes with him. We had heard of her, but he'd called her Henrietta, and we had never once been told that she'd had a little boy, or that she was dating a member of a motorcycle club.

"It gets worse." Henry cleared his throat while sliding over a much clearer image of the man she was with. In this one, he was alone, and his leather cut was easier to read. He was no mere member of that club...he was the president.

"So our aunt is dating the president of the club we're after..." I summarized, unsure how we were going to handle this.

We'd never met her, but that didn't change the fact that she was family, or that we owed her a certain amount of loyalty purely because of our blood relation.

My brother watched me, and it was with the same question in his eyes that I kept asking.

Did Dad know and would he murder us for going after her boyfriend?

Because we needed that land, and if they put up a fight, they'd die.

CHAPTER 41
GIO
PRESENT

I found my brother near the weapons room, discreetly filling a duffel bag with ammo.

"We stealing from them now?"

Kingston didn't look up, just kept adding in more ammo. "We're protecting them."

Ironic how this was always supposed to be Presley's role, and now we were the ones who were stepping in and ensuring everyone's safety.

"Henry texted and said the team is ready to take back the Manhattan strip."

I rolled my eyes, irritated that this was still something we were pursuing.

"She's family, King. I think we should leave this one alone; besides, whatever men we have, we need to reserve for our fight against Adrian."

My brother moved from one side of the room to the other. "Has Dad said anything to you about our new roles with El Peligro?"

I shook my head. "He and Mom are still going to the soup kitchen a few times a week to help Grandma cook. They don't seem to notice the amount of men who have stopped showing up, or the lack of support from the rest of the community. If they have, they haven't said anything."

Guilt flared like a burn across my chest. It was never our intention to take the thing my father was given and that he'd turned for the better of the community and twist it back to what our grandfather had made. Once our dad found out, he'd be heartbroken.

"What did Presley say?"

I glanced up and met my brother's gaze. "Exactly what you predicted."

The hurt in his eyes had mine dropping to the floor.

"So what now?"

Like I fucking knew. "I think she's still confused about us. She wanted to know where you were tonight. You're wanting to ruin her, I presume?"

The duffel bag slammed down. "I want to fucking protect her. I want her to know that she doesn't need Adrian Adesso, but you just proved that she won't believe that even if we show her or explain it to her."

I hated how his voice shook, how the pain so deeply rooted inside me was also in him.

"So we walk away?"

"No." He zipped up the last duffel and hung his head. "We try one last time to make her hear us in the only way she listens."

CHAPTER 42
PRESLEY
PRESENT

Gio's words were a stain on my conscience.

I replayed them, reshaped them, and tried to look at them from every angle and I just couldn't come to terms with it being the truth.

So I sought out the only person I knew that would help me unravel every possibility.

"He said his brothers are security when you visit?" Scotty clarified while writing something down in his notebook.

I sipped my hot chocolate and agreed. "Benni and Renzo Adesso. Two of Adrian's closest guards. I know them both...Gio said they are his brothers, and all three of them ordered the hit on Dad all those years ago."

Scotty looked confused. "There's no way they're connected to that family. The blame got put on the Yullivi family."

"Gio said they were connected to someone else...someone from years before that, back when dad was The Joker."

My uncle sat still on his stool and then took a sip of water. "That could be literally anyone."

"Well, Adrian confessed to knowing who I was at that ball we attended when I was sixteen."

I had yet to tell Scotty about the marriage proposal. For all I knew, he'd force me to accept before we worked through any of this stuff, and while I still didn't believe Gio, there was something that was bugging me about the entire thing.

"How would he have known who you were?"

I held my hand out. "That's what I'm saying. Was there anything that linked him to the men who made the hit on Dad?"

Scotty shook his head. "Nothing at all. I already checked all of that before agreeing to this."

So what the hell was Gio talking about, then?

"We need to have the twins come in here and just explain what they know because this is ridiculous."

I got up, about to head over to their room, when Scotty spoke up from his stool.

"It won't ever work with them, *Lánya*."

Pausing mid-step, I kept my eyes forward, which allowed him the chance to continue talking.

"They're putting on a show for you that the three of you could be together some day but really, they're just insecure about Adrian. They're working together to remove him; once he's gone, they'll make you choose."

I spun on my heel, eyes burning. "Why would they make me choose?"

"Because they don't know how to share you...they never have. It took them years to even admit that they cared about you, fought their own feelings for a decade, worried the other brother might get to you first. Now you're in love with them, and they might share you now, but they won't forever. You need to let them go."

I didn't even care that my uncle seemed to know more about my sex life than I wanted him to; I was desperate to have him see exactly how I could make it work. "What's wrong with sharing?"

"Nothing at all, *Lánya*. It's just that they don't know how to do it."

"So I just stop loving them?" I cried, frustrated beyond belief.

My uncle left his stool and rounded the counter until he was in front of me. "You never stop loving them, Presley. But you love them enough to stop hurting them. Let them go."

I was too selfish for that. I could never picture them kissing someone else. Loving someone else. Marrying someone else.

I'd die first.

Tears tracked down my face as I stood in front of my uncle, breaking. "Have you ever had to do this? Can you show me how?"

Scotty pulled me into his arms and whispered near my ear, "Yes, one day I'll tell you about the man I let go, the one I still sometimes watch through the safety of a lens. He's happy now, married and in love. He leads a life I could have never given to him. That is what loving someone looks like. You will tear them apart if you continue to give them hope. Say your goodbye in whatever shape it will take, but say it just the same."

An endless stream of tears burst from me with choked sobs and a broken heart.

I would break, so they wouldn't be torn apart.

I would break, so they would remain whole.

I would break, simply because it was about time I learned how.

MY COUSIN CARTER KEPT DISAPPEARING, which worried me. I had no idea who was watching her movements, or if there was more to her connection with the Ferros that we needed to look into. But my search for her had me over in her side of the manor, which is where the twins found me.

"What are you doing here?" Gio asked, popping a piece of candy into his mouth. He wore almost all black, just like his brother who wouldn't meet my eyeline.

Fluffing another cushion on Carter's couch, I grabbed her throw blanket to fold it and lay it over the back. "I'm looking for Carter. She hasn't been around the last few days, and when I do see her, she's passed out in here. I'm worried about her."

Kingston toyed with one of the plates left on the coffee table that had a half-eaten burrito on it. "Well, I saw her car leave about an hour ago. She's likely gone for the night."

It was almost nine at night, so that made sense if she just left and hadn't returned yet.

"Well...I was actually going to come and find you guys after I checked on her."

Kingston walked the plate to the sink and soaked it before asking in a sharp tone, "And what exactly were you expecting once you did find us?"

I hated when he acted like this. Scotty told me to let them go, and maybe I should, but it wouldn't be without a fight. "I wanted to apologize. I know you guys need to be able to share things on your own terms and not be rushed."

Gio hummed before popping another candy in his mouth. Kingston glanced over at the stairs before hitting the light switch and walking around the counter to gently hold my hand.

"Have you ever seen the view from this wing's fourth floor?"

I held on to him as he led us upstairs. Gio followed us up, tipping his head every few minutes to toss more candy back. "I didn't know this wing had a fourth floor."

We continued scaling each step, passing the second floor, and then once we were on the third, there was a door I'd never tried that Kingston opened. A new set of stairs appeared made of different, more raw finished wood. "Yeah, my dad told me about it. I guess it has its own loft that takes up the entire floor."

Sure enough, once we crested the top of the stairs, there was an entire furnished room before us. Various, thick rugs softened the space, along with deep armchairs, a long couch and by the window, a chaise lounge. Bookshelves ran along the back wall, a desk was in the center, and then on the opposite side, double glass doors that opened to a balcony.

Kingston released me and I made my way over, placing my hands on the bronze handles and pushing them open. Cool air grazed my face and hair as I stepped out onto the small cement perch with an iron railing.

Leaning my forearms against it, I stared over at the top of the barn, smiling at this view. I hadn't known the farmhouse was this easy to spot from here.

"Wow."

A dim light was clicked on somewhere behind me and then I felt them. Two hands landed on either side of my body. "Gorgeous, but it doesn't come close to the view we have."

With a smile and a tiny flutter in my chest, I turned around. The wind caught their hair, tossing it around the smallest bit, and I decided I'd cling to this memory forever. I'd always remember a set of amber eyes and starry gray that devoured me in a way that felt as though they'd pull my heart from my chest if they could.

What I saw there was unspoken but starved. A desperation I had inside me as well.

Curiosity threaded with absolute need.

Kingston's hand came to my jaw, pulling me into the room where our mouths slammed against one another in a rush. Our heads moved side to side as our tongues slid against one another, heated and wet.

A moan slipped past my lips as Gio's hands came around my chest, and instead of unbuttoning my pajama shirt, he yanked it apart, which sent the buttons in every direction. I didn't wear a bra, so my breasts were in his palms within seconds, while his twin continued to kiss me urgently and angrily.

There was so much venom under Kingston's tongue. It felt like every kiss was followed with a bite, and as unfamiliar as it was, it was also completely him. We needed this, to have our fight and argue with our limbs, and hopefully this would end with both of them finally taking that thing inside me that I'd always wanted them to have.

Kingston's mouth kept moving, but I was distracted by how Gio dropped behind me. His fingers were warm as they yanked my shorts and underwear down my legs. With a hiss, he gripped the globes of my ass. He played with them, lightly slapping and hissing as I felt them jiggle. I didn't have very much body fat, but my ass was the one place it went when I was able to keep it on. Scotty had helped me change my training schedule to be less rigorous because it was almost impossible to keep up with the calorie intake, especially when I wanted to add in farmhouse work.

Seemed the slowdown was helping.

"Gonna spread you, Pres, be a good girl and stand there for us," Gio rasped before he separated my cheeks and began licking along my crack. My eyes shot open, and I found Kingston already watching me with a wicked smile.

He also lowered to his knees, and while his brother licked me from behind, with his eyes on me, he gripped my thighs and used his tongue to lightly lap at my clit, then spear through my folds.

It felt unreal to have the two of them tasting me and moving their tongues over such sensitive places. Even more so was that they seemed to enjoy it as their groans began increasing with the speed of which they licked.

Even though they each held me in some capacity, I still felt completely unstable, so I reached out and gripped Kingston's head, threading my fingers through his hair. Those eyes I had grown up loving landed on me, and the way I saw his pink tongue dive through my center and circle my clit had my hips rocking.

It felt like a test, a challenge that I'd argue with them or tell them to stop, but I was too engrossed in how good they made me feel.

Gio stopped his ministrations to make a humming sound. "Let's start prepping her, brother."

Still holding on to Kingston, I wasn't sure what Gio meant, but seconds later, a finger began to push against that tight bundle of nerves in my ass that he'd been using his tongue to prod and lap at. Kingston used two fingers and slid them inside my center which felt...

"Holy shit," I gasped.

I felt too full with pressure in both places...I just—

"I—I, that's..." My hips moved forward and back into the weight behind me.

Kingston stared, mesmerized at where his fingers currently were. "If I push any harder, you're going to bleed on my fingers, Pres. Tell me to stop, and we'll have you bleed on one of our cocks, but to be perfectly frank with you, my fingers are likely going to be less painful. You've seen how big we are."

He wasn't saying it to be prideful; I could tell he was genuinely trying to ask what I'd be more comfortable with. Their cocks were much bigger and honestly made me nervous, especially because I had every intention of them taking me the way the couple had fucked in that video Gio had sent me.

Wetting my lips and widening my stance a bit more, I nodded. "Keep going."

"Okay, just breathe and tell me if it hurts. Gio, take a break for a sec, she doesn't need to be burning in both places."

I felt Gio remove his fingers and then he was kissing over my lower back and stroking up and down my ass before he stood and placed his hands on my hips. "King, let's move her to the chaise."

Gio stripped out of his clothes before carrying me over to the long chaise lounge and then settled in behind me. Being naked under me, I felt his cock bob against my back, but I focused on the way Kingston settled between my open legs, a hungry expression on his face.

"Fuck, you're perfect. You're gonna take our fingers then our cocks. Got it?"

I nodded eagerly and he smiled before leaning forward to lick through my center and circle my clit. Seconds later he replaced his tongue with three fingers then he slowly began pushing back into my heat.

Gio hissed by my ear while he began rubbing and playing with my nipples. "So fucking hot to see you get finger-fucked, Pres."

His words stirred the lust building in my stomach and I began rocking my hips into Kingston's hand.

"Yeah, just like always. You're drenching my fingers, Pres." I could hear how much I enjoyed it by the sounds echoing around the room. He pulled his fingers out, and lightly pushed them back in once more while watching.

There was pressure but he was gentle.

"Rock into my fingers, beautiful. I know how hard you can ride my hand, so start moving." Kingston leaned forward and circled my clit with his tongue while he continued to push his fingers inside me.

I tried to do as he said, but the pinching feeling from where his fingers had gone began to hurt, and it made my mind disconnect with the pleasure.

"Gio, rub her clit while I push in," Kingston ordered and Gio obeyed by bringing his hand over my hip and using the pads of his fingers to rub over my clit while Kingston had three of his buried inside my cunt.

"Oh shit." I rocked into both of them. Gio rubbed slower, and with a gasp I watched as he removed his fingers and Kingston spit on my pussy, right where my clit was, which Gio then resumed rubbing, right over his brother's spit.

It had me moving faster and faster against their hands.

Kingston watched me while lazily separating my center. "Tits bouncing, pussy dripping, God, I can't wait to fuck you." I felt something give inside me as I came with a gasp. It hurt but it wasn't horrible, but the cramping that came next wasn't comfortable.

Gazing down at King's fingers as he slowly slid them out, I wasn't sure how to feel when I saw the blood.

"That's perfect, Pres. Now, you'll be ready for us," Gio rasped from near my ear and I tried to relax further into him as he kissed along my neck, moving my hair out of the way. I couldn't stop Kingston or how even after he'd removed his fingers, he leaned in and swiped his tongue through my center, gently and so carefully that it nearly made me cry.

My legs began to shake, so Kingston pulled his hands free and I closed my legs and leaned into Gio's hold. I watched as King walked to the attached bathroom to wash up before returning to where we were.

Gio's mouth was on my neck, kissing and sucking. Kingston was there moments later, already naked. The two of them were on opposite ends of me, but as Kingston got on his knees at the end of the chair, between my legs, I couldn't stop searching all their ink and touching their skin. I wanted them closer, impossibly so.

"All these words you've printed on your skin."

Kingston's eyes shuddered before moving his head to the side, as if my touch hurt him. Which made me feel strange... I was about to ask what was wrong when his voice suddenly came out possessive and demanding.

"I'm going to stretch you with my cock now, Pres. Why don't you take Gio in your mouth."

I pushed down the question and focused on his brother. Gio adjusted us so we were closer to the edge of the chair.

"You on birth control?"

"Yeah...have been since I was sixteen...just in case we'd ever—" I trailed off, letting them fill in what I obviously meant. I wouldn't have been against it if they'd taken this when they were seventeen, but I understood why they hadn't.

"We're gonna fuck you bareback, Pres. Need to make sure you're okay with that," Kingston rumbled from his place near my knees. My pussy was sore, but as I felt his velvet tip begin to prod there, the pressure was incredible.

"Okay."

"So easygoing, I love it. Is that you just wanting us to fuck you that bad, or have you become used to giving us what we want?" Gio asked, gathering my hair in his hand.

Kingston's chest hovered over my stomach as he entered my body. He went slow, allowing me to adjust, and then he pulled out and cautiously slid back in. I watched in fascination each time his cock would disappear inside me.

"Oh fuck, that's good." Kingston shuddered before pulling out again and thrusting in.

Gio returned his fingers to my clit and began rubbing while Kingston stretched me. I pushed into Gio's shoulder while I muttered, "Fuck."

"Yeah, that's what we're doing," Kingston rasped, and I realized he had a grip on my hip bone and had found a solid rhythm of sliding in and out of me.

"King, you were only supposed to stretch her. If you want to fuck her then flip her so she can taste exactly what it does to me to watch her get fucked by my twin."

Without any warning, Kingston pulled completely out of me with a long groan and then he pulled my hips and flipped me.

"You heard Gio, Pres. Let him fuck your mouth and when he's ready, swallow every last drop of him down." I got to all fours and did as they told me, finding Gio's length hard and erect. I skimmed my thumb up and down the base of him, and then I circled the precum coating the tip. With my tongue, I licked it away and smiled at Gio.

"Oh shit." He touched my mouth with this thumb, and I sucked it into my mouth before releasing him and going back to his cock.

Kingston's palms jiggled my ass a few times before he slowly pushed into my aching heat. I focused on Gio as I licked over him, and then slowly lowered my mouth over his girth. Right as he hissed and gripped my hair, I felt Kingston slide all the way inside me and then freeze there.

I held my breath as he paused, before he began pulling out. The sensation made me nearly stop blowing Gio, but King thrust and returned to fucking me with gentle rocking and a few muffled groans. The discomfort of him stretching me had worn off and now as he moved, it felt like he was stoking a fire inside me. Each time he thrust forward, I moaned and sucked more of Gio's cock into my mouth.

He loved it by the way he rocked into me and gripped my hair.

Kingston began to lose himself as his movements became chaotic and he began to lightly slap my ass with a hiss. "Fuck yes. Shit, Presley. Holy fucking—" His rushed rasps had me desperately rocking my own hips to meet his thrusts all while Gio held on to me tighter and tighter, until he froze under me and began groaning as hot liquid hit my throat.

I swallowed every drop down and then slowly lapped at his crown as I watched Gio try to catch his breath and toss his head back into the cushion.

"Made us come at the same damn time, Presley. Shit." Kingston pulled out of me, and I felt liquid begin to slowly leak down my leg.

I turned to catch Kingston's expression, but I wished I hadn't. He looked as though he were saying his own version of goodbye.

The look would haunt me until I had a chance to talk to him and ask why he'd let the jar break earlier, and why each time he touched me, or kissed me, it felt like it might be the last.

CHAPTER 43
PRESLEY
PRESENT

We found blankets in the closet and made a bed on the floor, using the couch pillows as cushions for our heads. It took me back in time, being a kid and sleeping between them when I was little.

Everything felt so unstable, unless I was between Gio and King.

Even now, as we slept, I knew this would be the only place I wanted to be. I knew dawn was coming, and with it, a conversation that I would need to have with them. They didn't want to share where they'd been or why, and I had to respect that. Just the same, they might have to accept that I needed to do whatever was required to protect my family.

Adrian understood that it wouldn't be a marriage of love, but maybe with time...

"See, Elvis," Gio murmured, pressing a kiss to my nose, "we could have the future you talked about. The farm, each of us holding you at night. I know I once told you I couldn't share you, but I've had time to think about it, and we could work all of it out. We'd know when you're ovulating and we could use condoms during that time, or if one day we wanted a kid, then you could have sex without protection with only one of us, and maybe our kids would grow up not knowing any different except that they're loved. You'd be such a good mom someday, Pres."

He was half asleep and the way his thick lashes fanned against his cheeks made my heart flutter and my hand come up to his cheek to stroke just under them.

"Yeah?"

He nodded and pulled me closer, but Kingston yanked me back into his chest just as quick. It woke him up because seconds later I felt his erection grow thicker by the second against my ass.

"Hey, Pres, guess what," Gio whispered.

"What?"

His smirk was so cute I licked his lip.

Our kiss took off from there, all teeth, tongue and sultry moans from me because the twins were fucking fantastic kissers. I felt something behind me, a quick prod and then something warm being rubbed into my asshole. It made me pull my head back and Gio was still grinning. "I brought lube with me. King just found it."

Oh. That's when I felt it, the pressure I had been so consumed by when Kingston fucked me was now slowly pushing into my ass.

Gio lifted my thigh just the smallest amount and I felt Kingston's hand on my hip as he pressed in further. It burned, but every time I winced even a little bit, Kingston added more lube and then pulled out. He'd gently rock there, allowing me to adjust. Then he'd push in more.

"Halfway there, Pres. Fuck, this looks so good…I'm half tempted to take a picture of it so you can see how well your body molds to ours. It's like you were made just for us."

Gio began kissing my neck messy and loud as his own erection began sliding toward my pussy. This was it. I tried to breathe as I processed that they were about to both penetrate me, and I was going to be fucked at the same time by the twins.

Placing my hands on Gio's shoulders, I glanced down and watched as he began rubbing the crown of his cock over my slit. I knew some of the lube had leaked to the front, but I was also wet because what Kingston was doing felt so good.

"Already soaked, King. Our little slut loves to be fucked in the ass it seems."

"Knew she would. I wonder how hard she fucked her hand when you sent her that video and how long she's been thinking about us both fucking her."

Gio hummed then dipped to suck my nipple into his mouth. "I fucked my hand pretty hard just picturing it. I bet she drenched her shorts, and even her sheets. She's never gonna be okay with just one cock. She'll always want us both."

I didn't even have time to blush at their crass words before his cock nudged my center, until he was pushing deeper. The stretch was incredible, and the pressure from both was...

"Oh fuck," I gasped as Gio slid out, stared down at me, and then thrust hard into my core.

Kingston had more than adjusted behind me, and now that Gio had found a rhythm, I felt like I was emptied and filled back up, only to be emptied again. It was exhilarating and made me feel so insanely sexy to have these two men want me in this way. I slid my hips forward and pushed back, desperate to get as much of them inside me as possible.

The burn was gone and replaced with molten lust, which had my pussy dripping. The sounds we created in the room were purely pornographic and untethered. No one covered my mouth, nor tried to shy away from their own pleasure as moans and gasps erupted from us, and the slick sound of skin slapping filled the space.

They were both moving so fast in and out of me that my tits began to bounce and my eyes fell shut. Someone's mouth was fused to my nipple and the other was biting the skin along my back while lightly slapping my ass. It felt too good, all of it was so consuming that I came hard, with a shudder and a scream.

"Not fucking finished yet, Pres, so you're gonna have to just cream our cocks as much as you need until we fill you up." Kingston rasped heavily.

I felt weightless and as if I'd just simply fly away the second a breeze came through the room. Kingston pounded into me from behind all while his twin fucked my pussy with long, hard strokes, and Gio groaned about the ring of white around his cock from my cum.

"Almost there. Jesus. Fuck," Kingston yelled while gripping my hips tight.

Gio grunted and froze, pinning his forehead to mine while he muttered curses too quiet for me to hear above my own whimpering. Kingston quickly followed suit with a roar behind me, and then we all lay perfectly still while trying to catch our breaths.

We remained like that, all three of us breathing heavy, and two cocks filling me up. The second they moved, I'd feel empty and I didn't want to feel that way again. Kingston gathered me in his arms and pulled me into his chest as his dick twitched in my ass. Gio pressed forward and kissed me while his cock remained inside my cunt.

I loved it. This was all I ever wanted.

"You're going to be sore as hell tomorrow, Pres," Gio rasped, while slowly pulling out of me.

Kingston slowly slid out of me next, and with them both gone, I felt the wetness of their releases coat the inside of my thighs. Once they moved, I felt a shiver run over my skin from the cool air in the room. Gio brought me a warm rag to clean with. He glanced back at the lounger in the corner we'd used previously before joking. "That chair is fucked. I hope Uncle Decker and Aunt Mallory don't realize we defiled their office space."

I laughed, too tired for words, but I watched them both as they moved around the room.

Kingston pulled on his clothes with that same angry expression he'd had earlier and something dark dove inside my chest.

Sitting up, I asked, "Where are you going?"

He didn't look at me, so I glanced over at Gio. He too was dressing, tugging on all of his clothes, leaving me without anything to cover myself aside from ripped pajama top I'd have to hold closed. Something about their abruptness felt off to me. No one knew we were up here, what was their hurry?

"What's going on?" I stood, now getting angry.

Gio spoke first. "We know how long you waited until you reached out to us, Pres."

Silence stretched, and I tried to gather my thoughts. I knew they'd have questions so I decided to clarify. "You mean—"

Kingston cut me off with a snide tone. "You waited a year, Presley. An entire fucking year before you decided to take Scotty up on reading those texts, and even then, you didn't reply to a single one."

"So what, I was hurt. You both left me. Did you forget that?"

"We weren't given a choice!" Kingston yelled, his amber eyes practically glowed as his anger unleashed on me.

"And I didn't know that!" I yelled back.

This was ridiculous. I bent down to grab my own clothes and began pulling them on.

"So what, you guys decided to fuck me and then planned to leave me here?"

Gio's wince was answer enough. My heart felt torn in new ways, the hope I had completely gone.

"You're still going to be with Adrian even though Gio explained who he is," Kingston justified himself and his dickish behavior.

"I checked with Scotty. There is no connection between Adrian and my dad. If there's intel you have on it, then you should tell him because you know how thorough Scotty is. He was the one who suggested Adrian."

"But we told you differently. Why must you always believe him over us?" Gio asked, sounding exasperated.

I scoffed, rubbing at my forehead. "Why on earth would I take your word over his when neither of you will even tell me what you've been doing for almost two years? I'm not stupid, I know something has shifted. You're stronger, faster, and have men that follow you around. You did something, and call me stupid, but I assume it is something that might be able to help us."

Kingston stepped closer and seethed with fury. "I'm so fucking sick of our lives revolving around you and your family. Around if you're precious father is safe or not. My family has remained here as an ally to yours for almost twenty years and still you seek help outside of us. No one ever asked us. So no. Your family is on their own, and honestly, Pres, I'm exhausted by all this. I fucked you because I plan on taunting Adrian with it. I will ruin his family, so if you're aligning yourself with his, then we're coming for you too."

"What do you mean by that...what have you two done?" I had to focus on the specifics of what they weren't saying and not the impact of what they were. My chest felt as though they'd taken a spoon and carved a crater into it. They'd only fucked me to anger Adrian?

This hadn't even meant anything to them?

Angry tears spilled down my face and Gio tipped his head back and laughed. "This is so predictable, Pres. You cry and think we'll come running to fix it."

"This is why," I cried, swiping at my face. "This is why I didn't read your texts or listen to your voicemails because you crushed me into dust when I was only sixteen. You made me believe that I was nothing but a pity project to you. That I was pathetic and stupid for behaving the way I did. Here I am again, feeling stupid and naïve."

Pushing past them, I closed my arms over my chest to keep my pajama top closed.

"Thanks for making this really easy for me."

Their feet hit the stairs with an echo as they rushed after me. "What easy?"

I didn't look back as I replied, "Adrian proposed. I plan on saying yes."

CHAPTER 44

KINGSTON

PRESENT

Sometimes when I closed my eyes, I could see blood smeared on a wall, and a dead man's eyes staring at the ceiling. I could hear a man begging for his life. And I'd feel this darkness begin to swell inside my chest like a thundercloud. It used to be in small increments, anger and rage that would eclipse my good mood. Presley was the sun to most of those clouds, but now, all I could think of was how she'd chosen *him*.

She chose Adrian even before she agreed to marry him, so her bullshit excuse of why she decided to agree to this marriage was a lie.

I knew it was coming, and yet hearing the words leave her mouth made every dark place inside me quake. My heart spasmed and everything in me wanted to run in front of her to stop her. I needed to take her back into that room, rewind time and not get up. I wanted to go back and tell her what it meant that she'd let me be a part of taking her virginity. That it wasn't just something I did to piss off another man.

It meant everything to me. Yet I spewed a different version of truth, hoping she'd accept the lie.

314

She accepted it just like she did when she was sixteen, and now I was staring at her from across the room, completely out of reach as she stood next to Scotty and her father. She'd changed into real clothes and probably showered to get rid of any trace of us.

Something about that made the darkness worse.

I wanted her to crave us the way we craved her. The way we hadn't stopped thinking about her for nearly two years. The way even now, we both watched her every move as though she were the person who'd decide if we lived or died, and where our next breath came from.

She was our universe, and we'd somehow convinced her she was worth less than the soil under our boots.

"What's this about?" Dad asked, glancing between us and where Presley stood.

She lifted her chin, strong and defiant. "The twins have indicated they'd go to war with us, potentially Adrian, and while they haven't communicated with which army they'd be doing that, the threat is significant enough for us all to talk about it."

Our father didn't look surprised, even a little bit. He looked...sad.

I felt my twin stiffen as our father regarded us with that disappointed expression on his face. Amber eyes, same dark hair that was starting to grow silver along the edges, and more wrinkles than I remembered. "Tell me you didn't."

How were we supposed to respond? We hadn't hidden the hearts inked into our chests, but he'd yet to see them. But now, as he stood there, his gaze dropped to my chest, and I felt bold enough to reveal our truth. Tugging the hem up, I revealed my skin and looked over to see my brother copying my movements.

Dad's throat bobbed as if he were holding back emotions, but it was our mother making her way into the living room who saw them that had me shoving the fabric down.

"What have you done?" The fear in her voice and slight tremble had me backing up the smallest step.

Gio flicked his eyes at me. I saw the same guilt and the same shame I carried.

"Why would you do this?" Dad demanded.

Presley stepped forward, dark brows crumpled. "What did they do? I don't understand."

"They resurrected and now lead the thing their father worked nearly twenty years to bury," Scotty supplied with a blasé tone that had my anger surging.

"We wouldn't have touched El Peligro if we didn't feel like we needed an army," I argued.

Kyle laughed. "You fucking idiots."

Juan spun and glared at him. "No. Of all the people who will criticize them for this, you won't be the one."

"They threatened to take sides against us, Juan. That makes them my enemy."

My brother tried to smother a laugh, which had everyone glancing at us. "Sorry." He smiled. "You act as though we'd be in trouble if we were your enemy...what we have built, you would never be able to stand against."

I added, "You were so busy looking for an alliance for Presley, you skipped right over us. Dad had this powerful tool at his disposal all these years, and not a single time did he offer to pull on the power it could wield. It wasn't until we went to Mexico and we began to revive it, that we realized its full potential."

I'd never seen my father angry, not really to the point where tendons bulged in his neck or his eyes watered, but I knew it the second my mother walked up and slapped us across the face that this was more serious than we understood. "You have no idea what you've done. It wasn't a viable option for a reason."

"I thought I could wield that gang, the power it provided, but then we had a family, Son. We had people to protect and El Peligro isn't something you carry on your shoulders if you're trying to protect someone. You think what you've done will protect Presley, but it will end up being the death of her. The very reason you can't look in the mirror, the thing you hate most about your life."

I bit my tongue to stop myself from spewing all the shit inside my head that swirled and swirled and fucking swirled. Half the shit Presley lived through she wouldn't have had to if Dad had just asked us to step in and help him with the gang, but he never trusted us.

"We aren't worried about protecting Presley anymore. She's proved she can save herself and same with Kyle. I don't give a fuck what danger faces them. They're on their own but we have a score to settle with Adrian Adesso. If you align yourself with him, we'll be at war."

Presley blinked, and some sick part of me wanted to see her cry again. I needed to know that what we'd said bothered her. Kyle was the one who stepped in front of his daughter and settled his glare on us.

"You can hate me. I know what you saw when you were ten, Kingston. I know you witnessed us handling someone who had come in to hurt members of our community. You weren't given the context for the murder, but it was more than justified I can tell you that. You've grown resentful of me, and now you're misplacing your anger on my daughter. Speak of her again as if she's your enemy, and I promise you, we will be at war. Be considerate and don't make your father and I shoot one another because that's what will end up happening."

Gio shifted next to me and I knew this was getting too close to things we never wanted touched. Presley had her own category between us, and in everything, she was to be protected and kept safe. We would never harm her, but we had to give a good show that her choosing Adrian didn't ruin us. I would say whatever I had to in order to save face and not let on that she'd fucking gutted me with that news.

"Adrian Adesso is responsible for the hit placed on you ten years ago. I don't know how Scotty missed it, but he did. The three brothers were raised by a man named Markos Mariano." I explained calmly.

Our mom's head snapped up, her blue eyes blazing as bright as fire as she whispered. "What name did you just say?"

"Markos Mariano. He was the head of the Mariano family, but he had a business partner named Lucian Adesso. Someone Kyle had killed eleven years ago. Markos raised the boys, and for whatever reason, perhaps he just cared exceedingly for his late partner, but he raised them to hate you, Kyle. Their hatred for you goes deep enough for this elaborate charade he's pulling with Presley."

"Son of a fucking bitch," Kyle whispered, reaching for his phone.

Dad glanced over at Mom, his gaze narrowed in a way that meant they were communicating silently. I heard her walk up to him and ask, "Why would he go for Kyle and not us?"

Dad shook his head and pulled Mom closer. I looked between them, unsure what their connection to Markos was.

Scotty cleared his throat and stepped closer. "I've done my research. If there was a connection to Markos, I would have found it. This is baseless and, in my opinion, birthed from a place of jealousy and hurt over not being the person Presley could rely on."

Fuck. Him.

My jaw was tense from how hard I ground my molars together. It took all my strength not to attack him, when my mother harmlessly asked, "What does he mean, jealousy over what?"

Scotty smiled at us. "Presley has agreed to marry Adrian Adesso."

I pulled a gun out and aimed it at Scotty's head. Gio copied me without missing a beat.

I was prepared for Scotty to pull one in defense, or even Kyle, but I wasn't prepared for Presley to. She had the one we'd found that day in her closet pulled and aimed directly at me. She was a better shot than I was, so even if I did take a risk to shoot Scotty, her shot would land dead center in my chest.

"This is crazy, lower your guns. All of you," my mom cried, completely outraged.

Dad slowly moved in front of us, then he placed his hand on the barrel of our guns until they lowered. The second they were down, Scotty, Kyle and Presley lowered theirs.

"I think I more than proved my point," Scotty said before moving in front of Presley as if he was worried we'd actually harm a single hair on her head.

Everything felt too fast and out of control.

She wasn't really going to marry him. She couldn't.

She was ours.

"Presley, don't do this," Gio said, voice barely restrained. His fists kept clenching around the gun at his side.

She turned to look over her shoulder, but her gaze was empty as if we weren't there.

We'd broken something inside her.

I realized as she walked away from us, and it felt as though she took my heart with her, there were a few things I had to come to terms with: The most dangerous version of Presley would always be the one that didn't include us. We taught her about the beauty of stars and the importance of soil. In turn, she shared our passions with us; she had her cows and her ranch, but I believed it was all tethered to us. Without us, I didn't want to know what would come out of her.

There'd be nothing left but darkness.

CHAPTER 45

GIO
PRESENT

The smoke billowed from my joint as we watched Presley greet Adrian with a kiss and he began to pack things into the back of his car. She wore her hair down in pretty waves that bounced against her back.

"I heard her tell her mom she was only going to go with him for a week or so then she'd be back." Kingston blew out a cloud of smoke, mirroring what I was doing, his gaze pinned on her just like mine was.

"We won't be here." Our mother had put up a picture today that was meant to taunt us, and we knew she did it as a way to get back at us for reviving El Peligro, but it still hurt. In the image, she'd caught both Gio and I staring over at Presley while she was staring at the camera. It made us look like lovesick fools, and I suppose that's exactly what we were.

"What's the plan now since we lied to them about not using El Peligro to protect her?"

We had lied. I knew Kingston was trying to save face; I would have done the same, but the truth was, we never wanted this power unless it meant we could have Presley.

Kingston took another hit of his joint. "We need that strip in Manhattan; we'd have enough weapons if we took that back."

"So we go to war with a motorcycle club then?" That didn't exactly sound smart, but I knew El Peligro could handle it. Henry would help us ensure we had enough men to win.

Kingston continued to stare at the car Presley had just gotten in and then blew out one last smoke cloud. "We do whatever it takes to keep her safe. Even if it means we lose ourselves along the way."

He tossed his smoke down, but I kept mine between my lips, watching as the black armored car rolled down the drive. They weren't listening to us about Adrian, and it was the most danger they'd ever placed Presley in because of it. Just the idea of her going with him to Italy terrified the shit out of me, but there wasn't anything we could do beyond building our strength in El Peligro and coming for him.

The calling card for El Peligro was the king of hearts, perhaps that's all we were now.

Just two lost kings in search of our broken queen.

Grab Book Two Here

While you certainly don't have to read what the twins do next with that motorcycle club, you might enjoy it. My Darling Mayhem picks up right where this story ends and will bridge the gap between The Lost Kings and The Broken Queen. It's a great glimpse into how the twins process Presley's absence in their lives and their new role in El Peligro.

My Darling Mayhem

Here's a sneak peek:

Wren

. . .

"You need to listen to me, Henrietta. I have tried to stop them. I have done all that I can do, but a war is on its way. You need to be as far away from him as possible. If he really loves you, he knows I'm right. You and Cruz need to leave with us and go back to North Carolina, so you remain safe."

Archer cleared his throat, and I felt his hand find mine, lightly tugging me back. But I had to ask because I was so confused.

"Juan, who's leading El Peligro now, and wh—"

A clicking sound started near the front door, making me stop mid-sentence. All of us turned toward the sound, and I watched in horror as my deadbolt slid back and the knob turned.

Archer shifted in front of me, pulling me behind him right as my mother ran around me into Cruz's bedroom. My heart was in my throat as I tried to process what was happening, but it was all too fast.

"Fuck." My brother spat, running his hand through his hair while he took a position to stand in front of Archer, and a mere two seconds later, I realized why.

My front door opened, and a younger version of my brother stepped inside.

No.

Two near-identical versions of my brother stepped inside my house, smiling as if they'd found something extremely amusing.

"Hola, Daddio." One of them gave Juan a nod while swinging his focus to Archer. He was taller than my brother but years younger. He looked young, maybe eighteen or in his early twenties. His dark hair was thick and swept back, similar to my brother's. His skin was lighter, though, and his eyes were blue, which he must have gotten from his mother, or so I assumed. He wore a black hoodie over black jeans and thick boots.

The second twin stepped in, somber and seemingly more serious. His attire was identical to his twin's, but his hair was shaved closer on the sides and left longer on top. His eyes were amber like his father's, and like mine, and his skin was more tan than brown. But what set him apart other than his hair and eyes was the scar that ran through his left eyebrow. The way he watched us and surveyed the room gave off a sinister feeling.

Fear slithered into my stomach, deep down grabbing hold of old memories and tossing them around in my chest like shrapnel. These boys had the same look in their eyes that my father used to get. These boys were the leaders. While they hadn't said it, I knew it in my bones. My brother couldn't control them...and they were his sons.

This was bad.

Juan's jaw flexed as ten men filtered into my house behind my nephews. Finally, there was silence once the door was shut until Juan spoke up.

"I told you to give me tonight."

The one with blue eyes clicked his tongue. "Father, you should know that we don't bend to demands, even when they come from you. We know you have a soft spot for our aunt." His eyes flicked over to me quickly, then back to his father. "Whereas we do not, seeing as we've never met her."

Archer started laughing, making my head snap over to him. "These are the new leaders of El Peligro? Your sons. These are the ones you can't control?"

The twin with blue eyes seemed amused and took a step forward. "Tía, you may want to slide to the side if you don't want to get blood on your face. By the way, I'm Giovanni. You can call me Gio. It's nice to finally meet you. My mother will be happy to hear that you're well. She's requested we keep you that way."

Archer produced a gun, and in the blink of an eye, it was pointed at my nephew's head.

"My men will be here in thirty seconds if I don't check in with them. I suggest you leave before this turns into a blood bath."

Keep Reading Here

Also by Ashley Muñoz
Read in Kindle Unlimited

Stone Riders

Where We Started

Where We Belong

Where We Promise

Where We Ended

A Stone Rider Christmas

Mount Macon

Resisting the Grump

Tempting the Neighbor

Saving the Single Dad

A Macon Christmas

My Darling Mayhem

Rake Forge University

Wild Card

King of Hearts

The Joker

Royals of Rake Forge

The Lost Kings

The Broken Queen

Smalltown Standalones

The Rest of Me

Only Once

Tennessee Truths

Finding Home Duet

Glimmer

Fade

Anthologies/Co-Writes

What Are the Chances

Vicious Vet

Acknowledgments

This one is for every reader who ever messaged me, commented or told me in person to write Rake Forge second gen.

Honestly, enough time had passed I was contemplating just letting the idea of extending their world go and yet your messages continued to pour in, reminding me that you weren't done.

I really can't thank you enough for your love for my words, or your continued support.

Thank you to Amanda Anderson who helped me shape this series even knowing it would be stepping outside of my smalltown brand and setting us back a bit on everything we'd built for the past two years. You saw my vision and my heart to write second gen and helped me see that it happened.

A huge thanks to Erica, my PA. Honestly, I know for a fact this book got written because you took on so much responsibility. I am so grateful for your dedication and excitement for my words, and all of the things that make my world continue.

Gel, thank you for keeping up with all of my design demands and ensuring my graphics are always on brand

Savannah, thank you for being the best agent and always pushing my work and pairing me with the right audio publisher for this series. It wasn't easy and you managed it, and I'm so grateful for you.

Becky and Sarah, thank you for your incredible editing skills and helping me get this book exactly where it needs to be.

Melissa, I would have never made it here without your prompt and detailed feedback. I can't ever express how much it means to me that you're always willing to give me the hard truth of when something isn't working. You challenge me to always dig deeper and to pull out what the story needs, and the characters deserve. I think we did like four revisions before the final was finally given to you. The confidence I had in that last revision was so essential though, and I am honored to have you on my team.

Julia and Kelly, your eyes on the early revisions were so imperative. The way you each saw the story was so helpful and I am so honored to get to work with people who can tell me the truth, and exactly what could improve the book.

Thank you so much for your dedication to this series.

To my content team, I can't thank you enough. Truly. Your shares, tags and all your gorgeous creations are so incredible and they mean so much to me. Thank you for being so incredible and sticking with me through it all.

Same goes for all my Book Beauties, thank you for always loving my books and encouraging me with your posts and interest in literally anything that I do.

Lastly, certainly not least. The biggest thank you to my family:

You will always come first for me. This fictional world and all the others will never compare to the life you've all given me. Jose, thank you for being such an incredible business partner and dad. To my kids, you're my reason for doing all of this. Thank you for loving me and always making me laugh.

About the Author

Ashley is an Amazon Top 50 bestselling romance author who is best known for her small-town, second-chance romances. She resides in the Pacific Northwest, where she lives with her four children and her husband. She loves coffee, reading fantasy, and writing about people who kiss and cuss.

Follow her at www.ashleymunozbooks.com